THE BLACK MAGE

Candidate

RACHEL E. CARTER

Clean Reads
www.cleanreads.com

For every little girl who wished for a sword instead of a tiara. And for every little girl who wished for a tiara. Because tiaras are pretty cool, too. And for the girl that wanted both. Because that just kicks ass.

In truth, I have so many people to thank for continuing to support me on this journey. I honestly wasn't sure anyone would ever want to read about the crazy cast of characters inside my head -so thank you for proving me wrong. Especially the online community, my wonderful reader and reviewer friends who have helped my book get noticed. I love you all, even when you are posting updates about how you want to strangle a certain non-heir or hit Ryiah on the head. You make me laugh, you make me smile, and most of all, you make me feel like a friend —and that's what matters the most. So thank you. For making my dream real.

The People of My Life-

My mom. For buying me books —all of those trips to B&N for, yes, every single of the 56 Nancy Drew's, and that's before I even liked to read. For taking me on hikes in beautiful places. For letting me keep the family computer in my room. And most of all, for supporting my dream. *Always*.

My dad. For introducing me to more music than I ever would have listened to on my own. Especially that first Savage Garden CD. My book playlists are the result of your work. For the video games. For the good times. For everything.

Rotna. You get me —the whole me. The dark parts that no one else sees. The good and the strong. We couldn't be more different, and yet at the end of the day we are one and the same. You and Shelly are my Ella, and I know you will never let me fall. You will never let me break. And if I do break, you will be there to pick up the pieces. Because that's what best friends do. I love you.

Courtney. Because the second I told you I wrote a book you asked for it. And you read it the very next day. And you kept cheerleading me on every step of the way. Before I was convinced it would ever get published you were swearing up and down you were my #1 fan. You haven't stopped. And for that I owe you two things when I become famous: 1) a trip to England to stalk JK Rowling, live it up BBC-style, and listen to them speak in accents all day long, and 2) a dedication in this book. One down, one to go!

Last but definitely not least, to my new family! Susan, Gary, Thom, Amy, David, and Malachi (yes, books are cool, don't listen to your uncle!) —such wonderful, amazing people that I am so happy to share my new life with! You have all made me feel so loved & supported throughout this journey and I just wanted to say THANK YOU and I love you all.

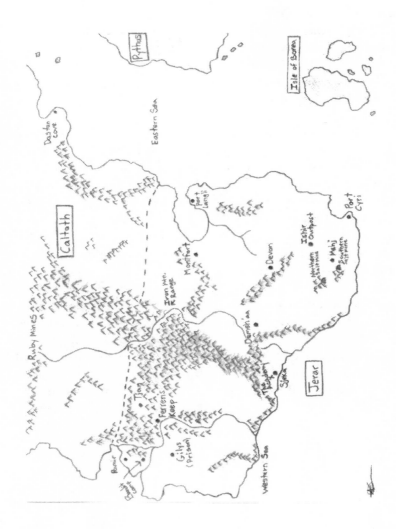

CHAPTER ONE

Darren laughed softly. It was like water. The sound of a stream cascading down rock, low and unhurried. Silky. Confident. "You don't really think you can beat me, Ryiah."

I put my hands on my hips. "How would you know? We've never dueled before."

"I beat you in that contest when we were apprentices in Port Langli."

"Yes, but we didn't fight with *magic*." I shifted from one foot to the next as the non-heir raised a brow and gave me a knowing look. He was tapping his fingers against his wrist, and I could tell he was torn between dismissing my challenge and outright intrigue. Prince Darren of Jerar, second-in-line to the throne, was nothing if not proud.

But he was also stubborn. Like me. And I knew he wasn't thrilled by the prospect of dueling his future wife.

I bit my lip. *How to convince him otherwise.* I watched as Darren's eyes fell to my mouth. Suddenly I was quite sure I knew the answer. Senseless attraction had made the past five years a misery for the both of us, but now it was going to help.

"How about a wager?"

"A wager?" Darren's tone was instantly suspicious. "What kind of wager?"

I took a step forward and lightly laid my palm against his form-fitting tunic. I had to swallow as I felt the flat layer of hard muscle beneath. *Control yourself, Ryiah.* Now was not the time to be noticing things like that. *I* was the one who was supposed to be seducing *him.*

"Careful, Ryiah." The prince was smiling.

"I win and you join me in Ferren's Keep." Ha. We'd spent the past week arguing over where the two of us were going to be stationed.

"You know I need to remain at the palace."

"Then win and you won't have to leave."

"What's my counter?"

I spoke without thinking. "Anything you want."

"*Anything*?" Darren's eyes met mine, and my stomach dropped. A flush crept up the side of my neck and stained my whole face crimson.

"I – I didn't mean a-anything," I stuttered.

"Then don't lose." His eyes were dancing. "Isn't that what you just told me?"

I folded my arms and stared him down stubbornly. "Fine," I said, "but if you get 'anything' then I get to add another condition if I win: you have to make peace with Alex the next time the two of you cross paths."

The non-heir cringed. He and my twin had a strained relationship at best, and even after the night of the ascension Alex was still wary of the prince. He had told me the morning after, four days back.

Which was ironic because Darren's brother, the crown prince of Jerar, *hated* me. Although to be fair, I shared the sentiment. There was no one I despised more than Blayne.

"Well, it's a good thing I plan on winning." I looked up and found Darren smirking. Gods, even when he was arrogant, he was attractive. Or maybe it was because of his smug self-assurance. It made me want to slap that silly smile off his face, and then grab him by the collar and kiss him until I couldn't breathe. Not necessarily in that order.

I concentrated on tugging my hair back into a knot—anything to appear unaffected. "Vanity doesn't suit you."

The prince just gave me a knowing smile and pulled himself off the wall, lazily walking to the center of the training court. I followed him until the two of us were standing ten feet apart in the center of a large stone dais. The palace's practice court was much smaller than the outdoor ones we had trained in during our apprenticeship, and it was also twice as elaborate. I suspected it was because we were in the nation's capital, where more coin was devoted to pleasure than practicality.

Normal arenas were in the dirt, outside under a radiating sun with a bare picket fence to serve as the border. Here, inside the palace of Devon, we stood on a raised stone platform surrounded by large, white pillars and a curved base of cushioned benches. On the same side as the empty seats was a thick glass wall, reinforced by a regular supply of the Alchemy mages' resistance potions.

This way the king's court could relax in leisure without the threat of a knight or mage's attack gone awry.

On the opposite side we had just come from was a small alcove featuring a display of training weapons and spare armor. Darren didn't bother to take any—he already had the most powerful weapon at hand. His *magic*. As Combat mages we were able to cast any weapon we needed, and while we would outfit ourselves in real battle, this was only a duel and we had both agreed the outcome would be decided by sheer prowess alone.

"Are you ready, Ryiah?" Darren was grinning.

I studied his stance, hoping for a small hint as to what his first attack might be. I had spent five years studying his form in casting, and while the prince was good, no one was perfect. He still had tells just like the rest of us. They might not be as obvious, but they were there. If Darren were to cast a weapon to hold he'd likely adjust his right hand—just the slightest widening of his fist to grip a handle. Likewise, he'd be more likely to dig in with his right heel were he to prepare for a substantial casting from his center of gravity, something akin to a heavy torrent of wind power or flame.

Right now, on the day I needed to read him the most, the prince was a blank slate. I scowled. "I'm ready."

"On the count of three." Darren's eyes met mine. "One ... Two ... *Three!*"

The two of us threw out our castings at once, our magic rising up and exploding in a collision of brute power and force.

And then we were flying back.

The two of us slammed against a pillar on each end of the arena. I barely had time to cushion my fall with a casting of air before I was staggering forward, running back toward Darren with a hand raised and magic flowing from my palm.

But he was even faster.

I narrowly ducked as a series of whistling daggers soared past my ear. Swiping a loose strand from my eyes, I met the prince's gaze.

"Having fun, love?" The words were full of unspoken laughter.

"Aren't you?" A blade appeared in one hand as my other sent off a blinding flash of light. The air lit up, and for a moment there was only gold as I barreled forward, bringing my sword up and down in a vertical slash. I threw all my weight into the heat of the attack.

But Darren was waiting. And the sound of two metals colliding sent out a noisy ring across the dais.

I withdrew and threw up a pine shield just in time to counter his cut.

"Nice touch."

"I learned from the best." I paused. "Well, *second* best."

He snorted.

We continued to trade blows for parries but within minutes Darren was walking me backward across the dais with a maddening smirk. His weighted blows were stronger than mine, and my arm was starting to strain against the heavy hits I was blocking, but only occasionally issuing.

I made a split-second decision to lunge forward with my shield. Darren blocked the move easily, but that was my intention. While he was distracted with the blow, I changed my sword to a knife.

Darren registered my decision a second too late as I threw a crescent cut low and out. I caught the side of his leg just before he fell back, and I was rewarded with a loud rip of cloth and the trickle of red.

I jumped out of the way of the prince's counter.

"Should have known you'd choose the knife."

"It always was my favorite."

We regarded one another for a moment in silence, our chests rising and falling after the first ten minutes of battle. I had drawn first blood, so I won by standard duel etiquette. But the both of us knew we were playing for more. We trained for Combat, and Combat trained to win. We were war mages. Our definition of winning was surrender—or death.

I adjusted my grip. *One victory down, and one more to go.* I lifted my hand at the same time Darren lowered his. Our eyes met and power burst from our fingertips. The dais rumbled and groaned, and I leaped to avoid a large fissure as Darren cast out a magicked globe, shielding himself from the storm of arrows I had sent flooding down from the ceiling.

This time there was no rest.

Fire tore a line across the fissure, sprouting even more flames as it chased me to the edge. I spun and doused it with a flurry of ice, listening to the *snap, crackle, hiss* as the flames met with cold.

For a second, heavy steam fogged up the arena. I shut my eyes and called up a memory for the next casting.

Darren and me. The night he told me he didn't love me. Blayne laughing in my face while the fathomless prince watched, unfeeling, as my heart crumbled to a million pieces.

My fingers tingled, and I felt the warm static building in my arm. These were the memories I needed. Weather magic wasn't like a normal casting: it was fueled by emotion. Extremities were best. And my years with Darren had certainly given me a large assortment to choose from:

"I told you not to trust a wolf. Because it would only ever want to break you... Haven't you figured it out yet? I'm the wolf, Ryiah."

A hot surge of anger leaped out of my core. I mentally harnessed the emotion and channeled its magic, letting the searing heat surge along my veins. Then, I released my casting.

A jolt of lightning struck Darren's barrier and shattered it. There was a shrill, earsplitting noise as his casting splintered like glass.

Darren released his magic and sprinted across the platform, a magicked sword in each hand.

I sent out a large funnel of fire, but the prince crossed his arms mid-stride and the flames came barreling back. I had just enough time to duck to my left, and then a terrible smell met my nose. Bitter and burned.

I lifted a hand to my head. The fire had singed off part of my hair, just above my right ear.

When Darren came again I was ready. Ice shot out across the short distance between us and met with the prince's swords. His metal froze over, webs of glistening frost spreading from the tip to the handle with a shrill crack.

Darren dropped his castings with a growl—nothing like the biting sting of frozen metal—and looked to his palms. They were now reddish-black.

I was torn between guilt and glee. I knew how they felt. I'd had that same casting done to me when I was an apprentice.

But I was here to win.

I barreled forward and prepared to end our duel with a knife to his neck. Or that was what I had planned. But, like usual, Darren was one step ahead of me.

The second the steel started to materialize in my hand Darren tackled me mid-stride.

Before I could get a good focus my casting disappeared—concentration broken by his attack—and we both hit the hard stone floor with a loud *thud.*

I felt the jarring impact in my side rather than the full at my back. I had somehow grappled my way so that Darren wasn't quite pinning me flat—one leg in and one out.

Darren was trying to wrestle me to the floor, but I knew the second he had my shoulders the match was as good as over. I would never be able to break the full weight of his hold if I couldn't push forward. I knew I would never win a contest with my arms—I simply didn't have the mass—but that didn't mean I couldn't fool Darren into thinking I'd try. He and I had never fought in hand-to-hand combat, so I could only hope that meant he hadn't been paying attention during my training in the apprenticeship.

Pretending to gasp, I made a huge deal out of struggling back and forth to break free. Darren took the bait. He leaned forward to pin me back and my second leg snaked free. It took me all of two seconds to dig my first heel into his hip and pivot to the side.

It was enough to give me some leverage against his weight.

I threw myself forward using the second leg to kick up and off the ground, rolling the prince underneath me. I was up.

But I was sitting too far back. Darren's reflexes were too fast. Or maybe he had expected the move. His hips threw me, and I toppled forward, palms slapping the ground while he used the strength in his torso to flip-roll me back. Hard.

I landed on my back with a curse. My lungs were on fire, and I wasn't sure I hadn't broken something in that twist. White-hot pain was eating away at my ribs, and Darren had my arms pinned out onto the stone ground beneath me.

"Time to surrender, love. Don't fault yourself, it's not every day someone goes up against a first-rank mage."

I grumbled a very unladylike word and Darren laughed, his whole body shaking.

"You are insufferable."

Darren stopped and his eyes met mine. The look he gave me was enough to forget the terrible pain in my chest and bring on a whole different kind of heat. "Well, I don't believe that for a second."

Blood rushed my face as the prince leaned in.

"Admit it." Darren's mouth was close to my ear. "You aren't suffering in the least..." His hand traced circles along the inside of my wrist. A rain of shivers followed wherever his fingers went. "*Are you*, Ryiah?"

I swallowed. For the first time I was conscious of the fact we were the only two in the room. And we were on the floor, which suddenly didn't feel quite so uncomfortable and cold.

Not when he was looking at me like that. Like...

I had a sudden flashback to that day in his chambers two years before. To what had almost transpired the last time we had been truly alone.

Gods, I hadn't been able to keep my hands to myself. And neither had he.

The memory was making me blush. Even now.

Darren noticed and his lips curved in a half-smile, his eyes hooded. "That's what I thought." The words closed the distance between us. I could detect the faint spiciness of his breath, like cinnamon and heat and *ice*. Something that was dangerous and dark and, to be honest, exactly what I wanted.

I knew we needed to treat our injuries, especially mine, but...

"If you are going to kiss me," I said brazenly, "you should do it now."

The corner of his lip turned up. "Oh, I intend to."

"Really, because I'm still—"

Darren placed a tanned finger to my lips, eyes dancing. "I haven't named the prize for our wager yet."

That silenced me real quick.

"Ah, and I see I've finally rendered you speechless." His smirk deepened. "And here I thought you would never—"

Before Darren could finish whatever taunt he had started, I dragged the prince down by the hem of his vest. His lips met mine, surprised, and for a moment everything was slow and languorous and sweet.

I could hear the unsteady beating of his pulse. The careful way he kissed me back had my vision swarming before my eyes. It might have been slow but my pulse was thundering inside my ears like a roar.

For once neither of us was rushed. There was nothing forbidden, nothing wrong, we had all the time in the world.

Darren's fingers slipped into the back of my hair. I looked up at him and his eyes were smoldering. This was *us*. He stared back and for once there was no challenge, no sarcasm or smirk, just Darren. And me.

After so many years we were finally together.

His fingers trailed the side of my face and my skin burned underneath his touch. *Could a person catch fire and still live?* I wasn't sure, but I thought the answer was yes.

His lips parted mine. I shut my eyes.

Dear. Gods.

"Ryiah..." His hand skimmed down the side of my waist...

And a startled cry fell from my lips.

Darren fell back with a start. "Are you—are you hurt?"

I pressed down on my stomach and bit back a long string of curses. Hot needle pricks flared in response. "My ribs." I avoided his gaze and silently chastised the god of chance. *Now?* The pain could *not* have resurged at a more inconvenient time.

Or maybe it is exactly the right time, my inner voice replied. *You know perfectly well what happened the last time the two of you got carried away...*

I groaned loudly to cover up the rest of my thoughts. Tomorrow morning I was supposed to set out to Ferren's Keep. I couldn't very well do a two week trek on horseback where I would be in constant motion with broken ribs.

I tried to stand and doubled over in agony.

Darren was there in an instant. I swatted him away with a weak wave of the hand.

"I'm a Combat mage." I stood and took a sharp lungful of air. "Not one of those damsels in distress you keep here at the palace."

He raised an amused brow. "I never said you were."

A scowl met his reply. "Tell that to the tutors your father ordered me for etiquette this week."

"I can never win with you, can I?"

I rolled my eyes, but inside I was smiling. Outside, my mouth was plastered in a grimace. "Just take me to the infirmary."

"So full of authority." Darren joined me as I started toward the nearest passage. He pointed the direction we were to take. "And I believe I told you I would never carry you."

I let him lead the way. "That was four years ago. And I'm not asking you to *carry* me—I just want your *company*."

Darren flashed me a predator's grin. "Well, don't expect me not to gloat on the way over. Because despite your injuries, love, I do believe I have maintained my standing as a first-rank mage."

I rolled my eyes. "For now."

I heard his chuckle echo along the barren palace hall. It was disconcerting. Usually the king's palace was filled to the brim with wandering courtiers, mages, off-duty knights, servants, and, of course, my favorite, his older brother by three years, Prince Blayne.

Luckily, today was not *most* days. The entire court— with the exception of a small sampling of its staff—had departed that morning for the yearly first-year trials at the Academy of Magic in Sjeka.

Traditionally the Crown—the king and his two sons— was supposed to attend, but Darren had been granted a leave of absence since his new service as a mage in the King's Regiment was to begin at the week's end.

The two of us continued on in a comfortable silence—well, as comfortable as it could be given my new injuries. It was nice. We had barely shared any time together since the ascension. After Darren had publicly declared our engagement most of his time had been stolen in long meetings with the king and his advisors, and I had been thrown into a parade of anxious courtiers eager to earn the favor of a future princess of Jerar.

King Lucius had not been thrilled with his son, and he definitely did not look favorably upon the former lowborn who had caused his son to make such a "reckless" decision in the first place. Darren and Princess Shinako of the Borea Isles had found a way to avoid their own impending marriages by promising her dowry to me in exchange for a renewed treaty between her island country and Jerar. It had been a brilliant move, and one no one had seen coming, but after the initial night of revelry there had been new problems to contend with.

There were many concerns about someone with my background taking on such a vital role within the Crown.

It didn't matter that said role was purely ornamental since Darren would never be king. It didn't matter that as an apprentice I had acquired a highborn status on my own. And it certainly didn't matter that I was hopelessly in love with the boy.

What mattered was that I had ruined a very strategic match between Blayne and an important ally. Now King Lucius was stuck in negotiations with Pythus. As heir to the kingdom of Jerar, Blayne needed to marry above Darren. And since the Borea Isles' princess's dowry had already been promised to me, Blayne was forced to pursue a new match with one of King Joren's daughters instead.

In truth, it was a great opportunity. The Borea Isles were a much smaller territory and couldn't provide the resources a large continent like Pythus could offer. But try telling that to Blayne. Darren and he had been intended for quick marriages to secure their dowries' funds as fast as possible, and now

Blayne had to find a new wife. King Joren was a much shrewder man than Emperor Liang. It didn't matter that the Crown needed as much support as it could get in order to go to war against its northern neighbor, Caltoth; to Blayne, I would always be the unruly lowborn who had managed to ruin all his plans.

And now he was determined to ruin mine. The very next morning after Darren's and my engagement, Blayne had petitioned his father to hold off on our wedding until he secured his own. When Darren had tried to counter his brother's absurd proclamation citing the impending war with Caltoth, the king had stiffly sided with his eldest, stating that the suggestion might motivate Darren to become more involved in Crown affairs. "*Besides*," he had added dryly, "*we need two dowries to finance an army, not one.*"

I wasn't sure I believed that. More likely, the king just wanted to punish Darren for the public humiliation he had faced the night of our ascension. Lucius had been all too willing to go along with his youngest son's strategy until he found out the second half of the arrangement: marriage to a lowborn. Since the king had already agreed to Darren's proposal and Emperor Liang's treaty had specifically mentioned me by name there had been nothing the king could do. Not if he wanted to keep the princess's dowry.

Needless to say, the last couple of days had not been pleasant. On the bright side, however, the king's general distaste had an advantage. Since he could hardly stomach the idea of me in his court, Lucius had been more than willing to grant my petition for service in Ferren's Keep. Darren hadn't been pleased, but he knew just as well as I that once Blayne's wedding passed I would be forced to take up permanent residency in the palace.

If anything, I think Darren envied my freedom. Now that he was done with his apprenticeship he was limited to the palace regiment. The same for me once that year was over.

It wasn't a bad thing. The King's Regiment was the most prestigious company in the land, and who could forget the palace housed the current Black Mage, Marius? But an eternity was daunting. Ferren's Keep was my one chance at glory, and I hadn't forgotten what the Combat mages said about its action: the northern border was the place to be.

We finished the ten-minute walk to the palace infirmary, and I was surprised to see two familiar persons already present as we turned the corner. The taller of the two, a young man with sandy-brown locks and easy blue eyes was chuckling at something the dark-skinned girl beside him had said.

Like most mages in the kingdom, neither wore their colored robes except for special occasions, but their status was still unmistakable. The two bore the air all newly ascended mages carried: one of barely contained excitement and pride. It was a sharp contrast to the calm of the palace healer in her red Restoration robe that greeted us upon entry.

"Alex! Ella!" I called out to my brother and best friend across the way.

The couple immediately turned toward the doorway. Ella broke into a grin, but my twin's smile faded as soon as he noticed my injuries and the person standing beside me.

"What happened?" His question sounded innocent, but I knew Alex well enough to catch the unusual lilt to his tone. My brother had already chastised me for too many injuries during the course of our four-year apprenticeship, and I knew he was anything but pleased that his sister had gotten herself hurt. *Again.*

I hastily made myself speak: "It's nothing, Darren was duel—" I corrected myself hastily. "*I* was practicing, and I think I broke a rib."

"Ryiah just needs a healer to look at her," Darren said. "Nothing too serious."

Alex's eyes narrowed on the prince. "I know what a broken rib is."

Darren stared at him. "I didn't say you didn't."

"Did you do this to her?"

The prince folded his arms defensively. "Your sister was the one who wanted to duel."

"That doesn't mean—" Alex never finished because at just that moment Ella placed a perfectly timed kick to his shins. Alex swallowed, scowling, and Ella finished for him with a small smile in Darren's direction.

"I take it Ry thought she'd give you a run for first rank?"

At her question the non-heir gave a small smile. "She tried."

"Did she at least get in some good castings of her own?"

"Depends on what you consider 'good.'"

I cringed. Now was not the best time to joke. Not with my brother seething in anger a couple feet away. "So about that healing…"

Darren and Ella stayed where they were, engaging in a strained but polite conversation while I followed Alex to one of the covered cots in the back of the room. He wasn't employed by the palace staff, but the healer was busy enough with two of the knights of the King's Regiment in the back so she didn't give us a second glance. The rest of her staff had undoubtedly left for the Academy trials with the rest of the court.

As soon as Alex started to make his examination I lowered my voice to a whisper. "There's no need to blame Darren for this."

My twin grumbled under his breath but said nothing.

"You can't continue to hate him, Alex. I already told you, everything he did during the apprenticeship, he had a reason—"

My brother cut me off. "I really do not want to talk about *him* right now."

I sighed and let him continue his work in silence. I felt the cooling touch as his magic seeped out of his hands and into my stomach, the terrible sensation of movement inside, and then the blissful sensation as my rib pain trickled away, bit by bit. It was a simple injury to treat—a broken or fractured rib could heal naturally with no magic within a month or two on its own—but I did not have the luxury of time.

Sitting up, I gave my twin a grateful smile. "So have you and Ella finally decided which city to take up service in?"

My brother's expression softened at the mention of her name. "Montfort."

I started. I had been expecting Ferren's Keep, or maybe Ishir Outpost. "Where is Montfort?"

"It's five days north. Ella wanted to come with you—you already know that—but after what happened last year I didn't feel comfortable stationed so close to the border, not that I like *you* going there either." He gave me a pointed look and I ignored it.

Neither Darren nor Alex could talk me out of a position in Commander Nyx's regiment. Besides, unlike the two of them, my station was only temporary: the Crown's advisors had made it clear that as soon as Darren and I were married I would be stuck serving close to home—and *that* would be the end of my grand adventures. I bit my lip. It was the one thing I wasn't looking forward to about my impending marriage.

"...Still close enough to the action to give her the excitement she wants, but they also have some of the best healers in the kingdom. Ronan is going there." Ronan was a first-rank mage like Darren—only his faction was Restoration like my brother's. The two of them had bonded during their apprenticeship, and while my brother was jealous of his friend's ranking, I knew he also looked up to him. In Alex's eyes, anywhere Ronan was stationed was worth going.

"And we both met with Commander Braxton during the ascension feast. He seemed friendly enough, and of course it helps that his city is hosting the Candidacy next year. As soon as he reminded Ella, she forgot whatever scheme she'd been cooking up to convince me to join Ferren's Keep with you."

I grinned. Ella was a true Combat mage. It didn't surprise me in the least that she had agreed to Montfort so easily after the Commander's mention of the Candidacy. It was a tempting opportunity, and if I hadn't been so set on Ferren's Keep, I would have probably begged to come along. The Candidacy was how our nation determined its reigning Council of Magic, known commonly as The Three. It was also how the Black Mage, Marius, had earned his title just nineteen years before. And in one year it would be my turn.

Even if I didn't win *the* robe—and the odds were I wouldn't—the prestige that came with any victory at all in our nation's infamous tourney was enough to elevate my status. I was a second rank now, but there were at least fifty other Combat mages with the same ranking, as I was only compared to four others of my same ascension year.

Still, if I won against even some others of my same rank, it would improve my standing. That I was better than the ones I beat, and any of the lower ranks of that person's own year.

"All done. Stop daydreaming." My brother clamped my shoulder lightly, startling me out of my thoughts with a jolt.

I slapped his hand away in mock protest. "What if you had missed something? That could have hurt." It didn't, but I wasn't about to let him off that easily.

My twin grinned at me. "You are just jealous you don't have my skill."

I rolled my eyes in good humor. "Jealous? *Hardly.* I believe the people up north call me a hero."

"Funny how she forgets they were talking about *both* of us." Darren and Ella had appeared beside us. I watched Alex stiffen at the non-heir's proximity. "Ella tells me you two are headed for Montfort," the prince added.

My brother opened his mouth, and then thought better of whatever insult he was about to say when he caught wind of my expression. When he finally spoke, it was the quietest reply I had ever heard him utter. It was also the shortest. "Yes."

"It's a great city. Small, but accomplished." Darren nodded to the red-robed woman on the other side of the room. "Jeanette hires most of the palace healers from there."

"How... nice." I elbowed my twin and he grated his teeth. "Thanks for the recommendation. It means—" Alex took a long breath and the words barely left his lips, "a lot. Thank you, your highness."

Darren's face was frozen in a polite smile. He was as uncomfortable as my brother, but years at court had given him the upper hand. "Anytime."

Ella winked at me. She could read the tension just as easily as I. "Well as pleasant as this little reunion has been, I do believe it's getting late and Alex and I have a long ride ahead of us. It was nice to see you both before we head out. Darren, I'm sure we'll see you in Montfort with Ry for the Candidacy next year?"

The lines seemed to leave Darren's shoulders—not much, but just enough to betray the real anxiety he had felt just moments before. "Of course."

I exchanged a quick embrace with my best friend and brother, and then watched them go.

As soon as they were out of sight Darren turned to face me. "He still hates me."

"Give him time." I squeezed his hand. "Alex has had the wrong opinion of you for so long. And he's never liked anyone I courted."

"He liked Ian."

"Ian was..." I paused, unsure how to begin. "Well, he's..."

The non-heir studied me in my hesitation. "He is everything I'm not."

"Ian is what *Alex* wants," I amended. "Not me."

Darren was silent.

"I chose *you*." I jabbed at the non-heir's chest with my finger. "I want *you*." I jabbed again. "I love *you*, you—" Jab. "Silly—" Jab. "Stubborn—"

Darren caught my finger with a straight face. "That's enough injuries for one night, don't you think?"

"Do you believe me?"

The corner of his lip twitched. "Gods know I am in for a lot of misery if I'm wrong." He tilted my chin up to his face and for once his eyes were serious. "I am going to miss you, Ryiah."

I looked down, heart sinking. "You could still come with me."

"You could still stay."

We were back to the same conversation we'd had all week.

Darren looked toward the ceiling. "Out of all the women I've met I *would* pick the only one who is too stubborn to enjoy my father's court." He returned his gaze to me, defeated. "I suppose there's no talking you around?"

I shook my head.

"I didn't think so." The non-heir groaned. "You frustrate me, you know that?"

I smiled. "And you are the most difficult person I've ever met."

He raised a brow. "Second only to yourself, of course."

"Darren."

"Yes?"

I sighed. "I'm going to miss you, too."

CHAPTER TWO

Trepidation filled every waking moment of the fourteen long days it took to reach the northeastern stronghold of Ferren's Keep.

Most of my trip was spent deep in thought, watching the passing of croplands and riverbeds of the country mainland. With the growing rebel attacks, Jerar's impending war with Caltoth, and my new position close to the border, the Crown's advisors had decreed that one of the King's Regiment remain with the future princess at all times. So, like the pack of guards that had once accompanied Darren to the Academy many years before, I now had Paige, a young knight four years my senior, for companionship. She wasn't very talkative, and what little sentences she did speak were of basic necessity.

When I had tried to expand on our conversation, the girl just frowned. I sensed she wasn't shy, but it was clear she hadn't warmed up to me either. The knight was sharp-tongued when she did utter an opinion, and I found myself regretting almost all of my attempts.

Paige was tall, brawny, and almost the female equivalent of Alex in stature. She only packed chainmail and men's clothes to dress. She had stunning brown locks she kept hidden in a braid to the side, and narrowed eyes that seemed to pass judgment the second they looked at you.

She was lowborn, but she was unlike any lowborn I had ever met. She despised small talk, scoffed at all my suggestions, and eyed every traveler—noble or not—with the same suspicious edge.

The third time I tried to engage her she snapped at me to pay attention to the road, and followed hastily with an unfeeling apology, "my lady."

I didn't know what to do. With all of our shared background, I had assumed a friendship was in order. Both of us were women who had risen above our station through hard work, and we were both young and stuck together for as long as the king ordained her presence necessary. It would have only made sense for us to bond—if for nothing else than the eternity we had ahead. But it was clear my companion had other ideas.

The rest of the time we traveled in silence, with the exception of one or two disagreements over direction.

I spent most of the hours enjoying our scenery. Which was very easy as we drew further and further west. Plains gave way to pine and thick clusters of sweet-smelling grass, thin streams joined and became one large coursing current. Foliage sprouted up along the banks, first and foremost my favorite: the dense green tree with its large, shiny leaves and clusters of tiny red flowers that dotted its branches.

The clove tree.

Before I knew it we had arrived at the small village of Demsh'aa. *Home.*

We were only supposed to be passing through for the night, but much to the chagrin of my traveling guard, I insisted on one extra day to visit with my parents. I hadn't seen either since my first-year trial four years before.

Paige left me to visit, scouring the local shops to replenish our supplies, and I took a tour of the new changes in my brothers' and my absence. I was pleased to see how much better we fared. Previously the apothecary had been an extra room in my parents' house, but because of the coin Alex and I had been sending home (Derrick's soldier salary was much less than that of a mage), they had been able to purchase a small building close to the center of town, and they had already apprenticed two young girls who had chosen to pursue a local trade instead of a trial year in one of the country's three war schools.

My parents apologized for missing Alex's and my ascension, but I had already known it would be too much to leave the store in the midst of the new apprentices' training. Besides, the mages' ceremony wasn't open to the public, and while I was sure they would have been able to attend the feast, it would have been a long journey to take for such a short event. I was just happy my parents had supported my studies.

Of course, I came bearing news...

But it had actually already arrived by Alex's envoy a week before. Although that didn't make it any easier to accept.

My father was in a constant state of shock. During my apprenticeship all my letters home had refrained from mentioning Darren—mostly because I hadn't known what to write—so to hear the prince and I had been falling in love all this time was something my father had never considered.

My mother was much more understanding, stating that she had suspected as much during the week of our first-year trials. "He wouldn't stop staring at you. I knew there was more to it than your friend led us to believe... I just never expected *this*."

It was a hard notion to ponder. A prince of the realm had chosen to take their lowborn daughter not as a mistress but as his wife.

My parents were happy, but confused. And I didn't have five years to explain exactly how it came to be. To be perfectly honest I was still reeling from the news as well.

Things like that just didn't happen. Not to me.

We discussed the coming Candidacy, and they promised they would be there to watch Alex and me participate. "The girls should be able to run the shop by then." We discussed the wedding, and my father was the first to inquire on the absence of a date. When I tried to explain my mother grew quiet.

It was only as I was saddling my horse the next morning that she finally spoke. "Be careful, Ryiah. I can't imagine the king is pleased with whatever his son did to win you a seat at their table."

I nodded, mutely. It wasn't something I hadn't already considered. My plan was to stay as far away from the king and his heir as possible. Yet another reason to accept Commander Nyx's offer.

From there it was a swift farewell and a return to the well-traveled dirt road that led up a steep trail to the great forest of the north. King's Road skirted the base of the Iron Mountains, and the remainder of our trip was uneventful. Paige and I spent each night at an inn along the way, and we made good time.

When we finally spotted a giant stone fortress built into one of the mountains themselves I let out a deep sigh of relief. Next to me, I heard Paige do the same.

It was a magnificent picture. With the setting of the sun just an hour behind us the great keep was made alive by hundreds of flickering yellow dots. The torches lined each wall, up and up each subsequent lookout until the light finally disappeared from a dark shadowy alcove into the mountain itself.

From where we stood I could catch the sheen of metal glittering off the wall's lowest sentries along the walk. It wound from the fortress's lowest point to the base of the mountain floor.

I gathered my reins, and then nudged my mare forward.
Ferren's Keep.
We had arrived.

"Please state your name and purpose."

Paige and I declared ourselves to the guard at the edge of the dais, holding our horses in place as we presented our official papers—my summons from Commander Nyx, and Paige's signed orders from King Lucius.

The soldier and his two comrades examined the documentation carefully, verifying the seals to make sure they weren't forgeries. When they found what they were looking for, the lead waved us forward with a rattle of chainmail in passing.

We continued along the raised walkway, horseshoes clattering against the paved road, until we reached the fortress's base: a protruding barbican with yet another set of guards guarding its gate.

We presented our papers again, and the gate was raised. Once more the process was repeated inside with another set of guards and another gate, and then we gave our horses to an awaiting hostler as we followed a steep set of stairs and then a long tunnel into the keep itself.

Spiraling floor after floor, chamber after chamber, everywhere we looked hundreds of supplies flooded the space of each storeroom. A giant well, barrels of grain, great mounds of firewood, weighted artillery, and racks. Racks of swords, knives, javelins, and every type of armor one could hope to imagine: chainmail, breastplates, arm guards, spare tunics, and breeches. The inside of the fortress was armed to withstand a siege.

I had seen it all during my last year of the apprenticeship, but I could tell Paige was impressed now. The frown she usually wore was nowhere in sight. The knight walked around with wide eyes and gawked unabashedly with each step we took.

After the storerooms we passed a locked set of reinforced doors—the Commander's private meeting chambers and her personal quarters, followed by an open, much larger space for regiment meetings. It was only a matter of minutes before we

reached the men's barracks, a long parade of rows with cots
lining the wall for as far back as the eye could see. Beyond
them, I knew, were the women's quarters, and just a bit further, leading out of the tunnel and through another set of
guards, was the small village of Ferren, named after the keep
because its only entry and exit was through the fortress's
guarded tunnel itself.

Ferren was settled in a small—very minute—valley and
decorated by steep, impassable crags on every side. Because of
its size and location, it had become home to the kingdom's best
blacksmiths, renowned men and women who furnished the
northern defenses and supplied the Crown's Army with the
finest steel one could buy. In some ways, the mass production
of Jerar weaponry was the most valuable resource the Crown
had, and as such the keep's village was reserved to local regiment and blacksmiths only—with the exception of a small but
hospitable staff for general upkeep.

I led Paige to the women's barracks and we began to un-
pack. The door was left open. Both barracks were empty,
which meant the regiment was taking dinner in the dining
commons on the second floor.

"Ryiah? Is that you?"

I spun around and caught sight of a stocky dark-skinned
boy with amber eyes and curling black ringlets at the barrack's
entrance. He was clutching a cloth in one hand and gaping.
Ray. One of my old factionmates from the apprenticeship, a
young man I had seen just three weeks ago during our ascension ceremony. "Ray!"

"I knew you would take Commander Nyx up on her offer!" He grinned. "And who is this you've brought with you?"

Paige gave the boy a stony look. "Her guard. And I do
not engage in frivolous conversation."

He started. "I-it was nice to meet you too."

My knight went right back to ignoring him, carefully
folding her shirts as she pressed them away into a trunk of her

now-claimed cot. I felt a surge of irritation. I would definitely be talking to my guard later. In private.

"Sorry about that." I gave my friend a sheepish smile. "*Paige* and I had a long ride here. Some of us are more irritable than usual." Actually she was born that way, but I wasn't in the mood to explain. "I was just unpacking before I checked in with the commander."

"She's still at dinner with the others . . . I could take you there, if you'd like."

I hesitated. I really wanted to clean up first—granted I'd had a hot bath at most of the inns we'd passed along the way, but I still had a day's worth of grime coating my clothes and hair.

And if memory served, the wait to one of the two small bathhouses in Ferren was easily an hour, though that had been with sixty visiting apprentices stationed in the keep.

Then again. Why not? The rest of the regiment had just served long hours sweating in armor so I would fit in right alongside them.

"Lead the way!"

A sea of faces swarmed my vision the moment we entered the dining hall. Ferren's Keep had the largest regiment north of Devon. The count was somewhere close to two thousand when all were in residence—which was never since fifteen of its twenty hundred-men units were always on patrols. Still, its regiment was one-fifth the size of the Crown's Army, double the size of anywhere else. Most cities' branches were closer to five hundred.

It was the perfect place to house a large regiment until more northern aid was needed from the Crown's Army.

That said, it wasn't the most prosperous. The contents were worn and meals were tubs of wilted produce, dry meat, and stale breads—the product of a city without local farming.

That, and five hundred sweat-stained faces fighting over the last scraps of food amidst tankards of ale.

"No better than a pack of ravenous dogs," Paige muttered.

I opened my mouth to tell her we didn't look much better, and froze. Even though the crowd was so overwhelming there was one person that caught my attention almost immediately. His broad shoulders and infectious laugh were impossible to miss.

Ian. Ian was *here.* Ray noticed my direction and nodded. "He arrived two days ago, right after me. Guess Port Langli wasn't to his liking. Jayson is here too, he's been promoted twice since his ascension—and if you look hard you should be able to spot Ruth from Alchemy. Ferren's Keep is a popular post."

"Well, this *is* a surprise."

I spun around and came face-to-face with the leader of Ferren's Keep, an imposing if slightly short woman in her early forties with a blonde mane cropped close to the ears and steel-gray eyes that missed nothing. The woman knight had one of the most sought after posts in the entire kingdom.

Commander Nyx studied me, arms folded across her chest. "It's nice to see you took me up on my offer, Mage Ryiah. I wasn't sure you would after the prince's announcement. A title can go to some people's heads."

I blushed. "It's not my title yet."

The woman raised a brow. "And what does the Crown have to say about that?"

"The king has agreed to let me serve on your regiment until the crown prince's wedding... But I will always be a Combat mage of Jerar. No title can change that."

"And you don't expect any special accommodations while you are here? A private room? Or a high position in my regiment, perhaps? Because I promote solely based on performance."

I stood my ground. "I would expect you to treat me the same as any other mage who enters your keep."

At this Paige made a choking noise. "Certainly not! My lady, you cannot possibly think the women's barracks are appropriate! You need a private chamber where I can see to your safety—"

"The barracks are fine." I scowled at my guard. "I will be surrounded by hundreds of brave women who fight for our country. Who better to protect?"

"Me! The knight appointed by the king himself!"

"Well, your job just got a whole lot easier."

Paige scowled and said nothing.

Commander Nyx cracked an amused smile, white teeth flashing. I was immediately struck by its oddity—like a sudden dunk in an icy bucket of water. The woman was made of frowns. "I assure you...what is your name again?"

"Paige," the knight supplied shortly.

"Well, Paige, my men and women are just as capable as your regiment in the capital. Ryiah will be in good hands." Nyx's gaze fell to someone behind us and she made a momentary gesture. "Now, if you'll excuse me, I have a meeting to attend. Ray, Ryiah will be serving on your squad with the rest of the newcomers. I expect you to introduce her to Sir Gavin first thing in the morning. Paige, while you are here you can serve alongside your charge so long as you defer to her squad leader's command. I believe the King's Regiment orders only decreed Ryiah's safe transport to and from my keep, did they not?"

Paige grumbled an unutterable reply as I thanked the commander for her time. Nyx withdrew back into the crowded hall and Paige made a sniffing noise beside me.

"I don't like the commander."

I stifled a snort. "You don't like anyone. You don't even like me."

"Well, I really don't like her."

Ray and I exchanged weary glances as the knight snatched a half-eaten loaf off someone's leftover plate and began to devour it all the while giving us an irritable expression. "What?" she spat. "I'm useless so long as you are surrounded by 'capable' others. I might as well eat. Or is that something else I must defer to this Gavin to do?"

Ray gave me a sympathetic clap on the shoulder. "I'm off to scrounge up a wash before the rest of the men get to the baths." He jerked his chin in the direction of Paige. "Good luck with... things."

As soon as he was gone I turned to my guard with a sigh. "You are going to be stuck with me for a long time. A little cheer once in a while certainly wouldn't hurt your cause."

"Cheer is for fools with idle minds. I am neither a fool nor idle."

And that was the end of that.

The next morning came much too soon. I had spent most of the evening before catching up with some of the regiment women I had met the year prior during the apprenticeship in our barracks. By the time the morning bell echoed down the keep's narrow walls I was ready to return to sleep.

Five years of the same routine, and I was still not used to early mornings. "*Mmmphf.*" I shoved the warm blankets aside, and then subsequently cursed as my toes touched the icy floor.

"Missing your accommodations back at the palace, my lady?" Paige's tone was anything but sympathetic.

I fixed her with a bleary-eyed glare. "All this hatred you harbor must be exhausting to maintain."

"You should have listened to me and asked for a private chamber."

"I thought you didn't care for frivolities," I snapped.

She threw her hands up in frustration. "I was the best knight of my rank and spent six years working up to a promo-

tion in the King's Regiment—*and for what?* You haven't listened to one suggestion I've made! I told you to keep west and
you insisted on that detour—"

"To see my parents!"

"—Then you bombarded me with banal questions about
the weather when you should have been paying attention to
the road!"

"I was trying to be friendly, and I *was* paying attention!
Contrary to your narrow-minded opinion I am capable of doing both!"

"My *only* purpose is to serve as your guard, and you insist
on harboring this foolish notion of sleeping out in the open
with six hundred other women where I cannot possibly fulfill
my duty should one of them harbor ill intentions!"

"Those women are soldiers, mages, and knights like yourself," I countered. "Hardly the type to wish me ill."

"How would you know? You are too busy smiling at everyone you meet. There are rebels in this great country in case
you've forgotten."

"Ferren's Keep is our nation's stronghold. It is the last
place a rebel would choose to stay."

"It is exactly where I would go."

I yanked my chainmail over my tunic a little too roughly. "Well, it is a good thing you are not a rebel."

Taking a deep breath I forced myself to reign in my temper. In a twisted way she was only doing her job, even if it was
in the most grating way she could do it. "I am sorry, Paige.
Please understand I wish to comply with your orders but the
king did grant me this leave. I can't exactly go around demanding my own chamber. I promise to consider all future
advice."

The knight tied her hair in a high knot and then looked
past my shoulder. "I don't hate you."

"W-what?" She had caught me off-guard.

Paige cleared her throat. "What you said earlier. I may
not enjoy your company, but I don't hate you, my lady."

And that was as close to an apology as I would get. I handed the knight one of her boots, and she took it without complaint.

Neither of us spoke another word as we trudged down the dank corridor and up the stairwell to the top floor of the keep. I was concentrating so hard on my own thoughts that I almost missed colliding with another in passing.

"Ryiah?" The boy did a double take.

Ian. I stopped and gave a nervous smile. "Surprise."

"What are you doing here? I heard…" He tried again. "I thought you would be at the palace."

I flushed. Our history and the awkward context of our present conversation were not lost on me. "No—I mean, yes, I will be, eventually, for the wedding, but…"

"She's here to make her mark," Paige interrupted, "the same as the rest of you."

Ian noticed the other woman and frowned. "And you are?"

"The knight charged with her safekeeping."

I smiled apologetically. "Paige is my personal guard. She was the only way I could serve outside the capital."

The two exchanged wary glances.

"King's Regiment?" Ian stared at the girl.

She met his gaze head on. "By Crown orders. To protect the *prince's* interests."

I changed the subject hastily. "You grew tired of Port Langli so quickly?"

He hesitated. "I got a better offer."

"In Ferren's Keep?"

"Well, this is where I grew up." Ian fiddled with a leather cord at his wrist. "Nyx and my parents are good friends. There has always been a position for me here. "

"Oh." I had forgotten.

"I suppose congratulations are in order."

I glanced up and saw Ian's poignant expression. There was no mistaking his meaning. "T-thank you."

An awkward silence followed. I was searching my thoughts for the right thing to say, and I could see Ian struggling to do the same.

Just then Ray appeared, sidling between us to grab me by the arm and spare the rest of the uncomfortable exchange. "Ry, are you ready for your first official day as a war mage?"

"Only my whole life."

"So, you are the infamous Ryiah?"

I stood silently, back erect, as the squad leader circled me slowly, taking in my narrow frame with a studious gleam. I was aware of every fault in my appearance—from the way his eyes lingered on the small tear at my sleeve to the slight pause as he caught my scarlet-red locks—still sticking up all over the place in my rush to make the morning's meet.

Sir Gavin took in my stubborn chin and the way I shifted nervously under the stare of all one hundred of our unit's members. He pursed his thin lips and nodded approvingly.

Apparently, I had passed inspection.

"You have quite a reputation," the knight admitted. His voice was rough and loud, but not unkind. "If I hadn't been present during the prince's and your heroics the year before I'm not sure I would believe it now."

Was that a compliment or an insult? I swallowed and hoped for the former. "Thank you, sir."

He nodded approvingly. "My squad is one of twenty in this keep. I understand the apprentices served with one of the inner patrols during field training but your experience will be quite different as a true member of the regiment. Commander Nyx has all recruits start with me, and *all* of my patrols are along the border. It's a right of passage for newcomers to help acclimate everyone to the more dangerous aspects of our work. For that reason there is a promotion every time someone joins the keep. You will have several opportunities for advancement, so long as you follow orders."

I perked up instantly.

"That said there are also too many deaths." The knight's expression was somber. "Everyone in the regiment understands that all lives are not equal. It is an unfortunate truth, but a mage's capacity for magic outweighs a soldier's life ten-to-one. During your apprenticeship this rule was undoubtedly brought up, but never is it so vital as the present. We have less than twelve mages per squad, and with your addition it comes to four Combat in this unit."

Only four? I counted mentally: Ray, Ian, me, and one other person—the lead mage. Four out of one hundred. Which meant there were less than two hundred mages total in the keep, and no more than eighty of them as Combat.

"You are, of course, expected to engage during any attacks that take place, but you *must* exercise caution. When we go on patrols, soldiers and knights take the brunt of dangerous tasks, however you will still have more than your fair share of opportunities to partake." The leader gripped the shoulder of a tall young man standing next to him. "This is Lief and he is the squad's lead for Combat. You will defer to his call in all circumstances that require a mage's judgment instead of my own."

Lief lifted his hand in silent greeting, choppy blond locks framing his square face as he did. He wasn't much older than the others. Maybe early-thirties at most. And he seemed friendly too.

A nice change from Master Byron.

The squad leader continued. "Now, we have far too many men and women to handle introductions, but I trust you'll come to know everyone in time. We have two more days at base, and then we will be setting out for another patrol. Five squads service the keep, and the rest regularly patrol specific sections of the border. We spend three weeks abroad followed by one week of respite and rotate with the rest of the units.

Should we be called to action, respite will be delayed as long as necessary. Have you any questions?"

I shook my head enthusiastically. "No, sir!"

"Good, and have you and your guard already been to the seamstress and armory to be properly outfitted?"

"Not yet…"

"Well then I will have one of your factionmates take you. Ray, you were just there the day before, I trust you can show Ryiah and Paige the way?"

"Yes, sir."

"When you three are finished please meet us in the strategy hall. Commander Nyx will be reporting on the latest activity for the squads currently present."

The boy nodded and led Paige and me away from the crowd, back down the keep steps to the third floor. As we turned the corner of yet another winding passage he turned to me with a hint of old humor.

"So, what do you think? Better than four years with Byron?"

"Are you kidding?" I kept a straight face. "Those were the best days of my life."

CHAPTER THREE

"During the patrols our squad follows a very specific formation," Lief began. "A handful of soldiers scout ahead, and the rest flank the very front and back of our pack. The knights are next and take center. Crammed in the very middle is us," The lead mage cleared his throat. "Sounds simple, right? It is. But every time a new Combat mage joins the squad they inevitably try to play hero and break formation at the first sight of danger."

"Has a mage ever broken formation just to run for his life?" Ian inquired innocently.

The lead mage rolled his eyes. "How I have missed your senseless humor."

Ian nudged his mare closer to Lief with a chuckle. "Admit it, you pined for me every night while I was away."

Ray and I exchanged smirks. The lead mage was also a Ferren's Keep native, and so the two older boys had a whole slew of insults to throw at one another whenever Ian deemed Lief's speeches too dry.

In the past two years I had almost forgotten what it was like to be friends with the curly-haired mage. Hearing him get along with our new leader now was bittersweet. I was happy to see Ian smiling again, cracking jokes and lightening moods, but also sad. Because I knew no matter how much time we spent together our friendship would never be like that again.

When Darren had first turned me away I had been devastated. What I had done to Ian was no better.

The difference was our motives. Darren's actions had been justified. He'd been trying to do what was best for the kingdom. Mine? Wrong, selfish, and cruel. I had used one of my best friends to shield myself from feelings for another, and when those feelings had finally gotten to be too strong I had tossed him aside.

Ian had forgiven me the day of his ascension, but that didn't erase the past. Our friendship would never be the same. And I had only myself to blame.

"We lost two Combat mages that day." Lief's story carried through my thoughts. "Sir Gavin doesn't usually yell but you should have seen him. He lost his voice after three hours of shouting at the rest of us. It didn't matter that the ones who had disobeyed his orders were dead—he held every one of us accountable. Told us if we ever saw one of the other mages try to march to the front of enemy lines we had better stop them unless we wished to be demoted and sent to some far away town with no action at all."

"That hardly seems fair," I said.

Lief raised a brow. "It's not meant to be fair."

Ray coughed. "And what if someone—say Ryiah—decides to take off on her own and threatens me with a pain casting?"

I guffawed and the boy winked at me.

"How am I supposed to stop her from breaking formation to help one of our injured comrades? I don't know about you or Ian, but the girl is second rank for a reason." Ray cast an apologetic glance at Paige. "My apologies but I don't think you can stop her either. Not without magic."

My guard glared at Ray in reply.

"Get help. Try to stop her however you can." Lief turned his attention to me with a furrowed brow. "You aren't planning to do something reckless, are you?"

Ian chuckled somewhere behind me.

"Of course not!" Even as I said it, I couldn't help thinking how grateful I was that the rest of them didn't know about my mission in Dastan Cove. Darren had blackmailed our leader Mira into leaving out my antics in our report to Commander Chen. Which was a good thing because if it had been public knowledge, then Ray would have realized his hypothetical scenario had actually happened.

"I am very good at following orders." Most of the time, anyway. "You don't have to worry about me."

Lief studied me for a moment in contemplative silence, and then with a sigh went on to explain the squad's routine. I listened attentively with my eyes combing the road ahead. It was our second day of duty. All around me were the remains of great pines, charred and needleless in the aftermath of the infamous Caltothian attack one year before. A quarter of the northern forest had gone up in flames.

I could still taste the bitter ash. My lungs constricted just remembering the fire, the way I could barely breathe, the way the world had thundered—just for an instant—as Eve gave herself to save the prince and me.

Some of the vegetation had returned, but for this patch the forest was just a field of black, towering trunks. In permanent mourning of those we had lost.

We crossed several small streams before making camp in a clearing fifteen miles later. The setting sun had transformed into a deep magenta.

Every man saw to his own horse, making sure it was brushed down, watered, and fed, but the soldiers saw to most of the camp's upkeep: pitching tents, preparing the meal, taking inventory, and collecting wood. They also did a rotation for sentry duty.

The rest of our party—the twenty-four knights and five mages—spent each evening discussing strategy with Lief and Sir Gavin. We learned the specifics of the territory patrols; the names of the bordering villages most destined for trouble; and reviewed general tactics.

At the third day's afternoon break, Sir Gavin addressed the question all the new recruits had been not-so-silently pondering.

"I've heard many of you ask your comrades when we should expect to run into the Caltothians. The answer is simple: not now, and not on the road." He cracked his neck as he spoke. "The enemy is far more likely to raid one of the small villages straddling the border than ambush an armed regiment. Even then, I expect their number to be few and ill-prepared at that."

"But what about the attack last year in Ferren?" The words spilled from my lips before I could stop them. "The Caltothians didn't seem ill-prepared then." Beside me I caught two of the new soldiers and Ray nodding in agreement.

Sir Gavin was silent for a moment while several soldiers exchanged knowing looks. When the lead knight finally answered it was with a bitter truth. "I am in full accord, Ryiah, but what you must realize is by now the Caltothians will have heard the rumors that King Lucius is actively citing Caltoth's most recent assault as a breach in the Great Compromise."

My confidence faltered. A break in the treaty was an open declaration of war. Everyone knew the participating rulers would automatically turn against the noncompliant country. It was what had kept peace between Jerar, Caltoth, the Borea Isles, and Pythus for almost a century.

"Previously Emperor Liang and King Joren refused to consider the Crown's complaints, but a direct assault on Ferren changed everything. The keep is too far south to be considered a territorial dispute." Sir Gavin paused and his eyes locked on all of the recruits, me included. "Now King Lucius's claims hold merit. Unless the king of Caltoth thinks himself a fool, he would be wise to hold off future attacks and focus his energies on disputing Jerar's claims. Any action at this point would not be advisable on our part *or* the Caltothians."

A short silence followed. The rest returned to their lunch, but I was too restless to follow. I downed the remains of my skin and then headed to the creek to refill it. I was lost in thought. *Sure, I knew war was coming...*

But what I hadn't realized was how much Jerar was depending on the other countries' blessings. I'd been so wrapped up in my apprenticeship that I had never paid much attention to politics, and what little I had heard had been limited to dowries. Sir Gavin's words were alarming. It meant that we were at the mercy of Caltoth until the other nations decided in our favor.

And even if Caltoth was smart enough to restrain from attacking Jerar while it was under observation, there was the added fear that King Horrace might somehow sway the other nations' favor.

Because even *with* Emperor Liang's renewed alliance to Jerar, the Borea Isles would not support a breach of the Great Compromise without the backing of Pythus. They were too weak. And from the fit Blayne had thrown during this year's ascension, it was clear even if the crown prince did obtain the hand of one of Joren's daughters, the Pythian king was not pro-Jerar.

And King Joren already had a sister married to one of King Horrace's brothers.

Which meant if we did not find a way to convince the others, we would end up at war with three countries instead of one. Something even a Pythian princess and my Borean dowry couldn't fix.

"The other rulers are cowards." Next to me Paige prodded the shore with a stick. She had come along in a bitter mood herself. "They use their distance as a crutch, claiming they are too far away to see what Caltoth is doing. We all know the truth."

"They shouldn't have signed the compromise unless they were willing to uphold it." My stomach was rolling. *What if they didn't?* "What if they leave us with no choice but to declare war on Caltoth without the protection of the treaty?" *Are they planning on siding with the wealthiest country, or the country with the greatest army?* Because Jerar was only the latter. *And do we really have the greatest army if we are facing three armies combined? From all sides?*

I looked down at my hands to see them shaking. Try as I might to appear unaffected, I was far from it. I hadn't a lot of free time to think about my mission in Dastan Cove, but I still dreamed of it. What it had felt like to kill. What it had felt like to almost lose Darren.

Fighting was easy until there were consequences.

I hadn't been close to Caine—or Eve—during the events of my second and fifth year as an apprentice, but that didn't mean their deaths didn't haunt me. Their memories were easy to ignore during the day, but they were always with me when I closed my eyes. I could still smell the singed flesh from the desert pyre. I could still remember the determined look in Eve's eyes right before she gave up her life to save the prince and me. A mage's "last stand"—a sacrifice she never should have had to make.

"We cannot afford to go to war against Caltoth, the Borea Isles, and Pythus."

"No, we can't."

I turned and found Paige watching me, her expression unwavering. "I do not believe you will let it come to that, my lady."

I frowned. If only it were up to me.

If only there was a way.

We picked up the bandits' trail almost immediately.

Unfortunately for us that was the only thing that came easily.

We had received the request for aid on our second week of duty. Sir Gavin's squad patrolled a hundred-mile grid in the northwestern territory of Jerar and three small townships fell into our route. Two of them reminded me of Demsh'aa, but the third, Pamir, was a sizeable city that was famous for its breeding grounds and the realm's best thoroughbreds. We had only just reached the border when several envoys appeared with tales of a theft that had taken place only three days before.

Apparently Pamir's Lord Waldyn had already sent out half the town's local regiment to hunt down the thieves, but they had returned empty-handed. Small town regiments were expected to stay close to home. They didn't have the resources for a long hunt. After all, most were needed at home to stand guard and keep a watchful eye on the remaining livestock in case the bandits decided to strike twice.

Since Pamir was a part of our patrols, it came down to Sir Gavin's squad to seek out the offenders and return the stallions to the desperate merchants.

"These are no ordinary bandits," the envoys had warned. And they were right. Within a couple of hours the thieves' tracks had all but disappeared.

"Forty horses don't just vanish into thin air." Lief studied the dirt. "My guess is they had someone with magic casting alongside them. It's the only explanation."

I nudged my mare forward. "Do you think it's the rebels?"

The lead mage shook his head vigorously. "The rebels don't bother this far north."

"Why not?" Ray was just as curious as me.

"All the Crown's Army reports state attacks south of the capital." Lief didn't seem concerned. "There hasn't been so much as a whiff near the border."

I frowned. It was true the Red Desert had the salt flats in the south, one of the nation's most profitable exports, but what about the armory in Ferren and the horse breeders in the townships up north? We traded with those too, did we not?

Ian noted my expression and drew closer. "The rebels don't bother us up here. There's no point. Caltoth does the job for them."

"Do you think King Horrace is the one financing their efforts?"

His eyes stayed focused on the woods around us. "Perhaps."

Next to me Paige scoffed. "If it were that easy all we'd need to do is round up one and beat the fool 'til he sings. End the war with Caltoth and those sorry rebels in one easy strike of the fist."

Ian's eyes flashed under the bright rays of the afternoon sun. "That's a bit—"

"What? *Cruel?* Well they shouldn't have turned traitors. My brother died serving in Port Cyri because of a rebel attack!"

Lief cleared his throat and took over for Ian. "No one is defending those rebels, Paige. But I can tell you that *this* isn't them. They stick south. We get thefts up north all the time because of the border raids. When their livelihood is destroyed, they turn to crime. It's not right, but it happens."

"With magic? An impoverished family wouldn't have mages with them." Bless Paige's skeptical heart, she wasn't ready to back down just yet. I hid a grin. I had to admire her resolve: she did not let anyone's explanation stand in the way of facts. Even when that person was scowling directly into her face.

Ray snickered beside me as Lief let out an exasperated sigh. "Yes, Paige, 'with magic.' There are plenty of people who apply to the Academy who aren't granted an apprenticeship but would still have enough magic to cast a simple enchantment like this. Hiding tracks and broken foliage isn't exactly an expertise."

My knight had the decency to duck her head. "Oh."

"Oh indeed." Lief gave her what I was sure was a tired smile. "It's against the law to practice magic unless you are a mage—or a part of the apprenticeship, but the desperate ones don't exactly play by the rules. I'm sure most follow the Code of Conduct where you grew up?"

"They did." Paige's cheeks were tinged pink. "They were tried with a higher sentence otherwise."

The young man laughed. "If only that worked around here."

I watched as my guard and the lead mage carried on into what could only be described as a friendly discourse. Ian, Ray, and I followed behind in an amused silence.

"Is she *blushing?*"

Ian stared. "I thought your guard hated everyone."

"Apparently there are exceptions."

"Exceptions with shining blond locks and long, *long* lashes," Ray chortled.

Ian grinned at me. "Apparently Paige *and* Ray are harboring amorous feelings for Lief. What about you, Ry? Are you pining after our lead mage as well?"

"Certainly. What with those long, long lashes." I winked at Ray. "How could I not?"

Ian opened his mouth to say something in reply, but it was lost on me as I caught wind of two knights' conversation behind us:

"*...Future princess can't even take her mage duties seriously, too busy flirting with the others.*"

My good humor was lost in a second.

"*I heard she only got offered the position because Nyx suspected her relationship with Prince Darren would be beneficial to the keep.*"

"*Was it that obvious?*"

"*After the attack in Ferren? Everyone knew. He was in and out of the infirmary every day she was recovering... Can you imagine what she must have done to convince him to leave Lady Priscil-*

la? She certainly wasn't practicing Combat, if you catch my meaning."

"I heard about that. I was in Tijan. So you truly think she's here because...?"

"Why else? From what I've seen she's nothing special."

I didn't even realize how tightly I was gripping the reins until the conversation died off and the second knight cleared her throat.

"Mage Ryiah, is something wrong?"

The false worry was like burnt sugar to the taste. My grip on the reins was so tight my knuckles were white. I could barely feel my fingers. I was sorely tempted to turn around in the saddle and tell the knight exactly what I thought of her "concern."

"What's wrong?" How about you *daring to pretend you know anything about me! Nyx offered me the position because of my performance saving soldiers from a Caltothian attack! Why did she offer you yours? Because of your talent for tasteless gossip?*

A slender arm slid into my field of vision and pried my hands from the reins, releasing the tension so that my mare was able to start forward once again.

"Ryiah." Ruth was leaning close to my face. I hadn't exchanged so much as a word with the Alchemy mage since I'd arrived—mostly because I had been too distracted to remember. "Come on, let's catch up to the rest of your group."

"Did you hear?" My voice cracked as she led me away from the knights, back to the center of our formation where the rest of the Combat mages and Paige rode.

The girl nodded once and I flushed.

For the past couple of days I had noticed conversations ending rather abruptly when I approached, but I had never thought twice about it until now. Was the entire squad talking about *me*?

Was that what this was?

"They don't know you, Ryiah." Ruth's discerning gaze was sympathetic. "All they can do is speculate."

"Do *you* think I was offered this post because of his feelings for me?" I didn't need to say whom. Ruth had watched Darren's and my relationship play out from a distance the entire apprenticeship.

"No." The girl hesitated. "But there are people who will always believe that no matter what you tell them."

"Are there..." I swallowed back my anger. "Are there a lot of them?"

Ruth didn't say anything.

Great. I felt anger fighting its way back to the surface. My entire squad thought I had received my rank *and* position because of my betrothal to the prince. My comrades gave me compliments to my face and speculated on my skill the second my back was turned.

Five years of proving myself. Gone. In an instant.

No wonder Darren had been so cold that first day at the Academy when Ella and I had questioned his place as a student. Doubtless, he had experienced what I was feeling now thousands of times. As a prince he probably got tired of proving himself again and again. Darren's angry retort that morning had been a culmination of years of false flattery and cruel speculation.

"*You will thank me one day for not filling your head with false compliments.*" Darren had been doing me a favor after all. If only I had realized it then instead of years after the fact. What I had thought was mocking irony was in truth the advice of an angry young prince who had been tirelessly lied to and talked about whenever he left a room. His entire life.

"Thanks," I told Ruth aloud, "for stopping me before I said something I'd regret." Although in truth I wasn't so sure. Those two knights deserved a piece or two of my mind.

Ruth patted my shoulder awkwardly, unaware of my internal conflict. "It'll get better, Ry, you'll see." She never was one for warm, friendly gestures. "And if it doesn't, well, you are only with us for a year before you have to return to the capital, isn't that right?"

That was a bleak prospect. I gave her a weak smile, and Ruth returned to her group of Alchemy mages as I followed behind Ian and Ray, lost in my own self-pity and fury.

"Ryiah. Ian. You two are going to go south with Jeffrey's band. Ray and I will head north with Sir Gavin's."

I tried not to let my disappointment show when we reached a fork in the road and Gavin had Lief split us up into two separate parties. Though the bandits' tracks had been missing for the first two days everyone suspected they had taken the stream north after the general resurgence of prints leading to the south.

As Lief put, "No one spends that much effort trying to hide their presence to suddenly stop trying." The thieves had clearly run out of magic and taken the stream to hide their route—leaving an abundance of evidence south to lead their pursuers astray. Still, Sir Gavin had to send some of us to investigate both options, and it was no surprise I got assigned to the group least likely to encounter the enemy.

The conversation between the two knights came echoing back: *"From what I've seen she's nothing special."* As I parted ways with Ray and Lief I had to keep from lobbing my apple's core at the lead mage's back. *Do you think I'm nothing special too?* I wanted to scream, *I am more than capable of handling a couple bandits on my own!*

But of course I couldn't say any of that. Because any fit of temper would confirm the skeptics' assumption that I was only here because of my relationship to the prince. Because a *true* war mage would never complain over their duty, no matter how menial or insignificant it might seem.

"You are unusually quiet." Paige sidled next to me on her mare after two hours of silence. "Is something bothering you, my lady?"

I clenched my teeth. Self-pity would not get me anywhere. "Nothing is bothering me." I studied the forest in front
of us and the moss-covered granite scattered throughout—it
would have been beautiful if I hadn't been so distraught. "Do
you really think the bandits would be this obvious?" I was re-
ferring to the droppings peeking out between dense patches of
grass and ivy.

The knight bit her lip, understanding my real reason for
asking. "No, my lady."

"I didn't think so."

Next to me Ian didn't say a word. I wondered if he was
upset to be assigned with the fifty of us clearly headed in the
wrong direction. The weaklings. It had to be an insult for Ray
to be given the premium assignment even though Ian was a
year older and more experienced. Chancing a quick glimpse I
saw the boy's face was a mask.

Since when was that boy unreadable?

We wove in and out of the thick-trunked pines dotted in
fuzzy growth, following the obvious indentations of crushed
foliage for nearly three hours before the prints finally turned
around and backtracked the path they had taken through a
nearby hedge.

"Well, isn't this a surprise," a soldier grumbled.

I dismounted and Paige followed by habit. The sun had
turned a hazy amber peaking out beneath the trees, illuminat-
ing our stop with shades of crimson and violet. It wouldn't be
much longer before it was time to set up camp. Some of the
knights nearby were debating whether to turn around now to
try and catch up to Sir Gavin's group to the north, or rest for
the night. Knowing how sinister the terrain could turn without
the sun's rays to guide us, I was in favor of the latter.

"Mages, would you mind collecting the firewood?"

Now that we were down to fifty, the soldiers needed help
with the tasks a hundred usually accomplished without the
mages' and knights' aid. I didn't mind. It gave me something
to do, and I needed a distraction. I grabbed one of the soldier's

empty sacks and Ian and Paige followed suit, the three of us scouting the west side of the trail while Alchemy and Restoration took the east.

"Everything is wet," Paige complained after ten minutes of fruitless searching. "It's so shaded here the dew stays on everything. Nothing is dry, look…" She snagged a branch in passing and attempted to split it—revealing a fresh-looking center that did not want to break. "I hope the others are having better luck."

"There's some light over there." Ian pointed to some brush in the distance that looked more aged than the rest of the forest. "Come on."

The two of us trudged after him, pushing past an assault of dense bramble to reach it. By the time we emerged on the other side I had small red lines all across my arms.

They itched like crazy.

Lovely, just lovely. I scratched my bare skin and made a face at nothing in particular. Service in Ferren's Keep Regiment was nothing like what I imagined. After an action-packed apprenticeship I had expected danger; so far this forest plant was the closest enemy I had encountered.

I kicked out at the nearest shrub with a vengeance and then swore as my foot collided against a large rock beneath.

"Ryiah?"

I looked up to catch Ian watching me with a cautious expression. A couple feet away Paige was pointedly ignoring us both, breaking off branches one at a time.

I made my face blank as I held the sack open for my guard. "It's nothing."

"Are you sure?" Ian stopped what he was doing. "You've been acting as though something has been bothering you all day."

Why deny it? He already knew something was wrong. "The others were talking about me."

Silence.

I picked up a piece of wood from the ground and yelped as my finger caught on its splintered bark. I yanked my hand away and plucked the infinitely small shard from my skin, watching as a small bead of red settled onto the surface. "Everyone thinks Nyx only offered me the position here because of my new status," I added.

Ian didn't look surprised. "I heard."

Thanks for sticking up for me. "Why didn't you correct them?" I swallowed and forced myself to ask the question I'd been secretly wondering since I arrived. "Are we... are you mad at me?"

"Ryiah." Ian folded his arms across his chest. "This has nothing to do with our past. Me saying something wouldn't change the facts. You are a lowborn who received second-rank status on the same night the prince told his father he was to marry you instead." The boy took the now-brimming sack from my hands and set his own empty one in its place. "What is everyone supposed to think?"

"Darren didn't ask Byron to do that." I felt frustration working its way to the surface and swallowed hard, forcing the anger back. "I earned my rank, Ian, you know that!"

"Yes," the boy said with a sigh, "and how convenient it was that Master Byron decided to have a change of heart the year of your ascension."

"It's not my fault Marius finally talked some sense into the old man!" I felt as if I had taken a punch to the gut. This was Ian. *Ian.* My former friend, or so I had thought. Maybe he was still mad. Maybe he hadn't forgiven me after all.

"Why am I being punished for impressing the Black Mage? Why am I being put down for catching Nyx's eye after I *saved* her regiment? Why does my new status have to mean anything here? I have proven myself time and time again!"

"You can't just pick and choose when to play the victim, Ry." Ian stopped ducking his head to look at me, really look at me. "Yes, people are going to speculate. That's what they do. But forgive me for saying you received plenty of privileges from your friendship with the prince, too. Or did you already forget how Darren got you a spot on that mission in Port Langli? Or how about the time you woke up our entire camp to yell at him—and were it anyone else Byron would have sent you packing in a minute?" He exhaled slowly. "And do you think the Black Mage would have been quite so eager to point out Byron's obvious bias unless Darren had drawn attention to it?"

"Ian, I..." My cheeks were in flames. I *had* received privileges. And here Ian was reminding me how silly I looked complaining over the prospect of one disadvantage when he would have killed to have any one of those. The boy whose heart I had trampled for another. "I'm sorry, I... I didn't realize—"

The young man held up his hand quickly to show me it wasn't what I thought. "*I* know you deserve your rank, Ry, but..." He swallowed loudly. "But the others are going to need a bit more convincing. And in the meantime don't bite their heads off for talking. Because their beliefs aren't entirely unfounded."

I wiped a strand of sticky hair back from my forehead. "Well, now I feel just terrible."

"As you should."

I opened my mouth and shut it as I caught his smile.

"I'm kidding, Ryiah."

I gave an embarrassed shrug. "I guess I've forgotten your humor. This has to be the longest conversation the two of us have had in years."

The boy chuckled. "It is a bit awkward, isn't it?"

"It was awkward for me." Paige's voice cut through my delayed response. I gave the knight a half-hearted glare. She was never very subtle.

"So..." Ian said.

"So."

"You and Darren."

"Oh..." I paused. "That."

The boy cleared his throat uncomfortably. "The non-heir turned out to be full of good intentions in the end. I can't say I saw that coming."

I shifted my feet guiltily. "I did... and then I didn't. He's..." I didn't know how to say it without making the conversation worse. "He's complicated."

"You could say that."

I cringed and hastened to explain. "But he wants to do the right thing. He doesn't always do it the right *way*, but he has good intentions." I cringed at the use of the same phrase as Ian. It made Darren sound so... complicated. *Complicated?* I had already used that word too. I was floundering here.

"I think you will be good for him."

My gaze shot up to meet Ian's. "T-thank you?"

"I'm not just saying that to be nice." The mage's eyes bore into mine. "You didn't grow up at the palace and spend your days wasting away in a convent. You will be able to advocate for others, affect policy..."

I laughed nervously. "You obviously have not spent much time with the royal family." King Lucius couldn't even stand to be in the same room as me, and I wasn't so sure his eldest didn't want me dead, despite whatever his brother claimed.

"Ryiah." Ian shut his eyes. "You convinced Darren to marry you. You have influence whether you want to believe it or not."

"He's not the heir. He can't—"

"Won't you at least try?" My friend's voice became increasingly strained. "Or does the lowborns' cause no longer concern you now that you are not one of us?"

That hurt. Ian knew full well that neither of us had been "lowborn" since our apprenticeship. "O-of course it does!"

There must have been something in my voice because Ian immediately looked guilty. "I'm sorry, Ry, I didn't mean—I know you are a good person. I just don't want this new life of yours to change you."

"It won't." I made myself smile as I reached out to touch his arm. "Believe me, it would take a lot more than pretty dresses—" A foul odor rose up and I wrinkled my nose, peering down at my boots. Horse droppings. I had managed to step into a mound of them, half-hidden by the dense forest floor. "Great, just..." I froze.

Droppings. Fresh—only a couple days old. Ten minutes past the brush where the bandits had supposedly turned around.

I glanced up sharply and took a quick examination of the surroundings, trying to locate any trampled foliage that had not come from Paige, Ian's, or my tracks.

There. I squinted. *There.* My eyes locked on some crushed ivy: and *there.* The bandits had come this way!

I drew a baited breath. "Lord Waldyn's envoys said their regiment couldn't find the bandits after two full days' search. But didn't their report state they went north, like Sir Gavin's group? Everyone thought the tracks leading south were too obvious. What if they weren't? What if it was a ploy?" I pointed to the mound at my feet.

Ian whistled. "The bandits *wanted* us to assume they took the stream."

I felt my excitement building. "It's why the southern trail looked so trampled. Because it was! They didn't just send a couple men to give it that appearance and turn around at our camp—they kept going: here!"

I was practically dancing in place. *Finally. Something to show the others I was more than the girl the prince favored.* "If the bandits had circled back they wouldn't have had reason to create false tracks this far south. My guess is they missed this or ran out of magic and figured they were too far south for us to search."

Paige groaned. "You mages make everything so complicated."

Ian gave the knight a victorious grin and hauled both wood sacks onto his back. "Things would be too easy otherwise, my dear."

The guard scowled and snatched back her sack. "I am nobody's 'dear.'"

I waved us forward. "Come on, let's go see where these tracks lead…"

"Oh, no, you don't." Paige grabbed Ian's and my wrists and yanked us back with a heavy tug. "You two will report back to the rest of your camp and let *them* decide whether to pursue the search now or in the morning. You know Sir Gavin will have my head if I let the both of you recklessly wander off to hunt the bandits on your own."

I made a face. We were already three days behind the bandits' progress. "It's not reckless. Lief said we could go in pairs and we'd only be scouting—"

"But *Sir* Gavin said you mages shouldn't be doing anything the soldiers can handle on their own."

"They sent us for firewood," Ian offered. "We are short-handed, we'd be doing the rest of them a favor."

"I am sure your leader will have a different priority for tracking criminals."

The two of us gave loud sighs as we followed Paige back to camp. She was right, of course, but I was itching to prove myself to the rest of our party. I chanced a glance at Ian and his expression mirrored my own.

"Feels like the old times, doesn't it, Ry?"

I smiled. Not yet. But I expected it was about to.

In the end our party voted to search the forest that morning. We were already three days behind the bandits' progress, and it would be foolhardy to try and ascertain their location at night when we could barely see two feet in front of us. Torches would give away our location, and the mages weren't about to use up magic tracking when we would need it for our inevitable encounter later on.

I spent a restless night tossing and turning. It was a warm summer night—cold in the shade of the forest, but still heated enough by fire to spend it under the stars instead of a tented canvas. Next to me I could hear Paige doing the same. She put on a brave act, but I suspected she was nervous for her first test of duty. When we went to battle, she would be undoubtedly glued to my side.

The entire camp was packed up and ready to go by the first morning's light. Ian, Paige and I were no exception. Every one of us was restless and ready for battle. Sixteen days of camping in the wilderness, and without the repetitive training routine of the Academy, I was itching to use my magic.

Five straight years of routine were hard to break. Here in the regiment we were expected to conserve our magic while on duty—one could never know when we could be forced to engage—and with the added pressure of my squad's disapproval I was ready to show it.

Luckily for us, the bandits' trail was easy to pick up with the discovery of the horse droppings the night before. The criminals clearly hadn't expected us to investigate this far south, so they hadn't bothered to hide the rest of their tracks. Everything was still a little wet with the morning dew, but by midday we had left the cool cover of the denser part of the forest for the sparser terrain deep in the mountains.

Summer heat beat down like the gods' pounding fists. In no time at all I was drenched in sweat and grime and my clothes were sticking to my skin. I was definitely happy Darren wasn't there to witness his betrothed's repugnant stench. Let alone the way the undershirt beneath my chainmail had turned brown and wet in the most revolting of ways.

Hours dragged by and the ground we passed became coarse. Jagged granite lined the narrow trail up and down into the heart of the northern range. Our stops became more frequent as even the horses grew weary.

It was late into the afternoon when two scouts finally returned bearing the news all of us had been anxiously anticipating: the horses and the bandits' base camp were just three more miles southwest of our current location. Apparently they had a small camp set up along the base of three nearby mountains. The heart of the Iron Range. Also desolate. A territory previously ignored by the regiment whose patrols had focused along the border and northernmost townships.

Which was probably the reason the outlaws had chosen it. And from the report the scouts had given, it had been in use for a year at the least. The horses were only a recent addition. There was livestock as well. Two cows and a small bay of pigs were stationed in pens at the edge of a roughly made fort. Several chickens clucking away in a wooden fixture nearby. Even several thin rows of mountain-hardy crops: red lettuce and stubby carrot heads.

The bandits' set up was far too permanent to be just a camp.

Paige scowled at the end of the scouts' report. "They must have been living there awhile."

"Explains the recent influx in thefts," a soldier nearby added. "All this time we thought the incidents were Caltoth. Never would have suspected it was on our side of the border."

"How many?"

"Thirty," was the scouts' reply.

"Only *thirty*? Why do they need forty horses?"

"Gods, Karl," someone drawled, "they are thoroughbreds. The bandits were probably going to sell them to the Caltothians, not ride them."

The head knight Killian cleared his throat above the soldiers' discourse. "The scouts may have counted thirty, but that doesn't mean there aren't more nearby. I doubt they expect us, but we can't be too careful. Ryder, I want you and half your band to take the camp with me. Avery, you are going to take the others and flank the outskirts in case there are others our scouts missed." He continued to list the names for each squad.

"What about Combat?"

"Ian, you are with Ryder's party. Ryiah—Avery."

My face fell. Not because I didn't admire Avery's conduct—she was a skilled knight, from what I had seen during the morning drills. It was that once again I was forced to join the action-less party.

Ian caught my eye and shook his head slowly. I bit my lip and took a deep breath. He knew exactly what I was thinking. Maybe I was wrong. Maybe our leader chose Ian for his seniority.

"Great, I'm stuck with her. If we run into trouble you had better hope we don't need a mage who can actually fight."

I tasted the copper tang of blood, and realized I had bit too deep in an effort to keep my comeback to myself.

Paige pulled up beside me. "Let's go, my lady," she said quietly.

I followed her back to where Avery and the rest of our group were gathering. My knight might not be my biggest fan, but she wasn't heartless. Silently, I thanked her for dragging me away before I said something I'd regret.

Adjusting my reins I listened to Avery detail our strategy.

We would be taking a slightly different route into the valley while Ian and Ryder's group took the main one. An Alchemy mage in each party had two potions on hand to give off a bright flare: red once the mission was complete, blue if they ran into trouble and needed backup. It wasn't as effective as lightning but it would serve our purpose given the close proximity while helping keep Ian's and my magic in reserve.

Assuming everything went to plan.

⚜

This time I was not going to be reckless—by word or by deed. It was a vow I had sworn my first night of service, and one I intended to keep. One that I was repeating over and over as I inched along in line with the twenty-five others of Knight Avery's lead. We skirted along a narrow trail of pine and stone, squeezing uncomfortably between the walls of two towering crags while the clip-clop of the horses hooves echoed our progress. The path got to be so tight that only one could pass at a time, and it took us the good part of an hour just to pass the worst of it.

I was beginning to wonder how the other party was faring when there was a heavy rumbling and then an earth-shattering thud. The ground quaked. My horse whinnied, then reared, and I just barely held on as the air filled with panicked cries behind me.

In the seconds that followed, I managed to calm my mare just long enough to dismount as Paige did the same. The two of us had enough sense not to stay mounted during an attack in such limited quarters.

I turned, one hand raised for casting as the other slid my sword from its hilt. Then I gasped. I heard the knights and soldiers behind me do the same.

An enormous boulder easily fifteen feet tall and as wide as the gap had fallen not five feet behind us, cutting us off from the rest of our group and the trail we had taken. There was the loud clash of metal on metal and shouting coming from the other side. I couldn't see—the obstacle was far too high—but I had ears. It didn't take much to ascertain that the scouts' count had been wrong.

The bandits and the rest of our men were on the other side.

And from the sound of it, ours were losing. They had the Alchemy flasks but were undoubtedly too occupied to use them. And even if they weren't, our location was shielded by two rocky walls with no end in sight. I doubted the others would be able to see us, let alone get here in time.

The fifteen of us listened to the fighting in a panic. Paige bellowed a string of curses and several soldiers were trying uselessly to move the boulder standing between us and the rest of our party.

I looked up instead and saw the tall ledge where the bandits had got the drop on us. It was high enough that no one had ever bothered to watch the ledge.

We were fools. The bandits had probably had a rotation of sentries posted at this entrance of the valley hiding, waiting for just this sort of opportunity. Bandits who built that sort of permanent camp undoubtedly employed various techniques to protect it: starting with the giant boulder that was keeping us out as they massacred the rest of our men.

"Ryiah, do something!"

I turned and saw Avery watching me with desperate blue eyes. The knight was frantic and the expressions of the soldiers and knights nearest were equally disturbed. Or helpless.

"We need you to stop them," she whispered.

"I…" My pulse was racing. Here was my opportunity to prove myself and I had nothing. The rock was too heavy to lift, too dense to cast through, too smooth with no holds to climb. I could levitate but it wouldn't help much—the others needed reinforcements, not one girl floating and trying to balance her casting at the same time. "Should I cast lightning to warn the others? Maybe Killian—"

"He'll come too late."

"Aren't you supposed to be powerful?" a man sneered. "You are a second-rank mage, aren't you? Save them!"

"I don't know what I can—"

"They are dying, princess!" another snapped.

"I'm not a—"

"Use your magic!"

"I don't know what to do." My voice quavered as I stared down fifteen sets of angry stares. Worse, I could hear the screams from across the way, echoing along the mountain passage. Bloodcurdling cries and shrieks. *They are dying because you can't think of a way to save them.*

"You are useless!" The same man who called me "princess" spat on me.

"That's enough!" Paige stepped in front of me to glare at the soldier. "She isn't useless, and your shouting isn't going to help her any so why don't you shut your big, ugly mouth before I am forced to do it for you!"

I swallowed. She was wrong. I was useless. This wasn't about my pride. I couldn't care less what that soldier or any of his friends thought of me. I was a fool to wish for conflict. The gods had done this on purpose to punish me. Silly girl wishes for battle to impress the others and this is what she gets. Stuck, useless, listening as innocents are slaughtered just a few paces away.

All my years of training had never prepared me for this.

I was helpless.

I didn't know what to do. I didn't know how. I didn't know anything.

My whole body was erupting in shakes and anxiety was seizing my veins. *Think, Ryiah.* I fought against the fear that was building, praying to the gods that my knees didn't give out in the face of my panic. *I have to do something.*

My audience's faces danced in and out of my sight, blurring and clearing as I held still. I couldn't do this now. I needed to be strong. I needed to think of something. Not to impress the others but to *save* them.

"My lady," Paige said softly, "you can't save everyone."

She was right. But that didn't mean I couldn't try. I breathed in and out through my nose, ten times. Then I squared my shoulders. "Everyone away from the boulder *now!*"

Three soldiers that had been trying to climb scattered and the rest backed away from the rock. I strode forward and placed my palms directly against the rock. Normally I wouldn't need to touch something to cast, but the amount of magic I was about to attempt would require every advantage available.

Let's hope I haven't reached my potential yet...

Clenching my eyes shut I called upon my magic slowly, piece by piece like kindling to a flame. I built up the projection in my mind, fanning the image until it was as real as the object pressed against my hands. I envisioned the casting I wanted to create, taking extra care to make sure my magic was equally projected along the five points in my mind.

Then I took a step back and threw my energy into the cold, gravelly surface for all I was worth.

The boulder started to... quiver? It was emitting just the slightest tremor, and I could hear the murmur of voices behind me. I dug my heels into the ground and forced my mind into a blank slate, wiping out the commotion of noises and smells and the beads of sweat condensing along my brow line. I ignored everything but my magic and strained against the headache that was building and building...

My legs started to tremble, blood pounded against my temples, a rush of hot and cold swamped my skin... but I kept focus and clenched my jaw, forcing my magic to stay with me even as I was ready to fall.

Someone gripped me by my armpits and held as my body set into convulsive shakes. "It's working," Paige whispered.

I peeked out beneath my lashes, and I fought to stay calm. I had *never* even remotely attempted something this heavy during my apprenticeship. Darren had, but even he had his limits. The rock was close to four tons—and the most I had ever lifted was two. Still... the boulder was hovering—albeit very shakily—a couple inches above the ground.

By the gods!

Behind me I could vaguely hear Avery giving orders for the others to take off their extra mail and plates. I swallowed. They needed at least a foot and a half—not two—to fit through the small crawl space.

"Paige," I croaked. "Your knife."

My knight wasted no time in placing the weapon into my shaking fist. I pressed the sharp edge into the palm of my hand. Lightly. Feather-soft at first, careful not to exert too much pressure and collapse the casting I had worked so hard to control.

The rock jolted for just a moment. It jumped another inch, and then three, before settling back a couple inches above the ground.

Ignoring the gasps behind me I let Paige take on the brunt of my weight as I dug the blade deeper and deeper—until blood was dripping down my wrist and the pain of metal against bone and muscle was almost too much to bear.

I opened my eyes again and saw the boulder was hovering two feet above the ground. Everyone was crawling as fast as they could to reach the other side.

A flare of white slammed against my eyes and everything became muted... Past experience taught me I had only seconds before my magic would end.

I stuck out the casting for as long as I could, gritting my teeth and willing it to stay, praying the others had finished making it across. The slight tremors in my legs and arms became sporadic jerks, and Paige struggled to hold on as I lost control of my limbs. I couldn't stop my body's response to the magic much longer...

No. I had to hold on. *You can do this, Ryiah.* I braced myself against the darkness for as long as—

Paige's awed voice broke the silence: "They made it, my lady, you can let go now."

And so I did.

CHAPTER FOUR

Our squad's mission was a success. Shortly after my stunt with the boulder our knights and soldiers were able to overpower the bandits that had ambushed us in the narrow mountain pass. Ian's party faced similar victory: the outlaws at the fort were taken with relative ease. In total there couldn't have been more than fifty men and women—three of which carried enough magic to warrant extra bindings in their ropes.

Our scouts sent a message to the rest of our regiment, and we met up at the stream that had first caused us to part. The soldiers led the prized stallions while our knights escorted the prisoners by foot. It was a slow, steady march to Pamir. Ian and I took turns exchanging stories with Lief and Ray along the way.

We were almost to our destination when Lord Waldyn's men arrived, praising our squad's quick capture and taking the horses off our hands. At the same time another Ferren's Keep regiment came to collect the prisoners.

I turned to Ian, curious. "Where will they take them?"

The mage watched the squad's progress fade off into the distance, disappearing into the thick cluster of trees. "The prison in Gilys. It's two days southwest of Ferren, Sir Quinn's unit covers that part of the territory."

"Will they be put to death?"

He frowned. "Do you think they should be?"

I gave him an incredulous look. "They killed three of our own."

"In self-defense."

Paige guffawed next to me. "They were also planning to sell our horses to Caltoth. They had every intention of supplying our enemy for war. That justifies a hanging in any trial."

Ian heaved a sigh. "I suppose you two are right... Still." He paused and his eyes fell to me. "You heard Sir Gavin— these ones came from one of the towns that lost everything in the fire. I'm not saying it justifies their actions, but... Perhaps that makes them a little harder to condemn?"

My stomach curled in on itself and I swallowed guiltily. The fire was because of me. "Didn't the king send coin?" Then I straightened abruptly, realizing I already knew the answer. "He *did*. Darren told me—"

Lief, who had been listening to our conversation thus far, interjected. "King Lucius is preparing for war. Any aid he sends, well, you can't imagine it's enough. Not with the heavy costs of maintaining the realm's largest army."

Ian met my eyes then. "Ferren and the logging towns received enough to rebuild, they are too important to ignore, but some of the smaller border ones... They aren't always as lucky when things like that happen, Ry. It's the reason my parents took up metal, so they could raise me close to the keep."

I didn't know what to say. The elation I had felt during the bandits' capture was fading fast, and confusion was taking its place. Had I made this happen? *Were the bandits my fault?*

"You didn't cause anything." Paige's biting words made me realize I had said my last thoughts aloud. My knight bristled at the insinuation. "*Caltoth* did this."

"Paige is right, of course." Lief nodded to my guard and then gave me a reassuring pat on the back. "You and the prince saved a great deal more people than you harmed. The fire was a necessary evil; no one would blame you for your actions, Ryiah."

I tried to smile and failed. The head mage had already returned to a conversation with Ian, too busy to notice. When he was finished, Lief turned to my knight with a grin. "Why don't you join Ray and me up front, Paige? I'm sure these two can handle any danger that comes their way." He winked at the two of us. "After Ryiah's little display in the mountains I don't think anyone is going to worry after her safety for a very long time."

Paige hesitated, and I saw her glance shift back to me, undecided. Torn between what she wanted and duty.

"Go on." I gave her a good-natured shove. "I'll be fine."

Her brows furrowed and her chin lifted. "I'll be keeping an eye on you the whole time, my lady."

"I wouldn't expect any less."

The knight huffed and then nudged her mare forward, following the lead mage with one last lingering glance to me.

Ian drew closer as soon as the guard had vanished into the crowd. "The King's Regiment picked well, didn't they?"

"They did." I thought about the way she had helped me when I was casting. "She's blunt, but I almost think it's a blessing. I never have to wonder what she's thinking, she's already told me."

Ian cleared his throat quietly. "What Paige said about Caltoth being at fault, she's not wrong. But Ry..."

I looked up to see his uncomfortable expression. Sweat was beading the boy's forehead and his eyes were conflicted.

I swallowed, mentally preparing myself for what came next. *It's your fault too, Ryiah, I didn't want to say this in front of the others...*

"The Crown isn't blameless."

I blinked slowly. Whatever I had been expecting him to say, that hadn't been it.

Ian pressed closer and lowered his voice. "What I said wasn't a lie. The north doesn't get the help it needs."

"You want me to talk to Darren." It wasn't a question.

"Don't *you*?"

"Ian." I sighed. "It won't change anything." The king was still furious with Darren for the night of the ascension. And preoccupied with negotiations with Pythus. And thanks to me he now hated lowborns a great deal more than usual.

The boy studied the ground. "So you aren't going to even try?"

"I will, but..." I waited until he looked up to continue. "But I don't want you to have any expectations."

"I know what I'm asking." His eyes were somber. "Thank you, Ryiah."

Hearing Ian say my full name was a bit unsettling. It was as if he were reminding himself to put a bit of formality to the end of his request. As if he were a subject, and I the sovereign. It pained me to hear that bit of distance, especially after our conversation in the forest, but I understood.

The north was his home, and whether or not I considered myself one of them, I was the Crown.

"A week," I breathed.

Ray echoed my words: "A *whole* week."

"Of freedom."

"Freedom," he repeated.

"A week."

"A whole week of it."

"If you two grow any more slack-jawed," Lief said, chuckling, "you'll become a pair of fish."

"It's standard for any service in all of the cities," Ian added.

Paige scoffed. "Not the King's Regiment."

I just shook my head in astonishment, still not quite believing we had a full week to ourselves. Three weeks of duty had flown by in the blink of an eye—well, not truly, at the time it had seemed like an eternity, but now...

"What does one do during this..." Ray paused. "Freedom?"

"What did you enjoy doing before the Academy?"

Ray's eyes were wide. "I don't remember."

The head mage's gaze flitted to me. "What about you, Ry?"

What did I enjoy before the Academy? So many years before... I found myself emitting the same response. "I don't remember."

"The novelty will wear off." Lief set his packs on his bunk with a groan. "By the second month we'll find the two of you in the taverns with the rest of our lot. Ferren might be known for its blacksmiths, but the true secret is Tijan's ale. Strongest brew around. Well, that and our women." His gaze fell to Paige.

My knight scowled in distaste. "*Hhmphf.* You must not have a very good selection."

I bit my lip. Tijan was tempting—not for the ale, but my brother. Now that I had seven days to myself, the world was full of possibility. And the best one: Derrick. I hadn't seen him in months, and now we were only a couple hours apart.

But there was also the Candidacy.

Ray was already throwing a pair of fresh clothes into his satchel. "When can we leave?"

"As soon as you are ready." Ian grinned and looked to me. "You coming?"

"I don't think so." My enthusiasm had already started to ebb. I couldn't visit Derrick, not with my dream looming so close on the horizon. "I think I'm going to stay behind."

"You serve the north," Lief said, "don't forget to live, Ryiah. We don't get paid near enough to risk our lives without a bit of fun from time to time."

"I know." I frowned. "It's not that... I just... I need to train."

"Train? For *what*? The apprenticeship is over. You already train every day in service." His tone was incredulous.

"For the Candidacy," I mumbled.

Ian and Lief exchanged knowing looks and Ray spoke: "Ry, it's months away. You can take a day off."

I looked down at my hands. "Not if I want to win."

"You really think you can beat him, don't you?"

I didn't ask who *he* was; it was obvious.

"Darren's not a god." I crossed my arms defiantly. "His potential isn't infinite."

"Master Byron ranked him first."

"For now."

Ray held up his hands in surrender. "Remind me to never challenge you to a duel. You are a bloodthirsty savage."

I just grinned in reply.

Lief grabbed Ray and Ian by the shoulders. "Are you two ready to head out?"

They nodded in unison and gave me a parting wave.

Lief tossed me his extra water skin in passing. "You better get training, Ryiah. We can't have our savage go soft."

Harsh crunching and then the ground gave a quivering sigh. The mountain of rubble rose into the air, twice the size of the boulder in the mountains. Thick granite hovered in the sky as I lifted my hand, higher and higher, watching my magic mirror its movement with the rock.

The rubble rose. Shakily, with small bits of dirt trailing down like a shower of rain.

My whole body trembled with the effort. I held steady, digging my boots into the soil as perspiration dripped down my eyes, blinding me with the beating rays of the sun.

Still, I held steady. And the rubble kept rising.

Then, it stopped.

My fingers started to tremble and shake and the sun's blinding light seemed to bleed itself right out of my chest. I could feel the casting sputtering inside me: a dying flame. My magic had reached its limit.

I bit my lip. A pain casting in the height of such power was too risky to partake. Not on my own.

Exhaling slowly, I let the rocks return to the ground and then took a deep swallow of mountain air to clear my head.

"That was amazing, love." Two hands slipped around my waist from behind, and I leaned into Darren's arms, letting the rush of victory wash over like the sweet scent of pine.

"I've been practicing." I knew I was preening. I had just surpassed his skill during our apprenticeship.

The prince smiled against the back of my ear, lips pressing into the skin just below. A shiver ran down my spine. "Yes, you have."

"Am I better than you?" The words spilled from my lips before I had a chance to catch myself.

Darren smiled and released me, pointing to a large shadow in front of us. I lost my breath: the mountain. He couldn't, could he? The prince took a step forward and raised his arm.

I watched as the giant base splintered and groaned, a terrible ear-shattering grate. Stones spewed out in every which direction as the jagged peak rose up into the sky, blacking out the sun so that the entire land was cast into shade.

The world became night.

The non-heir turned to me with a smirk. "Keep trying, Ryiah."

I woke up with a start.

My whole body was sore and aching, and every muscle felt as though it had been torn from my limbs and twisted back into place—the wrong place.

The summer heat hadn't helped; my sheets were pooling with sweat. I threw them off in disgust. Usually the keep was cool enough, but I suspected my dream had played a part in the mess I saw now.

I had spent the past couple days brushing up my routine while the three patrols on leave had all but disappeared from the keep. Sure, there were still stragglers and the squad in charge of the keep itself, but half of the men were visiting in Tijan or one of the nearby towns.

"Can't sleep?" Paige sat up on her bunk, rubbing her eyes.

"I had that dream again." I groaned. "I think the gods are trying to tell me to stop sleeping altogether. It's the only way I'll catch up to *him*."

The knight yawned. "The gods do not waste their time dallying in mortal affairs. That dream means you are worrying too much. It's playing on your fear—"

I shot her a half-hearted glare. "I'm not worrying. I'm tired. I'm sore. I'm even hungry, but I'm not worried."

"Whatever you say, my lady." She started to roll back on her side, and I tossed my pillow at her.

"It's time to go to the practice courts."

"Now?" She didn't even open her eyes. "It's too early. The sun won't rise for two more hours—and you, my lady, are *always* the last one to rise."

I ignored her and began changing into my clothes, one painful tug at a time. "The dream was a sign." I gritted my teeth. "I need to train harder." Another painful tug and the tunic was over my head. "If I don't..." Ow. "I'm never going to stand a chance against him." I bit back a sigh. "Or any of those other first-rank mages." And I wanted to. All those years of trials and tribulations. I was tired of being second-best.

I wanted *the* Black Robe.

Paige rose, with an exasperated sigh.

"That's the spirit." I shot her a grin. "Don't worry, I'll make sure to include you in my acceptance speech."

She followed me out the door, muttering under her
breath. At first I was too busy feigning enthusiasm to catch
what she was saying, but as we were sparring later outside the
keep it returned to me: *"And they told me to keep watch over a
'lady.'"*

I couldn't help but smirk. *A lady.*

I lunged and defeated her guard.

I was a war mage.

I spent the rest of the week in the practice courts. Endlessly drilling. Over and over until I was limping back to the
keep each night. If my guard had an opinion for why I was
pushing myself so hard she was wise enough not to comment.

Every single drop of sweat was a testament to how deeply I wanted that robe. I cast until I was hunched over the
ground, vomiting the contents of whatever meal I had managed to force down just hours before. Then I pain cast.

Paige had one of the keep's healers nearby, just in case.
Luckily, four years of Master Byron's scrupulous gaze had paid
off, and I knew just how far I could push myself before breach-
ing those limits.

By the time the week had ended I was ready to return to
service. Someone must have told the others how hard I was
drilling because I got nine reassuring pats on the back the
morning we set out. They didn't comment directly, but the
Candidacy was all anyone could talk about.

Like the previous patrol our three weeks of service went
by without much ado. Caltothians remained at bay, at least for
now. We didn't come across any outlaws this time around; our
patrol was conflict-free. All of the extra time led me to drills
and routine, anything to keep the non-heir from taking over
my thoughts. I wasn't going to let my anxiety get the best of
me, not after everything I had become. I threw myself into
practice instead.

"I can't—"

"Ry," Ray said plaintively. "You have done nothing, and I repeat, *nothing*, but drill for the last three months on end. You can afford one night off from your routine to take a drink with the rest of us. I know you want to concentrate on the Candidacy but the others talk. They think it's because you think you are better than them."

I glared in response. "You know that's not true."

"See here." Ian stepped between us. "We'll even take you to a tavern in town. Not Tijan, just a round with the squad, and then you can go back to torturing yourself for hours on end."

"Just one?"

"Just one," Ray promised.

I shifted from one foot to the next. In truth, they were right. I had heard what the soldiers were saying—I just hadn't wanted to think about it. I was also exhausted: mentally, physically... even my castings had started to falter. A night off was truly what I needed. During the apprenticeship we'd been given a reprieve, I could afford a couple of hours with friends now.

"Okay. You two win."

The boys exchanged victorious grins, and I promised to catch up the moment I finished putting away my things. In truth I wanted to pay a visit to the bathhouse—the stench following me was anything but pleasant. I doubted they would enjoy my company without it.

By the time I had finished washing up, Paige and I were ready for a reprieve. I was in such a good mood I almost missed the person standing next to the exit of the dining commons.

"*Derrick!*"

I caught sight of those blond tufts of curl and sprinted across the corridor as fast as my legs could run. Paige scrambled after me, grumbling about impatient charges. I knocked into two soldiers and spilled a whole tray of pickled greens along the way. I shouted an apology in passing. The dancing blue eyes of my brother were all I could see.

The young man broke into a grin, dimples on each side of his cheeks. "Ry! There you are. I've been looking all over for you!"

I squeaked and threw myself at him. Derrick was three years younger than me, but already twice as thick—sprouting a legion of muscle on every inch of his frame. "Gods, do you ever stop growing?"

Derrick ruffled my hair, setting me down with an unapologetic grin. "I have no intention of stopping until you can fit in the palm of my hand."

I snorted and even Paige—who had finally caught up after my mad dash across the room—almost smiled.

"And who is this? Your beautiful lady-in-waiting?"

And my knight was back to scowling. "You see the sword I'm carrying, no?"

His smile faltered under her stern expression. "Yes?"

"Say something that foolish again and I'll gut you from head to toe."

My brother backed away slowly. It didn't matter that Paige was half his size; the look in her eye was formidable enough.

"He's only teasing, Paige," I said. "Derrick doesn't have a death wish."

"It wasn't funny," the knight muttered.

"She's harmless," I promised.

Derrick raised his hands in peace.

A young man with coal-black hair coughed loudly beside Derrick. I wondered who he was until Derrick put his arm around the boy's shoulders and nodded. "Ry, and... *Paige.* This is my comrade-at-arms Jacob. He grew up here in Ferren—he was the one I wrote you about during the apprenticeship."

I studied the soldier and noted him doing the same for me. I started to smile and then stopped when I realized my brother's best friend was wearing a sour expression. *Not another one.* I tore my eyes away from the boy to regard my brother instead. "What are you doing here, Derrick? Not that I'm not happy to see you but I wasn't expecting—"

"I offered him a post. Here. At the keep."

I turned and found myself face-to-face with the elusive presence of Commander Nyx herself. She gave a small smile to the boys and then returned her gaze to me. "I had no idea Derrick was your youngest brother, Ryiah. Sir Borgan in Tijan does nothing but sing the young soldier praises, and Jacob, well, how can I say no to the son of Aldus? He is one of the best soldiers we have."

Aldus might have been one of the best, but he was also one of the older soldiers that continued to regard me with a perpetual dislike. Much like his son was doing now. Even after my performance in the mountains. I stifled a sigh.

Derrick elbowed me in the side. "Guess whose squad we are on?"

My eyes grew huge. "Mine? Really?" It was too good to be true.

"That's right." Commander Nyx nodded to a knight in passing and then continued. "Sir Gavin just promoted two of his soldiers to Sir Maxon's unit. When he informed me we had an opening I immediately contacted Borgan for recommendations." She folded her arms. "These two are already settled in and ready to start first thing in the morning."

The commander paused. "I must confess, Ryiah... I've been meaning to talk to you about what happened in the mountains. I know my men aren't the friendliest sort, but you've done some great work. I'm very impressed."

"Thank you, Commander."

"It'll be a shame when your time here is up." She dismissed herself and returned to the hall.

"She doesn't want you to return to the capital," Paige observed. "Most of them want you to leave, but not her."

"At least someone wants me here." I sighed.

Derrick made an offended noise. "Aren't you forgetting someone?"

"Fine. Two someones."

"What about Paige?"

My knight snorted. "Who would choose to stay in a wretched keep when they could reside in a palace?"

CHAPTER FIVE

Ryiah,

Blayne's negotiations with King Joren have gone better than expected. The Pythian ambassador is set to spend a week in Devon during the winter solstice. Father has demanded your presence—a letter was already sent to your commander issuing six weeks of leave from the Ferren's Keep Regiment.

I'd write more, but I haven't had a moment to myself. I've spent half my time on boring patrols and the rest in Crown meetings. I miss the Academy. Our time in the apprenticeship was a reprieve. I would trade most anything for it now.

When you get here I promise to ask you all about your time in Ferren. If you met anyone half as unbearable as me. If you are happy. If you are sad. If you miss me...

Gods, I wish it were sooner.

Prince Darren of Jerar, second son of King Lucius III

I stared at the letter, rereading its contents for the tenth time that evening, and then folded it into a neat little square that I tucked back into my pocket. Then I took it out again. I couldn't get over that last line: *Gods, I wish it were sooner.* I couldn't keep the smile from my face.

Darren missed me.

"It's a summons, isn't it?"

I nodded.

"Thank the gods!" Paige left the bench to grab a flagon of ale.

"You really have to go?" My brother sat down beside me, his face a puzzle of emotion. "I only just arrived."

"I'm sorry."

"Alex got to have all the fun," he griped.

"It's a Crown order, not a request, silly. If I don't..." I lowered my voice in conspiracy. "Paige will knock me over the head and drag me to the castle unconscious."

"You wouldn't do that, would you, Paige?" Derrick turned to my guard and she wiped the ale from her mouth with an evil laugh. He shuddered and looked away.

I touched his wrist. "Don't worry, little brother, we'll have plenty of adventures in the six weeks before I depart."

"You are leaving?"

I looked up to meet Ian's gaze as he walked past, his arms full of kindling.

"Not for a while. But I haven't forgotten what you asked me. I'll talk to him."

The mage smiled, but it didn't quite meet his eyes.

"What are the two of you hinting at?"

I gave my brother a nudge. "Nothing you need to worry about, Derrick. Just something I promised a friend."

"Are you going to tell Darren the promise was to *him*?" My brother grinned wickedly.

I glared at Derrick as Ian retreated to the other side of camp. "Please don't make this any more awkward than it already is."

"That's Ian, isn't it? The one Alex wanted you to pick. Over the prince."

"Yes." My teeth clenched. "Can we not talk about this anymore?"

"Only if you tell me what you promised him."

I groaned. "You've grown into a pest. I think Alex is my favorite now."

"That buffoon? Never." My brother prodded me with his fork. "Now spill, Ry."

It wasn't really a secret, I supposed. "Ian wants me to ask Darren to talk to his father about sending more coin north. To help the border towns—the ones that aren't prosperous enough to garner support when the raids hit."

"That's it?"

"What did you expect?"

"A secret affair—" My brother ducked my fist, laughing. "Well, he is *pretty*." He ducked again and this time was not so lucky.

"Pursuing Ian was a mistake," I said quietly. "I almost lost one of my best friends because I was a coward."

"Well then if it's not about him, why the secrecy? Why be ashamed to have the others hear you want to help the north?" My brother lowered his voice. "It might help, Ry. I've tried talking to some of the other soldiers, but a lot of them are set against you. They think you are a privileged highborn now that you are engaged to a prince—it makes no difference that you grew up in Demsh'aa and your brother is one of them."

I shook my head. "The king is furious with Darren. I promised Ian I'd ask, but I don't think it is going to help any." I pulled at a splinter that had gotten lodged in my finger. "I really wish they didn't hate me. I thought it would get better after I proved myself but…"

"But you are engaged to a prince." Derrick grew serious. "You haven't heard the rhyme have you?"

"What are you talking about?"

"It's the most common verse they have: 'north the poor and south the snout.'"

"The 'snout?'"

"Highborn Swine. Anyone who lives at court."

"Oh… how charming." I bit my lip. A prejudice that was undoubtedly inspired by the tragedies the Caltothians created.

The Crown was attempting to save for war, yet by doing so it had shirked its duties to the people up north. Border villages of friends—maybe even families—had been attacked, and they'd been left to fend for themselves. No wonder they had come up with such a hateful rhyme.

Commander Nyx and her regiment were attempting to help their people through patrols, but they could only do so much.

I needed to get that purse.

Derrick put a big arm around my neck, misunderstanding my silence. "Come, now, not everyone is going to like my big sister."

"Don't you even *think* about joining them."

Derrick grinned and pulled a simple leather cord out of his shirt to show me the copper ring I had given him years ago dangling at its end.

It made me smile to see he was still wearing it even in his soldier's garb.

"Never. Besides unlike our dear, *sweet* brother I actually like the fact that you are marrying a prince. I met Darren last year in the infirmary, remember? He's a good sort, Ry. You will always have my support."

I felt the tension leave my limbs. "Thank you."

He ruined the moment by picking me up and throwing me over his shoulder.

"Derrick!" I swatted at the back of his head. "Put me down."

"Hmm." The boy pretended not to hear my squeals. "That was too easy. You've got to work on your guard, Ry."

I lowered my hands and punched the side of his ribs. He set me down with a laugh.

"I don't need a guard around you. You aren't my enemy, Derrick."

My brother grinned. "That's the thing about enemies. You never know who they could end up being."

A week before I was to depart half the regiment was seeing to chores around camp, and the rest of us sat trading jokes or serving watch around the perimeter. I knew I should be helping out, but I was unwilling to leave until Lief finished his latest tale from the past Candidacy. Most of the regiment mages stuck around as well; Lief was a great storyteller and most of us were not old enough to remember the last Candidacy—I hadn't even been born.

All of us listened in rapture as Lief recounted the final duel between Marius and his final opponent, Mara. The Restoration and Alchemy sessions had been brutal, but nothing could compare to the head mage's recount of Combat. I am certain most of us forgot to breathe during his telling. *How in the name of the gods had Mara survived?*

Lief raised a brow as if hearing our unspoken question. "It took ten healers to save her life."

For a moment there was quiet and then Ian finally spoke: "And yet we are all mad enough to attempt the same ourselves." His raspy joke was met with more silence.

Several of the Restoration mages' faces were as white as a sheet; my nails were bitten to the quick. True, nothing Lief was saying was new. We had all heard similar stories during our youth, but hearing it now when our turn was less than a year away? It was an entirely different experience.

"A mage died in the last Candidacy." Ruth addressed Combat's head mage. "Didn't he?"

Lief prodded the fire with a stick. "The boy was seventeen, young for his faction and too young to be participating in the first place. One of those highborn mages that joined the academy at the tender age of twelve." His face filled with contempt. "The rules dictate very clearly that a mage must cease casting the moment his opponent surrenders. The boy never surrendered; he was overconfident and a fool. It was during the melee, he never should have made the mistake in the first place."

"I must be mad to think I have a chance at winning," I muttered to Ray and Ian as we started our evening drills. They chuckled.

The three of us took turns casting great bolts of lightning into the sky. We were a day's ride from the keep so there was no need for conservative casting. Not with so many nearby patrols.

"That might be true." Lief stopped observing to interrupt. "But what you mustn't forget, Ryiah, is how little of us there are to begin with. Only five Combat mages ascend each year, and by the time a man reaches his late fifties he has no magic left." He paused. "The youngest mage would be seventeen at the time of their ascension *if* they started at twelve. That leaves a little over forty years and five of us each year... Two hundred, but that number is infinitely smaller when you consider potential. Any mage past thirty is not going to consider entry—his stamina will have already begun to decline."

He paused. "For me, it's already too late." His gaze was wistful, but resigned. "Too young for the last Candidacy and too old for the present... But you, Ian, even Ray here... I doubt there will be more than sixty entries for Combat. You three have much better odds than you think."

I didn't say a word for the rest of the night. I wanted to best Darren and win, yes, but I had never stopped to consider exactly how many mages I would be going up against. Sixty was certainly better than I had anticipated. I was second rank. That put me at the top half of our faction's candidates... Of course there were those whose potential had grown post-ascension... but for most their limits will have undoubtedly been reached by the time they received their ranking.

And that's when I realized it: I really could have a chance.

I spoke too soon. That was the first thought that crossed my mind as I curled my knees to my chest, shivering and shaking under the heavy blankets of my cot.

Paige set a bucket on the floor. I cringed at the heavy thud of metal against stone. "Not so loud," I begged.

"You need to drink some of that tea the healers gave you, my lady."

My stomach gurgled and heaved and I clutched it with a groan. "Stuff was vile," was all I could manage.

"Well, you will never get better if you don't, and tomorrow we set off for the palace even if I have to tie you to the saddle."

"...Wouldn't...dare."

She snorted. "I will, and you know it well."

I didn't say anything else. I just clutched the mug and shuddered. Then I downed the contents, refusing to let the bitter, chalky liquid rest on my tongue any longer than it had to. When I was done I fell back against the bed in a heap. My belongings were already packed. I just needed this sickness to end. I'd spent the past three days tossing and turning in a sleepless fit, hot and cold, unable to do anything but writhe in my misery.

The Restoration mages in the infirmary said I had a "mage's cold." As one could surmise it was the result of too much magic. I had never experienced it before because Master Byron had been so focused on us learning to exercise what we had with caution. The few times I had been reckless with my magic I had ended up unconscious in the infirmary, so the cold would have just been a small part of my recovery.

"Why," I moaned, "why didn't I listen...?"

Paige blotted a cloth against my wet, sticky skin. "Because you are stubborn, my lady. Now drink and rest."

Gods, I prayed, *do not put me through this for another fourteen days.*

The gods never heard me.

CHAPTER SIX

"Oh dear, sweet..." I dismounted, running a hand through my frost-strewn hair as I fell to my knees in a broken promise, not caring what I looked like to the guards standing outside the palace gate.

Never, *ever* would I put myself through that again. I had spent the first week of travel drinking the healers' vile tea and recovering from my cold only to spend the final leg of our journey caught in an icy snowstorm that rivaled any Jerar had ever seen. I swore the moment I stepped foot in the capital city I would never push myself that hard again.

"My lady." Paige was working hard to hide her smile. "They are waiting for us."

I forced myself to stand, brushing off a layer of powder and scrambling to make myself presentable. Not that anyone would be able to recognize me under the layers of fur. I looked like a shaggy snow beast. The kind that terrorized children in cautionary tales told by their parents. Ella would be proud. She hated winter more than anyone else I knew.

Paige walked over to the two soldiers standing at attention. "I am escorting Lady Mage Ryiah of Demsh'aa, Prince Darren's intended—"

She didn't even get to finish. The palace gates swung open and one of the men grinned. "About time. You two were supposed to arrive this morning. His highness has been pacing the grounds like a caged animal. He'll probably find you before you even reach the doors."

The cold, my exhaustion, and everything else were instantly forgotten. Paige had to sprint to keep up with my progress as I threw my reins to the waiting hostler and searched the path ahead. I wasn't sure if I should be excited or nervous, but at the moment the only thing I knew was that my pulse was louder than whatever Paige was trying to say.

A hand touched my arm and I turned to face my knight.

She pointed to the left.

I looked.

Saw the gardens and the marble statue in the fountain's center. Saw the wandering nobility in their warm winter cloaks. And then I saw a scruffy gray mutt matted with snow and the person standing beside it, one hand absently rubbing its head—the other getting ready to throw a stick.

My heart stopped. *Breathe, Ryiah.* Darren looked... I didn't have words. *Has it really only been five months?* He was standing there in a dark brocade cloak and black leather boots. I was immediately reminded of the day we met. There was that gold chain hanging from his neck and the fading sun's rays caught the stone at its base, a hematite oval—the signature gem of the Crown. Ink-black, jaw-length locks framed his face, bangs falling just past his eyes.

I exhaled slowly.

Whatever people said about Blayne, he couldn't hold a candle to his brother.

Who had just looked up from his dog to catch me staring. Only this time I didn't have to feel guilty or ashamed. Because he was mine. And I was allowed to stare.

And he was staring right back.

For a second our gazes were locked and neither of us moved.

Then he was running and I was running, and we didn't stop until my arms were wrapped around his neck and his were locked around my waist, his face pressed in my hair.

"Five months is too long," he rasped.

My eyes watered, and I told myself I would never let go. "You smell like home."

I felt him crack a smile. "Would you believe me if I told you the same?"

I nodded and then held still, surrounded by pine and cloves, and for just once everything was right. The two of us in the middle of the courtyard, snow falling softly around us, lost to the rest of the world. I was content to stay that way for the rest of my life.

"Ah, and I see the prestigious lowborn has returned."

I started to pull away, but Darren held tight and growled at his brother who had managed to make an appearance unnoticed.

"Not now, Blayne."

"You don't have to use such a surly tone, Darren, I was merely making an observation." The crown prince's gaze fell to me, and he wrinkled his nose. "Might I suggest a nice bath before greeting anyone from court."

My cheeks burned as the heir to the kingdom sauntered away, a swing in his step.

"Don't listen to him." Darren's tone was resigned. "Blayne is just worried about the Pythians' arrival. Father has been... difficult."

I shook my head and stepped out of his embrace. "You don't need to explain." Blayne and I shared a mutual dislike. The king's temperament had no part in that.

I sighed. "Besides, Paige and I have been riding all day. I *should* probably get cleaned up before anyone else sees us."

"Then let me take you to your chambers." The non-heir caught my wrist and pulled me forward.

"What about Paige?" I glanced at my knight. She was trying to pick gray dog hair off her breeches with a sour expression. Wolf, seemingly oblivious to her reaction, continued to bark at her, demanding a playmate.

I stifled a smile.

"While you are on palace grounds, there is no need for a personal guard." Darren led me to the castle doors. "She will be on rotation with the rest of the King's Regiment."

"Oh." I followed him inside, and then froze as soon as I set foot on the marble. That's how long it took to recall his words. "My...chambers?"

He gave me a crooked grin. "You have the room next to mine. The servants spent the last week preparing it. Once we are wed, it will be a sitting room, but until then it's where you will stay during your time here. Your ladies-in-waiting have been..."

Darren rattled on, detailing the other changes that had taken place, but my thoughts had already been swept up by the first.

My own room. With ladies-in-waiting—*my* ladies-in-waiting. I swallowed, suddenly nervous. I had managed to avoid most of the changes from my new status in Ferren. The capital was a different story. I knew the king wouldn't let me run around in training breeches and a shirt unless I was in the practice courts.

What if they expected me to act like my new station? Highborn, well mannered, and fluent in whatever flowery tongue the nobility expected? I hadn't the slightest idea how to act like a true lady of court. Ella did, but she wasn't here to help guide me.

Not for the first time, I missed my best friend. Not just because she could tell me what to do. But so that she could hold my hand. We had gone through everything together.

For five years she had helped guide me through training and Darren and the etiquette of court; this time, I was on my own.

⚔

I couldn't keep from gawking even after Darren had finished showing me to my new chambers. This was it. My own room. In the king's palace. As the non-heir's future wife.

Nothing would ever be the same.

Two ladies-in-waiting had already called upon some servants to draw a bath in the paneled wood tub of a small adjoining room. I almost died of delight when I stepped in and the water was still steeping hot. I stayed until the water ran cold, rubbing my skin raw, and then soaking in the lavender-scented bubbles a bit longer.

When I finally did step out freshly pressed linens were waiting. *Bliss.*

The nearest girl, Celine, a young thing with long, brown tresses, helped dress me in one of the many gowns the king had commissioned for my stay. As the other styled my hair, Celine was quick to note that my first responsibility would be to visit the palace seamstress the following morning. I was in need of a whole new wardrobe. The beautiful clothes I had wouldn't begin to cover my appearances in court. Not of a princess-to-be. Even one who spent most of her time as a warrior mage.

I spent some more time taking in my surroundings: the flowery design adorning the walls, the delicate lace covering of a bed made of cherry wood, even the tiny nightstand with its golden vase of gently dried flowers—a bit of cheer in the midst of a white winter.

Like Darren's, the cold marble floor of my chamber was covered in luxurious fur rugs, thick and dense and seeping in warmth. I had to keep myself from cooing as I touched my toes to the ground. It felt so nice after a two-week's journey in nothing but soggy boots and on splintery inns' wood.

It was paradise.

Like all wonderful things, however, the charm did not last. And for me that was the moment I stepped outside the door, bidding my ladies to their own devices, and saw who stood outside it.

"Now, that is much better. Who knew you were capable of such contradictions?"

I braced myself immediately. Blayne was leaning on the wall just outside my chamber, and his stance made it clear it wasn't coincidence. "What do you want Blayne?"

"You, of course."

Panic slammed my ribs, and the prince's eyes narrowed in amusement. He laughed, a harsh, empty sound, and then continued.

"I wanted to *talk* to you, Ryiah. We've never had what one might call pleasant relations. I would like to start anew."

I was instantly suspicious. "Why?" Not only had he gone out of his way to threaten me during my time as an apprentice, he had also tried to rape my best friend. Prince Blayne of Jerar, first in line to the throne, was the last person I would trust. I already knew exactly what kind of person he was, and I had no intentions of "starting anew."

I was about to tell him as much, but a moment of clarity hit me. It would be reckless to alienate the heir, no matter how little I thought of him, and reckless was never a good move. Especially where Blayne was concerned.

Still, I doubted the prince would trust me if I acquiesced too easily. He knew we shared a mutual dislike. "Give me a reason I should believe a word you say."

He considered my question.

"Because one day I'm going to be your king, Ryiah, and I will be the last person you want as an enemy."

He didn't even bother to veil the threat. Well. I could play along. I didn't trust the heir's offer for a second. But I couldn't very well refuse.

"What do you say? Friends?" The boy held out his hand expectantly. It was pale. The pallor of a palace recluse. One who preferred darkness to light.

I made myself smile; praying the heir to the kingdom didn't notice how my eyes didn't match my words. "Of course."

I didn't know his end game, but there was one thing I knew for certain: whatever Blayne planned, it wasn't good for me.

The heir to the kingdom escorted me to the king's dining hall, the very same room that had changed my life during the ascension just six months before. Without the bustle of fifteen mages and the Council filling its seats the room was decidedly quieter. It was also more intimidating.

Now only the very end of the great table was set— enough for three persons. Two of the seats were already taken.

King Lucius sat at the end drinking from a heavy goblet of gold. His stark white hair pressed close to the skull and the trim of his mustache was barely more than a whisper, yet it framed the length of his hard face perfectly.

Our history told of kings that smiled and kings that conquered. He was the latter.

Darren sat at his father's right. He had changed into a crimson jacket and brown breeches that seemed at odds with the bejeweled velvet and heavy robes of his father. He was busy pushing a piece of cooked rabbit back and forth across his plate. He didn't notice when we entered.

Blayne wasted no time in taking the other chair. Then I was left standing, clutching my arms to keep from trembling as I waited for someone to tell me what to do. Did proper etiquette dictate I interrupt the king with a greeting, or simply stand and wait for him to acknowledge my presence first? I couldn't remember. I had spent so little time in court, and that short week of lessons before I had left for Ferren's Keep had slipped from my mind.

I wished Darren would look up and realize I was here.

The king finally spotted me. He watched me as the seconds passed, not a word was spoken.

Blayne cleared his throat. "Father, I invited Lady Ryiah to join us."

The non-heir looked up, startled. The king's gaze narrowed into two small pins.

What do I do?

Darren's eyes met mine, and he coughed loudly, making a quick gesture with his hand.

Memory returned and embarrassment flooded my cheeks. I dipped into a steep curtsy with a softly mumbled, "My liege."

The king's gaze fell from mine, and I was released from his spell.

Darren rushed forward to take my arm and called for a hovering servant to bring an extra chair. "Sorry," he said under his breath, "I didn't know you'd be joining us. I thought after the long ride you'd want to sleep."

"I didn't know I was," I whispered. I jerked my chin in Blayne's direction. "Your brother was the one who brought me here."

After the servant had returned with an extra setting, I took a seat at Darren's right, furthest from the king who had gone back to his drink. The room was uncomfortably silent. I wondered if it had anything to do with my added presence, or if this was how meals usually went for the royal family.

"So... Lady Ryiah, how have you found your stay so far?"

I forced myself to smile across the table. "Delightful. Thank you for asking, Blayne."

"And your new chambers? Were they to your liking?"

"They were."

Blayne continued to press one banal question after the other, and I continued to offer up stilted replies. Darren squeezed my hand under the table, resting his wrist against my lap. He was smiling at his brother, as if grateful to him for making polite conversation, but I didn't believe the heir's act for a moment.

Luckily the focus on me only lasted for a couple of minutes. The king finished his wine and growled at the servants for a new bottle. Then he turned to scowl at his sons, ignoring my presence.

"Blayne. My advisors tell me the ambassador is set to arrive by the end of this week. Have you seen to the preparations?"

"Yes, father. I met with the scholars just yesterday to discuss foreign policy."

"And custom?"

Blayne yawned, unperturbed. "Custom. Fare. Dress. And whatever else those barbarians insist on as part of their meaningless culture—"

The king cut him off. "It might be meaningless, but it will be one you breathe for as long as Duke Cassius is present."

"It will be my utmost concern."

"Don't use that tone with me, boy. If you had wooed the Borean princess the way you were supposed to we wouldn't be stuck hosting King Joren's brother in the first place. You know how I distrust those Pythians."

Blayne's eyes flitted to me—the real reason he hadn't been able to win over Shina. If his brother hadn't fallen in love with a lowborn, Darren never would have come between Blayne and Shinako in the first place.

I cringed and waited. This was why Blayne had been so kind to me earlier. I should have known. Trick the lowborn into coming to dinner, and then offer her up as the sacrificial lamb to his father's aggression. Admittedly, I hadn't expected the treachery so soon, but that didn't make it any less upsetting.

The corner of the prince's lip turned up, like the two of us were sharing a secret.

I am definitely a lamb. I looked to Darren panicked but he just shook his head. *What are you doing?* I wanted to scream. *Stop him!*

"Yes," Blayne said slowly. "Those Pythians are a nasty bunch. Don't you worry, father, I know my role well." He coughed loudly. "I can always have a lady or two keep him company when he grows restless."

"He has a wife," the king growled. "Unless you wish to insult him and make a mockery of our court, you will do no such thing."

"Come now, Father, everyone knows the noblemen take a lover or two during their travels. Even their wives. Why, it's a common enough saying: the longer at sea, the more lovers she keeps."

I let out a stilted breath of relief. Blayne had changed the subject with the barest brush of his words.

The king just made a disbelieving scoff and then turned to his youngest with a scowl. "And you, *you* will help your brother win their favor."

Darren didn't bat an eye. "Yes, Father."

"You understand how important the alliance is." The words were ominous.

The prince nodded.

"Good." The king sprawled back in his chair as a servant refilled his drink. He kept his eyes on his youngest. "Because if you don't, this entire kingdom will fall to Caltoth. And when it does? Your lowborn wife will be the first blood I spill."

My lungs ceased to work. The goblet I'd been drinking from sloshed scarlet into my lap. *I shouldn't be here.* I started to stand but Darren's grip on my hand tightened, pulling me back down.

"Blayne will not fail in his task," Darren said. Calmly. Rationally. "I will help him succeed, Father. Ryiah will too. She was with me when the Caltothians attacked. She has witnessed their brutality first hand."

"Which will be nothing compared to mine." The king set down his goblet just as a servant entered with a scroll. I watched as he skimmed its contents and then pushed back his chair, clearing his throat. "I am needed in the war chambers. It appears the rebels have struck Port Cyri again. I want the two of you to join me."

Both princes stood. "Yes, Father."

"And Darren, make sure this lowborn doesn't embarrass our court when the Pythians arrive."

Of all the exciting ways I had envisioned my time in the king's palace, spending my days in the Grand Chamber wasn't one of them. Two masters of decorum drilled highborn etiquette into my ears until I was certain I'd go mad. When it wasn't the proper address or the correct way to curtsy it was my expectations as a princess and those were even worse. I believe the phrase "sire a son" was repeated so often my cheeks would be permanently inflamed.

Darren wasn't even nearby. He was in the palace, but he might as well have been deployed. He and Blayne were stuck tending to Crown affairs the entire week. I didn't even have the pleasure of dining at his side—the king had ordered the servants to bring all their meals into the war chambers.

I couldn't bear the thought of the great long hall on my own so I spent most of my meals in the kitchens. Luckily for me the cook, Benny, was there, and he was more than willing to entertain an awkward girl.

True to his word, he had taken a bride shortly after Priscilla left the premises. When he wasn't feeding me pasties or complaining about his demanding new wife, he was telling me tales of Darren as a child.

It wasn't hard to notice almost all of the stories took place after the prince's sixth year.

"What was Darren like before?"

The cook pursed his lips. "A terror."

I started to laugh—until I caught the serious gleam in his eyes. "A terror? Surely you are talking about Blayne."

The man shook his head. "That one used to pick fights with anything that breathed. He was the complete opposite of his brother in fact."

I leaned closer on the counter. "Blayne was the 'nice' one?" What the palace must have been like if that were true.

"You see the boys as the men they are now." Benny pulled out another tray of scones and began heaping them on racks to cool. "They were much different back then."

"What changed?"

"Well…" The cook frowned. "One of the healers swears up and down the boys were brought into the infirmary one night—Blayne the worst of the two—and Darren still clutching a knife."

My stomach churned, and I set down my juice, all appetite lost. "Do you think Darren…?"

"All I know for certain is the king commissioned Commander Audric to start training him for the School of Knighthood the very next day."

"And Blayne?"

"Different than before. More outspoken, colder… I dare say like the one you know now."

What happened? I stared at my glass in dismay. *What would make Darren attack his older brother?* Blayne was terrible—I had my own experience to attest to that, but if what Benny said was true then the heir hadn't always been that way.

A wave of cold swept across my skin. "Did Blayne ever try to hurt Darren?"

The man shook his head. "If you had known him then, you would have never even thought to ask."

"Do you…" I swallowed, thinking of what Darren had done at our ascension. And what he was rumored to have done years before to his own brother. "Do you think Blayne hates him because of it?" Their discourse was always frosty, and while I had assumed it a natural progression to their relationship, I now had to wonder if it was something darker to do with their past.

"My dear." Benny's eyes met mine. "Blayne doesn't hate his brother. He loves him. Darren is the only person that boy has *ever* cared for, beside himself."

"But... *why*? If Darren—"

"Why not?" The man shrugged. "It doesn't have to make sense. They fight and they yell, but in the end they are brothers. Blood carries a much stronger pull than their hate."

"But—"

"Darren feels the same way about Blayne."

"He doesn't." I was certain.

Benny's eyes narrowed. "Have you asked him?"

"N-no, but I know..." I trailed off. *How did Darren feel about his own brother?* I had never bothered to ask. I had assumed he put up with Blayne as the heir but...*love*? Did he *love* the same person who had tried to hurt Ella? The same person who had tormented me? Was he struck by guilt for their past?

"They are brothers," Benny repeated softly. "That is a bond you cannot break."

"And we meet again."

I glanced up to see Paige waiting in the corridor. She had one arm propped behind her head and the other hand looped around her belt.

I grinned. "You have guard duty tonight? I was beginning to think my favorite knight was a figment of my imagination."

She slid into step with me as we turned the corner. Was that a smile I saw cross her face? "No imagination, my lady, they've got—"

A cloaked arm reached out and grabbed me by the wrist, yanking me into the dark hallway beyond. I opened my mouth to scream—one hand reaching for my dagger's hilt through my heavy skirts and calling on my magic to light the room—just as Paige leapt forward, her broadsword already drawn and calling for back up.

My attacker released me just before my casting or Paige's blade could reach him, chuckling as the black hood fell from his face.

It was Darren.

And he was laughing. "Good to know you haven't gone soft."

My guard shot the prince an irritable expression. "My apologies, your highness, but that wasn't very appropriate."

Darren just shook his head, trying to hide the half-smile from his lips. "How else am I supposed to make sure this one has kept up with her training? You, Paige, were *exceptional*, but Ryiah here was a little slow."

"Slow?" I took a step forward and shoved at his chest. "Let me assault *you* in a dark corridor!"

He smirked. "You are welcome to try."

I started to retort but Darren tugged on my hand and gave Paige a pointed look. "If my father sends men to look for me tell them I'm not here."

"I most certainly will not."

"Paige," I begged. This was the most I had seen Darren since I arrived, and five months prior. "Please?"

The knight scowled. "I will not lie when I say I did not see where you went."

"Paige—"

She huffed loudly. "My eyes are shut."

"Come on!" Darren pulled me into the great library behind. I was giggling so hard I was caught off-guard when the prince abruptly turned and shoved me up against the door, shutting it and trapping me in the same move.

"Darren," I stammered. "There could be people..."

He put one finger to my lips. "I sent them away before you arrived."

"How did you know I was—"

"Who do you think had the scholars send orders to meet?"

"That was you?"

"Ryiah." The non-heir was smiling. "Do you really want to talk right now?"

No. *No, I didn't.* I shook my head vehemently.

"Good." Darren tilted my chin. "Because I've been waiting to do this all day."

"Only today?" I inhaled sharply as he placed his hands on my waist and pulled me in close.

"Every day."

His lips found mine in the dark.

And just like kindling, my whole body went up in flames.

The two of us were lost. In a moment. He was barely holding me and already I was melting.

Then, he deepened the kiss.

And my knees threatened to give out.

"Darren," was all I could whisper.

His lips fell to the hollow at my throat.

I dug my nails into his shoulder to keep from crying out as he pushed me back against the door, garnet eyes flaring.

"Do you remember our first year at the Academy, Ryiah?"

"Yes," I whispered.

"You remember that time I kissed you in the hall?" The words were unsteady and ragged.

I nodded, not trusting myself to speak.

"That wasn't the first time I thought of kissing you." The corner of Darren's lip twitched as he fought back a smile. "It was just the first time I thought you wouldn't light me on fire for trying."

"It wasn't?" I exhaled softly. "But you hated me..."

"I never hated you, Ryiah." The prince laughed low. "I couldn't get you out of my head. You were the only girl who ever made it a point to tell me how little you thought of me. Gods—" His eyes danced. "You looked so proud that first night you came down the ladder spitting my words back in my face. I knew that moment I had made a mistake assuming you were like the others." He lowered his voice to a whisper. "I just refused to admit it."

"And to think that whole time I just wanted to strangle you."

He shook his head with a knowing smile. "Liar."

I blushed, remembering all the times Darren had left me flustered and weak.

"Maybe not the *whole* time," I conceded. "But you would have certainly deserved it if I did."

He leaned forward, pressing his palms against the wood at either side of my head. "Do I deserve it now?"

I rolled my eyes, and he smirked, removing one hand to tip my chin and kiss me. Softly. Slowly. Enough to send a wave of tremors from the pit of my stomach to the tips of my toes. Enough to let me know that *he* knew I had no real defense. Not against him.

But it wasn't just me.

I pulled him into me. *Closer.* So that it really was as if the two of us had melded against the door. As if there was nothing to separate us but the thin garments against the burning of our skin.

Everything around me was swimming.

My hands slid up his arms to wrap around his neck and then I willed myself not to faint. The way he shifted his hands to grip along my waist.

I could feel the non-heir's rapid intake of breath and the way his fingers dug into my sides. Hard.

And it felt so, *so* right.

In seconds his lips were back on mine. And I was gasping for air. And his tongue was in my mouth and his hands were fumbling with the top laces of my dress and I was ripping the shirt up and over his head.

And then...

And then the door I was pushed up against swung open, and I was sent stumbling into the corridor, tripping over my dress as I crashed into someone behind. Darren managed to catch himself against the knob, but I was not so lucky, falling against the stranger with a muffled yelp.

"And just when I thought the palace had grown short on entertainment."

I jumped at the familiar drawl and threw myself out of the stranger's arms faster than I had ever done anything in my life.

My face burned as I steadied myself, pulling up to straighten my dress as the crown prince stepped neatly out of the darkness behind Darren and me.

"Blayne." Darren's voice was a growl as he stepped forward, pulling me behind him.

"Really, brother." The crown prince folded his arms. "The library?"

The non-heir refused to rise to the bait. "What do you want?"

"Father sent the servants to find you, but I knew you'd give them the slip." The crown prince's gaze flitted to me and then back to his brother. "Lucky for you, I just asked them where *she* went and, well, here I am."

"Tell him I will be there shortly—"

"Now." Blayne cut him off with a sharp reprimand. "Do you think I like listening to those old men argue for hours on end? The Council isn't even present—they are still dealing with the rebels in the south. I'm not doing this alone. There will be plenty of time for romancing your bride *after* the Pythians arrive."

I nudged Darren, thinking about how angry the king had been just a couple nights before. I still didn't trust Blayne one bit, and I hadn't the slightest doubt he would tell the king who was responsible for Darren's absence if he delayed.

The non-heir gave a loud grumble. "Just give me a minute, Blayne."

"Smile, little brother." The crown prince gave his brother a hard clap on the shoulder and retreated back into the hall, calling out, "Just think, if we secure my Pythian princess, this happily ever after for you and your lovely, little lowborn can come that much sooner."

As soon as Blayne turned the corner Darren slumped against the wall and gave me a tired smile. It was the first time I realized how fatigued he really was—the shadows under his eyes hadn't been quite so evident in a dark library when my mind had been too consumed with feelings to notice.

"I doubt I'll get much sleep." Darren sighed. "The Pythian ambassador is ruthless. Father's advisors will spend the whole night debating how to proceed and nothing will get done."

"Is there anything I can do?"

He shook his head and took my hand, interweaving his fingers with my own.

I started to smile, and I was about to tell him to go, when I remembered something that had been pressing at my mind since arrival. "Darren?"

"Yes?"

Now was the time to ask. *Do it now, Ryiah, you aren't going to have a chance later.* "While I was in the north..." I swallowed. "Do you think you would be able to talk to your father about increasing the funds he sends to the border villages?"

"Ryiah." Darren's grip tightened on my hand. "We are preparing for war and trying to negotiate with the Pythians. The Crown's purse is limited. What little we send is all the treasury can afford. It costs a great deal to host an army as large as ours."

"But—" *What about the people whose livelihood was burned to the ground? What could they do?* I tried again. "How are the northerners supposed to fend for themselves?" I thought of my first month in service. "While I was on duty we came across a large bandit camp, Darren. They turned to crime when the

Crown couldn't help. Wouldn't it be better to find a way to help them and prevent the north from turning on its own?"

"That is why we have patrols. We can't save everyone, love." His eyes grew distant for a moment, and I knew he was thinking of what happened the year before. "*No matter how much I wish we could.*"

"Won't you at least try?"

"Father will never consider a petition from me." He squeezed my hand. "I was taught command, never policy, but..."

I waited for Darren to finish.

"He might listen if the request came from Blayne."

My face fell.

Darren wasn't a fool; he noticed the moment the expression crossed my face.

"I know my brother is difficult—"

You could say that again.

"But he cares about Jerar. If you take away anything from tonight that would be it."

I bit my lip. I had no choice. I had to try. For Ian. For all the northerners who had lost their home to the Caltothian raids. I just wished our plan didn't depend on Blayne. Every instinct was telling me it was wrong.

I didn't trust the crown prince for a moment. But Darren did. And try as I might I couldn't find a reason to refuse.

I just hoped I wasn't making a mistake.

CHAPTER SEVEN

"Tonight is going to be such a lavish affair!"

Sofia flounced around the room as she finished fitting me into a swirl of cream-colored skirts, oblivious to the frown that was written all over my face. "Just wait until the prince sees you in this gown—he won't be able to take his eyes off you!"

I squirmed uncomfortably. "I think you overestimate the ball's appeal. The entire production is to impress the Pythians—Blayne and Darren have orders to engage the duke the whole evening." I made a face. "Mine are to embarrass the Crown as little as possible."

"You won't embarrass anyone in this, my lady." She adjusted the top. "Even if you make a mistake you will be far too enchanting for them to take notice."

"Where have you been all my life?" I gave Sofia a mock curtsy with grand flourish. "You do wonders for my self-esteem."

The other lady-in-waiting, Gemma, scolded me for moving. The two proceeded to pile my locks into a tumbling array of curls, a couple loose strands to soften the hard lines of my face. Then they hung a small gold chain around the base of my hairline, a small sapphire hanging from its clasp.

I could admit I did feel a bit like Sofia described by the time we were finished. I had never seen Priscilla in anything half so nice as what I was wearing now. I knew the king had only issued such an extravagant order because of the Pythians' arrival, but there was no harm in reaping the benefits.

When I arrived at the hall outside the grand ballroom, I had another small victory when I caught sight of the non-heir.

He was staring. A lot. Lips slightly parted, I don't even think he realized that he was doing it.

Maybe Celine was right. *I should wear dresses more often.*

Darren muttered something as I took his arm—just loud enough for me to hear—and I was blushing uncontrollably. I looked away immediately, but out of the corner of my eye I could see his gaze hadn't left my face.

We waited for the herald to announce us to the awaiting audience.

When we were finally called, Darren led me across to King Lucius and the crown prince at the edge of the room.

We sat in silence and watched the courtiers mingle for the next hour. Finally, when I was fighting hard not to fall asleep at the chair, the herald returned to announce our guests of honor had arrived.

"Duke Cassius, brother and ambassador of King Joren of Pythus, and his attendants."

I watched as a towering man sauntered out into the hall, thick, corn-yellow braids swinging with each mighty stride of his legs. He bore a heavy cloak trimmed in fur, and heavy boots that seemed to crush the rug as they moved. Every step he took seemed slow and deliberate—a fact made even more evident by the quick patter of his guards.

When he finally reached the throne, Duke Cassius bowed the bare minimum afforded the Crown, for the bare minimum of time. Then he returned to a stand, the hint of a sneer playing along his lips.

"My dear, King Lucius. It's been years. You've grown a beard."

"And Duke Cassius. Always the charmer."

"Am I?" The man smirked. "I do not remember paying you a compliment."

Standing uncomfortably, I watched the royals proceed. For a moment there were false pleasantries, and then I heard Darren laugh—a little too loudly—at something the ambassador had said. As soon as the duke turned his back I watched the non-heir wipe his sweaty hand on his sleeve.

Blayne cleared his throat expectantly and addressed the duke with more force. "Care to take a tour of the grounds, Your Grace? I assure you it will be much more alluring than talk of old men's beards." He was using his courtier's charm, the one that might have fooled me years ago before I discovered his true nature. It was full of airy brevity and wit. Persuasive. I could immediately see why Ella had found him captivating before the incident that had forced her to leave court.

"I have only just arrived. Any gracious host would have already found me something to drink."

My head swerved in the duke's direction. It was impossible to miss the absence of Blayne's title, or the command in his voice.

Already I could see why the Crown had spent so much time preparing for the ambassador's arrival. In the two minutes that had passed since his introduction, one thing was already evident: the Pythian duke was not going to see his niece wed to Jerar's crown prince willingly. And whatever the duke believed, his brother—the king—was sure to follow.

How were we ever going to convince the Pythians to accept Jerar's proposal?

Blayne nodded pleasantly in return, and I wondered if he had heard the duke's underlying scorn. "Certainly, Your Grace."

Still, his expression didn't falter.

The duke adjusted his belt and watched the crown prince through narrowed eyes.

"Rupert!" Blayne snapped. *So he did hear it, after all.*

A nearby guard dropped his post at the young man's command. "Yes, Your—"

"Get the Pythians a drink. They are thirsty."

"Sir, I'm not supposed to leave my post," the man stammered.

"Then. Find. Someone. To. Do. It. For. You." Blayne flashed an apologetic smile at the duke. "I apologize for not anticipating your needs earlier, Your Grace."

"Do you?" He studied the prince with a furrowed brow. "I've heard you only anticipate your own. Why else would the Borean princess flee an arranged marriage?"

Ella would like this man. I bit my lip to keep from snickering. It was wrong to be feeling amiable in such hostile conversation, especially when the stakes were so high.

"You must have heard wrong." Blayne's smile never fell. "Princess Shinako didn't flee. In truth, she was so close to my dear, sweet brother that upon hearing his love for a lowborn the two of us agreed to call off the wedding and cede her dowry to the Lady Ryiah you see here before you now."

Duke Cassius took notice of me for the first time. His scrutiny made me want to squirm; I could feel his gaze taking in every inch of my uncomfortable appearance, from my burning face to the nervous wringing of my hands. "You are lowborn?"

I opened my mouth, wetting my lips to reply.

"My court heard the rumors, but I never imagined that bit to be true."

How could I explain? Blayne's explanation now was the Crown's interpretation of Ascension Day, and I was afraid of saying the wrong thing. I could see King Lucius watching from the corner of my eye.

Darren placed the palm of his hand on my back. "Lady Ryiah hasn't been lowborn since her apprenticeship. She earned a place in court of her own accord, as a *mage*."

"A mage to marry into the Crown?" His tone held blatant disbelief. "Doesn't your Council of Magic forbid it?"

I glanced to Darren but he just shook his head, eyes fixed on his father. Blayne and the rest of the duke's retinue had gone silent.

King Lucius corrected the duke with a curt address. "You forget yourself, Cassius, the Crown already has a mage in its ranks."

"Prince Darren?" The man scoffed. "I've heard the tales your traders spin in Pythus. Forgive me if I am a bit skeptical of a prince as prestigious as they claim."

The king's reply was instantaneous. "Darren will be a part of the Candidacy. I trust your brother will be sending his emissaries the same as the last?"

"He will. And I will be a part, regardless of however *this* plays out."

King Lucius's hand tightened on his throne. I could see him struggling to maintain composure.

Blayne took over for his father, trying to flatter the duke instead. "I recall you won quite a bit on a wager for Marius during your youth."

"Yes." Cassius didn't bother to hide his contempt. "What can I say? A Pythian never loses." His eyes stayed glued to the king's. "We take our bets very seriously."

"As do I." Lucius's words were ice. "And there is no surer bet than my son."

It didn't take much to recognize they were no longer talking about Darren or the Candidacy. The air was drowning in tension and neither the king nor the duke looked away. I wondered who would win: the brother of one of the most scrupulous kings in history, or our own?

The refreshments arrived just in time. Two sets of servants jostled around our circle, thrusting drinks into hands before the two leaders could pull out the swords and duel on the spot. Blayne took over the conversation, and slowly the tension began to ease into more pleasurable territory.

Sensing an opportunity to escape, Darren took my hand just as his father called his name.

The prince groaned. "I'm sorry, Ryiah."

Don't leave me!

My teeth grated. "Don't worry about me, I'll be fine." *As long as the courtiers don't try to engage me in conversation about their estates.* I forced an encouraging smile on my lips as we parted ways.

The few times I had been forced to partake with the court I'd been engaged in an endless barrage of conversation. It wasn't because I was charming, or debonair, or full of charming remarks.

It was because they all deemed me a gullible pawn in their play for power. One that I wanted nothing to do with. Every smile and eloquent aside held a secret, and I wasn't fool enough to pretend I could see through to the true intentions behind. Darren had warned me many would seek out friendships to secure royal favors, and I had yet to discern the ones I could trust.

I had never made a promise to engage in frivolities—if the ambassador was occupied then I had fulfilled my duties, and after the many cautions not to "humiliate" the Crown I told myself the best tactic really was evasion. I could not embarrass myself if I had no one watching to witness my courtly blunders.

Several minutes later I had made it to the palace kitchens, dress and all, and I was cackling away, sitting on the stool next to Benny as he finished the final touches to that evening's dessert, berating his least favorite members of court. The air smelled of candied ginger and mace. Mixed with the steady heat coming from the ovens I could almost pretend it was summer, and I was out in the field practicing my lunges with Ella instead of a cold, marble palace.

Benny finished icing his newest creation and looked up from his task. "How are the negotiations faring?"

"I wouldn't know." I snatched a tart that had not quite finished cooling and yelped, dropping it back to the rack. *Too early.* "The Pythians don't seem to like us much."

"The servants they brought claim their princess has already received an offer of marriage from Prince Klaus."

The Caltothians? "King Horrace's only son?"

"Precisely." The cook crooked a finger at me. "Two different heirs offering the shrewd Pythians their hand. Make no mistake, the prince that the ambassador chooses will decide the war."

My hunger vanished and the contents of my stomach plummeted. There it was. A reminder how important these negotiations really were.

I excused myself. *What was I doing?* I couldn't keep avoiding the festivities, not with so much at stake.

I had barely made it back to the ball when Blayne grabbed me by the wrist and dragged me out to the balcony. Darren was nowhere to be found.

It was hard to see with the absence of the sun, and the air frigid with winter chill. "Where were you?" he hissed. White clouds of air escaped his breath. "My father noticed your absence."

The lie slid from my tongue like butter. "I got lost. The palace is so large, and there are so many halls."

"You were shirking your duty." His nails dug into my skin, and they hurt. "You accepted your responsibilities the moment you and my brother decided to play me for a fool."

"I'm sorry." I wasn't, but I wanted Blayne gone as quickly as possible. My pulse was thundering in my ears. I was fighting every instinct not to yank my arm right out of his grasp. Or worse. The prince's expression was reminding me all too well of that moment in the hall my first year of the apprenticeship, the last time I had been at the receiving end of his threats.

What do I do if he strikes me? Defend myself and risk the king's wrath? Or take the hit against every instinct I have? I'd never felt more helpless—a black mage of Combat—and yet I was no more than a helpless little girl in the presence of the Crown.

My free hand formed a fist.

Blayne's gaze missed nothing. He took a step back, releasing my arm with a sneer. "I'm not going to hurt you, Ryiah." His tone was chaffing. "We are friends, or have you already forgotten?"

I said nothing. It was the safest reply I had.

"You have five minutes to gather your wits, and then I expect you to converse with the rest of them." His voice rang out as he left the terrace. "Do *not* give the Pythians a reason to question the hospitality of Jerar. A reclusive princess does nothing for our court."

I waited until the crown prince had faded completely from view, vanishing in the crowded floor of jewel-toned dress, and then walked to the edge of the balcony's rail and let out a shaky breath, clutching the cool surface against the frantic beating of my chest.

"That one truly is as pleasant as he first appeared."

I choked, spinning around in alarm. Standing in a darkened corner was the Pythian ambassador. "Duke Cassius!"

"I would have made myself known sooner," he noted, "but I never had the chance."

He had witnessed that entire conversation between Blayne and me. Panic clawed at my throat and I tried to remember what we had said. Luckily nothing to indict Jerar— but it hadn't been in our favor, either.

"If you don't mind, I would like to stay." The man didn't bother to wait for an answer. "The entire court has been a bustle of fools...I would like to converse with the one person who seems so eager to avoid it."

Earlier I had seen the spark of interest when he heard I was lowborn. Now he was studying me with that same glint in his eye, and it did nothing to assuage my nerves.

I knew I needed to stay. I didn't want to, but this was the moment the king's scholars had been preparing me for, the reason the king had summoned my presence in court for the Pythians' arrival in the first place. Friendly discourse that would earn their favor. An example of posterity with a prince of Jerar. *Especially the latter.*

"Nothing would delight me more," I squeaked. Was that really my voice? I swallowed the lump in my throat and spoke in what I hoped was a much more relaxed tenor. "I would be happy to converse. How fare the Pythian—"

He cut me off. "You fear the prince they intend for my niece."

I should have left.

"You are unhappy and uncomfortable amidst the grandeur of your king's palace," the duke continued. "True, a bit of that could be because of your lowborn upbringing, but there is more to it than that. You do not like a life at court. So why are you here?"

I didn't bat an eye. "Darren."

"He is quite handsome." His russet eyes were glued to mine. "You've found yourself a happily ever after in a time when there is none."

"Y-your niece could be very happy with Blayne," I stammered.

"Now you can't possibly believe that to be true. Not when you were cowering in his presence just moments before."

The man laughed throatily. "Your Blayne is pretty, but cruel. The Caltothian prince is but a boy and spends his time picking his nose." His lips curled up in disgust. "I seek your audience because you didn't grow up in court, my dear. You haven't learned how to lie. I can read every emotion on your face; I could tell how upset you were by the prince moments before, and I can see how nervous you are now. And that makes yours the most valuable opinion in this room."

He took a step closer, the heels of his boots a rattle. "Now tell me why I should pick King Lucius's son for my niece."

"I—I..."

I never should have gone off on my own. The king gave me very specific orders not to embarrass the Crown; his threats had stressed the stakes of earning the Pythians' favor. And now here the duke was, asking the one person whose face was, apparently, an open book. Because I was lowborn.

I struggled for a reply that would appear honest without putting Blayne in a negative light.

"The thing is … I don't really know him."

His lips twitched at the lie.

"Well *enough*," I blurted. "I don't know him well *enough*. I-I didn't like Darren either, when we first met. I hated him." *Nice, Ryiah, make him hate the whole family.* "B-but that was before I got to know Darren." No point in lying since he could read the truth. "I am still getting to know Blayne…"

I started to get nervous:

"I-I can't promise she would be h-happy… But if you choose Jerar you could save hundreds—thousands." I swallowed. "If you choose Jerar there will never be a war. Caltoth would never dare to attack us with your brother's support—"

"You disappoint me, Ryiah. Desperation and fear will never win you an ally." The duke gave me a pitying smile. "Thanks for your time."

Then he adjusted his cloak and left me standing there, clinging to the rail.

We were going to lose the war, I realized. The Pythians had already picked a side.

It wasn't ours.

CHAPTER EIGHT

Negotiations were fruitless. Three days into the ambassador's visit and it was clear the Pythians were not going to be swayed. There was nothing King Lucius's advisors could offer that would match the Caltothian's terms. And from the way the meetings had gone thus far, King Horrace had promised *a lot.*

I wasn't present for said meetings, of course, but the worry lines creasing the non-heir's forehead each dinner were enough. I had to watch Darren's haggard face each time he stepped out of the Crown Chambers looking worse than before. Over dinner he would practice strained conversation with the Pythians while I picked at my food and pretended things weren't as hopeless as they seemed. Even Blayne stopped trying to carry the pretense of self-assurance by that third night.

Duke Cassius was the only one enjoying himself, and he toasted his kinsmen every chance he got. Between his raucous laughter and that smug smile, it wasn't hard to see he was making a mockery of our court. Like me, he had four days left to his visit—but his was a mere formality.

"A shame…" The duke started to say, and then stopped himself. He didn't need to finish. The rest of his sentence was implied. *A shame your kingdom will fall. A shame King Horrace offers King Joren the world. A shame you can't offer the same.*

King Lucius was faring the worst. While Darren and Blayne continued to plaster fake smiles and flourishing compliments, their father was silent to a fault. The king spent entire evenings staring daggers at the duke, and from the way he tore into his meat and let the bloody venison drip down his chin, I suspected he envisioned it as the Pythian's flesh instead.

I lost all appetite after that.

The remainder of my time was spent in the practice courts—etiquette postponed in light of the Pythians' arrival. There were no more lessons on courtly decorum; the scholars were too busy poring over records in the treasury, searching for a way to appease the Pythians' demands.

I had just finished washing up from a particularly grueling session with some of the regiment knights when I heard Darren enter his chamber next door. From the way wood slammed against stone it was easy to assert the Crown had come no further in negotiations.

And then it slammed again. Two angry voices started on the other side.

Pressing a finger to my lips so Sofia and Gemma didn't give our presence away, I tiptoed across to the wall and cupped my hand against the surface.

I knew it was wrong to listen in, but Darren had refused to tell me anything since the negotiations began, and I was desperate for news. He was so busy trying to pretend things weren't as bad as they were, and if he wasn't willing to reveal the truth to me just yet, then I would find out another way.

"Never should have sent you off to that school!"

"Blayne—"

"You were supposed to be here, Darren. With me. Not her. Me."

"I'm here now." There was a bit of silence, then much quieter: *"Was he really that bad after I left?"*

"What do you think?"

"Blayne, I'm—"

"It's a bit late for an apology."

A reticent sigh. *"We still have three days. I'll figure out a way, there must be something we haven't thought of—"*

"We offered them everything. Everything! Didn't you hear the advisors? The only thing we haven't proposed is the country itself." A harsh laugh. *"Would you prefer Jerar go under Pythian rule, dear brother? We can't match the wealth of Caltoth, the only thing left is a crown."*

Something hit the wall with a shatter. *"They are supposed to honor the Great Compromise. Why won't they honor it?"*

Darren's voice: *"Caltoth has been attacking our border for years! They can't claim the incident in Ferren's Keep a territory dispute—"*

"King Joren will never choose honor when faced with his own country's gain." Blayne's tone was full of contempt. *"Why should one carry out a century's old pledge when he can further his own?"*

"It isn't right. We have supported the Pythians for years—"

"Loyalty is never built upon honor, brother. It is built upon blood."

I stepped away from the wall and asked Gemma to tell the king I was feeling a bit faint. I could not join them for dinner. It had been a mistake to listen in on Darren and his brother. The princes hadn't said anything I hadn't already assumed, but somehow hearing the words spoken aloud made it worse.

I could not sit across from that merciless duke and force a smile to my lips. Not tonight.

I had Sofia help me back out of my dress and then pulled on a fresh pair of breeches, yanking my long-sleeved wool tunic up over my head.

"My lady? You're training, again?" My lady-in-waiting blinked at me in confusion. "Aren't you exhausted?"

"I am." I grabbed my scabbard and swung open the door. "If Darren asks, tell him I am outside the soldiers barracks. But tell him I want to be alone."

Paige found me an hour later drilling myself in the soldier's arena to the east of the palace wall. I was fighting the flurry of cold with my blade, cutting a swathe through falling snow and pretending it was the Pythians instead. My breath came out staggered and hot, but I kept swinging and swinging until she finally dragged me away.

My guard pried the blade right out of my hands and tossed it to the frozen ground, handing me her flask. I took a long swig while she waited. And then another. I drank the entire container without even emitting a gasp as the searing contents tore a hole through my chest. Blood started to move and my fingers burned as they tingled, the warmth slowly working itself back to my limbs.

Paige studied my hands. "You should have worn gloves, my lady."

"Did Darren send you?"

"He did."

"Do you know what it is like to feel powerless?"

She didn't bother to reply.

"I'm powerless. They summoned me here to help win the Pythians' favor. Me. A lowborn." I hacked back a cough. "Lowborns can't lie. Did you know that?"

"I'm a lowborn," the knight scoffed. "I can lie."

"Well I can't. I mean…I can lie. But not well. Duke Cassius told me he could read the truth all over my face. I'm a truth-teller." I wobbled and then acquiesced as Paige led me back to lean against the barracks' fence. "And I couldn't lie and tell him to pick Blayne. He wanted me to give him a reason and I couldn't. He-he hurt Ella. And—and I couldn't. I couldn't do it."

"You don't trust the crown prince. So why are you trying to defend him?" Paige gave me a hard look. "Clearly the Pythian duke knows you are lying. You should try a different angle."

"Like pleading for our country? Begging for our people?" I choked back a laugh. "He doesn't care. They are toying with us, Paige."

She chewed her lip. I suspected she and the rest of the palace staff had already heard the rumors.

"They play to win."

"Perhaps you need to show them what they'll lose."

"How is that any different? They lose what cannot be won."

She shrugged her shoulders.

"Caltoth can give them more than Jerar ever could." I let her lead me back toward the palace, anger fading to cold. I was shivering and hot. I needed another searing bath, and then the chill of my bed. I needed everything and I needed nothing. I felt despair seeping its way back into the pit of my stomach.

"Thank you, Paige," I mumbled.

She clapped my back as she handed me off to Sofia and Gemma.

There was nothing else to be said.

The final evening of the Pythians and my visit was spent in a somber silence.

Our attempt at negotiation had failed. Darren and Blayne no longer feigned pleasantries as the night dragged on. The king didn't bother to eat the meal in front of him—his white beard was stained coppery red along the rim, and with every wine that was brought his eyes grew the icy blue of a storm. I kept waiting for the royal family to break, but the king and his two sons were well trained in the art of restraint.

Much more than I.

The Crown's advisors chattered the longest, but I could feel them growing quieter and quieter as the evening wore on. I was pushing mutton around on my plate, unable to stomach another bite with the knowledge that this man could reap the best of our harvest, drink our wine, and enjoy our hospitality all the while knowing he was sentencing the people he saw— and their kinsmen—to death. For the price of wealth. For the price of Caltothian rubies.

For a couple of sparkling red gems he was willing to watch us burn.

The Pythians were monsters.

"Well, hasn't this been just pleasant." The duke cleared his throat loudly, and held his goblet to toast the king with his other in flourish. "A shame, truly, that we couldn't—"

An unsuspecting maid scurried past the ambassador and caught her sleeve against his hand. Giant clumps of gravy coated his chair.

"Lucius, are your servants truly this daft?"

As the girl scrambled to apologize the duke began to tirade over the cost of his Borean silk and the incompetence of servants. His complaint was met with an outbreak of service. Servants scrambled to blot out the gravy as the maid fled the room.

I watched the whole scene play out with an invisible grip on my throat. I wanted to say something, *anything*, but it wasn't my place. The king hadn't even allowed my presence during the week's talks. *"You are ornamental, nothing more."* The tutors had repeated the reminder to me endlessly. *"Your role is to smile at your betrothed and give the Pythians a reason to believe in happy endings. Convince them their crown princess can have the same with Prince Blayne."* I was no one and it was taking every bit of resolve to keep the other Ryiah—the restless, reckless Ryiah—away.

I willed myself to take a deep, steadying breath. Beside me Darren was gripping his goblet so tightly I half-expected it to break. I wanted to reach out and take his hand but his ex-

pression was foreboding. Directly across from him, Blayne was
fighting to maintain an air of indifference as he ushered simpering apologies for the girl. If I hadn't heard him the night
before I would have easily believed his performance now.
There was only the barest lilt of anger, and given the context,
it could have easily been directed at the servant.

The king, in this round, resembled his youngest. His eyes
were like ice. The man did not bother with condolences. He
hated the duke. But like the rest of the kingdom, he had to re-
tain peace for as long as he could. So he said nothing.

I frowned. We, the people of Jerar, were so eager to appease. So eager to beg and plead and give the Pythians whatever they wanted. It was a paradox: we had the greatest army
in the realm, but we would lose the war.

The Pythians couldn't be bought. We would never be
enough.

"Desperation and fear will never win a Pythian's favor,"
the duke had said.

I studied the wet splotches of silk, watching the man
twist and squirm in his chair. Duke Cassius was too big for his
seat.

"Perhaps you need to show them what they'll lose."

Maybe Paige was right. It was reckless. But we had tried
safe. And if we were truly going to lose the war, then my actions wouldn't matter much longer anyway. We didn't have
the Pythians' favor.

We had nothing left to lose.

I pushed back my chair; it made a loud grating screech as
it went. I pretended not to notice, wiping my sweaty palms
across my skirts. My heart skipped a beat.

I didn't look to my betrothed or his brother. I definitely
didn't look to my left at their father. I had the eyes of the
room but mine were fixated solely on the duke.

At worst they could blame my words on a headstrong
lowborn. At best... I didn't bother hoping for the latter.

"Your grace, for the past six evenings you've regaled us with tales of Pythian grandeur. You tell us there is no greater fleet than your ships, and no prouder king than your Joren." *Don't stop, don't stop, don't stop.* "You tell us that a Pythian never loses, but you are wrong." I took a quick breath and let out my words in a rush. "If you choose Caltoth, the wealth their king promises you will be lost to war."

Silence.

I could feel King Lucius's gaze burning a hole through the back of my skull. Sharp intakes of breath and the duke's lips were parted in shock.

My legs started to tremble, and I clenched and un-clenched my fists at my sides. "B-because..." This was the hard part. The one I could live to regret. "Because..."

Darren's hand grazed the side of my wrist. He threaded his fingers through mine and abruptly shoved back his chair to join.

"Because we will destroy *everything*." Darren's voice rang out clear across the room. "Every village, every crop, every homestead. We will set the whole of Caltoth aflame." His grip on my hand tightened. I could hear all the frustration and rage from the past week seeping back into his speech. Darren wasn't his brother; his strength lied in passion, not policy. "We will destroy its ruby mines and melt them right into the earth. We will plunder and pillage until nothing is left."

The room was so quiet at this point a pin could have dropped and I would have heard it. Every single set of eyes was fixed upon us—the king, his eldest, the Crown advisors, the Pythians... even the servants had stopped serving.

This was the moment.

I swallowed and made myself finish. Because even Dar-ren couldn't anticipate where I was about to lead next. "In short, your grace, we will lose the war. Without Pythus we will lose. But we won't be the only ones losing." *Now. The final threat.* "Because *we* will also light *our* fields on fire. *We* will de-stroy every last inch of *our* lands. *We* will do this so that when

the Caltothians acquire their victory with you by their side
there will be nothing left to take."

My words grew bolder:

"Do you know the difference between a nation of merchants and a nation of warriors?" I followed through without
waiting for a reply. "Only one of them is prepared to fall on its
blade. King Horrace might promise you the world but in the
end you will reap the greater loss."

Absolute silence. Not a breath, not a cough, not a whisper. Nothing.

I forced myself to exhale, slowly, and then the duke
started to clap.

And then he started to laugh.

"Well, well," the man finally said, "just when I thought
negotiations had run their course."

I froze and Darren's grip tightened on my own, tugging
me gently back into my chair. Everyone was waiting for Duke
Cassius to continue, to decide whether or not to condemn my
actions.

I willed myself to breathe.

The large man leaned forward so that his elbows hit the
table, jostling his goblet of wine. His gaze was fixated on Darren's father.

"Now tell me," Duke Cassius drawled, "why is it that the
best argument I've heard all week came from a little girl?"

The king opened his mouth and shut it tightly.

"I do believe your stuffy board of advisors were a large
waste of my time, Lucius."

"My apologies." The king's reply was forced. "It appears
I have misjudged my men." The steel in his tone promised
quick recourse. There was a hushed panic at the other side of
the table as my victory turned sour.

Recklessness had a price. *Always.*

"I suppose I must send word to my brother." The duke
stood abruptly, thrusting his goblet into the arms of a scrawny
man that had been attempting to squeeze past, unnoticed.

"Are you not leaving in the morning, your grace?" Blayne's question was full of nonchalance. "Surely your news can wait until then... unless perhaps your visit is being extended?"

The duke waved an irate hand. "Don't play the fool, young prince, it doesn't suit you."

The king cleared his throat. "This is wonderful news, Cassius—"

The duke turned sharply around. "Wonderful it may be, but we still have much to discuss. A decision such as this will require great examination. I expect it to take no less than a month to find terms my brother will agree to."

"Whatever it takes." King Lucius did not bat an eye.

"We should stay." Paige sat down on my bed with a thump as I finished gathering the last of my belongings. She was rapping her fingers against the bedframe loudly. Every tap came harder than the last. "Now that the Pythians..."

"Paige." I looked up from my packing with an exasperated groan. "You know that isn't necessary." King Lucius had only ordered my presence as part of decorum—even with my feat the night before I was still excluded from the negotiations themselves. True, the Pythians were extending their visit for the time being, but only the Crown and its board of advisors could partake in meetings. Since I was neither, there was no point to prolonging my stay.

Well, there was Darren...I bit my lip in frustration. I would miss him; I missed him already—even now while we were still in the same city, the same residence. In the two short weeks since I'd arrived I had spent perhaps three hours in his company, and each time we had been in the midst of crowding nobility. Yes, we'd had a short exception in the library, but even Blayne had managed to interrupt *that*.

We might have been in the same place at the same time, but for all the actual time we had spent together we might as well have been miles and miles apart.

Once the alliance is forged it will only be a matter of time before you return to the palace anyway, as his wife. My annoyance began to fade. The two of us would have more time then. Without the stress of Pythian negotiations, Darren would be dismissed from most of the less pertinent Crown affairs, and the two of us would be able to serve together on the King's Regiment.

I wondered if the king would consider granting Darren and me service in the Crown's Army among its patrols. Once Blayne and his new princess secured an heir, surely Darren would be granted more freedom than before. Anything was possible.

In the meantime, I would return to Ferren's Keep. Crown politics took precedence here. Even Darren had fallen behind in his training, and the Candidacy was only six short months away.

I needed every advantage I could get.

"Ryiah…"

My guard ducked out of the room just as the younger prince appeared at its entrance, looking unusually out of sorts. Darren's hair was all over the place, as if he had run his hand through it one too many times and then given up completely. He studied the door for a moment and then heaved a great sigh and shut it behind him.

"If your father's advisors find out we are alone in my chamber they will flay us both alive." It was supposed to be teasing, but the comment came out a little more breathless than I would have liked.

One of the many things the palace scholars had endlessly drilled into me was the importance of a bride possessing certain *qualities*. Qualities that were becoming increasingly hard to keep during moments the two of us were alone.

A sad smile lit the prince's features, and when he met my eyes it wasn't what I expected. "Are you happy here, Ryiah?"

Panic gripped my lungs. Was something wrong? Why was he looking at me like that? "O-of course." *Liar.*

"What you did last night." Darren cleared his throat. "It was amazing. Ryiah, my father was impressed..."

I never heard what came next—it was all I could do to stand still and scream a silent thanks to the gods above. For a moment...for a moment I had thought Darren might be here to tell me the king wanted to call off our engagement.

"He would never go so far as to actually praise a low-born's actions, but he's agreed to your attendance for the remainder of the Pythian negotiations. I convinced him the etiquette lessons weren't necessary to your stay. You will be placed in the King's Regiment instead."

I hesitated. The conversation had taken an unexpected turn. "Darren, your father granted me leave until Blayne's wedding. Did he rescind his offer?"

The prince stared at me, a crease forming along his brow. "No, but...I thought you would want to stay." He ran a hand along his jaw and he seemed to be struggling against something unsaid. "Even after six months apart, you would still prefer Ferren? Even if you could be a part of the Crown negotiations and the palace regiment?"

I swallowed, an uneasy feeling entering the pit of my stomach. "I know you don't want to be here, either. Not truly." He had said it more than once.

Darren's jaw clenched. "Did you even miss me at all, Ryiah?"

"You know I did." I frowned. Two days before he hadn't seemed the least bit disturbed when we discussed my return to the keep. "What's wrong?" *What changed?*

"The two of us might as well be strangers for all the time we have shared since our engagement." Darren's gaze seared into mine. "And once King Horrace finds out the Pythians have extended their visit? It's too dangerous to patrol up

north. Caltoth can't be trusted not to retaliate. I don't want
you there if something happens."

"If anything, the Caltothians will be *more* likely to hold
off now that their alliance is at risk." I studied Darren's defensive stance. I didn't believe for a moment he thought the keep
was dangerous. There was something else bothering him, and I
was determined to get to the bottom of it.

"Darren..."

He started towards the door, and then paused, still facing
the wall. "When were you going to tell me *he* was stationed
there, too?"

I balked, thrown off by the sudden change of topic. "W-
what?"

"Ian." The non-heir spun around to face me, and his eyes
were twin pools of fire.

"*Ian?*" Was that all this was? Jealousy? I wanted to
laugh but Darren looked so serious I thought better of it.

"Commander Nyx's monthly report to the Crown arrived
this morning." Darren didn't bother to hide his disdain. "*His*
name was mentioned in your patrols. I checked the records and
he accepted a post and sent word the day after your ascension.
If I were a betting man I would say it was because he heard
you were to take up at the keep."

"It's been three years. Ian doesn't still harbor those feelings—"

Darren gave me a pitying look. "Believe me, Ryiah, a
man can carry the sentiment a lot longer than that."

I folded my arms. "Darren, Ian grew up in Ferren. His
parents are blacksmiths there." He had never once indicated
feelings of any kind, and he had been as surprised as I when I
arrived at the keep.

"And yet you felt guilty enough to hide his presence?"
The prince's expression was dubious.

I balked in offense. "I wasn't hiding anything! My
younger brother Derrick is there, too. Do you think I am hiding him?"

"I'm not a fool, Ryiah." Darren scowled. "I trust *you* but that lowborn's timing cannot be overlooked."

I glared at the prince. "Ian has never lied to me. He has been open and honest with his intentions since the day we met. Perhaps you are confusing his motivations with your own." I pointed a finger at the non-heir accusingly. "You were the one who pursued me *after* Ian and I got together, not the other way around—in this context only one of you has ever behaved honorably and it hasn't been you."

Darren recoiled as if he'd been slapped. "I apologize for not being as honorable as *him*," he snapped. "Not all of us had farmboy's freedom to choose."

"Darren, that's not what I meant." I scrambled forward to grab his wrist before he could storm out of the chamber. "Please." I took a deep swallow. "Please believe me when I tell you that you have nothing to worry about."

Darren's expression softened. "I can have your brother stationed at the palace if that is what you wish."

"I want to return to the keep, Darren."

"Stay." Darren weaved his fingers into my own. "I'll make sure you have everything you need."

I took a deep, steadying breath. "It's not the same. The Crown takes precedence here. You can't serve abroad. I've seen how little time you've had to yourself—even *you* have fallen behind in your training."

Darren released me and fell back in reproach. *"I haven't fallen behind!"*

"And maybe I'm wrong." I quickly retracted my words. "I just don't want to squander my chance of winning the Candidacy."

"Winning?" Darren arched a brow. "Love, I hardly think you need to worry about that."

My face turned to flames, and before I could stop myself the words came spilling from my lips. "Why? Because *you* are the only one who can?"

"I believe you are a great mage, Ryiah."

"But I'll never be as good as you, is that it?"

The back of his neck was tinged red. "I never said that."

I placed my hands on my hips. "You didn't deny it either."

Darren folded his arms and met my gaze head on. "This isn't some game, Ryiah."

"*Some game?*" Hot rage sputtered from my lips before I could stop. "*How can you even say that?*"

"Admit it, love." His expression was dark. "The people who choose this career don't do it for honor, they choose it for power. Prestige. The chance to make a name for themselves."

I dropped his hand angrily. "And what makes you so different?"

"Expectation. I've spent a lifetime training for the role."

Darren's pride was so great he wouldn't even acknowledge the *possibility* of me winning.

I swung my pack up over my shoulder. After everything we had been through Darren still managed to find just the right way to cut like a knife. There were words bubbling inside, words I knew I shouldn't say but just then I wanted to hurt him. To hurt him like he had just hurt me. "You know the difference between a prodigy and a prince, Darren?"

His mouth formed a thin, hard line.

"You can have the best training, the best tutors, the private lessons during the apprenticeship with Master Byron, everything that the rest of us—even the highborns—never had." My voice caught and I forced myself to continue, eyes blazing. "But none of that guarantees you a victory. None of that makes you a prodigy. It just means you were *privileged.*"

A flare of anger. "You have no idea what it's like—"

I cut him off, a new surge of indignation rising to the surface. "You know what? You are right. I probably won't win *the* Black Robe. But at least *I* will earn my place in that tourney. You? Well, you'll never know. Because a boy with the world at his feet? He's never truly earned anything."

"Better to be the boy with the world at his feet than the reckless lowborn who wouldn't amount to anything without my help." Darren's snarl was the last thing I heard before the door slammed shut in my face.

He didn't come back to apologize. I know because I waited. After fifteen minutes of hating myself, Paige burst through the door.

The knight ignored my red-rimmed eyes and started to drag me by the arm toward the castle exit.

"You'll have plenty of time for that on the ride back." For once she spoke without sarcasm, but her pity only made it worse.

I wiped my eyes, determined to keep from crying until we were on the road, and I could blame it on the bright winter sun. I didn't want any of the servants to report back to Darren. I needed to look strong; I wanted the court to remember my moments standing up against the Pythians, not the crippled girl who let a prince get the best of her.

"Let's get out of this place." I would prove him wrong. The non-heir might have helped me initially, but I had clawed my way up from the very bottom rung of the Academy, and I wasn't done. I had earned my rank and my potential was improving every day. I could still win.

He is just jealous.

Darren was falling behind, and I was in no mood to play the doting wife. I wasn't going to remain at the palace to appease his insecurities. He could fret over Ian all he wanted. I would train in the north, and while Darren was busy with Crown affairs, I was going to pass his blasted potential and shock the whole country when the former lowborn Ryiah was declared Black Mage instead. And only after I wiped that insolent smirk off his face would I accept his long, drawn out apology.

Because wrapped up in conceit the size of Jerar was *my* Darren. Somewhere. Deep, *deep* down. And that part I loved. With every bit of my being.

I just vehemently hated the rest.

Paige and I were five feet away from the palace doors when I realized who was waiting at their exit.

Would I never be free of the Crown?

I approached with caution. "Blayne."

"So full of distrust." The crown prince made a clucking noise at my leery expression. "And to think I came bearing gifts."

I fought every instinct I had not to scoff. Any present from him was not without its price. I waited for him to reveal this "gift."

The young man dug a drawstring purse from the satchel in his hands and tossed it my way. I reached out to catch it and almost dropped it from the unexpected weight.

Peeking inside I saw the leather pouch was stuffed to its brim with coin. Not just any coin, but gold. Enough to feed a village for a lifetime—enough to feed several villages, in fact. My arms sagged under its bulk, and it was all I could do not to gape.

"What—how?"

"It's all my father would allow." Blayne sounded pleased. "It's not much, of course, but you did ask my brother for aid. For the north."

"The north," I echoed, still not quite comprehending the wealth in my hands. I had forgotten all about my request until this moment.

"Consider it a parting gift. After your speech the last night, it was the least that I could do."

"T-thank you, truly—"

Blayne waved his hand in disregard. "Our interests are the same, Ryiah. Perhaps now you will be more willing to forgive the transgressions of our past."

I nodded dumbly and watched as he peeled himself off the wall and faded into one of the corridors behind.

I finished stuffing the satchel into my now-overflowing pack and followed Paige to the waiting stable-hands and our mares outside.

She waited until we had passed through the palace gates and the main city onto the King's Road itself before she finally spoke her opinion aloud.

"I thought you hated him." She didn't bother to say whom.

"I..." I paused. Anger at Darren was still taking up the majority of my thoughts, but Blayne was confusing me as well. *What was he up to?* Everything he did was surprising me. More than once he'd had the opportunity to make my stay difficult, and yet everything he did had been in my best interest. I didn't trust him, but it really did seem as if he were trying to make amends.

I studied the white tree line ahead of us. "My feelings don't matter one way or the other." Blayne was to be king regardless. "If he wants to claim amity, who am I to refuse?"

CHAPTER NINE

When Paige and I returned to the keep, our arrival was met with enthusiasm. Correspondence from the capital had preceded our arrival, but the commander and her regiment were eager to hear the news first hand.

"Of course a treatise hasn't been signed," I finished, fumbling under the commander's intense scrutiny. I could never tell what she was thinking. "But the Pythians agreed to extend their visit, and even their ambassador believes it is only a matter of time."

"Well, this is quite a...development." The commander grasped a hot mug of cider tightly in hand. "I think I speak for most when I say none of us anticipated this news." She paused and took a long sip from her cup. Her knuckles were white. "We hoped, of course, but hope never wins a war."

"That's not all."

The woman's eyes bulged as I took out Prince Blayne's purse and emptied its contents onto the table between us.

"W-what's this?" she breathed.

"I petitioned Dar -the Crown- to help the North... The king couldn't grant as much as I'm sure the border towns need—but I was hoping this would help?"

"Help?" The commander stared at me, studying my face for a sign of what, I wasn't sure. "It has been a great many years since the north received attention from the Crown." She inhaled sharply. "This will go a long way towards rebuilding their villages. I continue to underestimate your value to our keep." She paused in afterthought. "And the Crown."

"I-it wasn't just me." I scratched at my arm. I never would have even thought to ask without Ian's prompting, and it was Darren and Blayne who had actually seen to the favor. I tried to explain, but she wouldn't let me finish.

"We live in a world of kings. Like it or not, not everyone's request would make such an impression." Her expression was detached. "My men have sent the same petition for years, and this is the first time King Lucius has ever granted an exception."

Was that true? I cringed and realized her compliments weren't quite as innocent as I had been led to believe.

"Never regret your influence." The commander crooked her teeth in what I supposed was a cheery smile. "I will begin to make disbursements in the morning. I suspect many of the others will be a bit easier to contend with after they hear the news."

"You knew about that?"

"Some of my soldiers are a bit harder to please." She gave me a reassuring grasp on the shoulder as she showed me to the door. "I advise you not to pay them any attention."

I coughed uncomfortably. "Thank you, Commander."

"No, thank *you*, Mage Ryiah."

The level of gratitude was overwhelming, and as Paige followed me to the barracks I realized how earnest Ian's request had truly been. I had never grown up in the north. My stint of service didn't begin to cover the shortcomings resulting from the Caltothian border raids.

It made me upset to realize how much must have been behind Ian's petition to help. I was ashamed of my own ignorance, and a part of me was upset he had been right in assuming I could make the difference the Commander's appeals could not. I wasn't comfortable with that influence, and something about Nyx's words reminded me of Darren's speech several years before:

"People make mistakes all the time—some of us are just in more of a position to leave an impact when we do." Impact. Influence. Somehow along the way I had joined the circle of people whose actions dictated change, and it scared me how easy it would be to make the wrong one.

"Paige, will you tell me if you think I am making the wrong decision?"

"Wrong decision for what, my lady?" The knight had already collapsed onto her bunk, grateful to lie down after a long, cold week of travel.

I sat down on my cot, pulling the covers up to my chest. The rest of the barracks occupants were already fast asleep. "For anything."

"Gladly." She pointed to my water skin. "You're making the wrong one right now. You should always ask your guard if she requires the last drink."

"Paige!"

She rolled her eyes and settled in for the night. I heard soft snores coming from her just a moment later.

So much for help. I threw the water in her direction half-heartedly but she didn't move. I tossed and turned and I had almost fallen asleep when she finally spoke:

"You haven't made one yet, my lady."

I fervently hoped she was right.

My next two weeks at the keep flew by. Since my unit was still away on patrols for the first seven days I used my brief break to train alongside the Combat mages on reprieve. Most of them were older men and women closer to my parents' age than my own. Their focus was primarily on physical conditioning since the majority of their magic stores had started to diminish with age. They had to be extremely selective in casting, and I found it very interesting to study their process of choosing.

We trained hard day after day, and during our breaks they offered critiques on my casting. I exerted too much pressure in a lot of my magic—*still*, and while I was refined in my pain casting, I was lacking in traditional casting.

During my time at the Academy most of my masters had been so focused on revealing the depths of my potential they had never sought to polish the castings at hand. Master Byron had all but ignored me during the apprenticeship when he hadn't been openly insulting my technique, and so the older mages' feedback now was much more invaluable because of it.

Practicing a simple casting over and over to varying degrees of concentration was tedious, but after Darren's remarks the day I left Devon, I was determined to try anything and everything in the hopes he had missed something important on his own. Because now more than ever I was determined to win.

I had always seen Darren as a rival, but for the longest time I hadn't seriously contemplated my role. Our trial year I had just been lucky to snag an apprenticeship in the same faction. During the apprenticeship most of our competitive nature had been lost to an uncertain romance and Master Byron's bias. But now that we were training apart and with the Candidacy quickly approaching? Now that I was only one rank away from the non-heir's status? *Now that he said I would never be as good as him?*

Now our rivalry had reared its ugly head, and I for one embraced it. Some small part of me had always known it would come to this. Neither Darren nor I were blameless. No one ever made it into Combat without ambition, and those of us that did had been cultivating a lust for power for years.

Common sense dictated I accept my inevitable loss.

But I was tired of being second-best.

"So Ray got promoted while I was away?" I stared at the missing mage's spot in our riding formation. I had noticed his absence when my unit had returned from patrols, but I had assumed he had taken a leave of absence. Advancement so soon into our service hadn't crossed my mind, and even if it had I wouldn't have thought Ray would be the first to obtain it. Ian, perhaps, with his extra year of expertise or me. But Ray...he hadn't saved our unit during the bandit attack in the mountains, and...

You might as well admit the truth. I frowned as the bitter thought took over. *You* are *a better rank.*

Maybe I was mistaken. Maybe there was another reason.

"What..." I cleared my throat and tried again. "What wonderful news."

Lief didn't notice the strange lilt to my tone. "His performance was exceptional. He will do well in Sir Maxon's squad." The man gave me an easy grin. "Don't worry, Ryiah, I suspect you will be next."

But why wasn't I first?

I waited until the lead mage was busy in conversation with my knight before I pulled closer to Ian, slowing my mare's progress. Maybe now that our leader was gone he would be willing to share an opinion.

The next couple of minutes passed in silence.

"Great news for Ray," I prompted.

Ian adjusted his reigns. "I should say so."

"It doesn't bother you at all?"

The curly-haired mage gave me a puzzled smile. "Why would it bother me?"

"Lief just insinuated you would be last up for a promotion." He had also stated that Ray's performance had been exceptional—when *I* had been the one to save our unit from the bandits. But if I mentioned that now it would sound like I was jealous.

Maybe I was. Ray was a great person, and a good Combat mage, but even he had admitted to being less powerful than I. Why shouldn't Ian or I get the promotion first? I had the best rank and Ian was ahead of both of us in years of service.

It made no sense.

"Oh, that?" Ian shrugged. "I wouldn't worry about it. I trust in Lief's judgment. He sees things the rest of us miss."

Even Byron? *Well, the master was only paying close attention to Darren in our apprenticeship anyway.* Suddenly, I was nervous. What if I wasn't even second rank? What if it was supposed to be Ray, and Master Byron had just been too nervous around Marius to say so? The Black Mage had paid me special attention to annoy my training master—perhaps he had never noticed there was someone better.

Is that what Darren was insinuating the day I left?

No. I dug my nails into my palms to draw my thoughts away from the doubt. *Don't start to question it now. Lief just made a mistake. People make mistakes all the time.*

But what if it was Byron who made the mistake? My head hurt. I buried my face in my hands and groaned. *Stop thinking, Ryiah.* Any more questions were only going to bring out every insecurity I had ever fought since that first day at the Academy.

I needed to change the subject, fast.

I opened my mouth but Ian beat me to it. "So I heard some interesting news."

I started. "Y-you did?"

"Rumor is going around that Commander Nyx received a generous sum from the Crown." The corners of his eyes were crinkled. "You wouldn't have anything to do with that, would you, Ry?"

"It was your idea," I mumbled. "If you hadn't suggested it, I never would have thought to ask." For all the trouble I had put Ian through in the course of our apprenticeship, here was something that *I* could do for him.

He cocked his head to the side. "Did you go to the king directly, or...?"

"Darren. He petitioned his brother." I paused, guiltily. There were only three people I personally knew who held the crown prince with as little regard as I: one of them was Ian and the other two were my best friend and twin. Now was probably not the best time to mention that Blayne's aid was a form of "amends." "Blayne holds more sway with his father."

Ian looked away and studied his hands. "How was your return to the palace? I imagine the visit was much more pleasant with your new role?"

I snorted. "Hardly. I spent a week taking lessons in decorum and the rest of the time watching the court pretend I didn't exist—when they weren't trying to win my favor."

He raised an exaggerated brow. "I'm sure there were some advantages."

Getting picked apart by the Pythian ambassador and threatened by the king? I shook my head, and drew my hair back into a knot. "If there are I have yet to discover them." I paused, realizing how selfish I sounded even to myself. "Except for my own chamber. That was nice."

"Well I'm sure Darren was happy to see you."

"He was..." *Right until the time he found out about you.* I swallowed.

Ian caught my expression. "Let me guess, the young princeling found out I was here and assumed it was part of my nefarious plan to steal your heart." The mage chuckled and looked skyward. "Well, I can't say I missed him either. The next time you see your betrothed, please remind him not all of us sink to his level of treachery to get the girl."

I cringed. This conversation had not taken a favorable course. I wasn't pleased with Darren either but... But this wasn't making the situation any better. These two would never be friends, too many wrongs, and there was nothing I could do to set them right.

"Alright everyone, you know the routine. Tend to your mounts and then see to the camp." Sir Gavin's voice rang out loud and clear. Ian and I started from our thoughts.

The mage kept his eyes on the pine ahead as the two of us dismounted and walked across the clearing to where the rest of the party had started to tie up their charges. "In any case, I am happy he was decent enough to help you with the request."

I felt the tension leave my shoulders. I exhaled quietly. "Thank you, Ian."

He looked up, but the smile didn't quite reach his eyes. "I know you've been having trouble being accepted around here because of your new status, but I think this will go a long way toward changing the stubborn ones' opinions."

I nodded, not quite believing and still hoping desperately he and Commander Nyx would prove me wrong. So far I hadn't noticed a difference.

Everyone was still treating me with the same amount of hostility as before. Although, to be fair, I hadn't made that much of an effort to mingle.

In truth, since my return I'd been more isolated than usual. I was still upset over the way Darren and I had left things, and between my anger and his residual taunt I had become obsessed with my training both as a diversion and a way to prove the non-heir wrong. So much so that I had stopped taking meals with the rest of my unit. *Who realized how much longer it took to eat surrounded by conversation?* And while I was sure it didn't help my relations with the squad, it *did* amass an extra hour between the three meals of the day for drills.

An hour that before might have been part of some meaningless banter.

I wasn't so sure I cared what the soldiers thought of me anymore. I had proven myself—in my regular performance, in the bandit raid, and now my petition for coin. Quite frankly, I had done a whole lot more for my regiment than most men combined. If they wanted to complain about some privileged girl, there was nothing I could do to stop them. And I was done trying.

I finished brushing down my horse and set down my supplies. "I'm off to wash up before dinner, see you at drills after?"

Ian studied my face and then sighed. "You know, Ryiah..."

I waited for him to finish.

The mage cleared his throat. "It wouldn't hurt to spend some more time with the rest of the company. I know you want to train, but it's only the Candidacy. Relations here are going to matter a lot more than some contest."

I thought back to my first year of the apprenticeship when Ian had made a similar remark about Darren's time spent training with Byron. This was different. I *had* tried, and... And quite honestly Darren's methods had worked. Which one of us was first rank now? I should have been ignoring everyone and focusing on myself.

And now, for the first time, Darren was slipping. And I had the opportunity to rise. I understood Ian's concern, but it was time to turn to me.

"My friends are the people that matter. People like you and Ray and Lief and Ruth and everyone who got to know me for *me*. The ones blinded by the Crown? Well, it doesn't make a difference; I'll be out of here soon anyway."

Ian muttered something under his breath. I didn't catch it.

"What was that?"

The mage looked me straight in the eyes. "You sound just like *him*."

Ian's tone had an edge and even though I was still upset with Darren I flushed angrily in reply.

"Maybe I do. Darren is the most powerful mage of all of us, why shouldn't I want to be like him?"

He just shook his head. "I'm sorry I said anything."

I didn't continue the conversation; I just grabbed my things and left.

Derrick found me later that night. I was practicing my pain casting in a clearing with Paige's supervision. The guards at the camp's perimeter stood silently beyond. Most of the squad had gone to bed.

The evening's drills had been especially awkward. I knew Ian had told Lief our earlier conversation over dinner because when I arrived everyone had seemed especially uneasy. It was the quietest practice any of us had had.

Derrick waited until I had lowered the stump to the ground; my magic was still growing.

"Doesn't that hurt?" He pointed to my arm as I withdrew the small, serrated blade. Master Byron had made us pain cast with a variety of weapons, but the knife was still my favorite for practice.

I held a cloth in place as Paige wrapped it around the top of my forearm. Sir Gavin expected us in top health at all times in the event of an attack, but I usually waited until the last possible minute to seek out a healer. I was determined to become as accustomed to pain as possible.

I rolled my shoulders. "Every bit hurts." *But a high tolerance will give me an edge in battle.* I studied his anxious expression. "Why did you really come here, Derrick?"

"I overheard Ian at dinner while you were away." His face grew serious. "Ryiah, it's a mistake to withdraw from the rest of our unit."

Not him too. I scowled at my brother. Derrick had *always* taken my side in everything. Hearing him turn away now was something I couldn't take. Not willingly.

"Derrick." Tears were stinging my eyes. "I tried. You saw how hard I was trying before I left. I even brought all that coin from the Crown. But now they want me to waste my time making friends? The same people who want nothing to do with me?"

"I'm sorry, Ry." Derrick scuffed at the ground with his boot. "I just don't want them thinking the Crown has changed you. You are so much more than your title, and I just want you to give them a chance to see it."

"Who are the ones who are doing all of this 'talk?'"

"The names aren't important—"

"It was Jacob, wasn't it?" As soon as I said it I knew I was right just from the look on his face. "You know, your friend has done nothing but scowl since the two of you arrived. I would hardly consider him an expert on human relations."

Derrick bristled. "Jacob lost his mother to a Caltothian raid, Ry. And if you must know it wasn't just him. Everyone thinks you prioritize your training over the good of the regiment."

It took everything I had to keep my voice to an outraged whisper. "How is my training a *bad* thing? I am the best mage here —my power *helps* them!"

"We are supposed to be a unit, but you are looking out for yourself!" he countered. "Ry, the majority of our time is spent away from battle. One of the first things a soldier learns in the Cavalry is to get to know his comrades. Relationships are instrumental to trust—and you haven't bothered to build up any since you arrived. You perform your duties and that's it." He lowered his voice. "The only people you ever bother to talk to are your friends in Combat or Paige—and forgive me for saying it, but she is just as isolated as yourself."

Paige shot my brother a glare as I snapped, "People have far too much time on their hands if they are complaining I am not friendly enough."

"It's the reason Ray was promoted before you." Derrick met my eyes. "The orders came straight from Sir Gavin himself."

After… after all I've done for this place. Last year's attack and the bandit raids and the Crown's coin, and I'm the best mage in my unit and it still isn't enough. Commander Nyx tells me over and over how impressed she is, but she lets my squad commander promote someone else. All because I don't try to make friends with the people who talk behind my back.

For once, I didn't speak. My lungs burned and months of frustration were fighting to break their way to the surface. I kept trying to swallow, and all I got were sharp, angry gasps that seemed to build with each breath. That moment you are so angry you could barely breathe? I felt betrayed. I was sick to my stomach, and all I could think was that everyone hated me and once again I was that insecure first-year trying to prove herself to the world.

Would it be enough? Would anything I did *ever* be enough?

My brother drew forward but I raised my hand.

"Ryiah—"

"Go, Derrick." I exhaled slowly. "Just go."

His shoulders slumped and my stomach hurt. I watched my brother retreat wondering if I should have let him stay. Derrick was only looking out for me. He always had my best interests at heart.

The problem was they weren't mine; they were his. Derrick cared what this squad thought of me—I didn't. My brother and Ian's impassioned pleas only made me resent the others even more so than before. If Sir Gavin wanted to promote Ray before me then it would be the other squad's loss when they needed more magic than the other Combat mage could handle.

"I will not apologize for my own birthright." More than ever I understood what Darren meant all those years ago. If people couldn't accept me for me, then I was done trying to win their acceptance.

※

I could say the next two months flew by and that in time everything changed, but that would be a lie. Nothing changed. Nothing got better, and nothing got worse.

Well, my training continued. And my magic's potential continued to grow. But my relations within the squad were as barren as before. Ian and I were on shaky terms after our talk, and while Derrick had stopped trying to talk to me about the others, I knew he still wished I would try. Lief was clearly oblivious to the tension between the two Combat mages he commanded, and Sir Gavin had yet to notice any difference at all.

Reports continued to come in surrounding the Crown's negotiations with Pythus. It came as a giant relief when the king's summons arrived a couple weeks after that. A compromise had been reached and a date was set for the wedding. In three weeks Blayne and Princess Wrendolyn of Pythus would be wed in the capital. I was to pack my things and return to the palace much sooner than anticipated.

I would not be returning.

"Following the ceremony, you will partake in the king's annual progress to the Academy for first-year trials. From there, the progress will immediately proceed to Montfort for the Candidacy. Commander Nyx has been made aware of your discharge."

I couldn't say the summons wasn't welcome.

"So, this is it then?" Ian barely looked up as I bid farewell to Lief and our new factionmate, Killian, an older Combat mage who had transferred in from one of the Red Desert regiments shortly after I arrived.

I shifted my satchel from one shoulder to the other. "It is. I'll miss you all."

"A shame the two of you couldn't stay longer." Lief's eyes lingered on my guard, and then he strode forward to give me a parting clap on the shoulder. He stepped out of the way just as Derrick approached, a couple soldier friends trailing closely behind.

"Thought you could leave without saying goodbye to your little brother, did you?" Derrick pulled me in for a big hug. His tone was teasing, but I caught the grief in his eyes. I was sad too. I would miss him—my two brothers and parents were scattered across the realm in service, and I would be stuck in the capital.

Maybe I could convince them all to take up service closer to Devon? Give my parents an apartment in the palace? I would talk to the King's Regiment after the wedding. Perhaps something could be arranged.

"Don't you dare forget about me," I warned.

One of the soldiers gave into a series of coughs.

Jacob drawled loud enough for me to hear, "Going to a palace, seems like she would be the one to forget about us, don't it?" I bit down on my tongue to keep from retorting. Derrick shot his friend a disapproving look before wrapping me up for one final embrace. He stepped back with a lopsided grin. "I'm saving every bit of my purse for the Candidacy, Ry. You are going to make me a rich man, you hear?"

I laughed, a little too uncomfortable with our audience. "I'll try but... perhaps you should rethink your strategy, Derrick, I—"

"Sir Gavin already granted me the leave." He waved his hand. "I'll see you in two months."

I smiled. "That you will."

My life was about to change. If only I had known how much.

CHAPTER TEN

My horse lost its shoe. Somewhere trudging along the muddy mountain trail the blasted iron got stuck in a patch of high grass and ever-so-fortunately it was two hours before I noticed the limp. It took Paige and me a good part of the day just to find a farrier in the next village we passed.

Then, as we were preparing to set out, a spring storm arrived.

Thanks to the thunder and lightning we were forced to take shelter for the night, and when we awoke the next day the storm was still raging. War charges were better trained than most, but neither Paige nor I trusted a horse not to spook at giant pellets of hail and great flashes of light.

Needless to say, when we finally finished up the last leg of our travel we were two days behind schedule. We sent word with a local envoy the moment the storms let up, and then that final day we rode all night—much to Paige's distaste—just to reach the palace in time. The king's summons had stated Prince Blayne's wedding was to take place the following morning, and when we finally arrived at the palace gates we had barely an hour before the ceremony would start.

"Here to report the Lady Mage Ryiah—" Paige never got to finish.

A large, pompous woman I'd never met before shot out and grabbed my arm before the declaration was over. She hollered at my knight to attend to the horse as she dragged me down the palace walk, ducking through a side door for entry.

"You're filthy!" she snapped. "Not to mention late. The king had me attending the gates all morning. Do you have any idea what today is? The palace is filled with every noble house in the country and here you are, the mud-streaked lowborn who is supposed to marry the crown prince's brother? Do you have *any* idea what the Pythians would think if they spotted you? Why they might reconsider the wedding!"

"They've already met—"

"None of that sass! You have less than an hour to be presentable for the ceremony. In your state we will have to skip the herald's announcement and rush you straight to the prince's side." The woman shoved me into my chambers and began shouting directions at my ladies-in-waiting.

From the way the girls scrambled to attend I took the woman to be Madame Pollina, the head of staff and, incidentally, Benny's new wife. She'd been ill during my last trip to the palace, and I could see that had been a relief.

I barely squeaked out a greeting to Celine and Gemma before the woman had me stripped and tossed into an ice cold bath.

"It would have been hot," she continued. "If you hadn't decided to arrive two days late."

I didn't get a chance to reply. My head was dunked under the water, and then I was scrubbed and poked and prodded within an inch of my life. I barely got the chance to recognize the orange-scented oils before I was dried and shoved into a dress five times more elaborate than anything I had ever borne witness to. It was silken green layers, one after the other, with a gold corset and skintight sleeves edged in gold. Every inch seemed to shimmer in the light.

I barely had a chance to admire it. The bodice was so tight I could barely breathe, and I couldn't be sure it wasn't deliberately so.

Then came the matching stained slippers that were a size too small and the gold-and-green necklace, which hung heavily around my neck.

I was powdered and painted and my hair arranged in heavy curls at the back of my head, and then Madame Pollina dragged me out of the rooms and through the winding halls into the palace's holy room. I gasped.

Every inch of the chamber was packed as full as the keep. Hundreds of bright colors pressed together as highborns fought for a closer place to the front. A steady clamor of voices streamed across the rows of seats. Sunlight seemed to catch across every stained glass window, and the effect was almost blinding.

At the very front stood King Lucius and Darren in splendid red and gold, and Duke Cassius in a striking blue, the two countries' signature colors. Just beyond was the Council of Magic. The Crown's advisors and the king's most trusted families came next.

On the podium itself was a priest and Prince Blayne and a young girl with lovely blond locks—from the looks of it no more than fifteen. Princess Wrendolyn.

So young, I realized.

Madame Pollina pushed and shoved her way through the crowd with me in tow. Then she threw me at the foot of the stage. I scrambled to the side, dodging Mage Marius's amused eye as I stood beside Darren.

No one acknowledged my presence—all eyes were fixated on the priest, a small man with skin drawn tight across his face. He croaked on in countless blessings, praising the Crown and this couple for honoring the gods with their marriage and bringing a time of peace upon the land. The priest dipped his hand in a bowl of red wine and issued a prayer, blessing a pink stain across each forehead. Then the two completed their exchange of rings and vows.

The room erupted in cheers. Handfuls of flowers were tossed up into the air as the crown prince and his new wife made their way back. A herald proclaimed the beginning of a weeklong celebration of feasts, and the crowd began to disperse.

As everyone began to head to the grand ballroom I found myself nervously awaiting Darren's notice. Prince Blayne and his princess had already left the podium, as well as King Lucius whose only greeting had been a deep scowl in my direction before he followed his first son's procession.

What was Darren thinking?

I didn't know what to say after the way we had left things five months before. The two of us had let our tempers get the best of us and neither were blameless. As much as I still hated the things he had said, it was time to atone for the past.

"So..." The non-heir shifted stance so that he was facing me instead of the front. His tone made it clear he had known I was there the whole time. "You finally decided to grace Devon with your presence."

I pursed my lips. "We had bad weather. Paige sent an envoy."

"Did she?" Darren's eyes met mine and he forced a smile. "How convenient."

I folded my arms. "I'm not lying, Darren."

He gave a bored wave of his hand. "It doesn't matter either way. I have matters to attend to."

"Now?" This wasn't the way I had anticipated our meeting. I panicked. "Darren—"

"I assume you know your way around." The prince's tone was dismissive on the chance his words weren't abundantly clear. "The boy with the world at his feet is in need of some *privileged* company."

Before I could reply Darren stepped around and left me standing at the front of the room. Alone.

That... I was struck by the urge to throw something hard at his head. *How could he be so cold?* I had prepared an apology but now? Now I didn't want to apologize. Darren was mingling with a flock of highborn ladies at the center, his mouth curved in that half-smirk I mistakenly found attractive. And the girls were smiling back, batting their big lashes and touching his sleeve as they giggled overly loud.

My betrothed seemed in no hurry to leave.

I sucked air in angrily, and then pushed my way through the crowd. I didn't know why I had thought coming here would be any different than the keep. Either way I was alone with a horde of others who seemed to belong. And the one person I was supposed to have by my side? He was too busy nursing his wounded pride with a simpering flock of sheep.

I longed for Ella. She would understand. She had survived my twin, and she knew the games of court. If there was anyone who would know what to do it was her. But of course she was gone, serving in a wonderful, *appreciative* regiment in Montfort with my brother instead.

We had sent letters back and forth while I was at the keep. The two of them were as happy as could be. Alex had been promoted twice in the infirmary he served, and Ella's squad had frequent mock-duels in the same arena as the coming Candidacy. I was jealous.

I hadn't told either of them about my fight with Darren. Or my troubles in Ferren. I didn't want anyone to pity me. After hearing their happy tale, I just couldn't tell them mine. It was a far cry from pleasant.

Wallowing in pity is going to get you nowhere. I would not let Darren's cold demeanor stop me from enjoying the rest of the day. The bride and groom had a parade through the city for the commoners, but a feast was already being held in one of the ballrooms while the rest of the highborn court awaited the couple's return. I squared my shoulders and strode into the hall, determined to steal some of Benny's delicacies before the rest of the crowd finished them off. I wasn't the only fan of his cooking. Perhaps I would sneak away to visit Benny later. Although, now that his charming wife was back, perhaps it would be better to avoid the kitchens.

Maybe Wolf, I decided. I was still wary around the kennel—and dogs in general— but in my last visit I had made it a point to stop by once a day with a bit of the cook's scraps. I had even gotten myself to pet Wolf during that last morning. I had been hoping to surprise Darren the next time I visited, but now...

I pushed my frustration aside and stood there, stuffing myself. Eventually I was forced to stop—blasted corset. I was still hungry, but I couldn't manage anymore unless I ripped the silly thing right out from under my dress. Somehow I didn't think that would go over too well with the Crown.

All around me the highborn court flitted from one circle of acquaintances to the next, passing conversation until the heir and his bride returned from their progress. I stood idly by for the next hour wondering how much trouble I would be in if I attempted to escape before the festivities had truly begun. Darren had yet to make an appearance, and his father was busy reproaching one of the servants across the room. Maybe no one would notice.

"How fares my favorite new mage?"

I started from my thoughts to find Marius studying a platter of meats. The Black Mage grinned at me, white teeth flashing. "Or have I rendered you speechless once again, Ryiah?"

I quickly fumbled for a response. I was in a constant state of awe every time the two of us crossed paths. The towering mage bore the robe—and title— of my dreams. The gold lining was striking against the dark tint of his skin, and the silk seemed as fluid as water.

"I-I only just arrived." *Great, I already sound like a short-sentenced oaf.* "Have you and the Council really been away all this time?" I would have thought they'd have participated in at least some of the Pythian negotiations.

"Both a blessing and a curse." The mage gave me a con-spiratorial wink and tilted his head in the direction of his comrades. "Those two quibble like a couple of hens, but then again that's all the others do while we are here."

I glanced in the direction he indicated. A tall blond-haired woman a little older than Marius had her stark red lips pressed permanently in a frown while an older man with griz-zled, brown locks and soft, yellowed eyes conversed. Each bore their faction's signature robe with the prestigious gold trim that distinguished them from the rest. Though their hoods were pulled back, I could still make out a small fortune of sparkling gemstones lining each rim.

It was strange to think that in one short month these three great mages would give up their legacy. A twenty-year reign anew.

The grin left Marius's face. "We spent months in Cyri trying to put a face to the rebels in the south. All that time and no leads... Perhaps my successor will have better luck."

"I should have requested a post in Ishir," I muttered.

"We had half the Crown's Army combing the desert to no avail." The man heaved a sigh. "As much as I would have en-joyed your company, dear Ryiah, it would have done us no good. The rebels prefer sabotage to open attacks. Your experi-ence in the Mahj salt mines was one of a kind."

"There is no action in the north." I bit back a wistful sigh. "I thought there would be, with the attack on Ferren last year, but the closest encounter I had was with a small camp of bandits."

Marius gave me a crooked grin. "Here we are at the brink of war, and you are still itching for an opportunity to show off that fancy potential of yours." He gave a throaty laugh. "Don't you worry one bit, my dear, the Candidacy will push you to that brink."

I started to reply, but a curious nobleman beat me to it. "Do you think the new treaty will stop the Caltothians, Mage Marius?"

The Black Mage grumbled under his breath so only I could hear him, "And the endless assault begins." Louder he said, "My Lord Flavius, how pleasant to see you." He paused to have the man repeat his question. "No, I don't believe that nonsense for a minute. Yes. Exactly... The Caltothians haven't spent three decades assaulting our border to give up so easily... Not yet... I should say... No, I—"

A cluster of others arrived to pepper the mage with questions. I inched away. Marius caught my eye and lifted a knowing hand in farewell. The man would be busy for the rest of the evening.

Just as I was gathering the courage to sneak past the exit the herald blew his horn to clear the room. I stood a little straighter as Prince Blayne and Princess Wrendolyn were announced to the crowd. The non-heir emerged shortly thereafter, and it was only after he shot me an expectant look that I realized I was supposed to follow. *Well, how am I supposed to read your mind when you won't talk to me?* If Darren hadn't been so busy flirting with the ladies of court he could have warned me about their entrance.

I hurried to the front, ignoring the snickers as I took my seat at the head table and praying my face wasn't as red as it felt.

"I like your dress."

I glanced over to the speaker and found myself face to face with Blayne's new bride. Her eyes were bright.

"Thank you, Princess," I mumbled.

She smiled. "You can call me 'Wren,' Lady Ryiah. Is it okay if I call you just 'Ryiah?' Because if it's not I—"

Lucius stood, goblet in hand, and the rest of her words fell away. The king's voice as decisive as steel, and it was also the first time I had ever heard him address a crowd. The man's hair might be white but his manner cut like ice. There was no question he held the room's attention.

"Today marks the beginning of a new reign. For the first time in our great nations' history, Jerar and Pythus sit united as one. I toast to my firstborn son and his new bride, a lovely addition to the Crown. May the both of you live long and prosperous with many heirs to come."

My tongue grew heavy in my mouth. What did Blayne's marriage mean for Darren and me? The king had promised our wedding following the Pythian negotiations, but until now I had all but forgotten in the chaos that followed.

Darren caught me studying him, a muscle ticking in his jaw, and then he returned to scowling at the tapestry across the way.

I ground my teeth. *This is going to be a long night.*

Lucius continued on with a stern order for quiet. "This new treaty should dissuade the Caltothians for now, but it will not promise us peace. I have given Emperor Liang and King Joren my word Jerar will not initiate a war, but make no mistake—the next time King Horrace strikes we will have the strength of the alliance behind us."

A murmur of dissent started up in the back of the hall. It wasn't long before the crowd was in an uproar, baying for Caltothian blood. The new princess was one of the only ones who did not, and considering she could have very well married their prince instead, I understood her discomfort. I kept quiet, too. Death didn't excite me, and the prospect of war even after a new treaty was not something I wanted to ponder.

When the crowd finally settled, the king concluded his speech. "As tentative as our future might be, there is one thing for certain—and that is the Crown." His gaze narrowed to Darren. I swallowed, my mouth suddenly dry. "Today's union brings the onset of another. My youngest and his betrothed shall wed upon the progress's return from Montfort. Their marriage will bind Jerar to the Borea Isles, and our alliance will be complete."

"Here, here." Duke Cassius pounded the table with his fist. His cheeks were ruddy—and from his high spirits I was sure he was on his second bottle for the night. "To the New Alliance. May great fortune favor us all."

King Lucius's discerning gaze swept the hall as he held his goblet high. "To the New Alliance."

The sea of nobility raised its glasses in return, echoing the king's words.

There was a moment of silence and then the herald emerged from the entry, clearing his throat. *"Let the festivities begin!"*

A procession of entertainers poured in from the hall.

Almost instantly the room was a cacophony of noise. Music started as a group of performers wove up and down the aisles, stringed rebecs and lutes in hand. A group of jesters. A pairing of performers with masks of popular gods. Another man spun sticks of fire in a fast-spinning web.

It wasn't long before a dance broke out near the front of the room. The musicians filed into a corner and began their procession as courtiers flooded the ballroom's center.

Prince Blayne was one of the first to escort his new bride to a dance.

I waited until the king and Duke Cassius were deep in conversation, then I took a deep breath and turned to face the prince at my right.

Darren's garnet eyes met my own, but he made no attempt to smile.

"Are you going to ask me, too?"

His lip curled. "Really, Ryiah?"

"I am trying to make peace. This is your brother's celebration, so won't it be improper if we don't?"

"I pay no heed to what anyone thinks." He pushed back his chair, wood legs creaking against the marble floor as he stood. "Least of all you."

I flushed. "That's it? I return after four months apart and you are really so desperate to be rid of me? You don't even want to try and have a conversation."

"I'm sure you had a good cry and farmboy was there to comfort you in my place."

My jaw dropped. "Do you think so little of me?"

Garnet flared in response. "I don't know. Sometimes a person's opinion can surprise you."

"Darren, I'm trying to apologize."

"You wouldn't mean a single word." His words were bitter as he started to walk away. "The truth is told in anger, not regret, love."

I bit down on my tongue, and then followed Darren out into the hall, waiting until we were out of the public's eye. "You hurt me too! I'm not the only one who needs to apologize!"

The prince turned around and his expression was callous. "You want an apology, Ryiah? I'm sorry. I'm sorry I can't tell you the words you want to hear. *You won't win.* I believe you are good, love." His eyes were like twin pools of fire. "But you aren't me. And I'm sorry you never had that *privilege.*"

Then he left me. Darren strode out into the night without a backwards glance and left me standing in that bright hall listening to the peals of laughter just behind.

My whole body felt like it had just been kicked to the ground. Every part of me squeezing in, tighter and tighter, until my vision was black and spots were dancing before my eyes. I couldn't understand what had happened. My heart was hammering so hard it hurt.

Five long, shaky breaths. And then I was able to focus. Able to see.

On the night I had felt most beautiful Darren had made me feel my worst.

"Trouble in paradise?"

I didn't want anyone to see me like this. Especially not *him.* I cursed my timing and turned to face Blayne with a false smile to my lips, praying to the gods my eyes weren't as swollen as they felt.

"Leaving your new bride and festivities so soon?"

"I see." He ignored my barbed comment. "Well, you left my brother in quite a state yourself."

I didn't want to talk about Darren with Blayne. I didn't want to talk about myself. I wanted to be alone.

"You should know," the crown prince drawled, "he will never change."

"I don't want him to change! I just want him to talk to me!" The words came uninvited, and I regretted them instantly. I didn't want Blayne to know anything. But I had no one else.

I was alone. Ella was gone. My brothers were gone. My friends and family were across the countryside while I was trapped in the king's court. Paige was somewhere in the palace as a sentry but it would take me half the night to find her. And even then, she didn't like to talk about "feelings." I was trapped in the palace, and I didn't know what to do.

Blayne was the last person I trusted, but if what Benny said was true then he was possibly the one person who understood Darren. And that made me hesitate instead of sending him on his way, or sending myself on mine.

The crown prince glanced back at the dancers, looking for someone or something in the crowd—presumably his new wife, and then nodded toward a passage to our left. "Come with me."

"Where are we going?"

Blayne regarded me with a sneer. "You want my help or not, Ryiah?"

It was a challenge. A test of our supposed truce and my chance to find out more about his brother. I knew if I passed up this opportunity he would not offer it again.

Common sense bid I decline, but I was in no mood to listen to reason. I wanted to understand Darren, even if it meant spending time with the enemy.

I could only hope that Blayne didn't choose this moment
to suddenly return to his old nature.

"Lead the way."

I didn't know what I had expected, but the old queen's
chamber was certainly not part of the morbid possibilities in
my mind. When Blayne took me to the royal wing I was sure
he had made a mistake. But then he continued past the king's
chamber to the furthest door in the hall, one that had remained unoccupied since Queen Lillian's death many years
before.

I watched as the crown prince produced a large ring of
keys from the pocket of his trousers, and then unlocked the
door. Blayne paused as his hand stilled on the handle.

"You and I have our differences, but rest assured I love
my brother, Ryiah. I believe that is the one thing we hold in
common. What I am about to show, you are never to speak of
to anyone. Do I have your word?"

I nodded.

He swung open the door, and I followed him inside. Then
I took a step back, my back hitting the frame in horror.

Unlike the other royal chambers, this room had been
stripped bare of material. No bed, no furnishings, no sprawling
rug or tapestries. Nothing to suggest the queen had ever lived
in the chamber at all. But that wasn't why I had gasped.

Protruding from the back of the wall was a pair of
chained manacles that were approximately three feet in height
and a shoulder length apart. Another set rested along the
ground, built into a metal bar lining the floor.

The swirled marble tile was discolored beneath the
chains, as if someone—or two someones— had bled out repeat-
edly on its surface. The floor's design was an elaborate design
of red, gold, and violet swirl—the same as the rest of the palace— but the stain was much closer to rust.

"W-what is this place?" I choked. My heart was racing as I looked on and pictured a hundred horrible scenarios in my head. Reasons Blayne would need to show me this room. For the first time I prayed it was a ploy, that the crown prince's motives were malevolent—anything but what I was imagining now.

"This was my mother's room." Blayne walked over to a dark pine chest I hadn't noticed, reaching out to take one of the contents: a foot-long pole with a chain of small, sharp blades attached to its cord. He tested its weight in his hand.

"She was much younger than my father, much more lovely and had the most beautiful singing voice you could ever imagine. Darren was too young to remember her much, barely two years at the time of her passing. But I did." He dropped the whip, and I could hear him sigh. "My father was never a kind man. But losing my mother as he did, well I'm sure you've heard the stories..."

I swallowed. My parents had told me the tale as a child. Before I was born, Queen Lillian had been poisoned during a ceremonial feast. It was widely believed that her wine had been intended for the king. The aftermath was the stuff of legends. Following his wife's death Lucius had ordered the entire hall interrogated and then executed at once. Among the victims had been his current board of advisors, a handful of nobility, the serving staff on hand, and several of his guard. A culprit had never been identified and sixty-two men and women had died that night.

Scholars suspected it was the first of the Caltothian attacks. They also called it the "Lily Queen's Slaughter."

"This room..." My heart slammed against my ribs as he continued. "He had the servants *redecorate* after she passed. None of the staff was allowed to enter, and only the head infirmary mage knew."

The prince's voice was hard. "There was the palace dungeon, of course." The boy laughed, low and cruel. "But it would have been too much work to carry two unconscious boys

up and down the palace halls when this room was unused—
and so close to where we slept."

Blayne met my gaze head on. "So he took us here."

My knees threatened to give out, and I clung to the
door's frame for support. I could hear every word Blayne was
saying, and yet there was a thundering in my ears. I felt sick to
my stomach, and the pastries from earlier were fighting to rise
as I gulped in deep lungfuls of air.

"Any time we disobeyed orders, any time he had too
much to drink, any time he decided we were too *soft* to carry on
his line." The prince's lips twisted at the memory. "The man
always had his mage heal us when he was done. No one ever
knew, and if word ever got out...Well, he was the king and
there was nothing anyone could do unless they wished to find
themselves on the receiving end of his attention, like us."

"*No...*" The air sputtered from my lungs.

"When I was nine, I got into trouble with one of my tutors. Darren heard my cries from down the hall." The prince's
expression grew dark, and I realized Benny was right. Blayne
didn't hate Darren at all. "Instead of staying in his room, the
little fool snuck in and tried to save me... He never was afraid
of our father, even when he was beating him senseless."

My stomach surged, and I slid to the floor, clutching my
knees to my chest. My skin was clammy, and my hands were
still shaking as I took Blayne's proffered flask. I couldn't stop
picturing six-year-old Darren in a pool of his own blood, fists
and feet and a bladed whip coming from the man he called
"Father." A little boy trying to save his brother.

*Privilege. I accused Darren of a privilege the rest of us never
had.*

"Somehow he managed to pull a knife he had stolen from
the kitchens while our father was choking him—"

A whimper escaped my lips, and I clutched shaky fingers
to my mouth to let Blayne continue.

"Darren was overtaken in an instant, of course, and beat-
en within an inch of his life, but..." Blayne's voice seized. "—

He never stopped fighting. Later—when the healer had finished up with my brother and me—our father stopped by the infirmary. Told Darren he had finally done something right." Blayne didn't feign his disgust. "As second son Darren's duty was to me. He had finally proven his role. Father sent him off to train with our head knight the next morning so he could start preparing for the School of Knighthood and become Commander of the Crown's Army when I took the crown. Darren had *impressed* him."

My pulse slammed against my lungs, and I forced myself to swallow. Two sips of some bitter liquid that tore at my throat like ice. I wiped my sweaty palms against my dress.

"After that day…" I couldn't say it. "Did your father…?"

"Not with Darren."

I opened my mouth and the crown prince just gave me a sardonic smile. "It takes much more to impress when you are his heir. Darren wasn't always around. In any case I'm better for it now."

I didn't know what to say. I couldn't say anything. *What did you say to your enemy?* To the villain with the pitiable past? Everything Blayne had done, I couldn't help wondering if Darren would have turned out the same, were he the heir instead.

"Darren will never tell you any of this." The prince shut the chest with a *thud*. "I brought you here so you could see the truth for yourself. My brother pushes people away with his pride, and it doesn't take much to see he is doing the same to you now. Whatever happened between the two of you, I need you to forgive him, Ryiah."

"Why…" My voice caught and I tried again. "Why are you helping me? I-I know you want to make amends but—"

"Because he is my little brother. And as many mistakes as he has made, I want the best for him." The prince's gaze was bitter. "Even if that is you."

I found Darren leaving the training grounds just as I arrived. Before the training grounds, I had checked his chamber, the indoor practice court, the kitchens, and finally the kennels. *I should've realized he would seek solace in training.* Even in the middle of his brother's festivities. He and I were one and the same.

The scent of summer was thick in the air, fresh blossoms and cedar mixed in with the lingering trace of sweat and dirt from the barracks.

I stood anxiously, the warm breeze ruffling my dress.

"Darren."

The non-heir looked up, dark bangs falling across his eyes. Something like regret registered for just a moment before he clenched his jaw and turned away.

"What do you want, Ryiah?"

I took a deep breath. "I'm reckless."

His head jerked back as he regarded me in surprise. I could tell he hadn't been expecting *that*.

I rambled on quickly, "I judge too fast. I don't always think before I speak. I don't like to hear that I might not win. I lash out when I'm angry. I'm far from perfect, and I know I never will be. I make mistakes just like the rest of them."

With every confession I took a step closer, closing the distance between us. I waited until I was right in front of the prince, and then placed my hands on his chest, causing him to take another step back until his shoulders were lining the barrack's wall.

"You aren't one of my mistakes."

A lump in the prince's throat rose and fell.

"I love you." *And that's never going to change.* "I've been in love with you since that day in the desert, and today it's time for me to make an apology of my own." I leaned in close and watched his sharp intake of breath. "I'm sorry, Darren." My eyes rose to his, and I willed him to see the sincerity in my own. "I'm sorry I said you were privileged. I'm sorry I ever thought... Blayne told me..." I swallowed. "If I had known..."

Understanding, and then shame flared in response—but before Darren could break away I wrapped my fingers along the back of his neck and brought his lips to my own. I pressed hard, tasting the regret and anger that was perforating his.

Blood and salt mixed in with the sweetness of wine and I clung still.

He tried to break our kiss. "Ryiah—"

I pushed back harder; he was air and I was drowning for breath. "No." The word came sputtering from my chest. *No.* I wasn't going to let Darren turn away now.

I wasn't going to let his father win.

I kissed him again, a bit softer. Pleading. My lips brushed his, and I could feel his mouth trembling against my own. "I love you." I whispered the words again. Over and over. "Please don't shut me out."

I felt it the exact moment Darren stopped fighting.

Tension left his shoulders, and the non-heir's pulse sped up as his hands fisted in my skirt, pulling me in. Heated lips parted mine, and the kiss drove deep—neither one of us in control of our response. His eyes were shut, blocking out whatever memories he struggled to keep inside.

Darren's hands slid to my waist and then he swung me around so that I was up against the wall instead. My back slammed against stone, and the rough material dug into my skin, his fingers bruising my ribs. His breath was hot and angry as his mouth assaulted my own. I welcomed it, a hot wave of fury bubbling in its wake.

Pain and passion were so much easier to embrace. I didn't want to think about what the king had done to his two sons. I didn't want to pity the brother who had attacked my best friend. I didn't want to know how many times my betrothed had been pushed to the brink of death for the sake of his father's cruel, twisted games.

I didn't want to believe any of it.

All these years of coveting Darren's life only to find out everything I thought was a lie. Did he even want to be the Black Mage at all? Or was it just another role he was expected to meet?

Expectation. That's all this ever was.

I shut my eyes and tipped my chin, letting the prince's anger take charge of the moment. Praying, hoping that I could take it all away if I just held on long enough.

But I never could. And I was foolish to try.

"I'm..." Darren broke the kiss a couple minutes later and pressed his forehead against my own. I watched the rise and fall of his chest. "I'm sorry I said—"

I cut him off. "You don't have to explain."

His eyes seared. "But I want to, Ryiah. All these years..." Another lump in his throat as he swallowed. "I never got to be anything but what he wanted me to be—"

"Darren—"

"I don't even know who *I* am anymore." His whisper was hoarse. "And I *hate* it."

"What if you lose?" I studied his face, searching for a sign. "If you make it look like you are trying...?"

"He would know." The prince's laugh was bitter. "And he would punish me by taking away the only thing I've ever let myself be weak enough to want." His gaze met mine and for once he didn't hide. "It's not the first time he's used you against me."

The world rushed around me as I realized exactly what he meant.

The first time he tried to call things off with Priscilla.

When I had called him his father's whipping boy.

"Besides." Darren pulled away to rest against the wall beside me, shoulder to shoulder. He looked out at the night sky above. "With every second of my life devoted to this cursed role, a part of me wants it now... I'm so mad in the head I can't imagine a future in which the robe *isn't*."

I didn't know how to reply.

Darren took my hand, folding my fingers into his own. "If anyone beats me, I want it to be you, Ryiah."

I shut my eyes and sighed. "Perhaps the gods will surprise us and it will be neither."

"A true tragedy," he agreed.

"Of epic proportions."

His smile was just the faintest line in the shadows. "Two longstanding rivals."

"And only one robe to bear."

"Who will win?" Darren's tone was wry. "The handsome prince?"

I grinned. "Or his valiant betrothed?"

"I can't wait to marry you, Ryiah."

When I opened my eyes, Darren was watching me with the oddest gleam in his eyes. The soft expression in his gaze... it hurt to breathe.

Then a devious thought worked its way to the surface. "Even if I win?"

The prince's expression faltered, and then the boy from the Academy returned with a smirk. "Even if you lose."

CHAPTER ELEVEN

When we first entered the city with the rest of the Crown's progress, I wasn't sure what to expect. Heavy, towering pines of the Iron Range gave way to coarse, earthy fields and cracked riverbeds the further east we got. Montfort was a week's ride north of the capital, a week and a half from Sjeka and the first-year trials we had just left, and it shared neither city's natural splendor. While not as dry as the Red Desert by any means, it was certainly more arid and cool.

But what Montfort lacked in beauty it more than made up for in mass. The great city was famous for its architects, and the moment I spotted it from the road, I knew I was in for a shock.

Even two miles from the start of the city's residence, I could see the giant slabs of the Candidacy's arena towering above the rest. Like a giant stone mouth that longed to tear out the sky. The raised seats and spectator towers were easily fifteen houses tall from their lowest peaks.

The rest of the city was a bit simpler in nature—large square buildings and simple housing, flat roofs and rectangular windows, heavy curtains and chipped bricks in simple sundried mud, and the occasional stone-and-mortar mix. One raised building stood out among the rest: a steep dome roof supported by heavily decorated columns and smoothed walls, but even it paled next to the city's central feature.

Our horses kicked up loose dust as they made their way through the streets. I was stunned by the crowds. Every which way we moved were great herds of people, lowborn and high-born alike, flooding the markets and knocking on doors. That wasn't all; outside the city limits had been canvas tents as far as the eye could see.

As our tracks slowed, both Paige and Darren's guard, Henry, pressed closer to our side. The herald—who had been busy entertaining two women in our progress—broke free to blow his horn and proclaim our arrival to the crowd. In truth it did little—there was nowhere for the people to go.

"Like a bay of pigs, and just as brainless," Paige griped under her breath.

Wren giggled as I hid a smile. In the past three weeks the young princess and I had become close.

In some ways, she was the little sister I'd never had. Sweet—always saving me the last candied figs in our evening meals—and easy to laugh in a way that I was not. especially at my guard whom she had deemed "charming."

Wren was such a change from my loud, raucous brothers and their constant slew of insults and insatiable bellies. She didn't seem to mind my lowborn upbringing, and preferred my company to the rest of the court. She was a bit shy around Blayne, but that could have been their difference in age. Knowing what had happened to my best friend, I'd made it a point to ask about their wedding night when we were alone, and she had all but blushed furiously in reply.

Since the girl hadn't paled or given any sign of terror I took that to be a sign that Blayne had truly grown since the incident with my best friend. That, and I'd requested her la-dies-in-waiting report any bruises or marks marring her skin. I might trust the prince a bit more since the night in the old queen's chambers, but I was determined to do everything I could to ensure what happened to Ella never happened to another girl again.

"Fresh from this morn'! You won't get a better deal if you try!"

Our progress fought its way past the merchants to the ornate building I had admired before. As the hostlers appeared I realized it was where the Crown and its most important court would reside for the time being. Baron Cuthbert's manor.

The king's scholars confirmed it a moment later as they detailed our visit.

"During the last Candidacy it is estimated one-fifth of Jerar came out to watch, and with the Crown's own son a contender at present we expect close to a third." The man cleared his throat. "Not to discount the foreign embassies from Caltoth, the Borea Isles, and, of course, the Pythian court."

"That many visitors?" I squeaked.

Darren edged closer to lean into my ear. "Nervous, love?"

I rolled my eyes in jest, but in truth I was terrified. Hundreds of thousands of visitors. Every one of the stadium's seats. Filled.

And here you just thought they built it that big to look pretty.

Wait.

Caltothian embassy? I grabbed Darren's arm. "Caltothians?"

"You didn't know?" Darren took me by the hand, slowly edging along the standing crowd to peer at the back of the crowd, and tilted his head to the right. A stranger stood, engaged in conversation with a man who could only be Princess Shinako's father, Emperor Liang.

The man was tall and broad-shouldered, with curly, brown hair that fell to his shoulders. Foreboding, too—with cynical blue eyes that read the room in an instant. Self-assured, and not remotely perturbed to be surrounded by a room of potential enemies. I found myself wondering how he had found the courage to face the Crown in the light of what his kinsmen had done.

"Lord Tyrus of Gyr." Darren lowered his voice. "It's tradition to send invitations to each court, but for Caltoth it's little more than formality. Given the state of things I don't think anyone expected King Horrace to send a man. But perhaps with the New Alliance he is willing to make a bid for peace."

I snorted.

"Don't worry," he whispered. "Father's message was clear. One misstep and we will have ground to imprison Tyrus for treason. Blayne and Father have him and his guards flanked from dawn until dusk."

I started to nod, my gaze flitting back to the front, when I heard a familiar laugh in the alley. I spun around so fast I almost lost hold of my breakfast, eyes anxiously searching the faces behind us.

Sure enough, I spotted her leaning into my twin's shoulder in the middle of the street, laughing amber eyes as she looked up at Alex in jest. Her bronze skin glowed in the light of the early evening sun. She looked just as striking as always.

The crowd shifted, and I noticed Derrick and my parents standing a couple feet apart. Ella's parents and her older brother Jeffrey were there too.

"Ella!" Halfway across the street I screeched my friend's name and watched as she shrieked, charging in my direction like a blind madman.

I barely had time to speak before the two of us collided. Darren caught up a moment later just before my best friend and I took a tumble to the ground. Paige a minute after, spewing venom as she chastised me for leaving her behind.

"How can I protect someone who continuously neglects every precaution I have in place?"

By the time my guard had finished her lecture both sets of families had made their way alongside.

Ella's parents wore polite frowns as they regarded the prince beside us—no doubt recalling his brother—but mine, especially my mother, were eyeing him in unabashed interest.

"Mom, Dad, this is Darren." I couldn't help but notice how stiff and quiet our audience had suddenly become.

My father was first to break the silence. Unfortunately for me it was in the most embarrassing way possible. "Well, well, 'tall, dark, and handsome.' I can see why my daughter picked you. She certainly has a type."

Alex guffawed, and even Derrick had to hide a grin as the prince's face shot up in flames. Not even Darren was prepared for my father.

"Dad!" I hid my face in my hands.

"George." My mother elbowed my father for embarrassing his daughter in front of the prince. "Leave them alone." She smiled at Darren, her keen gray eyes studying our intertwined hands. "A pleasure to meet you, Your Highness. I'm Ry's mother, Liona."

"You don't have to call me by my title, ma'am." Darren's face was as red as mine.

An awkward moment ensued as Ella reintroduced the non-heir to her family, all of which he had met at court—albeit years before. Her brother Jeffrey looked just as dubious as Alex; her parents were better, they were at least attempting to take note of their daughter's acceptance of the younger of the two princes.

"As pleasant as it is to stand out in this stifling heat," Ella's father interjected suddenly. "I was wondering if everyone wouldn't mind joining us for dinner at our inn. Sable and I would love to get to know Alex's family. We've been hearing so much over the years, we'd love to share a round of drinks in person."

My family accepted as I promised a quick round for the prince and myself. I hadn't forgotten the endless parade of emissaries waiting back at Baron Cuthbert's manor, but we still had thirty minutes to spare and I intended to make the most of it. I also hadn't missed the exchange of incredulous expressions between my brothers when Darren spoke.

One way or another, I was going to find a way for them to make peace. I knew if Alex and Derrick just took the time to know Darren—without the Ferren's Keep regiment or my twin's past bias in the way—they would find a way to get along.

I hoped.

"Alright you two." Jeffrey set down his mug with a thud. "Spit it out."

My friend giggled as she and Alex exchanged grins. "What are you talking about?"

"Nice try." Her brother waggled a finger between the two. "Time to tell us what's going on."

"Alex has been sweating like a pig since we arrived." Derrick grinned. "Could there be a reason other than his distaste for the sun?"

My twin, usually so quick to retort to our sibling's wheedling, swallowed and stared at the wall behind us.

My jaw dropped—and I barely had time to think as Ella pulled my brother up off his stool. She nudged him forward and he swallowed again.

My parents and Ella's—who previously had been in the midst of a long conversation at the other side of the table—stopped to watch.

"Ella and I h-have news." My twin wiped his sweaty brow, beads of perspiration clinging to his forehead. "We wanted to wait until everyone was—"

"*We got married!*" Ella slapped a hand over her mouth as the whole table exploded in shock.

"WHAT?"

"*When?*"

"WHERE?"

"*Couldn't even wait for your own family!*" That was my mother.

Alex cringed and looked toward the ceiling while Ella responded to her own. "Two weeks back. We were going to wait for the Candidacy when the rest of you would arrive but—"

"But I couldn't wait." Alex's face was stained crimson.

Ella blushed. "He told me if he couldn't marry me that day he would die a thousand deaths."

"Alex?" My father was grinning. "*Alex* said that?"

I counted one, two, three seconds before I met Derrick's eyes across the room.

We were still cackling, tears streaming down our faces, five minutes later.

"Water!" Derrick finally wheezed. "I need water!"

"Yes!" I grinned like a fool. "I will die a thousand deaths if I don't get some water." It had to be the worst—and most hilarious—crack at prose my twin had ever attempted.

"They will never let me live that one down," Alex complained to Ella.

She smirked. "They are just jealous."

"Hey, Alex," I said, "how many deaths was it again?"

"Hey, Ry," my twin shot back, "*I. Forgive. You.*"

Darren, who had been silent thus far, choked on his drink, spewing ale everywhere. He was trying to keep a straight face, but his ribs shook with the effort not to laugh.

The adults remained clueless as I shot Alex a half-hearted glare, handing Darren a cloth.

The non-heir ignored it to grin at my twin. "That was a good one."

My brother gave Darren his first genuine smile. *Ever.* "I try."

As I stepped out onto the cobbled streets outside I was so focused on Alex and Ella's announcement I almost missed the man who had stepped directly into my path at the last possible second. I had just the barest sense to jump back before his black silk robe slapped me in the face.

I scowled and looked up to see the face of a charming stranger, and the recognition made me groan. Worn but sharp angles that gave way to a haughty gaze and thin, pursed lips. Lips that had scowled in my direction for the entire course of the apprenticeship. *Master Byron.*

He all but ignored me as he addressed the prince at my left. "Your Highness! What a pleasure to see you again!"

Darren hid a smile as his eyes flitted to my own.

"Master Byron, where do we—"

"*Silence!*" The man growled at a crowd of exhausted young faces behind him. Some I recognized as apprentices during my final year. "Go back to the barracks! Do not interrupt me while I am greeting the prince. He has more potential than the lot of you and the decency not to interrupt his elders when speaking!"

It was like I had never left. I arched a brow in Darren's direction and the non-heir coughed. "Master Byron, have you already forgotten Mage Ryiah?"

The man's eyes narrowed to slits as he was forced to acknowledge my presence. "How could I ever forget? It's only been a year." His tone was spoken with the warmth of an icicle.

Four years. Four years I had struggled while Byron all but ignored my training. The few times he had given me notice were to take down my gender and act as if I were the worst kind of mistake. I would never forgive the man for putting me through such a terrible apprenticeship. Which was why I said what I said next.

"Well, I couldn't, either!" I tried to sound as pert as I could, an extra emphasis on my vowels like an overeager convent girl. "And the two of us sharing the same rank. Imagine that, such an honor!"

"An honor." Byron repeated with a glare that implied it was anything but. Darren was watching me with a grin.

"Such a shame you lost your own Candidacy." I folded my arms and dropped the high-pitched tenor from before. Everyone knew the man had lost his final day's duel to a third-rank named Kara. My next line was five years in the making. "Perhaps I can make up for what you lacked, as a *woman*."

The expression the master wore as I walked away... it was priceless.

"No other tourney will be able to give you the same thrill for your purse. You will be able to place your bets at any of the booths along the stands before that morning's event. Combat is our most popular faction, but given the prince's high favor your coin might be better spent on Restoration or Alchemy where the odds are a bit more divided."

I sat next to Darren and our guards, two seats down from the king and another from Blayne and Wren on the left. We were listening to one of the Crown scholars explain the Candidacy rules to the seated emissaries and high-ranking nobility behind. Wagers were an important contributor to the Crown treasury, and in this at least I could understand. Mages *chose* to participate; the first-year trials were little more than a poor imitation, and one we'd had no choice but to partake if we'd wanted to continue our training.

Our seats were in a special center box in the first row of the stadium, raised and separated by a heavy stone wall perhaps eight feet in height from the ground floor of the arena. Most of the stadium's seating was little more than clay benches, raised row after row until they tipped up into the sky, followed by an outlying wall with more spectator towers for less privileged viewers to stand who could not pay for one of the Candidacy's prime seats at the front.

It was one of the few times I was happy to be part of the king's retinue. Our box was one of the few with a canopied roof to lessen the sweltering summer sun. I would be able to make out the contestants' details far better than I would further back with the rest of my family and Ella's. Refreshments were brought to the Crown's box before continuing on to the rest of the rows, and if the scholars' expectations were correct, each day of the weeklong event would last eight to ten hours trapped in our seats.

I recognized countless faces in the sea above. The scholars were right—it looked like every person I had ever met was in that crowd. Already the stands were brimming with color. I hadn't realized there were that many people in the kingdom, even after my tour in the apprenticeship.

One third of Jerar? Ha. Try at least half.

A couple rows beyond, I noted a tall, red-bearded man dragging his daughter through the stands, picking his way toward the seats at the front. *Really? A child?* It was like a punch to the gut. The girl couldn't have been more than six. And she looked scared, tugging at a yellow silk ribbon at the end of her curly black braid.

Why would somebody bring a child here?

Chancing a glance around, however, I saw she was far from alone. More children—some even younger than the girl— were scattered among the seats. *What is wrong with these parents?* I knew today wasn't Combat, but Restoration would surely show more blood than a child should ever be forced to watch.

Turning away, my gaze caught on the Caltothian ambassador and I paused.

The man was brimming with rage. Eyes locked on the little girl, I could see cold fury written all over his face. I started. *Was he upset by this brutality too?*

But then I heard a familiar laugh. Someone was talking with the little girl's father, and his voice was unmistakable.

My gaze flitted back to Lord Tyrus. He wasn't looking at the little girl; he was looking at the crown prince.

And his hatred was unmistakable.

"Darren," I whispered.

The non-heir glanced up and I pointed. His brow furrowed as he studied the man watching his brother. "I'll have Father put extra men to the ambassador's service tonight."

I shivered. There was something unsettling about the Caltothian's expression. When I snuck a glance again Lord Tyrus had composed himself, and if I hadn't seen the look myself I wasn't sure I'd have believed it was ever there to start.

The ambassador was not indifferent to the Crown, and he wasn't here for peace. That much was clear.

First up was fifth-rank Restoration. And it took me all of five minutes to realize I was wrong.

I had told Alex the Candidacy would be similar to the first-year trials, only more intense. What I hadn't mentioned—what I hadn't known—was that there was one minor difference. And that difference would matter the most.

The mages weren't casting on themselves, rather, the criminals of Jerar.

Men and women from the local jails were brought in to accommodate the total number of each rank's participants. Which should have been fine, except I kept thinking back to how the first-years had willingly chosen to succumb to ailments during their own trials, and these prisoners had not.

And the Candidacy ailments were far more serious than the light injuries of our trials.

Fourteen mages spaced out in a horizontal line across the field, facing the crowd. Fourteen criminals were brought with their backs to the audience, facing their candidate with a soldier beside.

Then the herald announced the start.

There was a horrible sound as the soldiers' blades cracked against the criminals' knees. Then each prisoner dropped to the ground, writhing in pain.

Screams were crowding the air.

The mages rushed forward to begin their first casting, each racing to treat their victim's five stages the fastest. The winner would move onto the next day's event, representing the best of their rank with an opportunity to advance.

The stages got worse.

Wren sucked in a gasp, and I had to clap my hand to my mouth to muffle a cry as one of the soldiers stabbed a thrashing woman three times in the chest.

Darren turned in his seat. "Ryiah?"

"This is wrong!" Violent crime was punished on the spot with a hanging, the men and women I was watching were guilty of little more than theft. The gaunt lines of their faces spoke the truth. Lowborns who had chosen to steal rather than starve.

It was the bandits from the north all over again.

Darren spoke my name urgently. "Ryiah—"

"Petty crime isn't enough to subject them to this!"

King Lucius's voice boomed out across our box. "Shall I replace the prisoners with innocents instead, Lady Ryiah?"

Darren's hand shot to my arm to keep me from replying.

"Your parents are merchants, no?" The question was a deadly promise. "Perhaps I can call on them first."

My stomach caved in on itself as cold panic flooded my veins. My nails dug into Darren's wrist, and it took every ounce of willpower I had to keep my magic at bay.

"That's not necessary, Father." Darren's grip tightened on my own. "She didn't mean anything."

"You might be too valuable." The king ignored his son to watch me like a hawk. "But your family is not. *Do you understand, Lady Ryiah?*"

"Y-yes." The word was barely more than a gasp. But inside every part of me was on fire. Wren caught my other hand in hers and squeezed.

"I have been patient with your stay thus far, but rest assured I won't hesitate to hold your family accountable for your actions."

A servant scurried past with the first round of refreshments for our box.

"Might I be excused, your majesty?" The words felt so heavy, my pulse beating against my throat.

"You have five minutes," the king growled. "Then I expect you back in your seat and cheering our nation's legacy."

I fled the box as fast as my legs could carry me.

"Ryiah, wait!" Darren caught up to me outside of the stands. I was gripping the stadium's back wall for support and trying not to think about what was going on on the other side of it. Paige was pacing at my right.

"I can't do it, Darren. I can't watch." There was no way I could go back and sit silently as men and women bled out for the mere notion of a *contest*. I couldn't pretend.

"You can't voice your disapproval over the Candidacy, he'll—"

"I didn't know it was going to be like this!"

What if the healers didn't treat their victims in time? The judges wouldn't interfere until each rank's hour was up. It was the first thing the herald had declared at the start of the day's event.

Darren waited until the stadium's clamor fell to a hush. "He changed it, Ryiah."

"W-what?"

The prince took a step closer, taking a look around and pausing when his gaze landed on our guards. Paige rolled her eyes and retreated to the wall's exit, with Darren's knight in tow—the both of them still close enough to jump in at the first sight of danger.

Darren spoke softly. "The old Candidacies still used prisoners for Restoration and Alchemy, but the worst malady was a broken limb, not... *this*. My father was the one who changed the rules."

I shrank back in disgust.

"It was one of the first things he did after my mother passed. Treating his own criminals to this as the emissaries watch... he wanted to send a message to any country foolish enough to break with Jerar. I thought you knew—you read all those books when we were first-years in the library."

"But..." I must have missed them. "I read about Combat."

"Combat stayed the same." Darren's contempt was quiet. "Our faction's tourney is already violent enough. But Restoration? Alchemy? The old Candidacies were far too tame for his liking. My father wanted blood."

Forfeit.

When they raised the white flag ten minutes into my brother's round, I prayed my eyes were playing tricks on my mind. But I had seen all of the signs.

The white face, the trembling hands, the heavy perspiration shining along his skin. The way Alex had swallowed as he watched the twelve soldiers lead their twelve criminals out across the field.

The look of naked horror when one had knocked the old man to the ground. The way the prisoner had bawled from the pain. The way my twin had dove to the man's side and whispered something into his ear, hands anxiously feeling out the injury for the break.

Alex had treated the man's leg, and I had seen the way his shoulders hunched and his hands kept drifting toward his ears to shut out the cries at his left.

He had treated the man and the soldier had summoned a Restoration mage to inspect his healing. After a minute the woman had nodded and the soldier had raised his blade to begin the next round.

My brother had jumped forward and grabbed the soldier's blade hand with a shout of command. I hadn't heard a word he'd said. The clamor of the crowd and the screams from the other prisoners had been too great.

But I saw the soldier raise his flag.

He hadn't known. Alex had been expecting the same routine as the first-year trials. It had always been the same. Until King Lucius.

A hushed silence fell over the stands. My brother started across the arena to the stadium's tunnel, oblivious to the change.

A silent scream tore at my throat.

Just two hours before I would have been proud. I would have sobbed tears of joy to see my brother stand up against the injustice. To know he wouldn't hurt an old man whose only crime couldn't have amounted to more than petty theft. But that was before the king of Jerar had threatened my family.

I prayed he wouldn't notice.

"Braxton!" The king's voice boomed out across our box.

"Your majesty?"

"I want that mage boy substituted for one of the prisoners in the final two ranks."

I jumped up just as Darren yanked me down, hard. "Don't say a word!" he pled. "He doesn't know!"

I fought the prince's grip and Wren clung to my arm. She didn't know what Darren and I were arguing over, but even she knew I was about to make a mistake.

"If the boy tries to heal himself, have him executed."

I was clawing in Darren's arms, every bit of magic threatening to burst—

"Ryiah," Darren's voice was a rasp, "*please.*"

"Yes, your majesty. Right away, your—"

"DON'T JUST STAND THERE TALKING. GET THAT BOY!"

Tears pricked at the corner of my eyes, and my heart was attacking my lungs, and I could barely hear over the blaring roar of my pulse.

ALEX.ALEX.ALEX.ALEX. I tried deep, shaking breaths, but as two knights sprinted across the field, dragging my confused brother by the pits of his arms, I broke free.

Darren caught me just before I reached the rail—he spun me around and his lips slammed against mine just in time to muffle the cry.

A part of me was shattering, and all that kept the audience from knowing the truth was Darren's hot mouth on my own. Strangling the shriek inside.

Preventing his father from knowing.

And that's when I heard Ella's rampant screams. And then my parents'. And then Derrick.

Two knights hauled my brother out into the center of the arena.

For thirty-nine minutes I had sat still, fighting the verge of panic as Darren whispered into my ear and Wren clung to my arm, pretending everything was fine. The king had been too busy watching the rest of the third-rank trials to notice, and during the brief break between rounds Blayne had hastily engaged his father in a long, drawn out conversation.

But now my brother was back.

I saw the look of horror as some of the candidates as they recognized their own among the prisoners. The soldiers were addressing their group and it was clear from their stance they were explaining the king's orders, pointing to the extra judge who would make sure my brother didn't attempt to heal himself during the second-rank trial.

And then it began.

I watched as my brother crumbled to the floor.

I watched as the candidate knelt to the sand and began to treat the first of his injuries.

I watched as the soldiers continued with beatings, and then, later, three stabbings across his chest.

The crowd's clamor was so loud during the final minutes of the round that my cry didn't stand out amongst the rest. I

was gripping the rail, eyes glued to the stadium floor, screaming at the top of my lungs until I went hoarse.

I watched as the soldiers hauled my brother away.
Healed by his candidate, but still wet blood dripping from his
robe, the whites of his eyes like saucers, the trembling of his
limbs...

And then they brought him out all over again.

I didn't have to worry about screaming. By the time it
was over, I had nothing left to give.

When the first day of the Candidacy had concluded, the
king had Alex brought to our box. I had to pretend that my
heart wasn't breaking, shattering into hundreds of tiny shards
as the king's men threw him before Lucius's feet.

Alex's gaze briefly met my own, and the betrayal was
enough to make me bleed out and die. There was so much pain
and confusion and anger, but I saw him swallow as the anger
vanished and he looked up to the king.

"What is your name?" the king barked.

"Rex." At least my twin knew better than to tell the
truth. He croaked the last words like he'd swallowed a mouth-
ful of rocks. "Your majesty."

"Rex. If you *dare* to humiliate your country like that
again I will have you beheaded. Today was a blessing, you
should count yourself lucky I did not de-robe you on the spot."

The knights released my brother, and he pulled himself
up, limping as he stood. Darren's grip tightened on my own as
I took in the full light of his face, a purple bruise still marring
his right eye and sandy brown bangs caked in blood.

He wouldn't even meet my eyes.

Darren half-dragged me out of the stands. I'd wanted to go to Alex, my family, Ella—but he had warned me to wait. He promised Paige would help me sneak out that evening after the rest of the manor was asleep, but I had to at least pretend for the sake of my twin.

After all, if the king found out it was my brother, the consequences would have only been worse.

When I finally did go to my family, it was in the dead of the night. My best friend was sobbing, and my parents couldn't even bear to look at me. Alex just stared at the wall, hands locked on the steaming mug in his hand.

"I'm so sorry," I whispered. I fell to my knees, taking his hand in my own and pleading for him to look down at me.

"You could have stopped them." Derrick's raging whisper cut across the inn's room like a knife. "You could have done *something!*"

Paige spoke up. "She would have made it worse. The king—"

"I'm not talking to you, bloody traitor! You might be a former lowborn, but you are just as bad as her. The both of you make me sick."

"Derrick—" My voice cracked. "I—"

"I hate you!" he spat the words in my face.

"Derrick." My father cleared his throat and looked to me with a pained expression. "If Ryiah said she couldn't do anything, your mother and I believe her. She is not a member of the Crown, she may not have as much sway—"

"She doesn't care about us!" His cry was hoarse. "Look at Alex. Look at what she let the king do to him"

"I didn't want to!" I was sobbing. My twin continued to ignore me as my little brother tore out my heart. "I love him—"

"Not more than that prince. You've forgotten all of us! First you act too high and mighty in the keep—"

"Derrick, I—"

"—Then you let your own brother be beat within an inch of his life for the Crown's entertainment! You aren't my sister. I don't even know who you are anymore!" He tore off his chain and threw my old ring at the floor. "You are nothing to me."

Then he stomped across the room and slammed the door shut behind him.

"Ry." My mother's voice was barely more than a whisper. "You promise?"

"I promise I never wanted..." My knees were shaking, and I looked down at her and my twin in anguish. "When I first saw the prisoners—I said something. The king made it clear if I did it again he would punish my family."

My mother choked and my father stumbled back against the wall.

"He didn't even know Alex was my family." I fell down beside my brother with a sob. "If he had, it would have been worse." My hand reached out to touch his wrist. Alex didn't tell me to move it, but he didn't acknowledge me either.

After a while my parents returned to their room across the way, and Ella finally walked me to the door. She hadn't spoken once. I prepared for another angry goodbye, but all she did was wrap her arms around me, shaking.

"I forgive you," she whispered. Her voice broke, and I could feel the tears through her shirt. "He will, too."

CHAPTER TWELVE

I watched the second day of Restoration without feeling. Each rank's winner challenged the winner from the next, and whoever won went on to challenge the next. It was an opportunity to advance from one's ranking during their own year's ascension, and a chance—albeit very slim—to wear the Red Robe should they win each subsequent challenge. In the past three Candidacies the most a mage had ever advanced were two ranks—and *none* of the factions had ever had the winner of second-rank best first.

Four matches in all, nine hours in total, and the final winner was a young man I didn't recognize named Torrance. He became Jerar's newest Red Mage, though the title was not to be formally bestowed until the Victors' Ceremony on the seventh day of the weeklong Candidacy.

Alchemy's trials were very similar to Restoration. The first day was the display of their castings' brews. Great fire flasks lobbed into the sky only to come crashing down and burst into an explosion of flame. Heavy gases that clouded the arena in smoke. Prisoners forced to undergo hallucinogens or paralysis in the blink of an eye. A swift display of potions-fortified weapons against the standard steel of the Crown's Army.

On the second day, each rank's winner competed against the next by poisoning their opposition's prisoner, and then scrambling to create the antidote for the one they received.

Two prisoners died before the appropriate cure could be completed.

As soon as the trials were over, I dismissed myself from our box and hurried out to the Montfort training ground to drown my frustration in rage. I needed to rest for my trial the following day, but if I did there was a very real chance the restless frustration would spill over into violence.

I would do something I'd regret—and that something would come at the cost of my family and Darren. Two things I swore never to risk.

The only person who followed me was Paige, and by now she knew my habits like her own. She joined me by sparring in silence.

I was leaving the Montfort training grounds when I spotted Lynn, my older mentor from my first year of the apprenticeship, quietly practicing her blocks, imitating some of the same moves she had taught me during my first few months of the apprenticeship.

It was a blessing in disguise. I was angry at the world, and I couldn't do anything. I couldn't save the prisoners, I couldn't stop the king, but right here—right now—I could right the past.

I was about five steps away when she spotted me. Her black bangs swung as she adjusted her stance, almond eyes cold.

"Do you need something, Ryiah?"

I made myself speak. "I'm sorry, Lynn. What I did during our apprenticeship—it wasn't fair. I knew you had feelings for Ian and I ignored them. I should have apologized before." I sucked in a breath. "You were a great mentor, and I never should have hurt you like I did."

She didn't say anything and after a moment I started to walk away. My conscience was clear.

"You know I actually pitied you." Her voice rang out behind me, and I turned around. "I kept thinking how hard it must be to have the master pick on you all the time. To care for that prince who so clearly could never return your affections." She laughed. "This was never about a boy, Ryiah. Ian was charming and handsome, yes, but it was more than that. I was your friend, too, and you didn't even have the decency to talk to me after it happened. Not once. Maybe I could have understood, but you never gave me a chance."

I looked down at the ground, shame-faced. "I don't expect your forgiveness. I just needed to let you know what I did back then was wrong and I'm sorry. I meant what I said. You deserved better."

Lynn resumed her drill, and I took that to mean the discussion was done, but then she raised her voice, pausing.

"We won't ever be friends again...but thank you, Ryiah." She gave a resigned sigh. "I can respect your apology."

I wasn't ready for my own Candidacy. Not after what had happened to my twin in Restoration. Not after watching a series of prisoners tortured for the sake of entertainment. It didn't matter that Combat didn't need prisoners since the candidates were fighting one another. I had no enthusiasm anymore.

Had I not feared the king's wrath, I would have withdrawn. But I couldn't. Lucius had heard Darren and me talk about competing several times over the Crown's progress to Montfort. While the kingdom might not know I had changed my mind, the king would, and he had made it perfectly clear what my missteps would bring.

You get the moment you were always waiting for, and you don't want it anymore. Irony, in every sense of the word.

Now every Combat candidate—regardless of rank—was crammed into the tunnels listening to the judge detail what we

could expect for our tourneys. There were eighty-one of us in
total. Far too many to be at their best potential. I could see
some participants that were past their peak, and I memorized
those faces in hopes I could use it to my advantage.

"Alliances happen, but make no mistake: the second you
trust a friend they'll betray you on the field. Happens every
rank. The melee is a battle to the end. There will only be one
winner." The man's brow furrowed. "You are encouraged to
surrender should a fight grow precarious. Should you fail to
speak the *ever so sensible word* there is a possibility we will be
finding a corpse before the healers can treat you. Deaths are
most common in Combat because so many candidates find
themselves unwilling to surrender when they should. If you are
unable to speak you must raise both hands, palms forward, to
indicate surrender."

Some of the candidates began to murmur amongst themselves. Ella gripped my hand tightly, no words necessary. She
was—if it were possible— worse off than I. She had already
put her name on the Combat roster the first day of the Candidacy. She'd wanted to withdraw after what happened to Alex,
but both of us had been too afraid the king would have someone checking the lists.

The tunnels were bright—a long row of torches lined
each wall and two gaping holes revealed sunlight at either end
of its mouth. Darren, who had been standing next to me for
the judge's speech, retired to the back soundlessly. I saw him
pass Ian on his way over, eyes momentarily meeting, but then
he just glanced away.

The non-heir had other things on his mind. Like winning.
Something I had wanted so desperately, but it was hard to recall now.

I saw other familiar faces. Lynn was here, standing off to
the side with another girl I'd never met, and Priscilla and Tyra
were closer to the front of the cave, the former refusing to
acknowledge Darren's or my presence.

I adjusted the leather straps of my vest—they pinched against the skin of my arms—and watched as Ian found Loren, Ella's old mentor during the apprenticeship, and the two sidled up to where we were standing.

I half-expected Ian to comment on what had happened to Alex. My brother was his friend too. But the mage said nothing, just gave us a smile and cocked his head in Darren's direction. "Your betrothed looks a bit nervous today."

I forced a nod and Ella cleared her throat.

"Think that makes all of us."

"I saw Lynn earlier," Loren added. "She looks good."

Ian and I cringed—we had both wronged the girl in our past. Ella was the one to speak. "Byron underestimated her. She shouldn't be fifth-rank. But I suppose it'll play out well against the others in her melee. Byron only gave Lynn that rank because he hated women."

"Well then, that'll make me a winner in fourth." Ian was met with confusion. "Come on, you three, have a laugh. Byron hated me just as much as Ryiah, which makes me much better than the other fourth-ranks, yes?"

Ella and I tried to make ourselves smile, but it was almost worse.

"Alright, I can see the two of you are too nervous to talk. Loren, how about that wall? *There.* Away from our favorite princeling?" Ian dragged our Loren away with a chuckle.

"So that was awkward." Ella glanced at me as soon as the boys were out of hearing distance. "What ever happened in Ferren's Keep? I thought the two of you were friends."

I shook my head. "We are but...it's complicated. I never got to tell you but—"

"FIFTH RANKS. YOU ARE UP. OUT ON THAT FIELD. NOW."

I watched Priscilla, Lynn, and Tyra hurry out onto the field with ten others of their rank. The audience's shrieks were deafening. No faction was more anticipated than Combat.

We weren't allowed to watch the other ranks' melees, but we could hear them. And we could hear the crowd chanting each winner's name. Fifth rank went to a young woman named Gwyn, fourth rank to another unknown named Argus, third rank, much to my disappointment, did not go to Ella. It went to a young man, Rowan, who'd been a fifth-year apprentice when Ella and I had been second-years.

Second rank was called and Loren wished me luck. He was one of the twenty first-years still waiting to go. We had nineteen second-years. Darren's eyes met mine briefly across the way and his lip twitched, a half-smile forming along his mouth.

"No luck?" I whispered as I passed him.

"You don't need it."

The first thing I noticed was the sun. When I stepped out into the arena I could feel it beating down my back, blistering against the crystalline glass of sand that crushed beneath my boots. It was midday and the glare was almost directly over the stadium.

I walked the five minutes—the arena was that large—to the stadium's center with the rest of the second-rank candidates. Everyone was dressed in similar fashion, tight leather vests and loose trousers for movement. Some—like me—wore fitted armguards, or in two cases: shoulder armor. One even wore a full chest plate—something I sincerely believed they were regretting now that they were out in such a humid arena.

As I was studying the other candidates, I realized two things. *One*: I was the only girl in the lot. Thanks to Byron's legacy of bias he had never awarded a good rank to any female in his time serving the apprenticeship. I was the only exception—not because I was the only girl worthy, but because it was I who had finally drawn the Black Mage's attention to Byron's injustice.

Two was Merrick, Priscilla's younger cousin. Somehow that insufferable boy had finished his ascension one month before and been awarded my same rank. Considering his lack of skill, I couldn't put it past the training master to have awarded him the rank on purpose. Byron had known my old mentee would get under my skin.

And he did. "I know we aren't *supposed* to make alliances, but the judge can hardly punish us for going after the girl. She's the weakest. We all know Byron only gave her our rank because she was betrothed to the prince."

I was mere seconds from ripping his face off. Merrick *knew* Darren hadn't proposed until *after* the ascension. But disputing the truth would get me nowhere.

Still, listening to some of the older men chuckle at the boy's joke was pushing my patience. I pretended to be oblivious, listening to the herald announce the candidates. His voice rang out in the arena thanks to a mage's assistance.

"So, Ryiah, how does it feel knowing you are going to lose?" Merrick's voice broke my meditation, and I saw the blond mage grinning.

"How does it feel knowing Byron only gave you this rank because he knows how much I loathe you?" I spat.

"Ohhhh!" Merrick raised his hands in mock surrender. "The girl got mad. Watch out, everyone. She's going to get us!"

My hands formed fists in reply.

"CANDIDATES, PLEASE TAKE YOUR PLACES ALONG THE ARENA. NO LESS THAN FIFTY FEET APART. IN TWO MINUTES WE WILL BEGIN THE TEN SECOND COUNTDOWN."

I began my jog toward the edge of the stadium. I wouldn't reach it, of course, but there was no point in keeping such close range with the others. Perhaps some of them would battle it out before they reached me. I wasn't sure if everyone else planned to follow Merrick's scheme, but I wasn't about to risk it.

I was still jogging as the countdown began. Putting as much distance between myself and the others as possible. Impatience and a restless rage were pumping through my veins. As the herald declared "ONE" I realized Merrick had done me a favor.

Because now I wanted to win.

I can do this. I made it this far. I can do this. I repeated the mantra over and over in my head as I watched the other candidates start sprinting across the arena, each trying to get a quick layout of the field without actually engaging in battle.

I noticed more than a few of them looking for "the girl." I knew this because I saw one point to me when the judge was looking the other way.

Well, two could play that game. My eyesight had always been better than most, and I could make out the oldest mages in a small triangle formation at the left side of the arena. They might've had too much pride to acknowledge their declining potential, but they were almost certainly lacking in brains to be clustered together for the taking. I couldn't be the only candidate who had noticed their age.

I wasn't. I kept one eye on my side of the arena as I watched a pack of five candidates approach the older ones from their front. No point in trying to hide their attack. The arena was a desert. There was nowhere to run.

The older candidates didn't stand a chance. I watched two call on their magic as the other fled. It was the smartest move that one could make—to win the Candidacy with gray hairs on your head you would have to conserve as much magic as possible.

I didn't have much opportunity to reflect. At that moment I spotted Merrick and another trailing mage at my left.

There was another on my right. I had two choices: let myself get backed into a wall fighting three mages at once, or take my chances and run toward the stadium's center and pray there wasn't a collection of candidates awaiting my approach.

I chose the latter.

"You can't run from us forever!" Merrick's screech followed me as I tore across the sand.

I ignored him, putting all my effort into the gapping distance between. My lungs burned from inhaling small grains of sand I kicked up along the run. I paid them no heed. Instead, I forced my attention to the casting I would need most: defense.

The globe went up not a moment too soon. Seconds later there was the sharp whistle of metal on wind, and then three subsequent thuds against the back of my shield.

My casting shuddered but held, flickering violet in waves as the candidates' javelins bounced off its surface. A moment later their weapons were gone; the mages had called off their castings.

I kept the shield up as I jogged toward the center.

The ground quivered beneath my boots. That was the only warning I had.

I dove toward the left, rolling hard on my side and blessing the arena for being sand instead of the marble training floor of the king's palace.

Two seconds later a fissure broke out—not two feet from where I had come. It spread across the arena's floor like a wildfire.

I hadn't been the only target. In seconds there was a web of shallow tunnels. I could hear muffled shouts as unsuspecting candidates got caught unawares. The pits weren't deep enough for anyone to get stuck, but they were enough to give several others an advantage in the moment.

I stifled a chuckle as I pushed myself up off the ground. *That* was a casting I could respect. It was hardly the type of magic to win a match, but it was smart. The older mages in Ferren had stressed the importance of conserving magic and that was far more strategic than Merrick's rapid fire of javelins (which were still hitting my shield as I ran). *Idiot*. He would run out of his magic far too quickly.

A shout to my right and I veered left to narrowly avoid two candidates who had stumbled into my path as they dueled with a sword in each arm and a shield at their backs.

Someone jumped out at my front and my first instinct was ice. White tendrils of frost tore up his blade and the burly mage was forced to drop his weapon with a whimper. I didn't bother to stick around and engage—the center was too open.

I sprinted past. A minute later I heard another man's cry of victory as he claimed the other's surrender. Then another shout of surprise as that man got caught unawares by another.

I ran around a cluster of three mages engaged in a battle of their own. Each one of them was wearing a globe like my own, but I could already see their shields showing signs of exhaust—the deep magenta had faded to an almost crystalline violet. They would have to call off their magic soon or resort to pain casting, *if* they had it.

There was a clap like thunder and my casting threw me forward. I stumbled, palms and knees skinning the sand as my casting shuddered and died. I felt a wave of heat rise up at its absence as the sharp, bitter scent of singed hair assaulted my nostrils.

"T-told you c-can't run!"

I cursed bitterly as I pulled myself to my feet, hardly daring to mourn the loss of my dignity for more than a second. Merrick and his friend were now throwing great balls of fire across the sand, huffing and puffing as they ran.

Fire? In an arena of sand? *Overconfident fools.* Every time they missed, their castings went out the second they hit the floor. Not to mention the boys' aim was beyond sloppy. I called up another globe the second I caught my breath and focus, but it was hardly needed.

Still, I was getting tired of the chase. I could run like this all day, but it was clear Merrick wasn't going to stop. I had figured I would lose him to others but the boy just wouldn't give up. Even if he was slower and weaker, I had to take him out. Sooner or later someone else would try to engage me in a fight, and I couldn't have Merrick as a distraction. Already he had caused me to lose focus, twice.

It was time to fight back.

I kept running my random course back and forth down the field until I was sure Merrick and I were far enough from the worst action at the center of the arena. I looked to the stadium wall, panting, and then turned my back to it, facing the highborn pest.

"Let's do this," I growled.

The boy stopped running, hand raised for another fireball, great globs of sweat dripping from his brow as he paused. He couldn't hear me, but something must have shown in my eyes because I saw him take a step back.

This is for the mock battle in Port Langli. I dropped my shield and my magic shot out like a bird of prey, a harsh whirl of shadow and the glimmer of metal in the sun.

For a moment his shield held, and then my sword broke the barrier and embedded itself in Merrick's side. Another soared across the sand and the mage raised his arms, shouting surrender before my blade had even reached its target.

I dropped the casting before it could finish. Both blades disappeared and the boy collapsed, clutching his wound with a gasp as a red-robed healer raced out from our side of the arena.

I wondered if any of my family had watched me just win my first bout. The audience faces towering the stadium seats looked to be little more than tiny specks of yellow and brown in the hazy afternoon rays.

Thwap!

I cried out in surprise as a sudden, biting pain tore across my thigh. I just barely managed to call upon my shield as a storm of arrows rained down from above. My casting flickered and held while I examined my leg with an angry self-lecture. *Stupid, stupid, stupid.* Why had I let my vanity get the best of me? I should have thrown up my shield the second Merrick surrendered, not preened like some foolish first-year over her first victory.

I gingerly pushed on the shaft, testing the arrow's depth. *Ow, ow, owwww.* It had embedded itself deep. And it burned like someone had stuck a white-hot poker into my flesh. Perhaps they had. It wasn't uncommon for mages to heat arrowheads before firing. It took more magic to cast, but if they hit, the cut was more effective than without.

The searing pain was enough to make me bite down on my lip, hard. I had plenty of practice with years of injury and pain casting but that didn't mean it didn't hurt. And the skin around the entry was already starting to swell. There was no way I could pull the head out without making the injury more at risk for infection, or bleeding out in the field which was a worse fate than the first.

Which means you are going to have to fight with the arrow in. It was on my right leg, too.

I looked up and watched as three candidates appeared clutching bows—for the moment, not shooting. They didn't need to just yet. I already knew what they were going to do, what I would have done if I were the hunter instead of the prey.

They were going to corner me against the wall. Shooting a quick glance to my left I saw two more approaching. Five on one. The odds were not in my favor.

I tested my weight on my leg and cringed. There was no way I could run fast enough to cut across the right in time. Not limping and hobbling like an old woman.

The leg was not the worst place to get shot, but it sure would have been nice if they hit my arm instead. An arm didn't stop me from running.

Well, I had been saving my magic for a reason. Running away for the first fifteen minutes had kept me from expelling as much magic as the others. I hoped the ones cornering me had used a lot.

"All to her barrier!" one of the men shouted. "Break it!!!"

I dug my heels in and held as the five mages threw out a large gust of fire. The crackle and burn of flames against my shield while it slowly faded lighter and lighter. I would not be able to hold on forever. I could already feel the raging heat warming my flesh.

I couldn't get cooked alive, but fortunately for me the others' fighting had weakened their stamina quite a bit. A minute before my shield shattered their casting receded.

I did a quick intake of my surroundings, preparing for the next attack. My opponents were on their last bit of magic and whatever casting they chose next would be intended to end our little standoff. I could see the two to the left had chosen a sickle sword and a mace. They were farther away than the others. I still had time before they drew close enough to attack—and I could tell they were wary to approach with the three at my front lest they become additional victims to the others' tally.

The three at my front were the true competition. If the four of us were lined up I wouldn't even reach the shortest man's shoulder. Not to mention the sheer bulk on the center mage—he was at least the size of my brothers. His arms were as thick as my legs. I prayed to the gods my magic held out long enough so I wouldn't have to find out how hard he hit.

Frankly, I prayed to the gods I made it out of this corner with any magic at all. It was all I could hope that they ran out of magic first.

From the discreet glances they were shooting one another I could tell they were reluctant to cast more magic as well. Probably because they knew they still had to fight one another after they finished with me. The man at the end took a step forward, and then they traded another set of cautionary glances.

Then they charged.

I sucked air in through my teeth.

Every casting that crossed my mind would only reach two opponents at a time, but as a slight breeze drifted across the arena my dilemma was solved.

A bit of dirt rose in the air, and my hand shot out in front of my face. I closed my eyes and called on my magic to join. Not only was sand an actual component to the arena— meaning it would cost me less magic to use—it was everywhere.

Then I pressed down on the arrow's shaft at my leg.

Sharp needles of agony exploded across my thigh. Pain and magic tore at my will, two savage beasts clawing and grasping for control. It felt like a thousand knives gutting my mind at once.

I took a deep, rattling breath and shoved them back, slamming my vision into the ravaging chaos with everything I had. My hands were shaking and sweat was stinging my eyes but I held on, bending the torment to my will. The darkness shuddered just once, and then suddenly all was quiet, an eerie sense of calm rushed out as my casting took hold.

A spinning funnel rose up from the ground. A plague of golden debris and wind, faster and faster, higher and higher, until it was a storm of its own.

I held my ground, heels digging into the earth, a couple strands of hair escaping their hold, and I watched my tempest give chase.

"She still has magic!"

"Get out of her range, Kai!"

The others froze. No one wanted to get caught in a sandstorm that would blind them to their allies' attacks. The two at my left started to flee, but the three at the front threw up a defensive sphere.

With the twist of my wrist the particles slammed together and melded with ice, my casting as solid as rock. Then I lobbed it at them. With every bit of concentration I had, I threw my granite wall, and then watched as their casting shattered like glass. The impact so great it sent the three sprawling backward into the dirt.

Run-limping forward, I set my projection to break.

A raincloud of sand rushed down on their heads, giant swells of dirt blinding while I cut our distance in half. Coughing and sputtering, they tried in vain to stand and draw up a new casting in time—but their magic was weak and they had more than one enemy to contend. By the time the haze had cleared three hovering blades were pointed at their throats.

I paused, one hand outstretched, as I locked eyes on my three victims. The metal quivered but held.

Slowly, white hot anger burning in the cores of their eyes, one, two, three sets of arms rose in surrender, palms forward. They didn't bother to speak the words.

I shot a quick glimpse to my left and saw the two remaining mages engaged in a bout of their own.

Now was my chance at escape.

I started toward the right, skirting the edge of the stadium. A moment later a gut-wrenching cry rang out behind me. When I peeked back the taller of the two was on the ground, blood pouring from his side as he whimpered the words for surrender. The other didn't bother to bask in his victory, like me he was already limping away, sporting a burn that ran up his arm and half his chest.

Two of our six still in play. I wondered how the others had fared in the rest of the arena.

It became my next objective to find out. I was hard-pressed to engage now that I was on my last bit of stamina, and my leg was almost unbearable the more I moved. Pain casting had been a smart decision at the time—I didn't have enough regular magic left, but now my whole body was throbbing in agony just from the effort to stand. Walking—or limp-running—was even worse.

I took a deep breath and headed toward the center. I needed to get a better idea of how many were left.

Six. After five more minutes of wary approach I counted five left, and me. And all of them seemed to be conserving their magic or hiding. Somewhere in the last fifty minutes of fighting we had gone from nineteen to not even a third of our original total.

Five. That was all that stood between me and becoming the best second rank. *Of all.*

The sharp whistle of a throwing axe, and I chastised myself for the momentary distraction. I threw up a hand and let my magic loose, a shield not a second too soon before the wedge could embed itself in my flesh. *You know better, Ryiah.*

One of the mages had drawn closer since the last time I looked. And he still had magic.

The man threw another axe, and I deflected it only to have the ground cave out right underneath my feet.

I struggled to catch my balance but my injured leg roared in protest. It went down and the rest of me followed. My balance was off and the slippery sand sent me flying on my back.

The mage took off at a run, and as I tried to push myself up off the ground he sent another rush of magic that slammed my head against the sand. My vision blurred and every part of me ached as I pushed up onto my elbows just as he closed in, magic casting an iron grip against my throat and another on my limbs.

"Surrender," he said.

Clearly, the young man had been conserving his castings.

I pretended to mutter the words, squabbling gibberish that wasn't hard to fake. Not when I was choking.

He drew closer, cautiously. One casted dagger in hand.

A couple steps closer and then his russet eyes hardened. "Surrender, *now.* Or I put this blade into your ribs. I won't ask you again. Raise your hands if you can't speak."

He released my arms from their invisible chains just far enough to lift. I could feel them vibrating, softly. His magic was waning.

I bit down on my cheek until I tasted blood. My casting sent him careening to the sand a couple feet away. His magic lost its hold, and I shot up and lunged. Pain was just a distant memory as I threw myself at the mage, a knife in hand.

The boy scrambled to rise and call up on a magic of his own when I was seconds away—but nothing came. His whole face was white and pooling sweat by the time my blade was against his throat.

"Surrender."

"I..." He coughed up blood, and I realized he was already bleeding heavily from a couple wounds at his sides. He'd had the good sense to bandage them with strips of his tunic and cover up underneath his mail, but now I could see why he had been so desperate to use magic to keep me at bay. "I s-surrender."

My knife vanished from my fist, and I quickly pulled away, gingerly shifting my leg as I stood. It was then I noticed the arrow was gone. *Huh?* I ripped off the hems of my breeches and wrapped them around my leg as tight as I could. I had barely made it two feet away before I saw two red-robed healers hurrying over to treat their newest victim.

There was another healer on the other side of the arena, half-carrying a different candidate—the one with the burns who was now bleeding heavily from his head. That explained my arrow's absence. But it also meant pools of blood were now seeping through my makeshift bandages every moment I stayed in the arena. *A good blow is not what usually kills an opponent—it's a loss of blood.* My stomach started to turn and I looked away, breathing deeply through my nose.

Four of us left.

I could see the three others from where I stood. A tall mage with black braids, dark skin, and a limp was farthest away. A bit closer was a stocky man in a full set of chainmail and leg plates, even a helmet. He had to be sweltering about now. The two were eying each other, but so far had made no move to attack.

The closest was a young man one hundred yards away who was bleeding heavily in—well, I wasn't sure where exactly; he was coated in sand and blood and clutching a wooden shield to his chest—the easiest defense, and also the weakest.

If no one else was going to lead the attacks it was going to have to be me. *Time to make it three.*

The throwing daggers whizzed through the air faster than my breath.

One caught the bleeding man in the shoulder, the other in the leg. Magic sputtered in front of him—the makings of a blast of fire—but it extinguished before it crossed even half the distance between us. The mage crumbled, and I skirted forward, watching as he tried again only to have the flames flicker and die at the tips of his fingers. He swore at me, raising his palms in surrender.

The other two met my eyes across the stadium as the announcer declared yet another candidate down. They had started to inch closer during my attack. All of us knew victory was bare minutes away.

I waited, gulping heavy drags of air in an effort to prepare. My lips were cracked, and sweat was pouring so hard and so fast that I had to keep wiping it away lest I go blind.

The wound in my leg? It ached worse than any injury I had ever encountered during my apprenticeship, possibly even more than that dagger to the ribs during the battle as a fifth year in Ferren. That had only lasted a couple minutes before I lost consciousness—this had lasted thirty minutes and counting. All my movement had tugged and pulled at the head so that my whole thigh was shiny red and tender at the slightest touch. I was quite sure with my pain casting earlier I had scraped against bone. The pain was even worse because it was only increasing every time I moved.

I thanked the gods my constant pain casting had increased my tolerance to bodily abuse.

When they got close enough to pause, the three of us made up a triangle—an equal distance apart.

My gaze flicked to the limping mage first. His expression was fierce and despite his limp I knew he wasn't out yet. The second man was still inscrutable and deadly. Now that we were on our last limbs of magic he had the best defense with his armor because it didn't cost him anything to keep it.

I swallowed. If the armored mage had lasted this long despite his lack of agility then his magic had to be great, his stamina even greater.

My eyes flicked back and forth between the two, my fists ready to cast at the slightest attack. A movement caught my eye and my chin jerked, ever so slightly to catch the limping mage's wink. He did it one more time, and then I casually returned my stare to the armored mage who was shifting from one foot to the next, no injury that I could see.

I prayed it wasn't a trick. After all, it made sense. We could waste our magic battling each other, neither keeping enough to challenge the armored mage on our own. Or we could both take him on first, and then let the best mage win.

Please, please don't let this be a trick.

Magic shot out of my palms at the same moment as the other. The armored mage threw up a sphere not a moment too soon—but cracks crept across, snaking trails of purple across his globe, and then the shield vanished and our castings sent him flying back against the sand.

The man struggled to rise, clunky mail making the stand difficult as twin bolts of ice shot at the two of us. One ball of fire from the black-haired mage deflected one as I sent up a gust of sand to overtake the second.

Back and forth our magic danced. After a couple quick bouts the armored mage dug his blade into his flesh. There was a ricocheting boom that echoed across the arena as the black-haired mage and I collapsed to the ground, spheres up just in time before a hot wall of fire cut across the gap.

I held back another cry as the bandage cut into my thigh, clinging to my casted shield with the last of my regular magic. The moment the wave passed my shield fell, and I pressed down on my wound, sending a set of three war hammers slamming against the armored mage's chains. The black-haired mage set his magic with a mace, and two of our castings pounded into the armored mage's flesh.

Chainmail might protect against sharp blades but it did not prevent a blunt but powerful force.

The armored man roared a surrender after his next pain casting barely charged—dying before it even reached the air. His magic had run out, and he wasn't in a position to out-match two of us still with magic.

I barely heard the announcer declare his loss. My eyes had flown to the black-haired man and his to me.

And then there were two.

This was it. I was so, *so* close. Every bit of me was crying out in pain as I pushed myself to stand; I could see he was struggling to do the same.

For a moment neither of us moved. He cocked his head, studying me as I studied him. The mage was definitely older— but not quite thirty if my assessment was correct. He was slimmer than most, and if he had survived this long he had to be my equal in agility and strength. He was down to pain casting just like me—and neither of us was faring well. His skin was clammy and red and he was shaking just to stand. I could see blood seeping through his bandages; blood was streaking down my leg.

That didn't stop him from casting, and it didn't stop me.

WHAM!

Our castings collided. His ice melded with my sand, and I snorted as the cluster dropped like a pile of crumbled debris between us. Clearly we had our favorite moves.

He scooted closer and I followed suit. This time neither of us chose a casting until we were barely fifteen feet apart. He knew his limits—well, so did I.

Another flare as this time I cast flying daggers and he arrows. Both of our castings fell as we threw up shields that crumbled the barest second after deflecting one another's casting.

I couldn't help but notice he had been digging a finger into his wound as I had pressed down on mine. Pain casting and we were already at our second limits. I bit down on my tongue as I added pressure but a wave of sickness roared up in its place. I bowled over and the other mage seemed to have a similar effect.

Our magic was gone.

I sucked in a deep breath and charged, every bit of me crying out as a fist feigned right and my leg swept at his feet. The man anticipated the move and caught my leg with both hands and pulled—causing me to stumble—before jerking back and throwing his weight forward so that I lost footing and fell to my back.

My hand had shot out and grabbed onto one of his long braids. When I fell the man came crashing down on top of me. The blow momentarily knocked the wind from my lungs and then the two of us were rolling and struggling in the sand.

When he had my hands and legs pinned—he was a bit heavier—I wriggled with all my might. Before the mage could make his hips and chest parallel to mine, my fingernails clawed desperately at the sand. I managed a small wad and shut my eyes and mouth just as I lobbed it at his face. The granules barely reached—my aim was severely hampered by the positioning of my wrist—but just enough took flight to catch in his breath. He started to sputter, and I thrust all my weight to the side, rolling with all my might until it was *me* on top of *him.*

I choked on my breath as my arms started to shake violently while he fought my grip. With his weight he had the clear advantage, and my arms were always my weakest strength.

He would win. He would outlast me in this, and then I'd be back on the ground, his victory at hand.

No. This couldn't be it. Already I was losing hold, my muscles screaming out in pain as the numbing pain in my leg echoed their call and begged me to quit.

NO.

I clung to my resolve and fought against every quivering fiber, refusing to let go of the victory so close at hand. The man shifted and squirmed, his eyes alight with a vigor I refused to accept.

My muscles contracted, and he flipped me back to the ground. One hand pinned my defenseless wrists, his other reaching for my throat.

"Surrender?"

"*No.*" I whimpered the word, and the man squeezed, hard. I choked as the pressure increased and pain lanced across my lungs. A searing heat was ripping at my chest and my skin was afire, every single bit of me raging as he continued to press. My teeth chattered violently as I gasped for breath.

You came this far, no one ever expected you to win anyway.

"Surrender n—"

The shuddering halted as a sudden, biting pain seemed to claw its way right out of my flesh. A jarring flash and then the abrupt pain—and the pressure on my throat—was gone.

When the dizziness faded I was able to push myself up with both fists and elbows digging into the ground for support. What I saw—it sucked the joy right out of my breath.

The other mage was sprawled out in the sand not five feet away. His limbs flailing up and down, eyelids fluttering and expression blank, as his lips flapped in some meaningless words. There was nothing *natural* to his bodily tremors.

Then I noticed the red marks on his palm, feathering down his arm like a snake. Master Byron had explained those symptoms before, though I had never seen them in person: lightning.

The heavy vibrations, the pain, the heightened emotions.

I'd been wrong. I'd still had magic.

We weren't so equal after all.

CHAPTER THIRTEEN

The mage survived. His name was Hadrian, I found out later. Lightning strikes, as the healers reminded me post-melee, hardly resulted in death if treated. My casting had only hit his palm. As far as injuries could go, it was quite possibly the best one he could get.

We spent the rest of the day being treated with the rest of the candidates in the local infirmary. Extra healers had been hired for the week of the Candidacy, so even though we had eighty-one injured by the time Darren's party arrived, every one of us were treated by no less than two healers a piece.

I was so tired that evening that I hardly remembered a thing. Except that the prince had also won. Not that I had ever expected anything less.

Before the sun had even finished making an attempt through the hazy morning sky, the final candidates were escorted to the special candidates' box. A section of seats reserved for the five best ranks and the Three Colored Robes.

A judge met with our group to go over the day's schedule. Not one of us spoke. We listened as the man instructed us on how to proceed.

Each rank's winner would challenge the one from the rank above. After the match concluded both candidates would be taken to the infirmary where an anxious staff of healers awaited. The next match would begin as soon as the winning candidate from the previous match was treated.

Most of our day—and the audience's—would be spent waiting for the matches to start. Now that each round was a duel, the contests took no more than an hour at most; healings, on the other hand, could take several hours—even with several healers working at once—to complete. Each winning candidate had to be at full strength and stamina before entering into their next match.

"No visitors!" The judge barked at a crowd of squabbling highborns that had attempted to push past the guards. No one was allowed to converse with the candidates until after the day's event was over. Too many bets had been placed and the stakes—though obviously in favor of the prince—were too at risk to have some sneaky spectator try to pay off a contestant, though I doubted it would work—all five of us had spent too much time training to let it come to that.

The fifth and fourth-rank candidates were called away to begin.

The judge came to escort the contestants with a pair of guards. Their expressions were equal terror and excitement. I noted that neither looked more than two years past Darren and me.

The loud rumblings of the audience quieted to a hush. It was as if everyone had taken a collective breath at once. The hazy sky—still unbearably hot—mirrored the abrupt mood, dark and light clouds dancing against the hazy morning sun.

Darren's gaze flitted to mine, and I swallowed hard.

And so it begins. My stomach coiled, and the little food I'd managed to force down threatened to rise. I pulled my feet onto the bench and rested my forehead on my knees, arms wrapped around my legs.

A hand pulled my clamped fingers apart. I didn't need to look up to register the sudden weight beside me, or whose

thumb was now pressing against my palm. The heavy pounding of his pulse matched my own.

He didn't say anything, and neither did I. We just
watched the stadium. And we waited.

Twenty-five minutes. That was how long it took me to
outlast my fifth-rank opponent in the arena.

I didn't even have to resort to pain casting. Gwyn had
been overconfident after winning two matches against the
fourth-rank, Argus, and the third-rank, Rowan. She was good.
Much more deserving than her fifth-rank status Master Byron
had so cruelly proclaimed. She'd advanced two ranks—more
than any Combat candidate had ever managed to do in the
Candidacy—but she lost to me.

My match the day before had made me more aware of
my surroundings. Toward the end of our duel it had started to
sprinkle—just a light misting of rain, but one I had embraced
in my castings. I'd funneled enough to evoke a quicksand-like
patch in the ground, and Gwyn hadn't noticed it until it was
too late.

While she had struggled to free herself, I'd managed to
break through her defenses with an onslaught of magic—
essentially forcing her hand. She'd surrendered—the both of us
bleeding heavily from our injuries in the arena.

I'd endured a broken arm, a burn down the side of my
stomach—so intense that the slightest wind had me convinced
someone had taken a tray of hot coals and thrust them against
my ribs, *and* a deep wound at the shoulder thanks to a throwing knife I had failed to deflect.

Gwyn's injuries had been worse.

"Is she fully well?" The judge pushed through my crowd
of healers and his sharp eyes bore into my own. "How are
those injuries, Mage Ryiah? Have you already tested your
magic? Full stamina?"

I nodded. My fingers were trembling, and I thrust them in my lap. There was no point delaying the inevitable. The team of Restoration mages had put me through a complete recovery both physically and magically—all within the course of three hours.

The burly man turned to the healers, and they affirmed I was ready.

"Good. I don't want anyone saying a prince of the kingdom won because his opponent wasn't up to potential." I cringed. Clearly the judge had already placed his bet. "Brenner, tell Godwin to bring His Highness around to the second entrance, I'll have Rhett escort her to the first. Make sure the announcer knows we are ready."

With the flap of his long black mage's robe he was gone. The healers handed me a new set of fighting garments to change into out of my clean shift. When I had finished, I stared out at my reflection in the mirror.

Supple deerskin boots that rose to my knees, skintight breeches of some stretchy material that allowed me the same freedom as my sleeveless top, a fitted leather vest that showed more skin than it hid, and arm guards that tied around my wrists. All candidates were given the same garb for our final day—no armor was allowed in these rounds. The only difference was the men went shirtless: something the women couldn't quite replicate on the battlefield.

I quickly braided my hair down the side. The plait I'd had the day before at the top of my head had come loose too easily, a down braid would hopefully be much easier to keep.

Gwyn walked up behind me—she was still in her shift and there was still a slight limp to her step. I swallowed, wondering whether she would wish me luck or misfortune after I had robbed her of the second-rank title.

"If it can't be me, I hope it's you."

I whirled around to thank her and her eyes crinkled. "Don't let the men get all the glory. It's our time to wear the robe."

I started to speak but Rhett—who had arrived and noticed I was finished dressing—took my arm and led me away before I had a chance to properly thank the mage.

I had to jog to keep up with the tall guard whose normal gait seemed to be a sprint, and by the time we had reached the primary tunnel blood was soaring through my veins—almost enough to distract me from the crippling anxiety that was beating at my chest.

Up until now I had managed to all but ignore who was waiting for me at the other side of the stadium. But then the announcer bellowed his name.

I could hear the raucous screams and cheers from the spectators like a giant clap of thunder.

"DARREN! DARREN! DARREN!"

The thick clay walls were shaking from the stomp of thousands of feet.

And then it was silent.

"Best of luck, my lady." The guard walked me to the edge of the tunnel and then looked my way. "My sister was a second-year apprentice during your last year with the prince. She convinced several of her friends to bet on you."

My tongue stuck to the back of my throat, and it was a great effort to swallow. "And you?"

"The prince. But I do believe you will give him a run for my gold."

"Thank you, Rhett."

"Good luck, my lady."

I strode out into the night.

Hundreds of cheers cut the air as I emerged from a tunnel of darkness to a somber violet sky. Rolling black clouds were speeding across the expanse, and I could barely make out the stands, bright blue mage's orbs lining the rows against a sea of shadowed faces.

Tiny sapphires of water poured down like glittering tears and made wet sand stick to the bottom of my boots as I ran. Thunder groaned and heaved, stark flashes of light sliced above like a waiting knife. The summer storm that had been brewing all day was here.

By the time I reached the center I was slick with sweat and rain, every inch of me alive.

The prince stood facing me, not fifteen feet away—dark garnet eyes and hair as black as coal. Droplets slid down his bare chest as he regarded me with the crook of a grin.

"It was always you," he said.

"TEN SECONDS, CANDIDATES! TEN. NINE. EIGHT..."

I gave Darren a shaky smile. "May the best of us win?"

"FIVE. FOUR. THREE..."

"They already have. But, yes..." His eyes danced, a streak of crimson in a shadowy night. "May the best mage win."

"ONE. AAAAAAND BEGIN!!!"

Twin blasts of power crackled and soared.

A brilliant flare lit up the whole arena as our castings shot out against the night—and then an awful ear-shattering screech as the brute strength of our magic collided. The sheer force of the impact sent the prince and me airborne, soaring back against the sand. Back, *far*, possibly a hundred and fifty feet between us when we landed.

I hit the ground with the air knocked out of my lungs and my whole back smarting from the unexpected blow. *Darren's magic was more powerful than any I had ever come across.* I had never hit his head on—not with the full force of an unrestrained attack. And now that I had, I wasn't eager to repeat the act again.

Funny, the two of us chose the same casting as the last time we fought.

My palms braced against the sand, and I leapt to my feet, kicking up a spray of dirt as I scrambled back up with a casted pole in the fold of my fist.

I relaxed the muscles in my arm and pushed off, right foot forward, metal edge of the javelin tipped slightly down as I sprinted down the way, counting the number of steps with my breath.

I could see Darren favoring an elbow as he also pushed up from his fall, his whole face a shadow across the gap. He was slower than normal.

The balls of my feet bounced along the stride and I sped up, letting the pole fall back to a full arm's extension as my right heel touched the ground and my left foot rose and fell, my shoulders aligned with Darren's direction.

Then I let the casting soar.

The pole whistled across the air, and I stood rigid, my mind focused on keeping its course against the heavy lilt of rain.

The prince ducked and threw up a soldier's timber shield, catching my javelin as easily as an arrow. The speared point absorbed into the wood and then dissipated as I released my casting with a bolt of power from my left.

He countered my attack with a thick beam of ice—drawn from the falling rain—that shattered and splintered into a thousand tiny shards.

Darren raised his hands to the sky. The clouds twisted and tore and I braced myself for an attack, swallowing down a gasp of shock. A torrential downpour of pellets rained down from above. Hail shot at me like an army of rocks, fist-sized lumps of crystalline ice that blinded me in their assault.

The storm of ice bounced as they hit the sand, hard. A cry fell from my lips as they violently pelted the sphere, the shield vibrating from thousands of tiny bits slamming the globe at once. I couldn't see out from my casting—the arena looked like a battle of stars. Arrowheads of milky white shooting in every direction, hitting the sand with a spray, hitting my defense with a crack.

I could barely hear. The noise was deafening. With each numbing crash the casting echoed, and it was all I could do to hold my casting as I squinted into the onslaught beyond.

Where is he? The pellets were nasty little things, but they were hardly the attack I would expect. *It has to be a distraction.*

There. A flash of light across the way. I couldn't tell what it was, but it didn't take much to guess: Darren.

I released my casting—not wanting to waste any more magic now that I knew he was far enough away—and then started toward the stadium wall.

My boot caught on a pellet in the sand and I tripped—

Shhhhlap!

The biting sting of metal slicing through flesh caught the top of my right shoulder in a searing cut. The dagger had only narrowly missed my back because I had stumbled forward at just the right moment.

It was a trap. I didn't have a chance to bandage the wound as I threw up my globe, blood streaming down my vest like little rivulets of red.

Darren was behind me. The light had been a trick.

The hailstones vanished and the rain returned, and I spun around just in time to see Darren charging my shield—a mace and chain in hand.

Then he leapt.

The spiked iron ball battered the barrier, and my heart slammed against my ribs.

He did it again. *And again.* Violet veins streaked down the surface of my casting and I stood there, holding my breath. The purple was fading with each subsequent attack.

Darren was going to shatter my defense.

I needed to find a way to counter his attack before it did, or the match would be over before it had truly begun.

An offense was a mistake; I was too close, and I would be the one caught off-guard when the barrier lifted. I needed to put some distance between us.

I hadn't wanted to expel this much magic right off the start. But I should have realized with Darren I didn't have a choice. They called him the prodigy for a reason and this wasn't a game.

This was what I had trained for. All those years of pushing myself to the brink. Neglecting friendships for a glimpse of power. This was *it*.

Holding onto my shield I dug deep into myself. Calling up two powerful castings at once was something I could never have attempted during that first year at the Academy, or even successfully as an apprentice.

Just beyond my shield the ground erupted in a quavering tremor and the earth trembled and heaved. A giant fissure spilled out right under the non-heir's feet.

Darren's eyes shot to mine in surprise as he staggered and fell. The mace and chain vanished before it could hit his chest.

Couldn't do that last year, could I?

I dropped my shield and sent him sprawling back with another raw burst of power. I'd been tempted to use lightning, but the casting was too risky in an arena filled with flying water and sand.

That bought me just enough time to tear up a quick makeshift bandage and tie it around the pit of my arm to the neck to stop the worst of my shoulder's cut. Then the prince was recovered, sprinting back with a dexterity that bespoke years of our iron-willed masters' training.

I cast a broadsword in one hand and waited.

His blade met mine with a resounding smack. I sucked in a breath as my shoulder throbbed from the hit.

Back and forth. Up and down. Cuts every which way were met with a parry of his own. I swiped up and to the right, Darren's blade swung down at my left.

I spun to the side just in time to avoid a slash to my ribs.

The two of us were circling in the sand, studying the other for a break in defense. His pupils were so wide his eyes were almost black—sweat and rain were stinging as my own locked on his.

Darren brought his sword down on mine—

I pulled away and countered with a sharp cut of my own. He danced to the side, the corner of his lip twitching up, dark locks plastered to his face. Thunder rumbled across the expanse and Darren lunged, bringing his weapon down on mine with all of his weight.

I fought to hold my guard. My whole body wavered viciously with the effort to match his pressure, my shoulder screaming against the weight as he bore down on my blade. I needed to do something as I shook, but it was costing all my magic just to hold on with my casting.

Every second it was getting harder and harder and I wasn't sure how much longer I could—

And then lightning streaked across the sky.

I shoved and his sword gave tilt, the flat end catching just the right angle... Stark rays of light shot across the blade.

Darren fell back, temporarily blinded.

But not before the edge of my sword caught his side.

And then his magic shot out like a snake. It threw me ten feet back, sprawling in the sand. My sword vanished upon impact.

I scrambled to my feet, one hand outstretched, as another bolt shot across the gap. My magic gave chase and for a moment our powers were matched—a brilliant misty blue ray in the shadows of the arena.

Then he started forward, one hand clutching the wound at his side, and my casting started to flare in and out, slowly receding with each step the non-heir took. I could feel raw power pulsating the air, and from the way my limbs were quivering I had only moments to spare before my magic ran out.

I broke off my casting and dove, my left palm slapping against the ground with a sickening crunch. A tearful cry escaped my lips, and I mourned the awkward way I fell, hating myself for not remembering my training in the heat of the moment.

I pushed off with my right hand, white-hot agony eating my shoulder as I rose.

And then screamed as an arrow lodged deep into my boot, its head digging into the side of my foot. My hasty globe rose just in time as another three arrows hit. *Darren isn't holding back.* I yanked the shaft out—knowing full well I wouldn't be able to run with it still in. The next second the arrow and the prince's crossbow vanished, and an axe appeared in each hand.

His favorite weapon.

Gods, no.

I didn't have time to bandage my foot; Darren was charging forward and in seconds hacking at my globe, his strong shoulders glinting underneath the fading purple defense.

I couldn't counter those with a sword. And my left hand was broken—my right shoulder all but aching at the slightest effort.

Time for pain casting.

I still had enough regular magic in reserve to produce a dagger in hand and pressed down against my left palm, blood trickling into the sand—the shoulder injury too far back to manage.

My sphere turned to ice and when his blades came crashing down, it shattered. Thousands of tiny razor-sharp shards shot out against the prince's exposed skin—tearing bloody trails down his arms, his chest, and his face.

Darren's axes faltered and my casted polearm came down without hesitation. The sickle blade made a terrible screech as it slid against the non-heir's globe.

I attacked. Again and again, high and low swoops as hard as my shoulder could manage—I could see Darren's defense losing color with every slash until it broke—

But as I lunged forward my own casting vanished, and I jerked to a stop, tottering. I needed the knife.

But nothing came.

The beauty of pain casting in real battle? A mage kept a knife on him at all times *for just that purpose.* In the Candidacy? There were no real weapons. We—*I*—had none.

Across the way I saw Darren's eyes flare up in understanding. His hand raised to cast—

But nothing came.

Like me, the prince had expelled all his regular magic.

Somehow, I had always known it would come to this.

Unlike me, Darren thought of a solution faster. I had just the barest moment to register his decision before the prince's fingers dug into the wound at his side.

Three daggers came at me at once.

"Surrender, Ryiah!"

They were almost here.

"No!" A nervous sweat broke as I clawed at my palm, sandy nails scraping against skin—the sensation of hot blood along the pads of my fingers almost enough to make me retch.

I was not fast enough.

Rain fell on the arena like sleets. Thunder roiled across an angry belly of shadow while stark flashes of yellow illuminated the arena.

I went down with a dagger square to the chest.

My giant burst of magic—it only swayed the last two.

"*Ryiah!*" Darren staggered forward and then stumbled as the sand roared up and caved beneath his boots. The last of my magic.

Two mages. Only one will win.

I was choking on air. Black, *black* air that I could no longer see. Everything was a shape.

Hot iron coated my lips, metallic and bitter. I clutched the blade, disbelief and fear taking hold of my thoughts. There was a strange ache building in the back of my throat, my stomach, my lungs. Like someone was pressing my chest against the flames of a fire. I screamed and I clawed, blood spraying from my mouth as I struggled to free myself from the pain.

Salty tears trailed down my frozen cheeks as strange hands fought to hold the fire in place. Raging, wild tremors took control of my limbs. Something was shredding me out from the inside. An anguish took over and every breath was like a thousand hot knives stabbing into me at once.

Hot air pressed against my ear, a familiar voice that begged for me to stay still. I whimpered and cried, nonsensical pleas as the pressure remained and the terrible darkness took over my world.

"You w-will be..." Someone else was breaking, too. Sobbing as the words became splintered and hoarse. The knives, I realized, they were killing him too. We would die together.

"The healers a-are almost here," he begged.

Pain ripped away at my flesh, and my scream was the last thing I heard.

Chapter Fourteen

When I woke up his red-rimmed eyes were the first ones I saw. There were heavy shadows under their lids, and his skin was so pale he could have been a ghost. His hands were gripping the rail of my cot, heavy tension radiating off the white of his fists.

Dried blood coated his chest and arms, and there were several bruises mottling his ribs. He looked like death.

I sucked in a sharp breath. We were in the infirmary.

A great ball of fire was climbing up my lungs.

A lump in Darren's throat rapidly rose and fell when he noticed I was awake. "Ryiah!" he choked out my name, and I swear I heard him break.

I opened my mouth and closed it as hundreds of raging needles stabbed at my ribs. A healer's palm shot out to cover it anyway.

"You shouldn't talk," the woman apologized. "It's only been a couple of hours since your match. Now that the prince knows you are awake—the both of you need to rest. Especially you, my lady. Your injuries were... grave." She glanced away quickly. "The Victors' Ceremony takes place tomorrow and—"

He won. The words snapped out like a whip.

"I-I'm so sorry." His voice was hoarse. "I never—I lost control, I—"

The dagger. My chest. The flames eating me alive. They were his.

Darren won the Candidacy.

"—Expected to partake, regardless of your condition—"

"Please forgive me."

"—The Crown has ordered no visitors to expedite the healings, but it will take all of our staff and a heavy night's rest just to have you walking around for the event." The mage leaned down to apply a salve to my skin, motioning for one of the others to come forward.

I lay mutely as the healers set forth to mend my maladies, crying out as bones shifted and scraped deep inside.

Darren's fingers reached out to brush my cheek, and I shut my eyes. His hand was trembling so violently the bed rattled.

The pain was terrible ... but I wasn't angry at him.

I was angry at myself.

A hot wash of envy threw up waves in the pit of my stomach, and I took a deep, rattling breath.

I was good. *But I wasn't great.*

Twelve hours of sleep; it made not the slightest difference. Sure, I felt less pain than before, but physical agony had little to do with the turbulence of emotions inside.

I had beat out every single mage in my rank. By all accounts I should have been happy. I had achieved what most people only dreamed. And if I hadn't achieved *the* dream, at least it went to the boy I loved. An adversary I could respect.

But I was a terrible person, and jealousy was a bitter seed. None of it mattered. All of those years telling myself one day I would be better... they were for nothing. Darren was the best, and he always would be. His pain casting had over-powered my own. His potential was the greatest.

Stop moping like a pitiful child.

I raised a hand and swiped at the corner of my eye.

"Ryiah?" Darren was still broken. All night long he had refused to leave that chair; I'd woken several times to see a mess of black locks against the side of my mattress. Now he was afraid to touch me—I could see it in the way he would reach out and then pull away, like I was made of glass.

He couldn't forgive himself.

The both of us were our own worst enemies.

"I'm fine." I swallowed. "Darren, what happened... it wasn't your fault."

"I lost control." His voice was hoarse and bitter. "I've never lost control, Ryiah. I could have killed you."

"And I could have killed Hadrian during the melee." It was killing me now just to utter the reassurance. I wanted to hole up in a wall and scream until my lungs were hoarse. "We chose Combat. We knew the risks. You offered me a chance to surrender, and I refused."

"It doesn't matter."

"Yes, it does."

His eyes shot to mine, and the garnet cut at my lungs.

"I'm sorry I hurt you."

I made myself breathe. "Please don't apologize." It only made me feel worse about myself.

"Would you like me to leave?"

I stayed quiet.

The prince slowly gathered his belongings and motioned for his guard Henry to follow. As he was exiting the infirmary he turned back to look at me. The self-hatred was written across his face.

"I'm sorry, Ryiah."

He had nothing to be sorry for. Every Combat mage had known what they were getting into the moment they entered that arena. But Darren's love for me had robbed him of reason.

I waited until he was gone, and then let out the breath I had been holding in. It burned the whole way up.

Jealousy had robbed me of mine.

A couple hours later, a retinue of servants arrived with my two ladies-in-waiting and Madame Pollina. Contrary to our previous interactions, the woman was nothing but genteel as she helped me dress for the Candidacy's formal ceremony. I suspected it had something to do with the way I looked. I hadn't had the courage to stand in front of a mirror since we arrived, but even a fool could see the bandage strapped to my chest and the tender purple patches dotting my ribs and arms.

I caught her looking at my back with a pang of sympathy when the others were plaiting my hair.

I wished the Candidacy had delayed the Victors' Ceremony by a week, so I could appear strong. I hated looking weak.

"Ryiah!"

My best friend's voice broke me free of my thoughts. "Ella?"

The girl burst through the room—looking every bit the daughter of nobility in her perfectly pressed appearance, her black mage's robe glinting in the light. She had an air I never would.

"How did you get past the guards?"

"Paige." She stopped grinning and her face turned serious. "I think she felt bad you couldn't have visitors. She turned us away last night, but she probably figured now that Darren was already at the ceremony the Crown's orders could be bent. Most of the king's orders were in regards to the prince anyway."

"Us?"

My parents stepped out from the corridor. "Oh, Ryiah," my father said softly. He was staring at the bandage that was still visible through the neckline of my mage's robe.

"I'm fine, Dad." The pity pressed at my lungs. I was suffocating in his expression.

"We have some herbs that might help. We will send someone to drop a sachet to your healers tonight." At least my mother was trying to maintain an air of normalcy. I prayed she would keep my father's sympathy at bay.

"Where's Derrick? Alex?"

"We thought it best if we came alone." My mother's eyes flashed a warning. It took me a moment to understand.

The king. They were too afraid the guards would recognize Alex—and Derrick, well, he'd been so upset. And he was so stubborn. He had probably refused to come.

A part of me deflated. My new life with Darren was supposed to be a dream, but so far it had only brought a whole string of complications. My own brothers couldn't—or wouldn't—see me. And right now I needed them more than anyone else.

We had all grown up to the same expectation. We had made the same choices. Alex, my other half; Derrick, the younger, headstrong version of me.

And now... now I didn't know what to do.

"Will they be coming tonight?"

My father shook his head, his eyes flitting to my mother.

"Darling," my mother said, "the ceremony is only for nobility. We could state our relation but we'd rather not..." *Draw the king's attention to our family* is what she didn't say.

A wave of fatigue washed over and I sat down quickly to avoid drawing their notice. My father's brows furrowed, and my mother sucked in a sharp breath. I wasn't fooling anyone.

"I'm going." Ella's fingers interlocked with mine as she sat down beside me. "Someone should be there to support my best friend."

Paige appeared in the room. Her expression was half-concerned, half-aloof. "The king expects your presence soon. The ceremony is about to start."

"Thank you, Paige." My father's eyes softened. "We won't keep our daughter much longer."

My parents came forward to each give me one long embrace, careful not to hug too tight. I found myself wishing I could prolong the moment. I saw them so little, and without tonight I doubted I would get a chance to stop by before we left.

As soon as they were gone, along with my ladies-in-waiting, Paige returned.

"Ready?"

I nodded as Ella helped me stand. I was still wobbly on my feet, and it had cost too much of my energy just in dressing.

The three of us left the infirmary and started the short walk to Baron Tybalt's mansion where the evening's festivities were to be held.

Paige walked at the front, one hand on the hilt at her hip. Ella pressed closer to me, drawing my elbow in as she spoke.

"I didn't want to say this around the others, but I want you to know that tonight means nothing."

I faltered, and she met my eyes—a persistent light reflecting across twin pools of amber.

"Darren might be the Black Mage, but I watched you from the stands, and I have never been so proud to call you my best friend."

My eyes started to blur, and I dug my nails into my palms to keep the tears from showing.

"Our titles don't mean a thing." Her grip tightened on my arm. "I know what you are feeling because I feel it too. *Of course* we want to be the best. It's what we trained for. But we don't need a title to validate our hard work, Ry." She raised her voice. "When we walk into that room tonight, it's going to be with our heads held high."

I froze and Ella jerked to a stop.

"Ry?" she asked hesitantly. "Is something—"

I cut her off, wrapping my arms around her and squeezing. Paige paused ahead of us. She didn't say a word—even though we were going to be late—she just stood to the side and surveyed the street.

I kept my arms locked around my best friend. My whole body was shaking and silent sobs were rocking my chest.

I kept my eyes clenched shut and clung to Ella until the tremors were gone. I hadn't let myself cry over the duel in the hours since it happened—I'd been too afraid Darren would blame himself, too guilty my parents would sympathize. Too angry at myself.

But here. Now. With my best friend. I let myself be.

"I love you, Ella."

She brushed the back of my head. "I love you too, Ry. Don't ever think you are not good enough."

The sprawling residence was almost as tall as the tops of the Candidacy stadium itself. Whoever had decided to call it a mansion had grossly underestimated its size. It might not be as big as the king's palace in Devon, but it was at least equal to that of the Academy's castle in Sjeka.

A giant circular dome made up the highest point of the building, several sections of the roof supported by heavy columns and a steep indoor balcony overlooking the grand ballroom at the center. The whole place was a wash of white stone and golden tile. All over were raised statues depicting the four previous victors of each faction. I recognized the current one closest to the door —Marius's crooked smile captured perfectly by the sculptor's hand.

I supposed Darren's would be next.

Heavy brocade curtains of blue and red adorned most of the many-paned windows, and a thick light streamed down from a hole at the center of the globe's roof. At the angle it was placed it would highlight the victors' balcony at precisely the right moment. I suspected that had been its intention.

The moment Paige, Ella, and I entered we were offered a very fine selection of wines. Their heady aroma alone made my stomach roll, and sensing my discomfort Ella passed. Paige, off-duty for the night but rarely ever sociable, passed as well.

As we took our places in the grand atrium we waited for the spectacle to begin. The room was packed full of nobility— ambassadors and highborns clamoring for the best place to stand. Darren and the other two victors, as well as the previous Council, were nowhere to be seen. I did spot the king and Blayne with Princess Wrendolyn a bit closer to the front, but I couldn't stomach the thought of standing so close to the man who had put my brother through such a horrible ordeal just days before. The room was so crowded, and there were so many important dignitaries around I doubted he would even notice my absence.

I felt Ella tense up as she noticed my stare. She had never trusted the Crown and I knew it was taking everything in her not to react. She put on a brave face, but she loved fiercely and was just as outspoken—if not more so— than I. It was killing her just to be in the same room as the man who had come so close to murdering her husband just to make a point.

I was sick to my stomach just thinking of the long years ahead, trapped in the palace with Lucius as my father-in-law.

Forcing my gaze elsewhere, I spotted Merrick glaring pointedly in my direction. As soon as he registered my attention he spoke loudly to his companion, proclaiming how big his winnings were from betting on the prince.

Oh, and that the only reason *I* had beat him was because he'd thought it only fair to give "the girl" a chance. *"Thought I would do her a favor, let the girls pretend they could win… for once."*

Arrogant little—

"My cousin is a fool."

My head swerved to the side and I heard Ella's shocked intake of breath as Priscilla emerged from the audience. She wore her mage's robe like a queen, and she didn't appear to look the least perturbed over her loss.

"S-sorry?" I stammered.

"You heard me perfectly well the first time, Ryiah. I'm not going to repeat myself."

"Priscilla." Ella wore a predator's smile. "What a delight."

"Ah, and I see *you* haven't lost your charm, Eleanor." The girl gave my friend a curling smile before turning back to me. "I bet on you. For the final match."

So she was here to chastise me for losing her coin? I bit back a groan. Priscilla had always known Darren was better. Everyone else had. "I'm sorry for your loss." I said it through clenched teeth.

The girl rolled her eyes. "I'm not sorry. Well, I *am* that I have to listen to that idiot rattle on. But I'm not sorry I bet on you."

Ella's jaw dropped to the floor, and I was sure mine followed.

"Stop gawking, you two. I just came to tell Ryiah here that I wouldn't have been surprised if she'd won. Darren was good, but he was *always* good." Priscilla crooked a nail at my face. "*You*, you are a cockroach. No matter how many times we tried to get rid of you, you kept finding a way to scuttle your way back. And as much as I don't like you, well, you are persistent. And even *I* can admire you for that."

I opened my mouth and she cut me off with a hand to the face.

"Don't even bother, Ryiah. We aren't friends, and I have no doubt you'll make a horrible princess. I just thought I'd show you a bit of kindness before you run this kingdom to the ground." Then she sauntered off like the lady of court she was.

Leaving Ella and me to stare at her back in shock.

"Did that really just happen?"

"It did."

A cockroach.

It was quite possibly the best and worst compliment I'd ever received.

When the herald called his name, Darren emerged at the open balcony, Marius at his left.

A collective murmur went through the audience as the Black Mage unclasped the robe from himself, placing the shimmering silk upon the non-heir's shoulders. Darren stood so still as the gold-lined sleeves slipped down his arms.

Marius stood beside him and raised its hood for the ceremonial pose. Sparkling gemstones danced across the stream of sunlight, the prince lit up like magic itself. His whole profile a heavy, ethereal glow.

Sheathed in heavy shades of darkness and light.

"Prince Darren, the new Black Mage of Jerar. A Colored Robe of the Council of Three. Lead Mage of Combat to the Crown. Representative for Combat upon the Council of Magic. We welcome you to your new role."

The roar was deafening. I pushed the twinge of envy aside as I screamed loudest of all. I could see Darren searching the crowd with his eyes, and when he finally spotted me beside Ella he gave a small smile. Fear was still written plain across his face, but he gained a bit of color after that.

That's the boy I love. For a moment I forgot myself and thought only of Darren. *He worked so hard, I'm happy it's him.* And I meant it.

After the first hour and a half Darren finally managed to break from the parade of endless courtiers and found me at the back of the room picking at the fresh array of cheese fritters, gingered custard, roasted leeks, and lamb and chickpea stew. His cheeks were flushed and from the way his eyes flitted to my bandage and then fell, I knew he still felt guilty from before.

I made a point to cut the tension before it became worse. "The robe suits you. You look…" I made a hand gesture. "Possibly *too* good. I don't like the way the other ladies have been admiring you."

I meant it. He looked like a god among men. And every woman in court was watching him—though, to be fair, they had never stopped. Not that I would ever tell him *that*.

The tension left the prince's shoulders as he advanced. "Have they now?"

"I've been struggling to keep from locking them in a tower."

Darren's grin turned wicked. "Perhaps I can wear it one night when we are alone." He lowered his voice. "If it truly looks that amazing I'd like to see what that means for you." The implication was enough for me to blush.

"Ryiah! Darren! Just the two I wanted to see!" Andy's voice rang out from behind.

We turned to find our old comrade from Port Langli's regiment, striding giant steps across the room with her stodgy cohort, the much quieter Cethan. We had spent a month serving alongside them when we were only apprentices, and in that time both Darren and I had gained a fondness for the two Combat mages of our past.

Darren smiled. "Andy, Ceth, it's great to—"

I shrieked and threw myself at the tall woman, forgetting my injuries until it was too late.

"Not smart, Ryiah." I stepped back with a self-admonished critique as the others hid a grin.

"Glad to see you both remember us." Ceth's smile was a bit strained given the room. He was uncomfortable at events like this—the man preferred sea with the silence of wind and a bit of bitter ale as company. Certainly not a crowd overflowing with nobility and wine.

"Gods, this place is a bit much, don't you think?" Andy hadn't outgrown her habit of speaking her mind.

Another familiar voice cut through the crowd like a knife. "Cassandra, that is no way to speak to the Crown!"

Andy made a face and I cringed.

Mage Mira appeared with a courtier's smile aimed at the prince. "Your highness, how pleasant it is that we meet again. I've just been conversing with your dear brother. Ryiah... I see you are still here." Her expression made it clear she didn't care for it. "Well, carry on. I won't keep you from your night of celebration, your highness."

"Thank you, Mage Mira." The words flowed so easily from the prince's tongue. "It has been pleasant to see you as well."

When Mage Mira had returned to the wretched hole she crawled out of Andy smirked at me. "Dragon Lady misses you."

"I don't miss her."

"She was cursing your name the whole way to the capital."

"Is she still in Langli?"

"Blessed gods, no. She's been running around the countryside in one of those fancy Crown's Army regiments with a promotion under her belt." Andy grinned with a nod at Darren. "Or did you forget your little stunt in Dastan's Cove? Our unit hasn't seen quite so much action since."

I started to laugh and then stopped—a moment of shame soiling the brevity. I couldn't believe I had forgotten our time on Caltothian soil so easily. The little girl and her mother. Our mission. *What had ever happened to them?* My eyes shot to

Andy, but she shook her head, already guessing my question from the expression on my face.

"Nobody knows." Cethan's gruff voice was a low rumble that blended in with the rest of the crowd. We were still under Crown orders not to discuss the assignment. Ever. I had to press closer to hear the rest. "We dropped them off at the city limits. Two men from the King's Regiment came and took them away."

I turned to Darren who frowned. He looked bothered that he had forgotten them too. Kidnapping a woman and child was something a person shouldn't be able to forget. But back then we had both been so busy with the apprenticeship and a tumultuous romance, it had happened anyway.

"I asked my father that year we returned to the palace." His eyes were on the king and the circle of ambassadors across the way. "He told me he couldn't recall."

Andy and Cethan stuck around for a couple more minutes, trading easy jokes about their time in Langli, but it quickly drew to an uncomfortable note after she mentioned one of the new recruits, a handsome young man with a great sense of humor and "golden-green eyes." "A shame he transferred to Ferren's Keep last summer. Took off rather suddenly after he got the summons."

Cethan adjusted his vest. "It was about a girl, I believe. She had just accepted a post there."

Darren's eyes shot to mine, accusingly, and I wanted to kick myself for letting this subject even come up. Why did they have to even know Ian? And what were they talking about? Cethan was mistaken.

"I swear to you he never said a word." My voice was barely a whisper. "Whatever Ian's reason for coming, Darren, it wasn't me." *I'm not lying. Please believe me.*

The prince's pulse was hammering against his skin but he forced himself to exhale slowly. "I believe you."

Andy cleared her throat uncomfortably after exchanging a glance with her comrade. They hadn't missed the conversation between us. "Well congratulations on your win, Darren. Ryiah, you gave a great effort. Who would have known we were in the presence of two prodigies that whole time onboard? Don't forget us little people while you are saving the world."

Darren's smile was forced, and mine wasn't much better. I wanted to find Ian and confront him over Cethan's accusation, but I was not about to do it around Darren. So I strung along and joined him for small talk instead. A long succession of well-wishers followed in Andy and Cethan's wake.

Last but not least were Blayne and his new wife. The crown prince and I still weren't close by any means, but since his revelation I found him a bit harder to hate. I understood him, and that almost made it worse. We still avoided direct conversation if we could, and I spent the majority of our reunion conversing with Wren instead.

Wren had a sweet tooth and was quick to describe each one of her favorite desserts since arriving in Montfort. *Such a lovely girl.* Even though she was boring me to death with talk of pastries, I still found myself eager to please. She was the complete opposite of her conniving uncle, Duke Cassius. Fortunately the Pythian ambassador was too busy filling his cup with drink to be much of a hindrance.

"Which one was your favorite, darling?" Wren tugged on Blayne's hand to draw him away from his talk with his brother.

The crown prince took a deep sip from his glass. "The raspberry tart, same as you, my dear."

"Would you like me to—"

"Blayne, you don't look well." Darren interrupted the princess with a start.

"You don't look that well, either, Darren." Blayne's tone was sardonic.

"True, but I'm still healing." The non-heir's brow furrowed. "You have nothing to be healing *from.*"

I studied Blayne and was alarmed to see Darren was right. A heavy sheen of sweat had broken out along his brother's forehead. Blayne looked pale—so much lighter than when he and Wren had arrived a mere five minutes before.

"Truly, brother, I'm—"

The crown prince never finished. His goblet fell to the marble tile with a loud clash. Darren caught his brother by the arms just as Wren started to scream for a healer.

"Healer!" Darren's voice roared out above the crowd. He had cast a defensive sphere in place. "Guards, get my brother a healer *NOW!*"

The floor broke out into a frenzied herd as servants and nobility alike came rushing to tend to the heir. Mage Marius and several guards formed a circle as a cluster of healers rushed in to help. I stumbled out of the way and almost slipped to give them space. Something was familiar. Something I couldn't place my finger on, but it had to do with Blayne...

Red seeped out on the marble floor beneath my boots. But it wasn't blood.

The wine.

His mother. Queen Lillian. And her poisoned wine.

The Caltothians had done it to her...

I started running to the front where I had seen Lord Tyrus last.

And I spotted him. Removing a dagger from the inside of his cloak. Right behind the king who was trying to push through to his son—

"To the ki-"

My hand shot out to cast as I cried—but it was too late. My magic was nothing but a whisper of flame. The potions the healers had given me had slowed its recovery to help speed my physical health.

I was helpless as the Caltothian plunged the weapon into King Lucius's back.

"FOR CALTOTH!" The man's blade struck out three times more as Darren's father stumbled and fell, blood spraying from his lips as he hit the ground with a *thud.*

I was still running as the room became chaos. Mage Mira was the closest to respond—she was able to cast what my magic could not. A bolt of lightning and Lord Tyrus went down without a fight. Before I had even reached the king, she had already sent two swords piercing his front to back.

Blood was dribbling from the man's wounds like a fountain, coating the tiles in red. Funny, how a Caltothian's blood was no different than a king of Jerar.

"Protect the Crown! It's an attack!" Commander Audric was running forward to see to the king as half the regiment on duty formed a circle around the two princes, the other half to their fallen king.

"Uncle!" Wrendolyn was running toward Duke Cassius in the crowd. She was sobbing and her eyes were crazed.

I fought the crowd, trying to push and shove my way toward the girl. Someone needed to protect her. I wasn't sure where the three Caltothian guards were.

"Wren!" I screamed her name. *"WREN! NO!"*

A servant snagged the girl's arm and another appeared, a quick draw of the blade, and then she was on the floor. A river of scarlet trickling from her neck, blond curls tinged in red.

I was chasing the servant as Duke Cassius and two of his men dropped to the princess's side. The Pythian ambassador's bellow shattered my heart. I pulled up short when I cornered the first. It wasn't a Caltothian in disguise.

It was one of the lower city guards I'd seen during my apprenticeship. *A rebel*, I realized belatedly as he pulled out his knife. *The rebels are working with the Caltothians.*

I had to warn the others. "Rebels!" I screamed. "They are here!"

My hand shot underneath the folds of my robe and I blanched. My dagger wasn't there. I reached for the sheath by my thigh. *Empty.* My outfit tonight had been for show. I'd spent all day in the infirmary; I didn't have a single weapon on me.

And my body was still healing. I was weak, sluggish. I had bruises speckling my arms and a bandage to the chest.

And no magic.

I wasn't the hunter; I was the prey.

The man's panicked expression turned sly, as he seemed to recognize the same. And then I was thrust aside as Paige's sword gut him from chest to belly, bowels and blood spilling out. A putrid stink filling the air.

I had to fight every instinct not to vomit.

"We've got to get you out of here!" My knight started to pull me away—one hand on my wrist, the other gripping her sword.

"Wren—"

Her voice grew thick. "She's gone, Ryiah."

"But the healers—"

"With the princes." Paige was dragging me across the floor, both eyes flitting back and forth, checking our surroundings for safety.

"Where's Darren?" Panic clawed at my throat when I didn't see him or his brother at the front.

"He got his brother out. Marius and some of the King's Regiment are guarding them in the eastern tower."

"Ryiah!" Ella rushed forward and stopped just an inch before Paige's blade impaled her throat. My friend shot her a reproachful look. "Paige, it's me. I'm here to help you, fool."

"Sorry." My guard looked apologetic, but didn't avert her gaze from the crowd. "I don't trust anyone right now."

"Ella." I grabbed my friend's arm. "There are rebels, you've got to warn Commander Audric—"

"They already know." My friend pointed to the exits, and there was another scream behind us. Her pupils dilated. "He blocked off the room until they can identify everyone in the attacks. The only ones leaving are foreign dignitaries and the Crown. You aren't safe here, Ry. Princess Wrendolyn—"

Paige cut Ella off. "She already knows. Help me get her out of here. If they went after the Pythian princess, Ryiah would be the next logical target."

"But the others!" I protested. "What about—"

"You are more important." Paige's reply had an edge. "Ella and I will return when you are safe."

I had never felt so useless in my life. I let them lead me through the maze of people, all the others begging to be free of the room. *Safe.* Not only was I without magic, and weak from injury, but I was also a part of the group others risked their lives to save.

I had trained my whole life as a warrior. But in that moment I was the damsel-in-distress.

CHAPTER FIFTEEN

Nine dead. On the final night of the Candidacy the new Council of Magic was brought into its official reign by the blood of a king of Jerar, a young Pythian princess, four high-ranking Crown advisors, two prominent noblemen, and one poisoning attempt on the crown prince—now new king of Jerar—himself.

Never in the history of Jerar had so many important lives been stolen away in the course of an hour.

The five rebels were all found and executed. The three Caltothian servants that had come with their Lord Tyrus? They never made it out. Commander Audric's men and the newly promoted Mage Mira ensured every single one of the traitors were put to death before the night had ended.

I doubted they had expected to live. In a room filled with so many of the Crown and King's Regiments? With so many high-ranking mages and the world's most powerful black robe? Their mission had only been to kill.

The Crown's progress carried King Lucius's corpse back to the capital in Devon. Duke Cassius took his niece's body back to Pythus by ship with the rest of the court from his own country. The Borea Isles followed the same.

We left so hastily I only got the barest glimpse of my parents and Alex and Ella before I left. Derrick was already riding off with the rest of his regiment friends for the keep. I saw Ian and Jacob alongside him, and a part of me wished I were returning too. Derrick hadn't forgiven me for what happened to our brother, and more than ever I wanted to make amends.

I spent the whole of our five days south quietly mourning Wrendolyn's loss. Quietly, because the new king had lost a wife, and both he and his brother a father. *All in one night.* Despite everything they had experienced at the hand of Lucius's reign, he was their father—and that in itself was its own kind of misery.

The speech Blayne gave at his father's funeral was a call for war.

"Gone is the benevolence my father gave to our neighbor in the north. For too long I have watched our great country suffer in the guise of peace. No more. King Horrace sent his chief ambassador to slaughter my father in cold blood... He took the life of an innocent young beauty, my wife—" Blayne's voice cracked and through the mage's amplification casting he swallowed. *"— Whose flower had barely begun to bloom—"* The young king ran a fist across his eyes. *"And several great house lords in the attack. Horrace has been paying off our men to weaken our kingdom and turn them against the Crown..."*

Blayne climbed the towering steps of his father's pyre; they led up to the sky. The red folds of his father's cloak flapped heavily in the wind.

"Jerar will no longer be victim to Caltothian greed. We will fight back."

The hoards of low and highborn alike shouted their consent, a roar that shattered the sky, as the new king of Jerar lowered his torch.

Flames erupted in a tempest of red. Against the bright summer sun it seared. Red like blood. Red like rage. Red like *revenge.*

"I PROMISE YOU THIS." Blayne's voice boomed down from above. "JERAR WILL NOT BE A VICTIM. PYTHUS AND THE BOREA ISLES *WILL* HONOR OUR NEW ALLIANCE, AND WE WILL GO TO WAR. IT IS TIME TO MAKE A STAND."

The streets of Devon were a rumble of cries. The hammer of footfalls and bellows for change. I screamed right along with them. I screamed until my lungs grew hoarse. I screamed for Wren and for Eve and for Caine and every one of our own. All the lives the enemy had taken. All the senseless violence.

It was so much easier to choose anger over pain, and so I screamed.

I didn't notice the boy with the garnet eyes walk away.

"But *where* did he go?"

Henry shrugged and I ground my teeth, frustrated. *How could the prince's own personal guard let him out of the city unaccompanied? So soon after the attack?*

"Your one job is to guard him!"

The man folded his arms, undaunted. "All apologies, my lady, but when the Black Mage orders you not to follow, you don't follow."

"It doesn't matter what he—"

Paige cut me off with a hand to my wrist. "He doesn't know, Ryiah, let him be."

"I know, I just…" I trailed off, my arms falling limp at my sides. "He shouldn't be out there, Paige." I wasn't really worried about Caltothians or rebels. They had never bothered to come after Darren during the attack, even when he was weak. After his display during the Candidacy he would be the last one anyone wanted to face. Not unless they had an army at their backs. "I'm worried."

Darren had been so busy playing his role as the new Black Mage to his brother he hadn't let himself *feel*. He had shut out that storm of emotions and been the man the others expected. The way he had dealt with everything in his life.

But tonight. Tonight, he had cracked. Whatever he had been feeling after his father's death, it had led him to leave. And now he was gone and he shouldn't be alone.

Not like this.

I started to sprint toward the stables where the regiment had boarded up our horses for the ceremony.

"Ryiah!" Paige chased after me. "Not you too! You don't even know where—"

I turned around sharply to stop her, panting. "No. You stay. Just this once, Paige. Let me do this on my own. *Please.*"

Her brown eyes narrowed to mine. She sighed loudly, muttering a curse when she saw my face. "Fine. Two hours. You have *two* hours to find him."

"But—"

"A minute longer and I will send out a search party. Henry and I would have done it regardless. The two of you might be the best mages in the realm, but you aren't invincible."

I started forward. "Thank—"

"Time started five seconds ago." She raised a brow. "I suggest you get going."

I tore out of the stable at a gallop. I took the empty backstreets to the plains just outside the capital; I knew Darren would have done the same.

As soon as I made it out of the city I came to a stop. Every direction the King's Road took was overflowing. Passersby and caravans on every branch of the path. Everyone who had come to pay respect to their new king, or to peddle their wares during the height of an opportunity. The air was thick with incense and chatter.

I veered off the main trail to the north. It was a different route from the one that wove around the mountain range to Montfort, and I could see recent hoof prints marring the grass headed east. It led to a dead end—the very back of the palace was actually situated over a cliff that ran along for a couple of miles in either direction, but I knew it would be the one he would take.

For thirty minutes I rode in silence. The last rays of the sun cut a somewhat abandoned path across heavy forest foliage. Bright flashes of gold mixed in with green, something beautiful and remote. The air was sweeter here, too.

I could hear the steady trickle of a stream as I drew closer to the clearing. When I finally cut across to the granite edge, I found him standing there, with Wolf at his feet, overlooking the ledge. A stream was snaking down its end; the soft hush of water against rock much further below.

The sky was teeming with stars.

The sound of hoof beats alerted him of my approach.

The non-heir—*or perhaps that title didn't fit anymore*—spun around, tottering. It was then I noticed the flask in his hand.

I dismounted, tying up my mare next to his own, and started forward. "Darren—"

He held out a hand to stop me, and I noticed he was shaking, violently. "I don't want you to see me like this, Ryiah." He slurred the words as he spoke. "Go home."

I stopped walking but made no move to turn around. My voice was gentle. "It's okay to be sad. He was your father."

The prince threw back his head and laughed. Like it was the funniest thing in the world. But the movement shifted his balance.

Darren started to slip—

My hand shot out without a moment's thought.

A blast of wind was all that saved Darren from the rocky abyss below. He collapsed onto jagged granite as I struggled to breathe, wind rattling my lungs. A part of me was furious it could have even happened. The other part terrified he might have let it.

And then I ran forward to drag him away from the ledge. There were cuts marring his hands but he didn't seem to care.

He didn't care at all. As I heaved one arm over my shoulder he was still laughing, madly. "Can you really call a man like him 'father?'"

I didn't know how to reply. So I kept silent and just kept moving him toward a boulder he could lean against a couple more feet toward the clearing, away from the drop. He was in no position to stand.

"All these years..." His words were faded. "All this time I hated him. When I... So many times I wondered what it would be like..." His head fell forward as I helped him sit. "I envied you, you know. I saw your parents that day... At the first-year trials... You looked so... *happy.*"

A part of me crumbled. *The little boy saving his brother, wishing for a different life.*

"I never loved him... I tried but what—what he did to us..." Pain lanced Darren's voice. "Blayne was never strong. Not like me... Maybe that was why..."

"Why?"

"The moment Blayne collapsed... I knew. I knew I should have gone to *him*... I was the Black Mage." His eyes met mine and suddenly I knew. "It was my job to protect him... But I chose my brother."

"You didn't know—"

"I suspected." Bitterness flowed through his words. "And I didn't do a thing... Could have had you watch Blayne... But—but I thought maybe it was better... So I didn't do anything." His whole body was shuddering. "I didn't speak a word."

I leaned against the granite so that my shoulders lined up with his. A slight puff of dirt settled as I shifted in my seat.

"If you were smart..." Darren drew in a sharp breath. "You'd run away and never look back." He exhaled. "I'm poison, Ryiah." The last words tore at my lungs. "Just like my father."

I clutched his bloodied fingers in my own, but he pulled away even as I spoke. "You are *nothing* like him!"

"Aren't I?" His laugh was low. "He wasn't always a bad man. He was never kind... but he wasn't always cruel. The servants... They say he changed after my mother died." Darren met my eyes. "Sometimes I wonder if that was who my father was always destined to be, and my mother just saved him from himself..." Garnet turned to black. "Or his love for her made him become it."

My heart slammed against my ribs.

His voice was so quiet. "I'm afraid of what my love for you will make *me*."

"Darren..." Now it was my turn to crack. "I—" I didn't know what to say. My palms were trembling, and I pressed them against the sand and rocks to hide their tremor.

"Sometimes I wish I was never a prince..." His eyes clouded. "And I wonder what it would be like... if I were just a boy, and you just a girl—without all of *this*."

I let my fingers slide to his. "It would have made everything a lot easier."

For a while there was just silence. The heavy patter of his heart next to mine, the rise and fall of his chest. The quiet in and out of our breath.

Then he shut his eyes. "We should be them, someday."

"We will." My grip tightened on his hand. Whatever he thought, he wasn't poison.

Darren wasn't darkness, and I wasn't his light.

The non-heir had proven time and time again he was more than his father's son. More than an arrogant non-heir who thought only of himself. And now I wanted to show Darren what he looked like to me.

I *needed* to show him he was fire. My fire. Something filled with light. Something good. Someone just like me but wrapped up so tightly in his own barrier of darkness it could burn. Unless you knew how to unravel him.

And so I kissed him. Tugging his face to mine, I held his face in the palm of my hands and kissed his mouth. Just once.

Pressing my lips to his I shut my eyes and channeled my one single promise.

I will never give up on you.

A spark seemed to light me up from the inside. Like tinder, my body shot to flames. And his returned. We were two coals burning in the dark.

When I pulled back his eyes were stars.

"Promise me, Ryiah, when this war is over, we leave this all behind. Promise we will be them."

"I promise."

The weeks following King Lucius's funeral brought with them a wave of change. Some good, some bad... well, they were primarily bad.

The entire castle was in mourning. It was a three-month duration in which we were required to dress in somber colors and postpone the Crown's weekly entertainment for the nobility at court. To honor our late king in longstanding tradition. Unfortunately, it also meant our wedding was postponed.

"Which is just as well because we don't have Emperor Liang's backing until we get King Joren to stop dragging his feet," Blayne had been quick to point out. "Until he acknowledges our claim, we have no reason to forsake tradition and expedite a wedding."

One of the other things to go from bad to worse. The Pythian king was now stating that he had received correspondence from King Horrace that stated his ambassador was acting without orders. His call "For Caltoth" could have been a "ploy" from Jerar to extract sympathies for a call to war. The letter even went so far as to say the attackers were executed before a panel of unbiased parties could question them. In other words, the Caltothians were blaming Jerar.

What surprised me most was that King Joren was even listening to their claims. After all, his own brother had watched his daughter get murdered before his very eyes.

How a king could just put aside the loss of his daughter and ignore the facts was beyond suspicious. A king so willing to listen to the man who had had his daughter slaughtered for show? There had to be more. Even to a girl like me with no knowledge of this sort of thing. Something else was afoot, I just didn't know what.

Were the Pythians working with the Caltothians? But then why go through all the false efforts to negotiate? Why marry a daughter when she could have been sent to marry the other king's son in the first place? Why pick the losing side?

Were they working with the rebels? But that wouldn't make sense either. Caltoth was the one who had been raiding and attacking our border for years. And if they had wanted to rule Jerar our treaty should have been enough—they hadn't needed to work up from the bottom rung of the rebels to seize control.

Or was King Joren so shrewd that he could sit upon his throne and deliberate? That he would ignore the facts and pick apart meaningless details to postpone promised aid after our call to war. To claim he sought the truth when he really just sought an escape.

Blayne sent two ambassadors to Pythus to plead our case. They would remain in his court as a constant reminder until he honored the New Alliance. An envoy traveled back and forth by ship, a new letter with updates on our progress every month to give us hope. Sooner or later Jerar would receive its promised aid. Our king refused to consider the alternative.

That wasn't the only change to pass.

Mage Mira was promoted to lead mage in the King's Regiment. Much to my chagrin she was my direct commander. I had only just come into my new role, and thanks to the Montfort attack she refused to send me even outside the palace gates. My new service was limited to guarding the Council of Magic's official chamber.

Four of the seven days each week, I spent dawn until dusk securing its entrance, growing more restless with each passing hour. The longer I spent watching Darren and the other two Colored Robes, Karina for Restoration and Yves for Alchemy, come and go for their meetings with Blayne and his new circle of advisors, the more I grew to resent my role, and in some ways myself.

He was better. It was the first sentence that came to mind when I woke. And it was the last before I went to bed. I hated myself for even thinking it, but every time I grew restless, every time Mira barked at me to stop my complaints, it was there.

If I were just a boy, and you were just a girl... If that were true I wouldn't be trapped in the palace. I wouldn't be "too valuable to send out on missions," as Mira had sneered. I wouldn't be serving as a sentry; I would be out doing things. Making a difference. Blayne had promised me as soon as we went to war I would be able to take on a more active duty, and he had made an effort to include me in his war council meetings on my days off... but it wasn't enough.

In all fairness, the whole of Jerar had grown silent as a front. Rebel attacks had ceased in the south; no more raids to the north. There wasn't action to be had, anywhere. Every pair of eyes was trained on Caltoth as we waited for good news from King Joren of Pythus.

A rampant hate was spreading across the countryside like the plague. Our king had been cut down in cold blood. Just a year before our stronghold, attacked. The Caltothians were ruthless, relentless in their pursuit of our land.

Any reluctance to war had disappeared under the latest attack.

Darren was at its head. Following his father's funeral, the prince had channeled his grief into rage. Rage that boiled over into his work. I hardly ever saw him outside the Council doors. Every waking moment was spent at his brother's side. Daring the rebels of Jerar to try an attempt again, daring Caltoth to send its army now. His mother and father had been murdered, his brother barely left to live. The Black Mage of Jerar was ready to lead us to war, and I was ready to serve.

Our enemies had to pay. Those heartless, faceless others who had stolen so much. It was a fire consuming the dark. Fanning us with its flames. Searing a brand right across our hearts.

Perhaps that was why I didn't notice when one walked right through the palace doors.

CHAPTER SIXTEEN

"Derrick?" I stopped dead in my tracks. Paige's blunt
practice sword hit me across the stomach, hard. I barely noticed.

My little brother was standing behind the spectator glass
of the palace's indoor training courts.

"Surprise, big sister." He gave me a small smile and my
heart did a flip. "Did you miss me?"

My casted polearm vanished, and I all but slipped across
the marble floor as I ran to meet my brother in the stands. No
one else was present except my knight who had returned to her
own warm-ups now that I had stopped our practice. The rest
of the court was still asleep. I would have been too, if I had
been able. Unfortunately my many late hours of restless duty
had left me unable to sleep for more than a few hours at a time.

"What are you doing here?" I threw my arms around
him, for a moment forgetting that I was covered in sweat.
"Why aren't you in Ferren?"

"I felt terrible after I left Montfort." His voice was muffled. "After what happened I realized the person I was really
mad at was myself. I—I was punishing you for something that
wasn't your fault—"

"Derrick." I pulled back. "I'm so sorry about Alex, I never—"

"I know." He cut me off. "I knew then, too, but I was so angry I just didn't care... After I returned to the keep I started to think about that night. Nine people were murdered, and my own sister could have been one of them. I wouldn't have been there to save you because I was too busy sulking like a child." Derrick drew a deep breath. "I would have never forgiven myself. So I wrote Darren and begged a position on the palace regiment."

"You did?" He had never mentioned it.

Derrick nodded, his arms tightening around my waist. "I couldn't let anything happen to my sister. He understood and I-I think he wanted you to have some family here... so you wouldn't feel so alone. He mentioned you'd had a hard time adjusting to the palace." My lungs constricted, just a little. Darren had noticed. All this time I had been envying his role, and he had been worrying over me. "I now serve with you on the King's Regiment. I've a cot in the barracks outside. I reported to their lead soldier last night—I was so tired it took me until this morning to come find you. I checked your chamber first but the guards told me you were in the practice court with her." His grin turned teasing. "Neither of you has changed one bit."

"Neither have you." I stepped back with an embarrassed laugh. His freshly pressed clothes were now damp with my perspiration. I pointed to his tunic. "Sorry, that wasn't my smartest moment."

"You couldn't contain your excitement to see me again." His eyes danced. "I'll take that as a compliment. Even if it does smell like an army of men rotting at sea."

I shoved him away and made a face. "I don't smell nearly as bad as the men we trained with in Ferren. And I wash regularly. Unlike the others."

"Well, why don't you wash up again? And then give me a tour of this palace? It's your day off, the guards said, no?"

"It is." I waved at Paige to let her know I was done for the morning. I could make up our practice later on my own. Or maybe Derrick could join me. "When do you start service?"

"Tomorrow."

Everything was better now that Derrick and I had made up from our fight in Montfort. Better even, because Darren was right. I *had* been suffering from loneliness since our return. I hadn't grown up highborn. I hadn't spent endless summers in the palace. I didn't have friends among the court. I had tried, with some of the regiment's soldiers, but most of them preferred silence in duty and the nobility were too eager to strike up a friendship with the Crown's future princess. I'd been wary of all but Paige, and now that Derrick was here I had another to turn to. Someone to confide my own thoughts so I wouldn't have to burden Darren with my jealousy and resentment.

Someone who—unlike Paige—could share in my opinion. The knight would never dare open her feelings up to the world. Even if she was formerly lowborn and now placed in a position of power. She preferred to stick to the task at hand and that was the end. Derrick was like me. He had chased power, pursued Combat even, and then turned to the Cavalry when his first dream got pushed aside.

"I was jealous of you and Alex," he admitted, one afternoon while we were drilling in the soldier's training court outside. "But especially you, because you had it all. The faction, the apprenticeship, you even made a name for yourself with Sir Piers and the Black Mage. You convinced a prince to call off his engagement. Our parents were so proud. They would talk about Alex, but it always came back to you. Every letter."

I swallowed as I blocked his blade with my own. "I had no idea."

He shook his head, tufts of blond, curling locks clearing his bright blue eyes. "And I didn't want you to. I was proud of you... Just, even if I *was* happy, it hurt. For years. It wasn't until Commander Nyx promoted me to her keep's regiment it finally started to fade. Until I started to make a name for myself."

I fell back and let Derrick take another swipe and kick at my feet. I twisted and parried his cut with ease. Hearing my own brother confess to his own insecurity, his own jealousy... it made it easier to breathe. What I was feeling was normal.

"Did you... did you ever start to believe you were a terrible person?"

"Every day. I would try to stay positive in our letters. It was easy because of the distance, and I really did miss you. But every time we were together and I watched you smile talking about your new life, I hated you. And I hated myself even more for thinking it."

Our match ended and Derrick sheathed his blade. My own casting vanished. The two of us went to sit against a bench. "I'm so sorry."

"You have nothing to be sorry for. It wasn't you, Ryiah. It was me. Something I had to overcome for myself." His gaze fell to my own and a smile tugged at the corner of his lips. "You wouldn't happen to have the ring your foolish brother cast away like a dolt?"

I tugged the leather cord from underneath my shirt. The tarnished copper band hung from its center, the letter "R" glinting along its surface. "Does this mean I am your favorite again?" My grin was wide. "Because I will only give it back if I am."

Derrick snickered. "Poor Alex never had a chance. The two of us are far too evil for the likes of a nice brother like him."

The next month passed by in a blur. My duties became more bearable after my talk with Derrick, and as much as I resented Mage Mira's obvious distaste where I was concerned, I embraced my role to the fullest. One thing was for certain: the Council chambers would be the most well guarded room in the palace.

And it was. Until the night I was doing a routine patrol down the hall and Darren appeared leaning against the entry with a wicked smile in play.

"Hello, lady mage," he said, "perhaps you can tell me why this chamber was left unattended for an hour putting our entire kingdom at risk?"

One eyebrow shot up as I fixed the prince with an incredulous expression. "It's been attended all night. *I* was the one guarding it."

He peeled himself off the paneling with an even deeper grin. "I think you are mistaken."

"And I think you have lost your mind."

"Then tell me why the inside is a mess."

"A-a mess?" I faltered. *Had I missed something? Someone snuck past me the moment my back was turned? Why was he still smiling like one of the palace cats who had gotten into the cook's cream?* "Show me!"

He produced a key and swung open the handle. I hurried past to check.

Not a thing was out of place. All the books still on their shelves, the giant maps of Jerar and its neighbors aligning the walls, the great Council table and chairs, the great chests still with their locks, even the flourishing tapestries exactly as before. Not since my inspection an hour ago had one object moved in the slightest.

I turned an accusatory finger back at the prince. "You see, nothing has changed!"

"But it will." Darren shut the door and locked it behind him, looking up at me from underneath long, sooty lashes. The side of his mouth was twitching to hold back a smirk.

Oh. I wanted to kick myself. *This.*

"I am sorry," he said, "that I have been so busy."

I sucked in a sharp breath.

"I've been going mad," he confessed. "Our wedding postponed. All the Council meetings. Only sharing meals. I..." He stopped as he drew up next to me at the center of the room. My back was pressed against the cold stone table, and there was nowhere else I could go.

Even if I wanted to. Which I didn't.

"I miss you even when you are standing in front of me now." The words came out in a rush as he met my eyes. "All I've been able to think about is you. We are going to go to war, and I'm the Black Mage and the whole time I am supposed to be leading those meetings I am thinking about you." His head dipped so that his lips were bare inches from my own. "I haven't stopped, love."

"I..." I could barely speak, my pulse was deafening. "I think about..."

"What do you think about?" His hands fell to either side of the table, pinning me in place. His eyes were like coals.

"You." His whole body was pressed against me, and it did odd things to my head. I was dizzy and too hot and too cold. All at once. All I could think about were his legs brushing mine, his chest rising and falling with my own, his hands on my skin.

"And?"

I licked my lips and his eyes followed the movement. A smile tugged at the corner of his own.

"Kiss me, Ryiah."

I rose to my toes, and he cut the distance in half. Sparks flared in the shadows as his mouth found mine in the dark. I heard him choke back a groan, and it was all I could do not to gasp.

"What else do you think about?" His breath was hot in my ear. His fingers were trailing down my ribs as he pressed down, my back arching against his.

"Do you think about this?" He bit down on my lower lip, and I couldn't stifle the whimper I emitted in response.

His tongue tangled with mine, and my whole body was ablaze. Hot, searing chills assaulted my limbs until I was panting for air. The prince of Jerar kissed me, and I swear to the gods I was catching fire because of it.

Heat flared in the pit of my stomach as he whispered the words. "What do you want, Ryiah?"

His hands lifted me against the cold marble top, and my legs wrapped around his waist before I even realized what I was doing. Shock and desire coursed my cheeks.

"Darren," I stammered.

"Ryiah." He was staring down at me, and I fought to break the spell that had found its way inside my head. His hands were pressed flat against the table on either side of me and heat was chasing through my veins, filling the pit of my stomach and up, up, *down*. The entire room was a haze. I wanted to pull Darren down to me and close any semblance of space between us.

I didn't want him wearing those clothes.

I swallowed. The thought should have stunned me but now... Now when every part of me was dying just for this.

I knew what he wanted.

I wanted it too.

"Ryiah." Darren raised one hand to lift my chin and meet my eyes with his own. His gaze was a bottomless abyss. Dark garnet swallowed me whole. The color reminded me of a setting sun: the moment red faded into black and became something else, something that pulled and drove you to madness, so beautiful you kept staring because you could no longer see anything else.

"I love you," he whispered.

I pulled Darren to me and kissed him. One long, slow kiss that told him everything I was too afraid to put into words. His eyes flared and Darren pressed into me in response, kissing me back in a breathless rush. His fingers slipped down, down to the hem of my shirt and my breath hitched.

My pulse thundering as I tore off his vest, my grip sliding on tile as his mouth found my neck.

There was a scratching, an odd creak, and for a moment I thought it was my fingernails against the marble top. But they were still in his hair, pulling as hot lips pressed into my skin, searing me alive.

Then the creak again and the soft squeak of a hinge.

I jerked back, my head banging against the table while Darren threw himself around, blocking me from the intruder, one hand casting a bright sheen of light against the chamber door.

"Derrick?" Darren's wheeze was echoed in my own. I struggled to right myself and adjust my top that had fallen low to one shoulder, snarled in my hair.

"Your highness... Ry? I–I'm so sorry, I didn't..." My brother's neck flushed pink as he stammered on. "I–I came to find my sister, a-and I saw the hallway was empty. I was worried and thought to check..." Derrick's voice trailed off as his eyes darted from one side of the dark chamber to the other, clearly getting an idea for why that was.

"Thanks for checking." The prince's gaze assessed my brother with a slight frown. "Wasn't that door locked?"

Something pricked at the back of my spine.

"It couldn't have been." My brother wore an incredulous expression. "How else would I have gotten in?"

My eyes darted to my brother, and he looked away as he added. "There must have been a catch. It swung open a-and then I realized..."

Darren looked away, embarrassed as my brother. The moment couldn't have been more awkward if he tried.

Derrick ducked his head. "I –I'll let the two of you alone."

"Derrick," I suddenly called, "why were you looking for me?"

His head shot up but he didn't meet my eyes. "I–I guess I don't remember."

The door shut and then it was just Darren and me in the dark. Only this time there were shadows creeping around my thoughts. Unease and fear were pounding at my chest. I pulled myself up off the table.

Darren caught my arm. "You are leaving?" He sounded so confused.

A part of me wanted to stay. To forget everything and recapture that moment, but... "I —Can you find me a replacement, tonight?"

"Of course..." He swallowed. "I'm sorry—I never meant to make you—"

"It wasn't that!" I cut him off quickly, blushing furiously and grateful for the dark. "I–I just..." Gods help me. "I haven't taken any of the potions to... help keep away a child... I... I wouldn't want to until a-after the war."

"Oh." The back of his neck was as red as my face, I was sure of it. "I... I, uh, can ask one of the healers to... if you want?"

I was ready to melt into a puddle of humiliation. But there was another part of me that begged not to brush his offer aside. She wouldn't let me run off in a childish fit; *she* wanted this. "I –I do." I squeaked the reply, and then ran from the room—confident my fit of "embarrassment" would be enough to explain my rough exit.

Darren didn't need to know the real reason was Derrick. To find my brother before he had time to recover. So I could corner him and force him to explain.

Only two guards—me, and a mage named Ike—had a key to the room. Ike took his role as seriously as Paige took hers. I had never seen him so much as yawn on duty once. The only others were the current Council of Magic and the Crown. Derrick was neither.

"You stole it from me, didn't you? That day in practice."
I didn't wait for a reply as I shoved my brother against the
wooded walls, hissing. "That time I thought I lost it. But I
didn't, did I? The next day when you told me you had found
it? You had taken it and made a copy!"

"I—" His chest rose and fell as he panted for breath. His
arms were twice as wide, his frame easily two heads above my
own—but just now he looked small, so much smaller than I.

"Why did you need it?" I rammed his shoulders, my fingers bruising upon impact. "*Why? WHY DID YOU NEED
IT, DERRICK?*" No one else was around. The building was
eerily quiet except for the soft crunch of hay and the shifting of
hooves.

Everyone else was at dinner. Or abed. Or on duty. The
closest guards were a quarter mile away: a couple at the palace
gates, the others the barrack walls. It was Derrick's shift at the
stables.

Or it was supposed to be. Except he had been attempting
to break into the Council chambers. Under the guise of visiting
me.

My brother stopped panting and looked me straight in
the eyes. "You know why," he said softly.

"No! No, I *don't*!" My fist hit the wall by his neck. A
trickle of blood dribbled down from my knuckles to the floor.

"You do." Derrick didn't falter under my gaze.

"No, I..." I did. My legs gave out from under me, and I
caught the wall just before I fell. "Oh gods, oh gods, oh..." I
slid down until I was sitting in the hay, my knees pulled up to
my chest. The name spilled over on my tongue like a disease.
"You are a rebel."

Derrick sat down next to me and said nothing.

"You... you d-didn't come back for me." My breath was
coming out hard and fast, and I was seconds away from heav-
ing. "You c-came here for *them*."

My whole world rose up to meet me. Hot flashes of sweat
and my skin became clammy and pale as I dropped on my

hands, vomiting into the musty straw, giant swells of dust and dirt clogging my throat.

Derrick held my hair back and waited for me to stop coughing, handing me his water skin until I had washed my mouth out and spat. Then he spoke.

"They aren't what you think."

"Cold-blooded murderers?" I choked the words out like fire. "They tried to kill *me*, Derrick. My first year of the apprenticeship. In Mahj. They tried to kill Darren. They killed Caine, they killed others, they attack our cities, they..." My voice cracked. "They killed Wren."

"They were after the salt mines, not you or Darren." His tone was sharp. "If the apprentices hadn't tried to play the people's hero their leader would never have attacked. The rebels care about weakening the Jerar coin through its exports, not killing off its youth. Finding out a prince of Jerar was present though..." He paused. "Well, they thought they might kill two birds with one stone. The Crown is our enemy, Ryiah." He exhaled. "You are just too blind to see it."

"You don't know what you are talking about." I felt sick. Twisted, gutted, like it was all a cruel test of will. Turn my little brother against me. Make him the enemy.

It was the worst kind of test. And one I would fail. I couldn't make a move to arrest him.

"They tried to recruit both of us, you know." He sounded pained. "In Ferren's Keep." *No rebel attacks in the north... I had always wondered why.* "When Nyx offered you the position after your apprenticeship, it was because she knew you would be powerful. She sent for Ian the moment you accepted. His parents are rebels—" *No.* "So was he. He'd been gathering information at Langli, helping her keep track of shipments—but then she asked for him to help watch you. To test you. After your engagement to the prince..." *He had been there for me. Darren had been right all along, just not for the reason he thought.* "She knew they would have to be careful. So she called on Ian... And then when you continued to mope she decided to recruit me. She brought on Jacob since his father was already one of them."

They were rebels. All of them. All quietly recruiting the lowborns to fight for their cause. 'South the Snout?' It was just another rhyme to turn the northerners against us. Why they had refrained from recruiting highborns. Even Ella hadn't been offered a position—but Ray, a rank lower, had.

Derrick's eyes met mine, and they were full of grief. "I didn't know, Ry. They didn't tell me anything until that first time you were called away to the palace. Sir Gavin's unit is where they put all the new recruits. Take them on missions, bond with them. Learn their secrets and if they pass the test— if they choose one another over the Crown in offhanded discussions, she promotes them. And then they tell." *Ray. He was promoted while I was in Devon.*

"They didn't promote me or Ian, of course," Derrick said. "Nyx needed us to get to you. You weren't engaged with your unit. You kept training for that blasted Candidacy and defending Darren. You brought the coin, and I thought it would be better—you had passed a test— but then you withdrew again. No one could trust you." His eyes flared in anger. "I begged and pleaded for Sir Gavin to give you a chance. But Ian wasn't convinced. He said you were too close to the Crown. That it didn't matter how much you could bring to our cause, you were too much a risk. That you would betray us to *him*."

I couldn't breathe.

"The bandits you found near Pamir. They were never taken to the prison in Gilys. They were recruited. Stationed in cities up north, given coin to survive." My brother's fingers dug into the straw. "The rebels don't abandon their people, Ryiah. They don't leave them to starve. They don't punish them for turning to crime when the Crown turns its back."

I forced down a deep lungful of air. "Derrick, the Crown doesn't have enough coin, it can't possibly support everyone when Caltoth is sending attacks..." My eyes grew wide. "The rebels, Derrick. Are they working with Caltoth?" *And why, if he was a rebel, why was he telling me all of this?*

Unless he knew I would never report him.

"Ry, Caltoth isn't the enemy."

"Then who is?" I spat the words back in his face. "The Crown? King Blayne? Darren? *Me?*" My eyes were swelling with tears, and I didn't bother to hide them away. I *wanted* Derrick to see me. His sister. His own flesh and blood. "TELL ME, DERRICK. WHO IS THE ENEMY?"

I wanted him to face me and say it. Because I was struggling to name my own.

My brother had the decency to look shamed, his cheeks flushing that of a stained rose. "It's not that easy, I—"

"TELL ME, DERRICK!"

"King Lucius."

I bit back a laugh. It choked at my lungs with the dust, and I was coughing for close to a minute before it finally stopped. "Is that the best that you can do?" I sneered. "A dead king. My own brother can't even think of a decent lie. *YOUR PEOPLE KILLED HIM NOT TWO MONTHS AGO AND YOU ALREADY FORGOT?*" I was hysterical. *He* was hysterical. My own brother, the world's worst liar. *How had I missed it over the course of a year?*

"No." Derrick squared his shoulders and shook me. "I'm not lying, Ry. King Lucius has been staging this war since the beginning. He had a sister, did you know that?"

I stopped laughing.

"Princess Kyra. She died on Caltothian soil—she was sick, it would have happened regardless. But his parents blamed their neighbor, and why not? Caltoth is the richest nation, you know." I did. "Lucius told his advisors he wanted to expand two months before his wife's death."

"How would you possibly know? It's just a lie they are saying to get you to join their cause!"

My brother ignored my question. "One of them, Raphael, disagreed. He didn't speak the truth to his king, but he warned his younger sister in the north. She was a head knight at the time in one of the regiments in Ferren's Keep. She went by Nyx."

Commander Nyx?

"They—with the help of their most trusted friends— plotted to kill the king. It was the only way to stop him. They knew Queen Lillian would be a manageable queen and better, she wasn't aware of her husband's plans. They never wanted to eliminate the Crown, Ryiah; they just wanted a ruler that wasn't corrupt and trying to cause a war between nations that would cost thousands of lives. They knew the princes would be better under the mother's guidance than the father."

Derrick stirred at the straw. "But Raphael mixed up the wines. Queen Lillian drank from the wrong cup. So King Lucius slaughtered the entire room that night. He probably guessed it was intended for him, after all, and he used the event as the first claim to Caltothian attacks."

I wanted to argue, to protest... but another part of me wanted to listen. I stayed silent. That part of me that wanted to believe my brother, to know he was not a traitor—it wouldn't be quieted.

And worst, what he was saying, *it made sense.*

"Lucius staged the border attacks, Ry. *For years.* Nyx started to suspect and sent some of her most trusted men to investigate. It was just small ones, innocent ones at first. But they started to grow. And knowing Raphael's secrets, she knew there was more to it." He sucked in a breath. "Nyx sent a band of emissaries to Caltoth. She had them petition his court. King Horrace claimed it was a farce. If he had been allowing the attacks he could have just as easily executed her spies, but instead he listened." My brother paused. "Horrace might have had the coin, but he didn't have the strength to combat a war. So he's spent years beseeching King Joren's favor, preparing him for King Lucius's claims. Because Lucius was hiring Caltothian fugitives, Ry, fugitives and bandits and assassins. He was paying them to attack his own people.

"NO." I tried to stand and caught myself against the wall. My limbs were like jelly. "Why would a king stage a war on his own people?"

"What better way to win over his people's support? What better way to show the other countries Caltoth had broken the Great Compromise?" Derrick paused. "That didn't mean there weren't raids from their own. Greedy lords that wanted more. Assassins that thought to pocket Lucius's coin and use it to their own gain... Like Ferren. Nyx told me you recalled something during the attack."

I sucked in a breath. *"You know the orders as well as I do, Wade, no survivors." "Not if we don't tell them." "Do you really want to take that chance? Two times a traitor would only bring a slow and painful death."*

"Lucius paid Caltothian assassins to attack one of the patrolling regiments during the mock battle. He had never expected his son to be far enough to stop it. You and Darren and the rest of your year were supposed to be in the keep." *Eve.* Something tugged at my lungs. She had died not to save us from Caltothian killers—but our own king.

She had died in vain.

"The lives we lost that day, Ryiah. They weren't because of King Horrace. They were the final proof Lucius needed to convince the others the Great Compromise was broken. From there he just needed to secure the Pythian's hand."

I was breaking, and it was all I could do to breathe. And then: *Wren.* And the others.

"You think the rebels are so noble?" I spat. "But they were willing to kill us in the desert, Derrick! You say that was for control of trade? Well, what about Montfort? What about *then?*" My voice trembled and caught. "Were you one of them? Did you somehow manage to escape—"

Derrick shook his head vehemently. "That wasn't us, Ry."

"You said the Crown is their enemy," I choked. "And they killed him, Derrick. Lucius is dead. They killed Wren. They tried to kill Blayne. They killed—"

"IT WASN'T US!" Derrick stood and grabbed both my arms, shaking me. "I swear to you, Ry, it wasn't the rebels. We wanted Lucius dead but it wasn't us. I was never there, and the rebels they caught, they weren't us—"

"*HOW WOULD YOU EVEN KNOW?*" I roared. "You just nod your head at every little thing Commander Nyx tells you! She's the rebel leader, isn't she?"

"She is but—"

"But you claim it isn't you!" I shoved him away. "Lucius was the rebel's enemy and now he is dead. *How convenient.* Who were those 'fake' rebels, then? Another group of fugitives set against the first? Pythians who were willing to kill their king's heir to the throne? If the Pythians wanted Jerar they could have just struck an alliance with Caltoth; they needn't have bothered with the farce of their negotiations! The death of their crown princess!" The words were tearing at my throat. "And the Boreans? They are the weakest country of all! Emperor Liang stands to gain nothing from the attack! The only answer is the rebels or Caltoth!"

I advanced on my brother, anger giving me the strength to stand tall. "Don't you see, Derrick? You've been played. King Horrace played all of you. He got the rebels to do his dirty work while he sat there laughing on his throne, sending his armies to weaken our border. Even if what you said about Lucius was true—which I might believe for some, King Horrace could have taken advantage. Maybe those men weren't your own rebels in Montfort. Perhaps they were *soldiers of Jerar bought by the Caltothians!* Did you ever think of that?"

Derrick glowered. "The ambassador shouted, 'For Caltoth.' Someone was clearly trying to frame Horrace and the rebels in one."

"Or perhaps," I said through clenched teeth, "Horrace really was condoning the attack and didn't care who knew. Or maybe the Caltothians aren't working with you at all, and Nyx bought off the ambassador!"

"The north can barely afford to outfit its own infantry!" Derrick raged. "You are a mage! You know nothing of what it is like to be a lowborn soldier with nothing to gain. The Crown sends us nothing. Nyx have no idea what it's like! Nyx would never betray us because she is one of us—*unlike you!*"

I tried a calming breath to prevent the rage from making me say something I would regret. I didn't know who the enemy was anymore, but whoever it was they were still out there. And I needed to convince my brother not to play right into the palm of their hand. "The enemy could be anyone, Derrick. Even your own."

"There is someone you forgot." My brother turned on me, twin storm clouds thrashing in his eyes. "Someone who was conveniently *not* injured in the Montfort attack."

"There were a lot of people not—"

"Someone important." Derrick took a step forward, backing me against the wall. His whole body was trembling. "Someone who stood to gain *everything*. Did you ever stop to wonder why?"

"Blayne?" I snorted. "Did you forget? He was *poisoned*."

"No." My brother's eyes flashed. "Not Blayne. No one knows if King Lucius shared his schemes with his sons. But there is one who stood to gain the most out of the king and his heir's deaths. Someone who could have decided it was time to take the throne—"

My brother stumbled back as my hand slapped across his face. Tears were stinging my eyes as I advanced on him, screaming, "*DARREN WOULD NEVER!*"

"Wouldn't he?" My brother caught my hand before I could hit him again. "You are blinded by love, Ry. *Did you forget Alex? Did you forget what you let happen to our own brother because you were too afraid to stand up to the Crown?*"

"Darren never wanted that!" I yanked free of his grip. "His father was evil! Darren *hated* him! You have no idea—"

"Perhaps he killed him over hate." My brother started to walk away.

"Derrick!" I chased after my brother. "We need to tell them what you told me. Darren and Blayne need to know the truth about their father!"

My brother turned around. "We aren't telling them anything. *You* won't tell them anything."

"You were searching the palace for proof of Lucius's orders, weren't you?" I was pleading. "That's what they told you to do, wasn't it?"

My brother said nothing.

"Darren could help you. Even Blayne. If what you said was true—"

"The Crown can't be trusted." Derrick's voice echoed across the stalls. "Even if the two princes weren't involved in Lucius's schemes, do you really think King Blayne would call off a war? With the Pythians' support Jerar will win, and the Crown stands everything to gain."

"Darren could help him see reason, Blayne trusts him—"

Derrick raised his hand. "Lucius raised Darren to be his brother's right hand. He will serve Blayne above all else."

"You don't know him!"

"I don't need to. They are the Crown. They will betray us."

"Derrick!" I was on my knees, begging him not to go. "You have to stop. If they find out you are with the rebels after the attack at Montfort—" *They will kill him.*

"You are going to have to tell them to stop me." My brother's jaw clenched, and I saw he was no longer just the boy I had helped raise, but a man. "I will keep searching. Because one of us has to. And if you turn me in—and I don't think you will—you will have to deal with my blood on your hands. And you can live your life knowing you betrayed your own brother. And when Alex and our parents cripple in despair, you will know it was *you* who did it. It will be *you* who destroyed your life."

I stumbled to my chambers—but before I did I made sure to dry my eyes. To clean my face. To brush the straw from my breeches. To hold my head up high and smile as I passed the regular patrol of guards.

As soon as I had reached my chamber I threw the door shut and fell to my bed, a muffled scream into the mattress beneath. I hated Derrick. I hated him for using my love against me. He knew I would never betray him to the Crown, and even if his tasks now were innocent enough, I would not be able to protect him if he got caught.

Why? Why does it have to be my brother who gets involved in this scheme? I hated Commander Nyx. Ian. *HOW DARE HE TRY TO CONVERT ME!* Ray. All of those angry soldiers at the keep. Jacob. Myself. *Why couldn't Derrick have been more like Alex? Why did he have to be like me?*

I hated every last one of them. I hated Derrick for asking me to choose. Because by asking me, he had known I would choose him. He *knew* I wouldn't betray him to Darren. Because I couldn't betray my brother, my own flesh and blood— the little boy who I had spent all those days chasing around a field, wrestling in the mud... Which meant Darren could never betray Blayne—the brother he had seen beaten and bruised, the one he had sworn to protect. And I couldn't count on Blayne not to condemn Derrick.

My brother had made me a traitor. And I would never, *ever* forgive him.

A sob escaped my lips.

"Ryiah?" There was a concerned knock at the door.

My chest squeezed until it hurt, and I had to dig my nails down into the blankets to fight back a cry. I couldn't talk to Darren. Not now. Not while everything I knew was falling apart. My brother had forced me to pick a side. And it wasn't Darren's.

I held my breath and waited until he left.

Derrick had implied the one I loved could be the traitor in our midst. But he was wrong. *Because deep down, I knew. If Darren had asked me to kill an evil tyrant and his brother? If he had begged? If he had told me it was all for Jerar?* I would have stood by his side.

The true traitors were the rebels. Or King Horrace of Caltoth. Or perhaps the Pythian king himself.

Had I known that this was how it would be? The life of a mage of Combat, betrothed to a prince? A kingdom in ruin. And with so many loose threads, something would tear.

And when it did, it would all fall apart.

CHAPTER SEVENTEEN

I had picked a side. But it didn't mean I was willing to embrace it. I was still determined to stop my brother any way I could.

Even if it meant becoming a traitor myself.

If I find him proof, he can go back to Commander Nyx. And that was all I cared about. Because as long as he was in the palace, he was at risk. And some part of me really did want to believe what he said about King Lucius. Because after all the man had done to his sons, anything was possible.

On my three days off for each of the next two weeks, I scoured every inch of the old king's rooms. Blayne hadn't transitioned over to King Lucius's chambers—after all, he was still in mourning—so nothing had yet been moved. The guards in the Crown hall only monitored its entrance, and since my chamber was a part of it, they never sought to check beyond.

I didn't need a key. I broke the lock on the second try. Rusting the metal until it cracked with just the slightest casting necessary. No one would ever suspect a thing.

And they didn't. Blayne was too busy in his war chambers, meeting with his board of advisors and Darren, whose counsel served to advise those in all of Combat with the other two Colored Robes following his lead. I didn't even miss not being a part of it; it was like Derrick said, now that I had my own mission, the envy was gone. My time was too busy spent searching, silently thanking the gods for sparing my brother and me thus far.

And praying we found whatever it was we were searching for before they found us.

But I didn't find a thing.

"The king would never keep the documents in his chambers!" Derrick admonished me one afternoon in the stables when I came to report my findings. "A man as underhanded as him? He probably burned them all."

"Then why are you still searching?" I threw up my hands in frustration. "Why are you still here? Go back, Derrick. Go back to the keep before they catch you." My voice broke, and I punched at the wall with my fist. "I can't keep doing this."

"No one is asking you to help," was his cold reply.

I stormed off, hating my brother even more than before. When Darren came to sit beside me that evening I was too busy stabbing my venison to notice.

"Ryiah?" The prince's hand slipped over my own. "What's wrong? You haven't touched your food in days."

"Nothing." I said the word bitterly, tearing off a forkful of roast and shoving it into my mouth.

"Did I do something to upset you?" The pain in his voice lanced at my heart. "I..." He lowered his voice so that his brother couldn't hear us over the other advisors and Council at the table. "I had the servants deliver that potion, but I..." His neck tinged red. "If that's w-what you are upset... I d-don't expect... If you aren't ready..."

My whole face flushed. "I-it's not that."

"Are you sure?" His eyes bore into mine until I was forced to look away, traitor that I was.

I fumbled for an excuse. "It's Wren." She was certainly a part of it. The lie flowed easily enough. "Every night your brother talks about Pythus, and I can't help thinking of her."

Darren's gaze drew dark and his hand tightened on my own. "Soon, Ryiah, we will catch every last one of those rebels. Blayne has me scouring all Marius's reports for something he might have missed. He was so thorough, but I've been talking with the other advisors, and I think he might have been going about everything wrong. What if they aren't in the South?"

My breath caught in my throat as he continued: "We always thought that's where they were. Because of all the attacks. But maybe that's what they wanted us to think. Maybe their base is in the north."

"YOUR MAJESTY, WE HAVE A TRAITOR IN OUR MIDST."

I slammed back in my chair, wooden legs scraping against the floor.

Mage Mira barged into the dining hall, leading two of her favorite mages and *Derrick*. His head was hung and his arms were dripping blood, all of his weight shifted to one leg.

My heart slammed against my ribs so loud I couldn't hear the next words she shouted. *NO. GODS, NO.*

King Blayne shot out of his chair, his brother a second later. Blayne's eyes flitted to mine and then Mira's, and then back again. An inscrutable expression.

Darren staggered back, mirroring my movements only a moment before.

"We caught this one in the war chamber." Mira had her men jerk my brother forward, and I heard the whimper as he was thrown to his knees, a sickening crack as his bad leg slammed against the marble tile. *DERRICK*. "He was making a list. Looking at the books. Keeping a count of each city's regiment. Writing names." She spat the words and a drop of saliva hit my brother's shirt. He made no move to wipe it away— he couldn't, his hands were bound behind his back.

Lists? Numbers? My pulse stopped as the facts came into play. My brother had never been looking for proof. His whole story about King Lucius was a lie. He had been gathering information for the rebels on the Crown the entire time. And he had been using me to get it.

Betrayal cut across my chest like a knife. And what was worse? My heart still bled for him. Even when I knew the truth. Even when it was staring me in the face. "It has to be a mistake!"

"It's not." Mira's eyes lobbed daggers at my own. "And for all we know *you* were helping him! He's your brother, seems to me a traitor wouldn't fly far from the nest."

"I wasn't—"

"*If you ever accuse my betrothed of treachery again,*" Darren's voice rang out low and ominous without a second glance my way. His fists were white on the back of his chair. "*You will be disrobed and tossed in a cell to rot. Do you understand, mage?*" He didn't even address her by her name.

A hot flush of shame threatened to drown me in air.

"That's enough, Darren." Blayne's eyes were glued to my face. "Mira, have your men take him to the dungeons. Ryiah, Darren, you will come with Mage Mira and me. To the war chambers. *Now.* The rest of you, continue your meal. You breathe a word of the rebel's presence to anyone, and I will have you thrown in a cell right along side."

"Ryiah." The king met my eyes, and his ice-cold gaze bore into my own. Even though he was a good deal younger, I could see his father staring right back. Lucius had trained his son well.

I could only hope it was still Blayne on the other side.

"Did you know your brother was a traitor to the Crown?"

Deep, slow breath. No sudden movements. Shock plastered on my lips. Terror in my eyes. Fury and betrayal burning in my lungs. "No, I-I didn't."

It's not a lie. It's not a lie. I thought he was a *good* rebel. I thought he cared about the kingdom. I didn't know he was helping prepare the Caltothians for a war.

"I told you, brother!" Darren's voice whipped out and struck his brother's accusation in a rage. "Ryiah would *never* betray us!"

"If you can't keep that temper in check, I will have you tossed out of this chamber!" Blayne snapped. "Gods all know your beautiful betrothed can do no wrong. Any fool can see the way you look at her. But *I* am not blinded by love, Darren, and *I* am asking her a question. As her king. It would do you well to remember your place."

"It would do you well to remember she tried to save our father!" Darren shouted. "Ryiah tried to save Wren! She was *attacked* in Mahj! You tell me I am blinded by love, but she would be the last person in the world to betray the Crown, and it would do *you* well to remember I answer to you as your Black Mage, not a servant."

"ONE MORE WORD, BROTHER." Blayne's voice boomed across the room. "ONE MORE WORD AND I WILL HAVE YOU THROWN IN THE DUNGEONS TOO. I AM YOUR KING, AND YOU WILL NOT SPEAK TO ME LIKE THAT AGAIN."

Darren wrapped his arms around my waist. He didn't say another word, but his stance was a statement of its own. I shivered in his arms and prayed the brothers' fight had kept Blayne from noticing my lie.

"I say we string the rebel up like the lowborn scum he is—" Mira's eyes made a not-so-obvious slant toward my own, daring me to counter her claim. "And then feed him hot coals. One at a time. It has been a while since the people saw a traitor choke on his own deceit. If I recall, the screams are something unlike any other. While they last."

Darren's arms and the look in Blayne's eyes were all that kept me from tearing *her* apart, limb-by-limb. Fingernails dug

into the palm of my hands, and I imagined it was her skin instead.

"*Please,*" my voice came out a croak. "Let me talk to
Derrick first. You don't know anything about the rebels. M-
maybe he has information—"

"Which we will get after a couple hours of torture," Mira
drawled.

"How would you know?" I countered. She was so eager
to get to my brother, and a part of me knew it was for the sins
of my past. "All the other rebels have never succumbed to
questioning, they chose death or found ways to take their
life—"

"And maybe they haven't been questioned by *me.*"

"Maybe it's time to try *something else.*" I slipped out of
Darren's hold to fall to my knees in front of his brother.

"Ryiah—" Darren tried to protest but I shook my head.
If I had to beg, I would. "Please." My head shot up to
look at the king. *Please don't be your father.* "H-he's so young.
Derrick didn't know...If he confesses to his crime? I-if I can
get him to tell you who they are, *where* they are..."

"Go on."

"If h-he does all that...Can you spare my *little brother's*
life?" I emphasized the term, hoping to draw on Blayne's relationship to his own.

The king folded his arms, his steel gaze unwavering. "For
you, Ryiah, three days. If you can get your brother to confess,
if you can get him to give my men the information you claim, I
will consider it payment for his life."

"Thank you. Oh gods, *thank*—"

"But, Ryiah," Blayne's voice was sharp. "I give Mira
permission to start her methods the second day."

My heart hammered against my ribs, and Darren knelt
down to help me stand, shooting a glower at his brother. "You
don't have to scare her," he snapped. "Ryiah's brother isn't a
bad person. Whatever fool decision he made, he's young. She'll
get him to talk."

"You'd be surprised what kind of villain can reside under a person's skin." Blayne's tone was curt. "Or have you forgotten our father so soon?"

"Derrick is hardly—"

"Anybody is capable of anything." The king's gaze flitted to mine and then back to his brother. His expression was dark. "It would do the two of you well to remember that. Do not let your love for anyone blind you from the truth. Those are the ones we stand to lose the most, when they betray us."

Mira and Darren led me through a series of halls, following a torch-lit corridor, passing stone stairs and rusted gates and all sorts of foul smells, before we finally reached the end. Through a narrow tunnel we came across a final set of doors bound by iron bars and a set of two guards in King's Regiment garb.

The palace dungeons.

"She's not going in alone!" Mira snarled. "She could be plotting his escape!"

"Do you not trust your own mages against one shackled soldier?" Darren gave the woman a hard look. "The rebels never responded to an inquisitor. Ryiah's brother will be less willing to talk with anyone looming over their conversation."

"It isn't *right*—"

"Mira." The prince swore. "I am not happy about finding a rebel in our midst, either, but there is nowhere that boy can escape. As your superior, and your prince, I am asking you to stand down."

The mage shot me a sour look as she gave the two others a nod, indicating they should let me in. I swallowed as the men turned the heavy key into the door's lock, praying the guilt wasn't written all across my face. *Did Mira see it?*

The guilt was eating away at my lungs, but in that moment there was nothing to stop me from seeing my brother and

convincing him to take Blayne's deal. *Nothing*. I would see him
live.

The door swung open, and the second it did the terrible
scent of decay and fresh urine was so overpowering I had to fall
back. My hand was covering my mouth and nose, but it didn't
make a difference. I felt as if I had inhaled a cloud of death and
rot; the air was so thick I could feel the particles pressing
against my skin.

Iron bars separated ten cells between the door and the
wall. Manacles were secured to the bars inside. Blood stained
the ground beneath, along with seeping buckets of what looked
like old human waste.

Then I spotted my brother. The only prisoner, furthest
from the door. His leg was sprawled out on the dirty floor, and
he was clutching his ribs. Blood stained the rags that barely
covered his form, nothing more than an old potato sack,
threadbare and worn. *Of course they would have made him
change; they could never allow a prisoner to wear the uniform of a
guard.*

Not three feet from where I stood was an iron chair, covered in spikes on every inch of its surface—even the arm rests.

A whimper escaped my lips. *The Prisoner's Chair.* I'd
read about it in the history books at the Academy. It was a
longstanding favorite of inquisitors. Criminals were strapped in
and then straps were tightened. The pain was supposed to be
terrible, but most wouldn't die. They would writhe in agony,
for hours holding their breath wishing the pain to end. And
then they would be removed.

They would bleed to death in their cells. *If they were
lucky.* If they survived there were other methods far worse.
Mice trapped against the flesh that would eat a person out
from the inside. Devices that would stretch and then rip the
limbs out of their sockets. Mutilation. Fire. Hot metal poured
onto screaming flesh.

The kings of Jerar had many ways to interrogate their
criminals. Most methods were usually too complex to waste the

time. A normal crime that warranted death was done by hanging. But most prisoners didn't carry secrets that could reveal a large grouping of traitors to the Crown.

"Derrick!" I threw myself against the bars of his cell, trying to hold my breath against the stench.

"What are you doing here?" My brother's cough was labored.

"What do you mean?" My fists clung to the iron rods. "I came here to convince you to turn them in."

Derrick said nothing.

"DERRICK!" My arms rattled the bars. "YOU HAVE TO TURN THEM IN!"

"I'm not telling the Crown anything." His voice was empty, toneless. "You know this, Ryiah."

"How can you say that?" My hands hurt from how hard I was gripping the steel. *"They are going to have you killed, Derrick!"* Tears were stinging my eyes as I fell to the ground outside his cell. "You have to tell."

"If I have to die, at least it won't be their blood on my hands."

"Their blood? What about Alex? Our parents? What about me, Derrick?" My voice raised wildly. *"Do we mean nothing to you?"*

"I would give my life just to keep the four of you safe." He raised his gaze to mine, and his fists were clenched tight. "Just as I would for that of my comrades."

"WHY?" My voice boomed across the chamber, and I didn't care if Darren and Mira heard me. "WHY WOULD YOU PROTECT A GROUP OF TRAITORS? SELLING OUR COUNTRY'S SECRETS TO A CALTOTHIAN KING?"

"Ryiah—"

"You lied to me!" My fingers dug into the hard metal bars. I inhaled sharply and the stench burned at my lungs. I made myself lower my voice so it didn't carry across. "About

everything. You were never even looking for proof, were you? You just told me what you thought I needed to hear—"

He shifted his leg, and I could see how hard he was fighting to keep the pain at bay. "I wasn't lying. King Lucius—"

"You are still lying to me now!" I bit back a scream. *"And you know what is worse? I don't even care!* I begged Blayne to spare your life, Derrick, because you are my brother and I love you." The bars groaned as I shook them again and again. *"I can't lose you.* I need you to beg the king's forgiveness and tell him everything!"

"That man isn't my king." My brother's words were bitter.

"They will torture you, Derrick. And then they will kill you. They will do it in the worst way, Derrick, because you are a traitor!"

"Many great men have died the same."

"You are a bloody pawn!" I shrieked.

"And you are a bloody fool!" he spat. "I wasn't lying! Everything I said was true!" He lowered his voice to an angry hiss. "I *was* searching for proof. I may have neglected to tell you the part about getting the lists for Nyx, but that was only because I knew you would try to stop me!"

"I don't care. *I don't care.* I DON'T CARE!" My fists were beating against the metal, jagged ridges drawing blood. I lowered my voice to a snarl. "You are going to tell them EVERYTHING." My eyes flashed steel. *"Or I will."*

"No, you won't." My brother's gaze matched my own. Impenetrable walls of stone.

"Yes, I—"

"Would you give up your life in the palace?" His words hit my chest like a thick slab of ice. "Would you give up *your prince?* Would you willingly sacrifice Ian? And Ray? And all those lives in the north?" His laugh was cold. "Just to save me you would be condemning yourself. The Crown would never trust you again if they found out you knew about the rebels—"

I was choking on air.

"They might spare your life, because of *him*... But you will be right here alongside me. To live out your life in the dungeons, a traitor."

He was right. My fingers slipped from the bars, and I slumped to the floor. Waves of nausea threatened to attack my lungs.

"Maybe King Blayne would spare me, but I would rather die a traitor than give up the others' lives just to live rotting in these cells." His next sentence cut into me worse than any blade ever could. "*And you and I, we are one in the same.*"

"Derrick..." I was breaking. "Please, w-what about Alex?" My voice grew higher. "Mom? D-dad?" *What about me?*

"I'm so sorry." A flush of shame covered his face, and for the first time I saw emotion in his eyes. Regret. "I love you, Ry."

"But they'll never know!" Shards of glass were ripping me apart. Our family. "Three days, Derrick, they won't even know until I tell them!"

"Tell them I'm sorry." He tossed the leather cord and the copper ring clinked against the floor.

"Derrick, no!" I beat at the bars and blood sprayed across the room. "DERRICK, PLEASE!" *There has to be a way!*

"GUARDS!" My brother raised his voice and it cracked. "Please take my sister away."

"DERRICK, NO!" I reached into the cell and grabbed his arm. I saw him flinch. "*PLEASE, DON'T DO THIS!*"

A rough pair of hands dragged me back, hauling me away from his cell.

"*No!*" I clawed at my captor, fingernails tearing apart skin, and the hot liquid streaming down like tears.

"Ryiah!" Another pair of hands caught me and pulled me away from the first. Garnet flashed before my vision and tears burst out like a stream, clouding the room so that I could no longer see.

"I will bring you back tomorrow," Darren whispered.

"He's not going to tell!" My voice was hoarse from the screams. *"He's not going to tell!"* And I couldn't either. I was a liar. And a coward.

And I—

"We need to get her out of here." The prince's panic was a distant call as my body crumbled in his arms. Moments later my legs and waist were lifted and swung, my head falling against something soft. Pine and cloves muffled the stench of blood and rot, but they only made it worse.

Home.

I was struggling to breathe. Cool glass was pressed against my lips and someone was begging me to drink. I opened my mouth to protest and a bitter liquid hit my tongue. *Derrick.* A steady stream that forced me to swallow, again and again as pungent sweetness and herbs assaulted my lungs.

Derrick.

The deafening pounding of my pulse slowly gave way to a lull. The frantic struggle fell from my limbs.

Derrick.

A sense of calamity, and then... I never remembered the rest.

CHAPTER EIGHTEEN

The second day my brother refused, Mira set to work on his inquisition. It was supposed to be the Black Mage who interrogated prisoners of high treason, but Darren had petitioned Blayne for a reprieve.

A part of me longed to have him do it. Mira was bloodless and cold; it was hard for me to separate her from the enemy. My brother may have committed the crime, but I was in no state to consider reason. I had to be dragged away from the dungeon doors—and even then his screams still echoed in my head. They never went away.

I couldn't sleep. I couldn't eat. I refused to drink. Darren was on his knees pleading with me just to breathe, and all I could do was stare at the wall. I needed a way to save my brother, and even if I were to reach out to the rebels, they were too far away. I had no way of knowing if he had a contact in the city, and Derrick refused to give me the answer for fear I would try and trade the life of another for his.

He wouldn't have been wrong.

I had fallen to madness by the morning of the third day. Mira's methods had left my brother in a state so terrible that Darren had to drag me from the dungeon cells, kicking and screaming and threatening to kill the woman who had done it.

They tried to put me in my chamber with Paige to stand guard, but I broke down the castle door with my magic. When she tried to stop me, I cast a sword and held it to her throat, shaking as I begged her to take me to the king.

She could have stopped me, but something in her expression cracked and she sheathed her blade and let me by.

I fell to my knees on the cold marble tile. By now they were purple and bloodied—fresh wounds reopening so new stains mixed with old—so many times had I dropped and scrapped and begged for my brother's reprieve.

"I'm truly sorry, Ryiah." Blayne looked down at me from his throne, and his expression was full of regret. "I can't let his crimes go unpunished. Not unless Derrick can give us the answers we need."

"*P-please.*" Darren was holding me as I cried, tears flooding the floor with pieces of my heart mixed up in between. *"I'll do anything."*

"You have until dawn tomorrow." Blayne looked away. "Too many lives are at stake. I want to spare him, Ryiah, I do. You have shown nothing but loyalty to our Crown..." His voice grew sharp. "But your brother put everyone in this kingdom at risk. Crown law dictates a traitor die after the first night, and I have given him three. More than my father would have ever done."

A part of me was shattering out on that floor. Darren and Paige helped me back to the dungeons where I fell apart, screams and sobs as I begged my little brother who lay dying to talk.

Eventually, I was taken away. Where I was put back in my chamber with Darren sitting outside the door, his back to the panel as he spoke quietly to me inside.

As the hours drew to a close, his voice grew hoarse. "I'm sorry, Ryiah." Then I heard the soft pad of his boots as he retreated to his own.

‡

I tossed and turned but I was never asleep. A thousand ideas crossed my mind as I fought reason for heart, and heart for reason. Every minute I considered bursting through that door to confess. I told myself I would tell Blayne everything and he would spare my brother.

But then Derrick's words came rushing back:

"Would you give up your life in the palace?"

I would.

"Would you give up your prince?"

I would love Darren from afar, in my cell, until the day I died. I could give up his love for me for my brother's life. It would kill me to do it, but it wasn't even a question.

"Would you willingly sacrifice Ian? And Ray? And all those lives in the north?"

To sentence hundreds of people to death...

"And you and I, we are one and the same."

He knew I couldn't do it. *Derrick knew.* I could give up everything for myself, but I couldn't give up the others.

So many times the idea of breaking him out had come to mind. It was as often as my breath... But even if I somehow found a way to do it, all I could think about was the Caltothian king and my brother's lists. A part of me knew if he escaped King Horrace and the rebels would have everything they needed to start a war.

Hundreds, thousands of lives would be lost.

So much more than just my brother.

I couldn't do it.

Three hours past the midnight hour alarm tolls rocked the palace walls.

I shoved past the blankets with a start. Every part of me knew what this was. I didn't bother to think or change or even *breathe.*

I knew what to do.

I could hear Darren through the thin walls of our rooms utter a muffled curse, and then the loud thump as he left his bed to go put on boots.

The rebels were here.

I didn't bother to change out of my shift or copy the prince. I had only seconds before Darren would reach the hall, and I had to get there first.

I had to get to Derrick first.

I took off at a run. Slip-sliding with my feet against the icy marble I tore past the corner—no guards in sight. I could hear the panicked shouts heading toward the palace barracks.

We were under attack.

As I got closer, I found two sets of guards crumbled and bleeding from their heads.

I was going to stop my brother, and it had to be me.

When I reached the end of the corridor I found Jacob half-carrying my brother out of his cell, one of the dead guard's keys dangling from a chain at his hip.

The Ferren's Keep solider regarded me with a sneer. "Come to stop us," he challenged. "I always told Derrick you were never to be trusted."

My hand shook as I held it out in front of my chest.

"You are his *sister*, but you chose the Crown." The boy took another step, and my brother's head lolled against his friend's chest. My heart skipped a beat as Derrick sucked in a raggedy breath.

"If you don't let us go, you sentence him to die." Jacob was only a couple steps away. His eyes were glittering with malice and hate. "Is that what you want, *swine?*"

"N-no!" I stuttered the words as my hand shook violently.

"He loves you, you know." Jacob's words lashed out like a knife. "He kept telling Nyx she was wrong. He pled for the others to tell you every night you were out there practicing your blasted magic for the Candidacy."

You've got to stop them, Ryiah. Do it. Do it now before he talks you out of it—

"Kill him." Jacob shoved Derrick forward so that he was directly in front of my trembling hand. My brother's face was streaked in blood and swelling with cuts. His body was nothing but red, and he was struggling just to breathe.

Derrick's blue eyes met mine and I saw defeat.

"At least then it will be at the hand of his sister," Jacob said. "Instead of an executioner."

I knew I had to do it. All those lives. The war. *I had to.*

But my hand stilled. *I couldn't.*

I slumped to the wall, letting the two rebels pass. Jacob's knowing smile caused a burning rage to sweep up deep inside, but to see my brother... my brother was all I could think about.

A shout and then a thundering boom.

Jacob and my brother were sent flying against the dungeon door. There was a loud, splintering crack of wood.

I heard the sound as running steps drew closer, and I forced myself up. I made no move to form a casting as I stood in front of my brother and his friend.

"STOP!" Darren's voice shot out. "ANY FURTHER AND I CAST TO KILL!"

The prince reached the end of the hall and recognition flared in his eyes. *"Ryiah?"*

"Darren..." My voice broke. *"Please."*

He stood frozen in place.

"Please don't let my brother die."

The prince's gaze never left my face.

He stepped to the side.

Jacob finished pulling Derrick to his feet, and then they were off. Twin sets of footfall racing down the hall.

Darren never made a move to stop them. He just stood facing me, his chest rising and falling with my own.

He chose me.

The words filled me, warmed me, made me whole. I couldn't speak, but it didn't matter. Darren reached out his hand and I took it.

And then a flash of white lit up the hall.

I started to run, cutting across the corner to find Mage Mira standing above two crumbled bodies, twin burn marks protruding from their chests. Directly at the heart.

Lightning still crackled just below her nails.

"You missed something," she said.

And then I started to scream.

"She tried to stop them and she hesitated—you can't blame her for not killing her own brother!"

"She would have let them escape, Blayne!" the woman screeched. "She's no different than a rebel herself!"

"If that had been Marius—"

"And he were a rebel?" The woman sneered at the young man. "I would have put a blade through him myself!"

"Blayne!" The young man was pleading. "If it were you I never could have done it—"

"Because your king would never be so foolish!" The woman snorted. "And you were with her—"

"I was trying to stop her! Ryiah's magic is just as good as my own, and she caught me off-guard. We were at a standstill when the boys escaped—"

"For all we know you were helping!"

"ENOUGH!" The third party roared. "I'm trying to think."

"It's Ryiah, Blayne! You know her. She fought to save Wren and father during the attack! She lost her brother today. She made a mistake, but she would never be one of them. Please, don't hold this against her!"

Silence, then: "We will not hold Ryiah responsible for last night's actions. The distraction the rebels caused in the gardens was done without her help. Her rooms were already searched—"

"BLAYNE!"

"Silence, brother. They came up empty. All the guards report no unusual activity, and her past actions demonstrate nothing but loyalty to the Crown. Her knight reports that the young woman has never been approached, and her family is loyal to the Crown." He paused. *"That said, I believe the Caltothians are recruiting at least some of their rebels from the border. The boy and his friend were both serving in the Ferren's Keep Regiment. Since it appears Commander Nyx was not aware of her men I would like you, Darren, to send your top men to investigate. Marius had no luck locating the rebels but I trust you will be more thorough."*

"Yes, brother."

"And Mira, write to your brother in Langli. Tell him I want him to return to his investigations in the south. He might not be the Black Mage any longer, but I need all our best men on the job."

"Yes, your majesty..."

One day screaming and dying in bed. One day of rejecting the truth, burning it, tearing it right out of my lungs, and feeding it to the shadows that chased me as I slept.

Tears were stinging my eyes and a burning hate was strangling my lungs.

For one day, I allowed myself to shatter.

I wanted to lose. I wanted to let the darkness take me right there. But I couldn't. And so I took the potions the healers offered me. I listened when the boy begged me to eat. I smiled when all I wanted to do was scream.

And then I begged to leave the very next morning. It didn't matter that I was on the verge of losing myself to grief, it didn't matter that I was breaking, that I could barely go a second without my heart screaming his name.

I still had to tell them.

And it couldn't come as a letter. It couldn't wait.

Even if I was never ready. I couldn't give in to grief. Not until then.

But I needed to do it alone.

He understood. And so did his brother.

The five days' ride to Demsh'aa was the hardest of my life. I rode on with four guards at my back and Paige at my front. Since the rebels had attacked the Crown not once but twice in the last couple of months I was far too valuable to have just one guard in travel.

Let them try.

Now, I had two Combat mages, two knights, and my head knight, Paige, to protect me from the dangers of my brother's betrayal.

But they did nothing. They could not save me from myself. They could not spare me from the crippling shame that was eating me out from the inside. They could not hide the truth.

Derrick was dead.

It made no difference that he was a rebel, a traitor to the Crown.

Whenever I thought of him a cold fury slammed at my lungs. My hands balled to fists as I choked on a silent scream.

How could he? How could he betray us? How could he get caught?

How could he make me be the one to go home and tell them? Their youngest was dead. Derrick. The one with the dimples. The easiest smile. The one who made us all laugh.

I stifled a sob with a sharp, hitching breath and stared angrily out at King's Road. I had the barest of two hours before I reached my parents. Darren had sent two envoys—one to my mother and father, the other to Alex and Ella in Montfort—telling them to expect me at my parents' homestead in exactly one week. The journey for Alex and Ella would take a bit longer to reach.

Just enough time for me to tell my parents on my own.

I pulled at the leather cord at my neck. My skin there was rubbed raw. The copper ring glinted out in the sun. The "R" stared back at me, reminding me of everything I had lost.

A ring for each twin. A boy and a girl who couldn't be more different. And then came Derrick, the feisty little boy with blond curls, three years younger but outspoken and always brandishing a stick in hand. He had stolen my heart the second he was born, and he had continued to steal it with every breath... until the end.

I had given him the ring meant for me. Told him that each of my favorite brothers had a part.

And now I had one.

The more the grief welled up inside, the way my parents looked as I told them when I arrived home that night. One thing was clear: *the Caltothians had to pay.* King Horrace had tricked Commander Nyx and her men, and my brother had died because of it.

I would not turn in the rebels. I had thought of it countless times in the day following his death, but I couldn't. A part of me was ripped apart at the thought. Derrick had died for their cause. If I betrayed them now it would mean my brother had died in vain.

So I stayed silent. And I watched my parents fall. Dishes clattering, muffled cries, and puddles of tears. Angry, disbelieving shouts followed by stark betrayal and then grief.

I joined them. And another part of me shattered. I knew by the time Alex arrived there would be almost nothing left to break.

How many times can a person shatter?

At least one more.

Paige and the rest of the guards from the King's Regiment remained outside. She was able to grant me that much when my twin and his new wife walked through my parents' door.

"Ryiah," Alex looked around the room, confused. His brow furrowed when he saw my parents in the corner clutching hands, their faces turned away. "What is it? Why were we summoned here?"

Ella caught my expression before Alex understood. "*No.*" Her arms went around her husband just as he noticed the cord on my neck. I had never taken it off.

"Derrick?" My twin rasped. "Where is he?"

I opened my mouth, but the words couldn't come out. Tears started to swell at my eyes.

"Derrick!" Alex's voice turned raw. "WHERE IS HE, RYIAH?" He broke free of Ella's grip and crossed the room, shaking me while I struggled to breathe.

I can't tell him. But you must. *I can't.*

"Ryiah!" My brother was screaming in my face. "*WHERE IS DERRICK?*"

My father's sob was all he needed to hear.

"NO!" Alex stumbled back; his eyes were streaming tears. "NO!"

"He's dead, Alex." My mother made herself reach out and catch my brother's arm. "Derrick is dead." Her voice caught, and my father's hand shot out to her shoulder.

"*What happened?*" was Ella's whisper.

"WHY DID YOU KNOW FIRST?" My brother's eyes never left my face. "RYIAH, WHY ARE YOU THE ONE TO TELL?"

"Derrick was a rebel." My whole body was trembling. All of the darkness—it was coming back. And it was threatening to take hold. "A-Alex, he tried to steal information to help them—"

"NO!"

"—He g-got caught—"

"NO!" Tears were streaking down his face.

"Alex, I t-tried to have him confess. I t-tried—" I bit down on my lip to keep from sobbing. "—But h-he wouldn't l-listen."

My brother sank to the floor, and Ella fell down beside him.

"The rebels...T-they broke him out." I lowered my voice to a whisper. "Darren and I l-let him go but h-he still got c-caught by one of the g-guards—"

My brother was up in an instant. And then it was me being slammed against the wall, my back and shoulders flaring up in agony as he pounced on me, his voice a low snarl.

"Why was he a rebel, Ryiah?"

"Alex," I whimpered.

My twin shoved me harder and my parents cried out in horror. "There's something you aren't telling us, Ryiah!" he whisper-shouted. "You wouldn't look this guilty—"

"Alex!" Ella staggered to her feet. "Let her go!"

"Not until she tells us what she's hiding!" My brother's eyes stayed locked on my face.

"I'm not—"

"NO." My brother cut me off. "Stop lying! *This is me.* I know every expression you make, Ry. I know you like I know myself—and right now I *know* you are hiding something." He dropped his shoulders, letting his forehead press against mine, whispering. *"What are you hiding, Ryiah?"*

My gaze fell to the doorway where the guards were still waiting. So far they would have just assumed our conversation was that of an angry brother in denial. They had heard the same from my parents that first night I arrived.

But the one thing I hadn't counted on was my twin who knew me like the back of his hand.

I grabbed his arm and spoke softly. "You need to lower your voice." My gaze darted to my family and Ella as I pulled them to the furthest corner of our house.

"I k-know who the rebels are."

"WHAT—"

Ella slapped a hand over my brother's mouth. *"Alex!"*

"You know?" My mother's gaze searched my own. "Why didn't you—"

"It's dangerous." My voice was pained. "Darren fought his brother just to grant me a reprieve. If Blayne suspected I-I knew anything..." I trailed off for a moment, and then forced myself to continue. "They are looking for traitors, a-and after Derrick I d-didn't want them thinking any of you were one of them. T-that you know something you shouldn't."

"Why did Derrick join the rebels?" My father was shaking. "What did he tell you? Why was he at the palace and not the keep?"

"What I tell you now." My voice was barely a whisper. I made myself stand strong. "It can't ever leave this house. None of you can ever breathe a word of it to anyone, *ever*. Not even to each other." I didn't want to tell them, *but how could I not?* They deserved to know why their child was dead. Alex deserved to know why his little brother would never come home.

And so I told them. I told them *everything*.

My parents and Ella were horrified, but Alex...

I shouldn't have told him.

"How do you know Derrick wasn't telling the truth?" my twin whispered furiously. "Did you see what King Lucius did to those prisoners? To me?" His voice quivered. "To Ella? Did you forget what the king allowed Blayne to do to her? What Darren did to you during the course of the apprenticeship? No—" He caught my protests before I could speak. "What Darren did was wrong, Ry. No man leads a woman on while he is betrothed to another! He lied to you, humiliated you in front of the court, he lied to you every gods' blasted day for two years before he was finally man enough to do something about it—"

"I told you why Darren did that!" My voice rose. "Don't you dare—"

"That whole family is evil!" My twin was struggling not to shout. "Maybe Derrick was right. Maybe the brothers did know what their father was doing the whole time. Maybe your precious prince decided to murder his cruel father and his brother in one night, only he missed. Maybe this has been his plan all along. You said yourself you believed what the rebels said about King Lucius was correct. How do you know they aren't telling the truth about the attack in Montfort?" Alex's breath was coming out faster and faster, his chest rising and falling as his face grew red. *"What if it wasn't them or King Horace? You let our brother die for nothing!"* Hot tears were streaming down his face and he shoved Ella's hand away when she tried to reach his wrist.

My brother grabbed his saddlebag and threw it over one shoulder; his eyes twin daggers as he regarded me with hate. "The Crown has done too much to the people I love—"

"Alex, no!" My father's face was full of terror, and my mother raised her voice. "Alex, don't you even—"

"My little brother was murdered. And I didn't even get to see his funeral because our new king has his body hanging from a pike in the capital square." His tone could have cut glass. "If asked to choose between a tyrant and a misguided group of people trying to make a change, I choose the latter. The rebels had the right idea all along."

"Alex!" Ella was shaking, trying to stop him from leaving. "Please, Ryiah didn't tell you this so—"

"I'm sorry, Ella." My brother's shoulders fell as he looked across to his wife. "You don't have to come with me."

"Alex—" I reached out and he jerked back, eyes flashing.

"Go ahead and turn me in!" he snapped. "You already let one brother die, what's another!"

My best friend and parents were screaming and sobbing as my twin stormed out the door. A second later a cloud of dust was trailing in his wake.

I could barely breathe. *Why had I told him?* My misguided guilt had turned my second brother against me, and now my own betrothed was going to be hunting my own while his brother called on a war.

There was a flurry of movement, and I realized Ella was running toward the door.

"Ella!"

"I'm sorry, Ryiah." Her voice was hoarse. "I'll try and stop him."

And then she was gone. A second horse's bray and then a second misting of dirt hitting the air.

Then it was just me and my parents.

"I'm so sorry," I whispered.

"First Derrick..." My father could barely speak. "And now Alex..."

My mom just stared at me, and the way her nails dug into her palms I knew she was fighting not to speak her thoughts aloud. But her eyes were sad, and my mother was never sad. She was *strong*.

And now my parents were breaking.

I heard what my father didn't say, what my mom fought to swallow. *Ryiah, how could you?*

I didn't have a reply. There was nothing I could say to repent the pain I had brought them both.

CHAPTER NINETEEN

I returned to the palace and my days were written in red.

I saw Derrick's face around every corner; every young man in the crimson soldier's tunic was his ghost. Every stain against the cold marble was a pool of his scarlet blood.

I looked into Darren's eyes. Dark garnet was the color of my soul, and the Shadow God was counting down my days.

I was a filthy traitor. To the boy I loved because every word from my mouth was a lie. To my little brother who had died because I was too much a coward to speak the truth. To my twin because I had to be the one to break his heart, and then send him on his way. To my parents, because I was supposed to look out for my little brother, and I had failed. To my best friend whose husband was now joining the wrong cause, all because I had told the truth when a lie would have been warranted instead.

I was a traitor to everyone I loved. And I had only myself to blame.

I wasn't sure how a person like me could sleep. The shadows that consumed my thoughts, I should have been writhing in terror each night. But the pain was helping. It kept me from the grief. It kept me from breaking one final time; it kept me strong.

I went about my duties in a haze.

A couple more weeks passed, and they assumed I was in mourning. It was understood the sister of a traitor might be experiencing a bit of despair. But I wasn't depressed; I wasn't crying myself to sleep... I was numb.

The flames of the castle's sconces danced for me as I passed. They taunted and beckoned, telling me they knew all my lies. That they knew my heart was really black.

I should have turned in the rebels. If not for Derrick, then Alex now. I should have gone to Blayne. I should have confessed everything and begged for Alex's amnesty and condemned myself to the cells. I should have saved the lives of thousands by turning my brother and the rebels in.

But I was a coward. Too afraid of what it would mean if the king decided my second brother was an even greater traitor than the first. Too afraid to take another brother's life. Too afraid of his blood on my hands, so I sacrificed the others.

I was bound for the pit of darkness in the Shadow God's realm. It was only a matter of time.

When the king announced that King Joren had agreed to our terms, that he would fulfill his end of the New Alliance, I felt not a moment of relief. The crowds rose up in Devon's square, but my eyes were glued to the rafters.

Darren had finally convinced Blayne to take down Derrick and the other rebels' bodies. They'd been burned the previous night. *Then*. Then I had felt something.

"Pythus has promised us forty warships. They set sail in two months." Blayne's words echoed across the crowd and everywhere, screams and cheers, frenzied cries of justice. The clamor of fools. *Didn't they know they were calling for blood?*

"Our Caltothian enemies will feel what it is to suffer. They will feel Jerar's wrath." The king's eyes sparkled as he raised his fist in the air, his Black Mage at his side. "As your king, I promised you peace. And peace you shall have. Emperor Liang has renewed his treaty as well. A fortnight from today, my dearest brother will be marrying his betrothed. The two most formidable warrior mages our kingdom has ever seen, prince and princess of our realm. The Crown has never been more powerful."

Darren's eyes fell to mine, and I looked away. I didn't wait for his face to fall. A tempest of emotions were threatening to burst. I needed to keep them inside.

When the proclamations were done I was first to exit the square.

He found me. Three knocks at the door in which I feigned silence. I wanted him to go away. I wanted to be alone, but Paige let him in anyway.

I heard her turn the key in its lock, an odd gravelly sound that scratched at my ears.

My room was a den of shadow. I didn't want any light. And he didn't try.

Darren pulled up beside me on the bed.

"I wish it didn't have to be like this," he said.

I didn't speak. I was too afraid if I did the words would fall away. Too afraid in the darkness I would confess my sins, and I couldn't speak a word. I couldn't stand the blood.

"You haven't spoken a word to me since it happened." I could hear his pain. It hurt me worse. "When Eve and Caine... when my father died..." He swallowed. "It was never like this. Derrick was your brother, and you loved him. He was the youngest, the one you were sworn to protect..." Darren shifted on the bed. "I know you, Ryiah. You are blaming yourself. It's what I would have done."

Silence was my only response.

"You think you could have stopped it, but you can't stop a person from their mistakes. When you returned to Demsh'aa, they blamed you, didn't they?" Silence. "Alex always hated me. I'm sure he made me the villain... But we did nothing wrong."

Yes. I did. I made myself blink away the tears.

"We never talked after..." Darren's voice fell to a whisper. "I would have let him go, Ryiah. I know it would have been a mistake. Gods, after all the rebels have done..." He was quiet for a minute, and then he made himself continue. "I swear to you, Ryiah, if I had known Mira was there, I would have stopped her. *For you.*" His voice broke. "No one should ever have to watch their brother die."

My whole face was wet, and my hands were trembling in my lap. I shoved them under the cover and held my breath, waiting for him to leave.

"I wish I could take it all away." Darren's hand pressed against my wrist as he stood to go.

There was the shift of shadows, and then he was walking toward the door.

"Stay," I whispered.

The outline of his shoulders froze, and I heard the soft pad of his boots. They grew louder until he was at the edge of my bed.

I was curled up to my knees, sitting against the frame. The tears were drowning me. I didn't want to be alone.

Not tonight.

Darren's arms wrapped around my waist, and he pulled me against him, my back pressing against his front.

He held me.

The rise and fall of his chest carried me to sleep. His chin resting on my shoulder. Pine and cloves enveloping me whole.

Darren's whisper was the last thing I heard.

"I love you, Ryiah."

Over the next two weeks it got easier to breathe. In. And out. With Darren's arms around me as I slept. He came to my room each night, each morning a pressed flower next to my head. Without fail.

The prince was going to cure me of everything Derrick had taken that night. Everything Alex had stolen the day he joined the rebel cause.

All Darren ever did was hold me. But that act alone was...*everything*.

It was a drop of sunlight in a prison of ice. It warmed the part of me I was afraid I'd lost. It took the fear, the doubt, the terror, and it pushed it all away.

And that morning I awoke. My ladies-in-waiting came to the door, and I smiled. It was small, barely a tug of the lips. But it was real.

I could be happy.

And today I am marrying my best friend. Because that's what Darren was. After all these years. Ella was one—she had held my hand and carried me through the trial year and our apprenticeship—But this last year had been Darren. The two of us had held each other through the darkest part of our lives, and never once let go.

Madame Pollina and Celine and Gemma helped me bathe. Soft-scented rose water and oils that made my skin glisten. They brushed my hair, pinning just a couple strands behind my head with sparkly pins. The rest remained down, loose waves framing my face.

The powders they applied were bare and set to highlight my narrow cheeks, the softest gloss to my mouth, the lightest shadows to darken the corners of my eyes.

Then they brought out my gown. A cream yellow, light ruffles running diagonally down its silken skirts, a fitted bodice of gold and orange beads. Nothing like I had ever imagined, and everything that I had never known I wanted. With its matching satin slippers it was fit for a princess.

The loveliest thing I would ever wear.

I stood on a small raised stand as they helped me into the dress in front of a gilded mirror studded with pearls.

They laced the bodice, and I held my breath, my arms free from the weight of traditional sleeves.

It was then I read his letter: *"This dress reminds me of the midwinter solstice, our second year in the apprenticeship. Your arms were bare and Priscilla told you it made you look common...I remember your friend asked me what I thought, and I remember your face when I didn't reply. Ryiah, I want you to know that you looked beautiful. So beautiful, that I couldn't stop staring even if I tried. And then I asked you to dance—and even though I knew it would only bring the both of us heartache—it was the best night of my life. And now I want you to wear a dress just like it, today, as you become my wife."*

"Don't cry!" Celine snatched the card out of my hand before I could read it again. "We just finished with your face."

"I-I'm sorry," I stammered. But I wasn't. Not after reading Darren's letter.

I started to smile and then grimaced as the extra inhale stabbed at my ribs. The dress was tighter than anything I'd ever worn.

My eyes were a bit blurry, and ever mindful of Celine's warning I lifted a cautious finger to swipe away the water that had started to form at the rims.

I blinked twice, and then regarded myself in the mirror.

And that's when I saw it.

What I had been missing all along. What I had failed to see until the moment that yellow silk caught the light.

"Might I have a couple minutes," I rasped, "alone?"

"My lady, you don't have much time before the ceremony!"

"Please?" I was gulping up air, my fingers trembling as I pressed them together in hopes no one would notice.

Madame Pollina sighed and then motioned for my ladies to go, trailing after them to the door. She ducked her head in one last time. "Ten minutes, my lady!"

I waited until their mindless chatter trailed off down the corridor.

I took one last look at my dress. My *yellow silk* dress.

Then I shut my eyes and let the memory come flooding back:

A scared girl, no more than six, tugging at a yellow silk ribbon at the end of her curly black braid.

A man who looked nothing like his daughter, dragging her along to meet with a crown prince in the stands of the Candidacy.

The black-haired Caltothian ambassador looking on, no longer indifferent, cold fury written across his face, fists clenched at his sides, eyes locked on the same pair as me.

And then Blayne's voice: "*Come now, Father, everyone knows the noblemen take a lover or two during their travels. Even their wives. Why, it's a common enough saying: the longer at sea, the more lovers she keeps.*"

The woman we kidnapped. During the apprenticeship. In Dastan's Cove.

Lady Sybil was awaiting her husband's return.

I left the dais to press my palms against the side of the wall. This couldn't be happening. Not now. Not like this.

But now that the gates had been thrown open, the memories wouldn't stop: Three years ago the lady had had a three-year-old daughter. With black curls.

The mother adjusting the pale silk ribbon on the waist of her daughter's dress.

Little Tamora. Who looked just like that girl in the stands. The same blue eyes, the same age, the same fondness for silk. The black hair of the mother. The curls that mirrored Lord Tyrus. The blue eyes that matched both.

The cold fury on his face...

He couldn't have been Baron Cyr. The other dignitaries would have recognized...

Was Lord Tyrus the lover?

Was Tamora his daughter?

Cold steel cut at my chest, and my whole body seized: *Had Blayne known?*

But *how*? How would he—

And then I remembered.

The Caltothian traitor. *Flint.* A sentry who had served among Lady Sybil's men. The man who had mapped out the terrain for Dastan Cove. A common soldier who knew the in's and out's of Baron Cyr's castle. A husband who was away at sea for many months at a time.

Master Byron's words returned: *"Lucky for you Commander Chen has recently received orders from the Crown itself."*

"Just think," Alex had said, *"a month at sea on a secret mission. Imagine all the stories you'll be able to tell us when you return, Ry"*

And finally, Mira's threat as she informed us that our mission was, *"never, ever to be discussed with anyone unless you have permission from the king himself."*

The Crown had ordered a kidnapping. But on whose orders? King Lucius?

"I asked my father that year we returned to the palace," Darren had replied. "He told me he couldn't recall."

What if the reason the king couldn't recall was because the orders were never his?

Blayne and Darren had hated their father. But Blayne... Blayne had suffered much longer at his hand.

The crown prince just gave me a sardonic smile. "It takes much more to impress when you are his heir. Darren wasn't always around. In any case I'm better for it now."

Had Blayne planned all of this? Had he been planning this for *years?*

Crown orders for a secret mission nobody knew about. Kidnapping the lover and child of the head Caltothian ambassador?

Blackmailing Lord Tyrus with his child's life. Had the girl been brought to the Candidacy, within the lord's sight as a reminder? A promise to keep her alive, in exchange for his crime? Murdering a king in front of a room of soldiers and knights and the world's greatest mages. The man had never expected escape.

"For Caltoth!" It had been a cry to remind the audience it was an attack. To show the other country's ambassadors the ultimate breach of a treaty.

No one would be able to tie Lord Tyrus to Baron Cyr's missing wife and child. No one would have known she had a lover.

No one but a traitorous sentry, one who had managed to explore every inch of Baron Cyr's castle unnoticed. One who had perhaps seen Lord Tyrus visit Lady Sybil while her baron husband was away.

Perhaps Flint had been one of the traitors hired by King Lucius to stage the attacks on the Jerar-Caltothian border.

Maybe Commander Nyx and King Horrace had never lied. Maybe Derrick was telling the truth.

And maybe Blayne, tired of being in his tyrant father's shadow, had decided to bribe his father's man to learn Caltothian secrets. Something to use to his advantage. *Because perhaps his father had told him about all of the staged attacks.* After all, Blayne had been groomed as King Lucius's successor for years. *Why wouldn't the king share his secret with his heir?*

And perhaps Blayne had needed a mage to help accomplish his mission. Not a commander, not the current Black Mage, but the jealous sister, Mage Mira. The one who would love more than anything a position of power. Something to distance herself from her prestigious brother. *Something to rise.*

She stepped in like a hero to kill the king's murderer. It had been so easy. So convenient. It had earned her a place as King's Regiment lead mage. Blayne's right hand in castle affairs.

Blackmailing Lord Tyrus with his lover and child would have accomplished two goals with one act:

First: *Kill the father.* The man who had tormented him for years. The king who had taken a sweet boy, and made him a monster.

"You see the boys as the men they are now," Benny had said. *"They were much different back then."*

Second: Convince the other countries that Caltoth had broken the Great Compromise in one indisputable act. Kill off a Pythian heir, an added blow to the shrewd King Joren who was so reluctant to pick a side?

Blayne had been poisoned, of course. But what if it had been a farce? What if one of the healers had already had an antidote on hand?

It took a mage precious minutes to identify a strange poison's symptoms, and even longer to cast the correct balance of magic mixed with the herbs and powders on hand. I had seen the Restoration mages struggle during their Candidacy trials just to concoct the correct casting for their prisoner's ailment in time. And those took close to an hour.

The crown prince had been healed within twenty minutes.

I slipped to the floor.

This past year. Everything Blayne had done to win my trust. I hadn't ever trusted him, not completely.

But I had let down my guard after he had shown me a bit of his past. *Isn't the best bit of truth always woven in with a lie?* Blayne had never lied about the cruelty of his father. But he had used it to garner my pity.

But why hadn't he tried to kill me, too? Why didn't he just get rid of the girl he hated and force his brother to marry Priscilla instead?

The crown prince had hated me from the moment we met. The second he saw the way Darren looked at me that second year at the ascension fest—

And then I paused. *Darren.* That was it.

"My dear," Benny said. *"Darren is the only person that boy has ever cared for, besides himself."*

Blayne hadn't been able to do it. Not after he saw how hard Darren had worked to trick his father into accepting me as his betrothed. An infatuation he could ignore. But love? As much as Blayne had hated me, he loved Darren more. *The*

*younger brother who continuously fought his father to protect him
from the blows.*

Blayne had probably felt indebted to Darren. And so he
had made me a part of his plans. He had changed his game, he
had shown me vulnerability, sympathy in his father's cruel
acts to win me to his side.

It was all to further his ploy. Like Blayne had said: *"The
two most formidable warrior mages our kingdom has ever seen...
The Crown has never been more powerful."*

He had been building his indisputable reign. All along.

My head pressed against the chamber wall. I kept my
eyes clenched shut as the wave of nausea hit, breathing heavily
through my nose.

Derrick.

I slammed my fist to my mouth. Teeth scraped against
skin as the scream ripped me apart. It clawed up from my
chest. It was so long and so hard I had to slap my other hand
over to muffle the cry. Blood coated my tongue. I was choking
on hot metal that was melting my lungs.

DERRICK!

The screams rippled across my skin, one after the other,
until all will left my limbs, my hands and arms went limp
against the cold marble floor.

*I let him die. I let him die, and I could have helped him es-
cape.* I was the second best Combat mage in the realm. I could
have taken on a whole legion of guards. *Why hadn't I done
something?*

That first night, after he was caught. *I could have done
something.* I would have been caught, of course, and tossed in a
cell to rot. But Darren would have convinced Blayne to spare
my life.

And *I* could have let my brother live.

But instead I had called my own brother a traitor. I had blamed him for not telling me everything about the rebels' orders. *And why would he?* He'd known the Crown was tainted. He had suspected the wrong brother, but he had been close.

Why didn't I listen? The answer had been staring me in the face the entire time.

Blayne was evil. What he had tried to do to Ella, the way he had treated me when he thought I was just a distraction...

I had known all along. I had known, and then I had looked the other way. Because the black wolf had dressed up like a white lamb. And the fool that I was, I had seen the wolf become the lamb and never bothered to wonder whether the one was still the other. Because a person couldn't ever be good and evil at once.

Little girl, don't you know? The world is made up of shades of grey.

I was one of the few people who had served on that mission to Caltoth, and I was the *only* one who had seen Tamora at the stands in Montfort. I had even seen the way the Caltothian ambassador looked at her and the prince. No one else could have added up those two clues but me.

I had condemned my little brother to death. My family was right to hate me. *I* hated me.

The pain I had suffered after his death: the agony, the torment, the rage, and self-flagellation. *The guilt.*

It was nothing compared to this moment now.

But it was also different. Because this time I couldn't be a victim. I couldn't be the little girl who shut out the world. I couldn't break apart any longer. I had to do something. And I knew exactly what I had to do.

I had to keep Darren and Marius from finding out the rebels' identity. Blayne had given them orders to investigate, and it would be my mission to sabotage.

I had to find the proof the rebels were looking for. Anything I could use to prevent a war.

I had to gather as much information as I could. My position in the Crown granted me access to things that would raise questions were it anyone else. I had proven my loyalty time and time again—even Blayne had agreed with Darren. I was not a rebel; I was not a threat. *But I was now.*

I had to convince the Pythian ambassador not to honor the alliance with Jerar. He had seen me try to save his niece, he had respected my negotiations—he would have to convince King Joren.

And then. Then I had to find a way to stop the king of Jerar.

My fist closed around the dagger. The casting had appeared at a moment's notice.

I could kill him now. Darren wouldn't be able to stop me. He wouldn't be on his guard. He wouldn't be able to save his brother...

A rage was boiling in the pit of my stomach and spewing to the surface, deadly tendrils of anger piercing at my ribs. My fist clenched the blade so tightly that blood had started to slip down my wrist. Small splatters of red against the skirts of my dress.

It would be so easy. I could do it now.

But I couldn't. For the same reason Blayne couldn't kill me.

Darren.

Darren didn't know about any of this. He didn't know what his brother had done. He didn't know what Blayne was capable of. He didn't know his brother had set fire to the world. Just so he could watch it burn.

All he knew was he loved him. That he had watched his older brother suffer blow after blow, and that he had been the one to save him. King Lucius had raised Darren as Blayne's right hand.

As twisted as the king might have been, he had been wise beyond his years. The best way to preserve the throne was to encourage unswerving loyalty in the other, and what better way to unite two brothers than through terror and hate? Like his eldest, Lucius had planned their relationship all along.

Preserving his son's reign.

And perhaps, *perhaps* Lucius had even seen it coming. From a tyrant, another tyrant had been born.

That day I had begged and pleaded for my brother, hoping beyond hope Blayne wasn't his father.

Blayne was crueler.

I should have been hoping it was his father, and not Blayne, staring back.

The ladies-in-waiting returned for finishing touches before the ceremony began. Pollina was aghast to see the fresh stains on my skirts and my fist.

I told them I fell. That the bones of the corset had been too tight. After all, they had found me on the floor. The tears in my eyes? Just from losing my breath.

I was nothing more than an anxious girl before she married the boy of her dreams.

Even though inside I was nothing but screams.

You will lose him.

As soon as the thought entered my mind, I knew it was true.

I couldn't tell him. Even if Darren believed me, he would insist on confronting his brother. And his brother was king. Blayne would have me beheaded at a moment's notice. I might stand a chance against a small collective of mages, but an army?

And what proof did I have? *Nothing.* I had no papers, no witness, nothing but a memory of a little girl with a slip of yellow ribbon in her hair.

Darren had never seen that little girl in the stands. He'd only seen the ambassador.

Everything else was a miles-long conclusion that would sound like the ranting of a madwoman determined to clear her brother's name.

And Blayne was *his* brother. Darren wouldn't be able to keep a secret or turn against him. Even when I had believed Derrick capable of putting thousands of future lives at risk, *I had still let him escape*. I had still chosen him.

And Darren would choose Blayne.

I would lose Darren. By keeping these secrets, by turning a traitor, by ultimately betraying the Crown... I would lose. *But sometimes the sacrifice is worth the cost.*

My cost would be Darren.

I would keep him safe. From the rebels. From Blayne. From myself—except for my lies. And when this was all over. When we had his brother in chains and the country was safe from his family's tyrannous plague.

Then I would fall to my hands and knees. And I would beg his forgiveness.

And maybe, *someday*, we could be that boy and girl he talked about. And we would leave this all behind.

I entered the ceremonial chamber, and the sun's rays caught on my dress.

The glow of butter-yellow against scarlet-red locks and steel-gray eyes.

Down the row I walked, head held high as I strode across to the priest.

My eyes were locked on the tapestry behind him. It depicted a king in a gilded chair, a crown atop his head and a hematite pendant at his throat. With a man in ceremonial black robes at his right. His Black Mage.

The king and his right hand. Blayne and Darren.

My slippers glided along the soft carpet lining the walk, and it was only as I reached the end that I let myself look to my left.

Darren stood there. His face a wash of emotion. Ink-black, jaw-length locks and garnet eyes—everything I had ever loved. In his robe. Just like the tapestry.

He held a hand out as I climbed to the top of the dais.

The priest garbled on, almost incoherent in his speech. And then he stopped. He dipped his thumb into a bowl of crimson wine and pressed once along my forehead, and then once along the prince's.

He issued a prayer.

And my eyes slid to the king waiting below, a cruel smile painting his mouth, his soul stained red with the blood of hundreds. Every life lost in the name of the Crown.

I wasn't sure how I had missed it before. It was the same smile I had seen countless times over the last year, only this time I could see it for what it was.

Evil. Corruption. Greed.

"Do you, Prince Darren, First Prince to Jerar and Black Mage to the Crown, take the Lady Mage Ryiah of Demsh'aa, as your wedded wife, to have and to hold from this day forward and keep thee only unto her, so long as ye both shall live?"

"I do." Darren's voice rang out across the hall. His whisper after was enough to bring me back, and break me. *"Always."*

"And do you, Lady Mage Ryiah of Demsh'aa, take Prince Darren, First Prince to Jerar and Black Mage to the Crown, as your wedded husband, to have and to hold from this day forward and keep thee only unto him, so long as ye both shall live?"

My hands were trembling as I made myself look left and into the eyes of the boy I would betray.

"I do."

The End

ABOUT THE AUTHOR

Rachel E. Carter is a young adult author who hoards coffee and books. She has a weakness for villain and bad boy love interests. When not writing, she is usually reading, and when not reading she is usually asleep. To her, the real world is Hogwarts and everything else is a lie.

The Black Mage is Rachel's first YA fantasy series, with many more to come. She loves to interact with fellow readers & aspiring writers, and here is a list of places you can find her online:

Official Site: www.rachelecarter.com
Facebook: www.facebook.com/theblackmageauthor
Instagram: https://instagram.com/rachelcarterauthor
Twitter: https://twitter.com/recarterauthor
Pinterest: www.pinterest.com/recarterauthor
Tumblr: http://rachelcarterauthor.tumblr.com
Goodreads: www.goodreads.com/rachelcarterauthor
Email: rachelcarterauthor@gmail.com

CPSIA information can be obtained at www.ICGtesting.com
Printed in the USA
LVOW10s1521050216

473888LV00004B/331/P